Sign up for our newsletter to hear
about new and upcoming releases.

www.ylva-publishing.com

OTHER BOOKS BY G BENSON

All the Little Moments
Flinging It

PIECES

G BENSON

ACKNOWLEDGMENTS

Thanks, as always, to my amazing beta and sensitivity team. You all supply endless feedback, honesty, and encouragement. My books would never get anywhere without you all.

A big thank-you to the editing team, who had their work cut out for them with this one. A huge thanks to Michelle—your patience and funny comments always make the editing experience that much easier.

Finally, thank you, as always, to the Ylva team, especially Astrid. A content editor, a publisher, and a friend all rolled into one. And who got me this cover (thanks Adam!), which I adore.

DEDICATION

For Katja, beta and friend extraordinaire—*Pieces* feels like it's half yours.

CHAPTER 1

THE DAY OLLIE SAW THE girl who was all cheekbones and shadowed eyes, something stilled in her chest, and for a second, she forgot how to breathe. High school was transitioning, was flowing. Her sixteenth birthday had come and gone, and everything was that little bit different. The summer had passed, hot and hazy and filled with days by the pool, chlorine drying tight over her skin, the sun leaving her even darker than normal. She thought maybe she could float through the rest of her life.

But that girl brought Ollie's feet crashing back to the ground.

Ollie blinked, her gaze tearing from the girl across the cafeteria. "Who's that?"

"Who?" And, of course, Sara turned, staring obviously, dark eyes narrowing as she took in the scene. "That chick? She was in our class four years ago and disappeared for a while, then came back a grade below us. Um…Carmen?"

There was something about that girl's clothes; they hung a little loose, a little haggard. Something sat around the edges of her expression that Ollie didn't recognize but wanted to know. She did look slightly familiar—a kid Ollie had circled but never collided with, comets skimming past each other.

The imagery whirled in her mind, and she slipped her sketch pad out of her bag, pencil in hand and gaze still half on that girl.

"Why do you care, anyway?"

Ollie tore her gaze away a second time, warmth crawling along her cheeks. "I don't."

And then she'd forgotten her as Sean had slid into the next seat, his tray clattering on the table and his arm clattering over her shoulder. She sank into him, the solidity, the heat of him.

One by one, her friends dropped into their places, and laughter started up as Deon told a story about Mr. Warren and the costume he'd worn to history class that day. Sara put some straws and forks together to make some kind of catapult, sending fries and grapes to slap across people's cheeks, her teeth flashing white against her dark skin. She was a year older than they were, in the same grade after missing so much school when she was younger. Insanely smart, she could solve a physics equation faster than Ollie could wake up in the morning.

Though that wasn't hard.

Ollie's friends distracted her, and she disappeared into them, as was so easy for her to do.

At home that evening, Ollie slipped in and out of her usual push and pull with her parents. They hovered and then were absent, as if they knew to give their teenage daughter space but then couldn't stop themselves from missing how they all used to talk.

Ollie, once upon a time, had spent hours with her mom, asking her about the hospital and patients and how the heart worked, but that had ebbed away as she'd grown and become more attached to paper and color. Sometimes her father would try to nudge her art more toward design, as if hoping she'd fall into architecture or engineering. But he'd do it gently, his eyes soft.

They always ended up asking how her day was.

"Fine."

"What subjects did you have?"

"I don't know. I did math." She pushed her potatoes around and wondered why it mattered.

"Any tests coming up?"

And she shrugged, like she did every time. Impertinence settled over her shoulders, familiar and grating all at once. She didn't even know where it came from. She did know that these questions, every night at dinner, were like the third degree, even as a small voice inside her told her she was being ridiculous.

But then, later that night, her mom brought her a hot chocolate and quietly left it next to Ollie while she studied, and guilt prickled in her stomach as she mumbled a thank-you and tried to offer something more tangible than grunts and shrugs. Filled with warm, sweet milk, Ollie tucked her feet under herself at the computer chair, her mother leaning against the doorframe. "There's a party this weekend."

"Oh?" Her mom seemed to hold back a smile. "So now you want to talk to me?"

Ollie rolled her eyes. "Only a little."

That made her mother laugh, and Ollie smirked.

"Whose party?"

"Sara's."

"Are her parents there?"

"No."

She may sit in her own house some days, an inexplicable frustration crawling into the back of her mind, but Ollie didn't lie to her parents beyond a white fib; she'd never needed to.

"Who's going?" Her mom cocked her head.

"Both soccer teams and a few extras. Deon."

That girl, Carmen, maybe. Would she go?

"Will Sean be there?"

"Of course."

Her parents loved Sean. He was polite and nice and respectful. Ollie loved that he was all of those things, but at times, a restlessness was in her feet she couldn't explain. Something mediocre that tingled in her fingertips. They'd been friends for a while, and the dating was new, unsettled, and not something she felt sure of.

"Will you stay there?"

"If that's okay?"

Her mom's lips pursed, and her father appeared behind her.

"Is what okay?"

Ollie rolled her eyes again.

"Be careful, they'll roll out of your head, and then how will you show me you think I'm lame?"

He made the worst dad jokes. Her mother actually snorted.

"Is it okay if I stay at Sara's? She's having a party."

"A party?" He clutched a hand over his heart. "Teenagers like…parties?"

Her mother was going to strain herself repressing her smile.

"You're not funny, Dad."

He kind of was, even if he mostly just tried to annoy her these days.

"It's fine with me. Lou?"

"It's fine. As long as you call us if things get out of hand. I'd rather deal with messy, drunk you then messy, drunk, missing you. Okay?"

When Ollie nodded, her mother added, "Just don't do anything we wouldn't do."

A belly laugh emanated from her father, followed by a wink from her mother, and they both turned to walk away.

"You're both gross!" Ollie called after them.

Their only answer was determined kissy noises.

The next week, she saw the girl, Carmen, again. Ollie's art class had gone out to the sports grounds to draw people in live action.

To sit and let the charcoal spill over the page, to shape the things that moved and melded into something tangible in front of her, was easy for Ollie. A corner filled with feet tackling a ball, the fluidity caught and held on her paper. Trees spilled over a side of her paper, a shirtless teenager who should have been doing other things caught climbing the tree, his muscles tightening and pulling and evident. The flick of a ponytail as someone went to take a shot at goal. Ollie's eyes traced the grounds for something else to capture and stopped again.

The ponytail on her page belonged to Carmen. Ollie's fingers stilled over the notebook, and it felt like charcoal was seeping into her blood to permanently stain her insides. Maybe it would leave the memory of Carmen there forever. Skimming her eyes from the paper to the soccer game for the next half hour, Ollie watched as Carmen's PE team won their soccer match solely thanks to her. Carmen's eyes held a glint, a spark absent the other week in the cafeteria, and Ollie's hands moved of their own accord, capturing that look and immortalizing that gleam on paper. Heat spread through her chest, and she swallowed hard, wondering why her gaze was glued to the muscles in Carmen's arms, to the pull of her calf when she kicked.

Carmen's skin was a dark bronze, her eyes a brown liquor.

Ollie spent the afternoon trying to ask her friends subtle questions to learn more about her, but none of them had anything solid.

"I think her last name is García." Deon lay back on the grass near the football field, his skin as dark as the rich earth they lay on. He gave a shrug. "But I'm not sure. She's not in any of our classes now."

Sara shifted, jostling Ollie's head where it lay in her lap. "Yeah, she's a year below. One of the others in the Queer and Ally Club mentioned something about her being in their class."

Since Sara had finally stopped wiggling, Ollie relaxed, an arm thrown over her eyes. The sun was weakly warm, as if trying to cling to summer. Over the last month, they'd been doing the same thing, staying by the pool on weekends and ignoring the bite to the water, wearing shorts and tanks that brought forth goose bumps. But now the utter lack of warmth was obvious. The sweater Ollie had begrudgingly pulled on was not doing much to warm her. "Is that movie night for the club tonight or tomorrow night?" she asked.

Sara's voice, rich and warm, drifted toward her. "Tonight. We're watching *But I'm a Cheerleader.*"

"I love that one," Ollie said.

Gravelly and filled with sleep like it always was just after lunch, Deon's voice chimed in. "You love the actress."

"Truth."

Ollie knew she liked guys *and* girls. *Bisexual* was a label she claimed easily in the safety of her friends. Her parents didn't know, yet, but it seemed unimportant until it was necessary to tell them. Sean didn't care, and her friends all flittered under the queer umbrella with her: her acceptance was here, and one day, she figured she'd think more about it.

The next day at school, Ollie saw Carmen walking away from her locker, and before she could stop herself, she accidentally-kind-of-on-purpose shouldered Carmen as she walked past, her mouth dry and her heart pounding while she had no idea why. Ollie was never shy. A faux apology spilled from her lips, and Carmen gave a one-shouldered shrug, the light brown, almost amber, of her eyes caught on Ollie's.

"It's okay."

It wasn't okay, because Ollie didn't want just an acceptance of an apology and for it to be over. Dark smudges sat under Carmen's eyes, but somehow that made their color more vibrant. There was a forest in those eyes, the bark and wild growth of secrets and depth that Ollie wanted to disappear into. She wanted to draw that complexity, to find a color that completely matched and layer it thick over paper.

Ollie licked her lips, which suddenly felt chapped, and the fact she'd been rushing to meet Sean slipped to the back of her mind. She leaned against the locker next to Carmen. "Are you coming to Williams's party this weekend?"

Those eyes widened, eyebrows climbing. "What's a Williams?"

Carmen's lips quirked up in a way that Ollie wanted to see more often. Anytime she'd spotted her, Carmen had seemed so serious, and now that curve was a surprise. She gave a huff of a laugh. "Sara Williams. Foster sister of the captain of the guys' soccer team?"

"Oh." Something flashed, a shadow that flittered across Carmen's face at the description. "I, uh, hadn't heard anything about it."

"You should come. It's kind of open invite. Her parents are away."

Carmen gave a vacant nod and shuffled her feet, a hint that Carmen was about to move on. A trill of desperation ran up Ollie's spine.

"Maybe." Carmen's gaze was on the ground, somewhere near Ollie's feet.

Before Carmen could leave, Ollie blurted out, "Why aren't you on the team, anyway? I saw you score six goals in class the other day."

The words had left her lips before Ollie had contemplated them, before she had considered the fact they proved she'd been watching Carmen. She wanted to regret them, to reel them back in to sit somewhere no one could pick them apart, but Carmen had pressed back against the lockers, in a mirror of Ollie's position, and Ollie couldn't feel any regret at all.

"I don't like soccer."

She didn't have to know the girl to know this was a lie. "I'm Olivia." She stuck her hand out, stiff and awkward, and cursed herself for it. "But everyone calls me Ollie."

"Carmen."

They shook once, hands dropping quickly, Ollie panicking that she'd hold on too long, so she let go too soon. Carmen pushed her hands into her back pockets.

"I know," Ollie said, hoping it sounded smooth and not like she was a stalker. The hesitant smile told her that maybe she'd managed it.

CHAPTER 2

THE NIGHT WAS STIFLING, LEAVING Carmen's skin itchy.

There were nights she dreamed of crawling out of her skin. Of pulling at herself until her seams fell apart in threads and she could scatter grains of herself over the floor. Some nights, when her house had been without an adult for more than a week, she felt like running. She'd jump a bus and then a plane and disappear into another country, never to be seen again. Her feet would lose themselves on paths built centuries upon centuries ago, fruit she'd never seen would explode over her tongue, and her fingers would trace ruins time itself hadn't been able to erase. And slowly, painfully, like stretching a canvas until it was the size it had been made for, she'd become who she was meant to be.

But then Mattie would shuffle into her room in the dead of the night like he had tonight, rubbing sleep from his eyes. His cheekbones were sharp like hers, but his black curls and dark mahogany skin were both from a father who wasn't hers at all. His father had never known he existed, and her father had died not long after Carmen had been born. Carmen sometimes let herself wonder if everything would be different if he hadn't died—if her mother had gotten that vacant look in her eyes from his death or if it had always been there.

But then, if he hadn't died, Carmen wouldn't have Mattie.

Like he did tonight, he would curl into her bed, too big for it at eight years old, but she'd never send him away. Carmen would lie there, and the warm, even breaths against the crook of her neck would stitch up those holes in her, would pull her feet back until she accepted that she had to stay where she was.

She always would for Mattie.

That girl in school had been staring at her lately, the girl with a mess of curls on her head and eyes that were the blue of oceans and skies in flashes.

With her hands stained in paint and wishes and her skin a deep dark brown, Ollie had left a feeling of normalcy in Carmen's chest. It was a light feeling that sat next to the heavy stone her mother always left inside her as Carmen walked her brother home from school, as she made him dinner with the last remnants of pasta in the cupboard, and even as she made sure he did his homework, brushed his teeth, went to bed.

The gas was out, so they had no hot water; she had boiled the pasta in the kettle and hoped they didn't lose the electricity too.

That stone inside her just grew heavier. Would her mother be back tomorrow? They really were out of food this time. She would have to scavenge soon.

She hated doing that.

That was how it started. Too many times without lunch at school got noticed. The hang of clothes, the distracted look in a hungry kid's face. All that sent them down a road Carmen and Mattie had gone down twice before. And Carmen couldn't walk it again, had promised Mattie they wouldn't as his nails dug desperately into her neck after the last time they had been separated for far too long.

Her mother would be back the next day. She would.

She had to be.

Carmen buried her face into Mattie's hair and breathed him in, the smell of kid—grass and school and pure Mattie—settling around her.

If her mother came home, Carmen had a semblance of a chance of going out that weekend. Shame flashed in her belly that *that* was a huge part of the reason she hoped her mother would come back. If Mattie could go to a sleepover, there would be an adult around, just in case.

And Carmen could feel like other teenagers, just for one night.

The next afternoon, though, she wasn't there, and Mattie and Carmen sat at the table that wobbled, with marks cut into it where her mother had once chopped at white powder. When Carmen had walked in and found her doing that, she'd taken Mattie's hand, dragged him out, and hadn't taken him home until stupidly late.

Mattie's fingers ran along one of the lines, his thumbnail following it like a train on its track.

At times, Carmen felt like that: like a train on a precarious track where just one waver could derail them all.

"She's been gone a week." His voice was high, nerves plucking at his vowels. Carmen was pretty sure kids his age didn't normally keep track of time like that.

"Yeah, she has. But…" She waited for him to look up, his eyes deep and dark, and Carmen could swear they had been like that when he was a baby: knowing and wise and too pure for what he'd been born into. "…I got us dinner."

And those eyes lit up. He didn't ask where, and Carmen didn't tell him. She pulled out a container from her bag, followed by a second one, and they ate until they thought they'd be sick. Carmen didn't tell him she'd pulled money from a teacher's bag, her heart in her throat and her hands clammy. She didn't do it a lot, especially now, but there was no way she'd risk listening to her brother's stomach rumble emptily next to her in bed again. They'd had nothing to take to school. Lies dripped from both their tongues, adept at covers and half-truths, but it really would be noticed soon.

The cafeteria lunch for kids with no money was almost as bad as not having any lunch at all.

Her mother needed to come back, and anger itched under Carmen's skin that they needed her at all.

"I love noodles." His plump lips rounded, and he slurped one up.

Carmen's laugh, rare and unheard in that house, bounced off the walls.

Their mother didn't come back the next day, but she did Friday. She had blown-wide pupils and a slur to her voice and was clutching money too closely that Carmen didn't want to ask about.

Mattie, no longer tiny and easily supplicated, gave his mother a grim smile, his eyes only lighting up a little when she handed him a new Nintendo DS. He quickly said, "Thanks, Mom."

And Carmen's heart swelled, pushed against her ribs, and choked her at the way he really did mean the words.

So, Saturday night, Carmen found herself at a party far from the city center.

People spilled from room to room, the house huge, the property huge, the atmosphere huge—Carmen had walked a mile and a half from the bus to get there, a bottle in hand pilfered from her mother's bag.

Their hot water still wasn't on, so Carmen had taken a cold shower. Before Mattie had gone to his friend's house, she'd heated the kettle to make a bath that wasn't freezing and forced him into it.

He gave in. They knew how to cover.

When Carmen left the house, her mother had already been gone for hours, eyes glassy as she'd taken her keys. She'd smelled like vodka. It'd made Carmen hesitate before leaving. If something happened and Mattie needed to go home... But she'd pushed it aside. He was safe at a friend's.

Carmen hated alcohol, hated the burn, the smell. Hated the way it made her mother into someone Carmen swore she hadn't been once upon a time. But that may have been a false thing to swear to, a lie to sit heavy on her shoulders. Because, really, Carmen barely remembered a time her mother wasn't high on something, gambling away what they had, forgetting she had two children at home who needed her to be something.

But even Carmen knew, in her zero experience with this, that you never turned up to a party without something. Her heart thudded at the amount of people—the laughing, the shrieking—and she uncapped the bottle and took a swig, purely with the hope of faking some confidence. Her face scrunched up at the taste. She'd never spent much time with people her own age outside of school. She wasn't sure she could slide in comfortably and pretend she fit in among them, worried about kissing, tests, the next soccer game, and anything else in between.

Her feet ghosted from room to room, and something inside her clenched as she realized she didn't really know anyone. That missed school year hung wide between her and everyone else, and she hadn't exactly tried very hard before anyway. She never knew how: the ground that was meant to be common had always been foreign under her own feet, and she couldn't expect someone else to attempt to step over it.

Somehow, Carmen found herself in a conversation with an old classmate that started awkwardly but ended up flowing, a river in its bed, smooth and easy. They shared a drink and a laugh, and another boy joined in and held his hand up with a grin. "That goal in PE the other day? Like, *seriously*."

His hand hung there, and Carmen stared at it. With raised eyebrows, he wriggled his fingers, and Carmen laughed, the sound too obviously like relief to her ears. She slapped her hand against his.

"Why aren't you on the team?" he asked.

He had kind eyes and a kind face. A shadow shaded his jaw. His eyes were a little unfocused, probably from the drink sloshing in the red cup in his hand.

The question made her swallow and eye the room. Could she sidle away, out of this conversation? Her cheeks were already growing hot. She couldn't afford the registration, the equipment, the cleats, the time to train. What if Mattie needed something? Their mother was gone more often than not.

"You really should join. The girls' team is kickass, and you'd make a great striker. Hey, dude." He turned to his friend, Jacob, the one Carmen had started talking with at first. "Isn't there that program now? Money to get girls onto the soccer team, to pay for stuff 'cause they're desperate for decent players?"

He said it innocently, but maybe he wasn't so oblivious after all and didn't want to offer it to her like charity. Hope, or something like it, ballooned in her throat.

"Yeah, I heard the coaches talking about it."

The guy whose name she still didn't know turned back to her. "You should totally talk to them. I'll recommend you, if you want."

And that's when it clicked: he was the captain of the boys' soccer team. This was his house.

She smiled despite herself. "Okay."

Overwhelmed and a little light-headed, Carmen slipped away when they started talking about starting a chugging contest. After wandering though rooms full of people, Carmen didn't see Ollie and ended up outside, surrounded by cool, still air. When she sat down, the cold quickly seeped into her jeans from the grass, but she didn't mind, because as she tilted her head up, the sky was a blanket of whirling stars and black clouds. She took a sip from the bottle between her legs and watched the patterns overhead with her tipsy gaze.

Maybe she could play soccer.

That was like something beyond her reach, something silly.

Someone plopped down next to her, fingers brushing over hers to steal the bottle from between her legs. Carmen was too hazy to be surprised, and a giggle washed over her as she turned her head. She was struck by the sight of Ollie tipping the bottle back to take a sip. A loud "ugh" followed the swallow.

A husky laugh fell from Carmen's throat, unfamiliar, and she watched Ollie's profile as she ran a tongue over her lip. Something pulled low in Carmen's stomach. "Hey."

"Hey." Ollie looked at her. "You made it."

"That I did."

Ollie held the bottle out, and Carmen couldn't say no to the stormy offer in those eyes. She took a long sip.

"Are you having fun?" Ollie asked.

Something like delight painted across her features as she watched Carmen swallow the burning liquid down. Her skin was such a delicate shade of brown, yet the blue of her eyes was bright, an intriguing contrast that left Carmen tripping over her words.

"I am."

"You sound surprised."

Carmen looked around, the noise filtering out of the open doorway and people trickling through the doors, their laughter loud and raucous. Couples were making out in every darkened corner, one even on a trampoline. "I suppose I am." She turned back to Ollie. "This isn't usually my scene."

"Hmm." Ollie clicked her tongue and pressed against Carmen. Her shoulder was warm, a heavy weight of young comfort.

She was so easily affectionate, and Carmen didn't want to stiffen at the touch, but she did a little. But Ollie didn't even seem to notice. She tilted her head to stare at Carmen. "And what is your scene?"

Carmen would have waded into Ollie's eyes and never come out again if someone offered her the chance. She shrugged and said nothing and instead offered the bottle to Ollie for another sip.

When Ollie held it out toward her again, Carmen tried to take it back. With a laugh, Ollie held on, their fingers slipping together against the neck of the bottle, sticky with spilled spirits. Ollie tugged, gravity happened, and they tumbled together, a tangle on the ground. Ollie's hair splayed out around her head, and Carmen's fingers trailed over it, like tendrils of fog against her skin. Ollie's hand was stuck between their chests. Surely, she would be able to feel the thumping of Carmen's heart through muscle and bone and skin.

"Ollie!"

And with that, they were pulled away, hauled onto their feet.

"This is Sara." Ollie threw her arm easily over the girl's shoulder.

With nimble movements, Sara pulled grass out of Ollie's hair, her big, dark eyes throwing a wink at Carmen.

Brashness normally made her uncomfortable, but the motion sat easily on the shoulders of the plump Sara, and Carmen found herself smiling.

They were called inside to a game with a ping-pong ball and cups. Carmen remembered the party game from a book. Turned out she sucked at it.

"I chose the wrong team," Ollie declared with a wide, cheery grin and a nudge to Carmen's shoulder after tossing a ball over the table and missing all the cups. She blew a kiss to the boy across the table, Sean, one of many names thrown Carmen's way over the evening.

The other day, Carmen had seen Ollie nuzzle his neck in the corridor at school.

Sara grinned at them, bumping her hip against Sean's. "It doesn't matter whose team you're on. You always suck."

The ping-pong ball landed with a *splat* in a cup, and Ollie pouted but picked it up and drank the contents. She put the cup back down with a twist of her mouth. "Who put Jaeger in the cups?"

"You did." Carmen said it with a laugh, and Ollie rolled her eyes.

"True. Well, I have terrible ideas. You'll learn that." Ollie closed an eye, lined up her shot, and threw the ball. It bounced off one of the cups' rims, and Sara and Sean crowed. "My ideas are about as terrible as I am at this game."

There was another *splat* as Sean got the ball in a cup that was for Carmen.

Ollie winked. "But you suck too, so we can suck together." She held the drink out, swaying a little. Or maybe that was Carmen? "Bottoms up!"

The alcohol was burning in Carmen's stomach, but she didn't care, because Ollie really was an affectionate person. Her hand ran down Carmen's arm at one moment, and later her arm slung over Carmen's shoulders. She was full of fist bumps and high fives and cheers and loud groans when they had to drink again. At some point, she pulled the snapback cap off the head of one of her many friends—a kid named Deon. It sat backward on her head, ridiculous. If Carmen stumbled, it was into Ollie, who giggled and pulled her in closer. Everything was a blur, but it wasn't a bad feeling.

When they lost their second game, Ollie threw up her hands and shook her head. "God, no. No more. We're shit."

Their place went easily to others more than willing to take it. She led Carmen to the bathroom, a smile on her face, and when they fell through the door and against the sink, they were wrapped up in each other.

"I thought you had to pee?"

Ollie shrugged, her nose against Carmen's neck and her breath sending shivers down Carmen's back. "Not anymore."

Carmen pushed the hat away and it fell into the sink. It had sat too low on Ollie's forehead. She wanted to see her with no shadows falling over those eyes.

When Ollie's lips pressed to the sensitive skin over Carmen's pounding pulse, Carmen's own parted in a sigh. No one had ever touched her there, like that, with softness and uncertainty. She swallowed heavily and felt the lips against her throat curve up in a smile. They trailed to her mouth, and it seemed so simple to kiss her, to fall into the safety of Ollie's warm mouth, the wetness of her tongue against Carmen's own. Carmen's first kiss, drunk in a bathroom. Her first kiss, delivered in a way she'd always thought she'd never want but now wouldn't change for anything.

Ollie's glasses fogged up, and she giggled, the sound a delight. She pushed them on top of her head. Fingers buried in her hair, and Carmen's nails scraped skin she exposed by plucking at Ollie's shirt.

Carmen had known, had known she could fall into Ollie and not crawl her way out, because why would she want to?

Hours later, Carmen stumbled through her front door, a thousand memories of her mother doing the same thing crashing into her. The smell of alcohol and disappointment dragged itself inside, not far behind. Something rebellious stirred under the knee-jerk disgust that swelled up in her. Carmen was sixteen, was smart, was young, was desperate for something that tasted like normal—she could do this just once.

Squaring her shoulders, swaying only a little, Carmen stumbled down the hallway, her keys rattling on a table before they dropped heavily to the ground. For a moment, she eyed them, then decided they weren't worth the effort. Before she could turn to go to her room, she froze. Her mouth was dry. Water. Water would help this situation. She turned for the living room, but paused in the doorway. A blurry shape on the sofa slowly came into focus.

Carmen's hand gripped the doorframe, fingers biting into the wood. "Mattie?"

He was huddled in a ball. The clock above him said three in the morning.

He said nothing, so Carmen, dread rippling in her belly, hurried over to sit next to him. When her hand ran across the plane of his shoulder blades, they quivered under her palm. "Mattie? Why aren't you at your friend's house?"

"Mom picked me up. Then she went out." His voice was hoarse, probably scratched from hours of crying. "She went out and left me alone."

Carmen never left him alone. Never. Her lips were numb. "Why did she pick you up?"

"I don't know. She was saying all kinds of stuff, weird stuff, then left the house. She didn't even say why."

Guilt flared. Carmen wrapped her arms completely around Mattie, pulling him half into her lap, not caring how his legs didn't fit anymore.

"She was gone, but so were you."

His sobs were hot against her neck. Hot and wet and everything she had promised herself she would never play a part in. Carmen would never be their mother. But the smell of spirits clung to her clothes, it was early morning, and her brother was sobbing. Disgust at herself curled in her lungs, her breathing halting at the choking sensation of it.

She wanted to tell him sorry, to fix it, but instead she held him to her chest and rocked him, the way he'd liked when he was small, the way her mother had shown her to do before she went away for a few nights, before Mattie could even crawl.

Sniffling into her shirt, he pulled his head back, his face wrinkled. "You smell."

"Sorry."

He opened his mouth to say something but snapped it shut, and he whipped his head around, staring out the window.

It took Carmen longer, but her drunken brain registered the blue-and-red lights washing the room, washing Mattie's face in a ghostly image of wide eyes and open mouth.

"Not again," he whispered, his words settling deep in Carmen's chest.

CHAPTER 3

CARMEN'S HEART WAS THUDDING, A beat so fast she thought she was going to be sick. In her arms, Mattie was shaking; his eyes still hadn't left the window. And in a moment, everything shrank to a kind of clarity, a focal point. Carmen bit her lip, looking from out the window and back to Mattie, the broken look on his face shattering her insides.

"No." His voice scraped out, rasping, grating over Carmen's cheek. His eyes screwed shut, and he shook his head again and again and again. "No. No. Carmen. No. Not again. I don't want to go back."

Something in Carmen's throat expanded, a lump growing bigger and bigger, and she couldn't swallow past it. She could only hope the evidence of it didn't leak out of her eyes. The sound of a door slamming shut, followed by another, echoed in her ears, and anxiety flared deep in her gut, so far down, clawing up and trying to fight at the rest of her. How were they here again?

"I can't, I can't, I can't, I can't." The voice was a whisper in her ear, but Mattie may as well have been screaming.

Their chests expanded in time, too fast, oxygen saturating their blood and too much carbon dioxide expelling from their bodies as they drew shallow, panicked breaths. Carmen desperately tried to grab on to a solid thought. "Mattie." She didn't recognize her own voice, the desperation, the plea. "Mattie, look at me." She clasped his burning cheeks, his hair curling at the edges of her fingers. He shook his head in her grasp, and she clung to him, her voice low. "Mattie, please."

He forced his eyes open, and the look in them cracked her down the middle.

"Mattie, listen to me carefully. Take a breath in, slowly."

He did as she said, and that was all she had time to let him do. Knocks pounded at the door, echoing alongside the flurry in her chest, and Mattie's breathing sped up again.

"I need you to go to your room."

When he stood, she pushed him on shaky legs in the right direction.

Fists pounded at the door again, and Carmen waited until she heard the *snick* of her bedroom door. Of course he went to her room and not his own. She pulled open the front door.

The lights were even brighter outside, and Carmen closed her eyes for a moment, squinting when she finally opened them again. A man and a woman stood in front of her, both with grim expressions that did nothing to ease the tightness in Carmen's chest. The constantly flashing colors coming from their car bounced off their metal badges and reminded her of the party she'd just left.

"Carmen García?"

She nodded, gripping the door. She waited, like last time, to be told her mother had been arrested again. Once for drugs. Another for leaving minors alone, which constituted neglect. What had happened now? Carmen had made sure no one could think neglect this time around, hadn't she?

"We're really very sorry to tell you this, but there's been an accident."

The rest of their words filtered out, were nothing. Their mouths moved, and Carmen watched them silently, the indistinct sound buzzing in her ears, getting louder and louder.

Her mother was dead, and that meant foster care would be permanent this time.

CHAPTER 4

ON MONDAY MORNING, OLLIE WAS finally hangover free. Sunday had been spent with her friends and Sean by the pool, avoiding their questions of where she had been for hours the night before. Instead, she'd lain in the sun and run her tongue over her lips, as though it could evoke the same sensation Carmen had caused the night before.

It couldn't.

She walked the school corridors with the memory of lips and tongues and teeth, of bruising kisses and fingers that caressed her skin languidly, delighting in every tremor and ripple. Ollie hadn't known it could feel like that. She hadn't known *girls* could feel like that, or even if they were supposed to, despite her feelings that she *liked* both boys and girls.

Her gaze swept the classrooms, the cafeteria, the gym. She walked with intent, in the hope she would bump into Carmen. Ollie would lean into her, look up at her from under her lashes and hope, just hope, that she wasn't freaked out by the other night, but rather that she was as utterly delighted as Ollie.

If Carmen regretted it, Ollie would swallow all of this down and smile. And then spend the next year convincing Carmen to do that again and again, if she had to. Never mind the boyfriend Ollie had.

On Wednesday, Ollie still hadn't found her.

Over lukewarm food and souring milk, she tried to ask casually, "Have you guys seen Carmen?"

"The chick from the party?"

"Yeah."

Sara laughed. "That girl was fun—would never have known. I don't remember her speaking much when she was in our year." She shrugged. "Haven't seen her, though. Ask her to the next party, yeah?"

No one else had seen her either, and Ollie didn't ask again.

By Friday, Carmen still hadn't appeared, and Ollie was beginning to think she'd imagined the entire thing.

Floating through the weekend was easy, something comfortable. The past week of school faded into the recesses of Ollie's mind, and she tried to forget the touch of Carmen's fingertips against her cheeks and the bite of her teeth on her lips. She had moments of contented boredom, of stretching out in the backyard, layered in clothes, as they'd finally had to accept the warm weather was leaving. Her friends were laughing around her. In the early afternoon, the sun burst out, and she made the most of it, stripping to her bikini.

When Sean rubbed sunscreen on her back, his fingers smoothing over muscles, Ollie tried not to remember other hands on that spot the weekend before. Instead, she smiled up at him, the sun glinting behind his head and casting him in shadow. She imagined him flattening her pieces back together, running her parts over each other until she fit back together seamlessly. But for reasons she couldn't name, that thought left her squirming to get away.

She ended up next to Sara, the ease of her friendship sometimes more comfortable than the expectations Sean carried in his eyes.

"I have news." Sara was sprawled on her back, blinking up at the sky.

"Is it what I think?" The smile was already pulling up Ollie's lips, for the moment letting her take her mind off the mystery that was Carmen García.

"Maybe." Sara was grinning so hard her cheeks had to hurt.

"There are two options."

"Yup."

"The official adoption papers have gone through..." Ollie paused hopefully, but Sara's face stayed perfectly neutral. "Or your parents think you've finally won and you can get your name legally changed?"

"What if I told you both?"

Now Ollie was grinning. "No way."

"Way."

The foster parents Sara had been placed with when she was eleven had been fighting to adopt her the last six and a half years, and fighting to get her name legally changed from her deadname for just as long. When Ollie had first met her, Sara was quiet, yet explosively angry at unexpected times.

There were moments at school Ollie didn't quite understand, in which some teachers called Sara "him" and others "her." Or used an entirely different name, the deadname Sara would soon be able to leave completely behind her.

And then there had been the day Sara's parents had come in, their faces colored in anger.

That afternoon by the swings, Sara had whispered to Ollie that she was a foster kid and a year older than all of them.

It had been a new word—*foster*.

Sara had explained her foster parents were new but wanted to adopt her, that they didn't try to use the name Sara hated but had had pushed onto her for years in the foster system. They just used *Sara* like she asked. They arranged for appointments to talk to someone who helped, they let Sara wear whatever she wanted.

Wide-eyed and not completely understanding, Ollie had nodded.

They'd become fast friends, easy friends. Sara was outrageously smart and Ollie outrageously protective.

"Sara!" Their hug was sun-warmed and smelled like the coconut in their sunscreen. Sara held out her hand, up in the air between them, and Ollie linked their fingers. The sun was a bright, lukewarm ball the knot of their hands blocked out.

"Next to me, you look pale," Sara said.

Ollie burst out a laugh. Her father was black and her mother was white, but Ollie was still dark skinned. Her blue eyes threw people, she knew. Being much darker, though, Sara liked to tease her. "I'm not even close to pale," Ollie protested.

The teasing was all for play. It's what they did. Jokes and fun, but careful questions when needed.

Ollie had been there when Sara had first been approved for puberty blockers, which had taken years due to Sara still being in the foster system. Then later, the day she'd finally started hormone replacement therapy, Ollie had filmed the start of her transition video. Sara had a huge following online.

That night, Ollie flopped over the huge sofa in her basement in a pile with her friends. Legs were thrown over her own, a chest under her head as she watched a film flicker over the screen with a heartbeat thrumming in her ear, keeping the time of an easing adolescence.

Halfway through the movie, her dad brought more popcorn down the stairs, and the smell of butter and salt made them all sit up. From the corner of her eye, she saw him shake his head at them all before throwing her a wink, the sight stitching itself across her ribs.

When Sean kissed a grain of salt off her lip and tucked her hair behind her ear, she sighed into his movements with a smile and tried to stitch that feeling into herself as well.

CHAPTER 5

Group homes were full of strange sounds, of bumping footsteps and the clearing of foreign throats. Of kids with darkness looped into their eyes and track marks along their skin. Of forgotten kids, of unwanted kids, of kids who were wanted but lost, of kids who craved running and kids who wanted to stay and kids who wandered around with sad, vacant eyes.

Now Mattie's eyes were full of ghosts, of flashing blue and red, and of a look of slight betrayal. In her bed that night, with the terror of knowing that after a week she had to go back to school, Carmen stared at the ceiling. She stuffed her hand in her mouth and bit down on it so she could stifle the sob that burned at her lungs and pushed at the insides of her ribs. A stain stretched over her head on the ceiling, and she traced it with her gaze over and over again in a pattern until she started to feel like she could breathe. Her eyes were seared with exhaustion, the feeling creeping along her bones to settle in her marrow and threatening to overcome her.

She was tired of talking to a therapist who could never get it, of sitting with Mattie and trying to get him to talk to her. All he asked, though, was *where after this, what after this?* The knowledge sat in his eyes of the last two times before, one when they were together that he barely remembered and another alone that he remembered all too well. He clung to her like he hadn't in years, his fingers clawing at her shirt, at her hands, his body against her side. In his therapy sessions, since he wouldn't talk—only grit his teeth and stare—Carmen talked at his therapist. She talked and talked and tried to convince her that unlike the last time, they needed to go to a placement together.

That was what Connecticut was supposed to try to do, to place siblings together.

No one told them anything, though.

Except rules. There were so many rules. Rules to use the TV, to eat, to shower, to see each other, to leave. The girls' and boys' sides were separated. Three times in the last week, Mattie had snuck out to slip into her room and curl along her length. His fingers burned holes into her arms with their grip as he cried for a mother Carmen had always tried to shield him from the truth of. After the third night of him being physically dragged out of her bed, they left someone permanently in his hallway. After that, the hollowness under his eyes grew deeper, and he pushed his food around his plate, asking her when they could finally leave.

Sixteen was too young for her to take guardianship, and Carmen wanted to rage at them, to tear down their stupid rules and scream that she'd been doing it since she was eight. Why was she suddenly too young now?

Mostly, the anger bubbled under her skin—at her mother, at herself, at adults who played God—as she stared upward, sleepless, teeth grinding, with no idea what to do.

On Monday, Carmen was back in school, cloaked in rumors and with something glinting in her eyes Ollie didn't think had been there before. The rumors reached Ollie first, words like *drunk driving, syringes, dead on arrival, pileup,* and *cause of death* flowing through the school corridors, unstoppable as they always were. Other words rose up, of foster care and group homes, and Ollie wanted to cover her ears and tell them all to go to hell. Carmen's life was not a juicy story, was not something amusing to exchange between toilet stalls.

Especially since barely anyone had known her name before this.

Their table at lunch didn't buzz with the news, though, and Ollie fell into the comfort of her friends, unable to find Carmen beyond a glimpse in the corridor. The only thing mentioned was a "hope she's okay" from Deon.

Sara gave a one-shouldered shrug and then propped her chin in her hand, straddling her seat. "Sometimes the system works out okay."

And they all hushed and clearly remembered that, of all of them, she would know. Something was in her eye, though, that made Ollie both want to ask more, yet also turn away, to not push for things she didn't really want to know. Instead, she did neither and threw Sara her pudding cup, earning a wink from her and a sigh from Sean, who had been eyeing it.

That afternoon, Ollie slipped out of Art, under the pretense of finding supplies, and watched the PE class troop into the locker rooms. One figure walked behind, taking her time, and Ollie watched her walk behind the bleachers when the teacher wasn't looking. Ollie took a breath and, not knowing why she was going, followed, ducking behind. What she saw stopped her dead.

Crouched on the ground, face buried in her hands, Carmen looked small and defeated. Lost. She looked nothing like the girl Ollie had found sitting under the stars with a smile on her lips and a bottle of whiskey in her lap.

Ollie hovered, torn between leaving her be and walking forward.

Again she decided on neither. "Carmen."

Carmen's head shot up, and instead of cheeks covered in tears, Ollie just saw red-rimmed eyes and flushed cheeks, a tight jaw, and lips in a taut line.

"Ollie."

The word was hoarse, was a run of vowels, and Ollie thought she could listen to her name being said like that forever.

Carmen stood, and Ollie leaned against the wall beside her, the brick rough under her palm. The amber of Carmen's eyes was a storm of things Ollie had no name for, as much as she pushed at her mind to find the words.

"Are you okay?"

The question was a terrible one, clichéd and unhelpful. It was useless and nothing that Carmen could need. Instead of the scoff Ollie expected at it, or the anger or the eye roll, Carmen swallowed so heavily Ollie could see it. Her lip quivered just slightly as she looked up at Ollie, as if willing herself to not fall to the floor in parts, shattered and so scattered as to never be put back together.

Carmen shook her head, her eyes brighter and magnified by the tears that swam in them but never fell. "No. I'm not."

And then Carmen surged forward, pushing Ollie against the brick where it scraped at her back, a groan ripping out of her throat. Hands threaded in Ollie's hair, and lips pressed to her own, kissing her like Carmen wanted to coax something from Ollie that she didn't have to give.

But Ollie tried. She surged against her, their bodies flush, and let Carmen turn her inside out, let her fingers flay her open, expose her insides, and leave her with nothing left to hide. Nails dug into her scalp, and Ollie pulled her closer, Carmen's shirt fisted in her hand. The kiss tasted of salt, of desperation, of what sadness would taste like. Of loss and grief and hurt, and Ollie wanted to tear that feeling out from Carmen, even if just for a minute, so she could be free of it.

When it ended, it was as if Carmen had to rend herself in two to detach, the kiss pulling apart like something was tearing. She dropped her forehead to Ollie's for just a second, their lips grazing once more before Carmen sucked in a breath and turned on her heel to go back to the locker rooms. Ollie was left gasping for breath as she watched her walk away.

The group home was no different after a day at school, walking the eclipse of her life, but Carmen moved about with the shadow of Ollie on her lips, and it made her feel like something was under her control. Mattie wouldn't speak about his day, his jaw set and his eyes hard, even as his fingers dug into her shirt. He sat next to her on one of the sofas, staring at the television screen without emotion.

They didn't have a TV at home. Normally, he'd be enthralled. Through the fog of her own uncertainty, Carmen tried to coax him out of the vacancy in his eyes that didn't sit right, to poke his side and draw out *something*. But her heart wasn't in it, and she gave up quickly, asking him if he wanted to play his DS.

"Someone stole my games." His focus stayed on the TV.

Carmen just put her arm around his shoulder and shifted closer. His rigid body softened slightly.

They stayed there until their counsellor appeared and led them to one of the small meeting rooms, all hard plastic chairs and hard plastic atmosphere. They sat among it, and the woman looked at them with a smile as plastic as what Carmen sat on.

"I have some news."

Later, Carmen would be grateful she hadn't used words like *great* or *exciting* or even *good*.

"We have a foster home, available tomorrow."

Carmen twitched and felt Mattie do the same next to her.

The group home was bad, but a foster home could be worse. Her last had not been a pleasure, and Mattie had refused to speak of his. He'd come home a mess, though. Their first was one Carmen was glad Mattie hadn't been old enough to really remember.

The memories of that place had lain thick over her skull. The early relief that responsible adults had appeared to look after them had faded quickly, and instead, a new relief had filled her when they sent them back to their mother. How her mother did it, Carmen would never know, but she had proven herself reformed to the courts, even if she had quickly fallen back into old habits. But at least she left them in peace.

Carmen just stared at the woman and waited.

"Unfortunately, it's only for Mattie."

Something caught in her stomach—caught and held and didn't let go.

"Carmen, at your age, as you know, placement is hard. We're trying to get you a place in a smaller home for girls on the other side of the city."

It seemed to take a moment for the words to hit Mattie, only when Carmen closed her eyes, her hands clenching in her lap, did she hear his seat scrape loudly against the floor. He must have stood too quickly, because the chair clattered backward, the door slamming loudly behind him.

CHAPTER 6

ALL NIGHT, CARMEN LAY AWAKE, bouncing her leg nervously, biting her fingers until they bled. In this state, rules were supposed to be followed that ensured siblings saw each other, even if placed separately, but she knew from last time how quickly that promise could fall apart.

And that was only if anyone actually made it happen in the first place.

At least they'd been together in the first house, when Carmen had been eleven. The second time, two years later, had been a mess. Three foster homes in as many months. The last one she'd been sent to had left a trail of scars through Carmen's mind she didn't think would ever fade. She'd only lasted there a week. Over the few months she'd been in the homes, Carmen had gotten to see Mattie twice. Each time, he had withdrawn a little more. She'd only seen more of him after the third home because she'd run away and taken matters into her own hands.

When they were finally back together at home, he'd been like a shell—one Carmen hadn't been able to crack open for months. The three different schools they went to as their mother moved them around didn't help.

He was older now. What if it happened again? What if that shell grew thicker, more impenetrable?

Whatever happened now could be permanent.

Her mother, God, her mother. Carmen jammed her hand into her mouth again. The scrapes from her teeth, from doing this again and again in the last week, cracked open as she bit down. She needed to stifle the sob that threatened to break her open at the thought of her goddamned, fucking mother. She was dead, they had no semblance of a home now to go back to. No way to try to make everything as normal as possible for Mattie. She'd be on the other side of the city in a new school, too far away to help him.

Who knew where he'd be, what his placement would be like. That lack of information was an unknown that loomed so big it shadowed Carmen's eyes with its ferocity. The lump that had taken permanent residence in her throat grew at the thought that he would most likely end up shipped from house to house... She'd seen some of those kids and where they ended up.

Maybe if she could keep him from shattering again over the next year and a half, she could then take guardianship. But then she'd need a job, money, a house. How could she prove she was able to take care of him?

She had nothing.

When someone knocked on the door to rouse the six of them in her dorm, Carmen was still staring upward, her eyes red and the edge of an idea in her mind.

She wasn't doing this again.

She couldn't.

The day after Carmen had kissed Ollie and torn her apart, leaving her to pull all her dizzy pieces back together, Ollie went to school, leaving behind a trail of clothes scattered around her room. She'd thrown them on and off again, in an attempt to find an outfit that would make Carmen and her grasping fingers want to tear her into little pieces once more, with her tongue slipping against Ollie's own.

It was a little embarrassing and not at all like Ollie to stress over an outfit.

"Babe."

Ollie kept her eyes on the door of the cafeteria. "Mm?"

"Babe." Sean's voice grated a little. "You're so distracted."

Hurt laced his voice, and her stomach twinged with guilt. "Sorry." She turned back to him, trying to keep her attention from flitting from person to person. To focus on him and her friends. The sound of their voices as they rose and fell in patterns was a sound she normally melded her own voice to easily, but today just even hearing them was a struggle.

Ollie laughed at something someone said, only slightly forced, and Sean's shoulders relaxed next to her, tension seeping from his body. But Sara just watched her, head slightly cocked. So Ollie ignored her and went back to watching the students who floated in and out.

In the bathroom, Sara cornered Ollie, a hand on her hip and eyes lit with curiosity. "Were you watching for Carmen again?"

"What?" Ollie heard the high lilt at the end of the word, but couldn't stop it. "No. No, I'm just…distracted today. Big test in Chem."

One she'd fail, because instead of studying, Ollie had drawn the same eyes over and over again in her notebook all last night. Her own eyes had burned as sleep evaded her and the look she was trying to capture on paper did so as well.

What was Ollie doing with Carmen? She didn't know. Something fun, she supposed, a distraction from the feeling of monotony that sometimes cracked against her bones. But also, there was something about her eyes and the way she seemed to wander around, lost, that made Ollie want to follow her.

But Sara wouldn't let it go. "Don't lie to me, Ollie—I've known you six years. You blink three times in a row when you lie."

"Do not." Ollie's eyes started to water as she tried not to blink at all.

"Now you look constipated."

With a snorting laugh, Ollie rolled her eyes, and some of the tension that had slid in between them dissipated, filtered away in shared, knowing smiles.

"So why can't you keep your eyes off Carmen?"

Ollie sighed and decided on a half-truth. "I don't know. We've been getting to know each other. And if those rumors are true…"

"You're worried about her?"

Ollie shrugged helplessly, not sure how to put the feeling curling in her chest into words. "She's not here again today. Yesterday, it seemed like she was back." Back and wreaking havoc on Ollie's mind.

"Just add her on Facebook like the rest of the world when they're trying to get in touch with someone. Or Snapchat." Sara leaned toward the mirror, fingers at her hair, and missed the flush Ollie could feel heating her cheeks.

"She's not on either."

Sara froze. "Who isn't on Facebook?"

"Exactly."

Straightening, Sara pulled her phone out of her pocket. "Twitter? Tumblr? The school's forum? Instagram?"

"Not that I could find." So maybe Ollie hadn't *only* been drawing last night.

Jamming the phone back in her pocket, Sara pursed her lips for a minute, a sure sign she was thinking as quickly as she could. "Well, we need to get someone on this who knows more than we do."

"Deon?"

"Deon."

Ollie grinned.

"But not yet, you giant stalker."

Her grin fell. "Why?"

"Because she was here yesterday. It's only been twenty-four hours. Maybe it was her mom's funeral or something…"

Ollie pressed against the wall, crossing her arms. Sara made a good point, and if Ollie pushed, Sara would ask questions, and Ollie was answerless. She had no idea why she cared or what exactly about Carmen left her reeling.

But something did.

And that was enough to break up with Sean, with a fast sentence and a twist of guilt in her gut. She did it after school and said sorry and tried not to dwell on the fact he didn't really look surprised, even as hurt crept into his expression.

On the bus that took them to school, Carmen sat close to Mattie, who grudgingly allowed it, despite his mood. The bundle of bills Carmen had taken from the social worker's bag that morning were lead in her pocket. Her fingers had slid in easily, muscle memory helping her pluck them out and slip them into her own pocket in a split second. She'd ignored the flare of guilt, the quickening of her heart. This morning, she'd made short work of shoving the things into her oversized backpack that she'd managed to think to bring the blurry night the police had come knocking. The pack sat at her feet, ratty and worn and matching her heart. She didn't have a lot, as mostly she wanted anything warm and her toiletries, along with some extras. As her teeth worried at her lip, she had slipped in a textbook, weighty and unnecessary. At the bottom was the sleeping bag she'd now had for years.

Next to her, Mattie resolutely stared forward. He hadn't spoken since last night, not one word to her, no matter how much she tried to promise him it would be fine, that they'd see each other all the time. All he did was stare ahead, his jaw tight. The reassurances had tasted bitter on her tongue, and she eventually stopped spilling them forth.

When they got to Mattie's school first, he stormed down the aisle to get off the bus, and Carmen let him be angry, let him walk away, and dropped her forehead against the bus window, the vibrations giving her a headache.

At her own school, she got off and waited for the bus to turn away. Once it was out of sight, she just walked down the street, her hood pulled over her head and her hands buried in her pockets, fingers plucking at the money that was burning her.

She wandered all day, ending up in a park and pulling out her favorite textbook. While the breeze played at her hair, she devoured it and tried not to think of how Ollie had felt, between her body and the wall. She could almost feel the clinging of her fingers, the way Ollie had pulled her closer and closer, taking the desperation Carmen needed *someone* to absorb. And Ollie had definitely done that. So Carmen tried not to think of it but to concentrate on the text in front of her.

Beyond all of that, she tried not to think about Mattie, about her mother, about what was to come.

Hours later, when school was due to finish, she ended up near Mattie's school, waiting until the bell rang to seek him out. He barely showed surprise when she curled her fingers around his arm and drew him around a corner into the shelter of some trees. Cool shade ran over her skin, and spots of light through the leaves danced over his cheeks.

"Mattie…"

"You're leaving."

He knew her too well. "Not the city, I'll… I'll be here when you need me."

His lip quivered, though Carmen thought she may have imagined it, because the next second his jaw was clenched. "No."

"Mattie…" How did she explain that she had to? She couldn't be where she had been before, just couldn't. If she'd been placed with Mattie, maybe, but in one of those places? Alone?

"No! Last time I barely saw you. They—they kept us apart."

Carmen fell to a knee in front of him, the coolness of the grass seeping through her jeans. "When I left last time, I saw you more than when I was in the foster homes. I could stop by the school, like I am right now."

He stared at her, his eyes narrowing, his voice baby-soft. "But this time we can't end up at home."

"I know… I'm going to fix it, Mattie. I am going to make sure I can be with you when I turn eighteen."

He shook his head. "No. I'm coming."

Somehow, she'd expected that, yet the words still hit her like a slap. "What? You can't. You have school, you need…a house." The argument was weak, but the basic idea was a truth Carmen couldn't deny.

"And you don't?"

Carmen blinked at him, because she had no retort to that. "You—you know I can handle myself." She gave a half-hearted wink he didn't even acknowledge.

With a fluid motion, he pulled his backpack to his front and unzipped it to show it was stuffed with clothes, a toothbrush poking out, and his DS crammed on top.

Panic crawled along her skin. "You were going to run? No." Her fingers dug into his bicep, too hard, too frantic, but he didn't flinch. Horror crawled up her throat at the idea of him alone on the streets. They were going to collect him from school that afternoon to take him to the new place, and he hadn't planned to be there. Carmen couldn't even be mad—she'd done it before, and she had been about to do it again. She was the worst of all influences. But she hadn't been eight; she'd been thirteen—and this time, sixteen. "Mattie, no. You can never run away. You'd be alone. The streets aren't something *fun*."

He stared her straight in the eye, her little brother who was growing too tall too quickly, his face thinning and his baby fat dropping. The glint in his eyes was something most adults didn't have. "I wasn't going to go alone. I knew you'd run too."

For a second, the need for a reprieve broke her, and Carmen dropped her head, still clinging to his bony arms. Too thin; he'd always been too thin. He needed school. He needed food. He needed a roof; he was only eight.

With a breath to inflate her, to build her up, to give her the strength to walk away, Carmen looked up. "You can't come. Once they stop watching you to find me, I'll try and stop by the school to see you, like last time."

His jaw clenched. "They might make me move schools."

"I'll find you."

"How?" He shouted the word at her, his eyes red and brimming, yet nothing on his cheeks but a blazing-red anger.

"I just will, Mattie! I always do."

"Carmen." His voice was rough, hoarse, strained, and she hated what the world was doing to him. "You can't leave me."

"I'm sorry."

She tried to wrap her arms around him, but he pushed her off, planting his hands on her chest and shoving her backward. She landed hard on the ground, but all she could see was how tears streaked his cheeks now, the way his jaw clamped tight.

With hands in the dirt and grass behind her, she watched his chest heave as he dragged in air. She shook her head. "I'll see you soon."

And she turned to leave, his broken "Carmen" hitting her square between the shoulder blades.

She only made it two steps before she froze, her eyes closed tight. He would run anyway. And then where would he be?

She'd promised him she'd never leave him alone again. And he, the boy with shattered promises at his feet, from a mother who didn't know how to keep a single one, had believed her.

With regret in her chest that weighed her down too heavily to breathe, Carmen turned back, feet thudding against the grass with her steps, and took his outstretched hand. Their fingers laced together tight, and they walked away, step by step, from the school, away from any sense. The thought pounded in Carmen's mind that maybe this had been what she was always going to do.

She was too selfish not to.

She could tell herself it was because she'd worry he'd run alone. Hell, it wasn't even a worry; she *knew* he would. She could tell herself it was all for *him*.

But she'd be lying.

CHAPTER 7

For one night, Carmen pretended they could do it alone. They covered themselves in the sleeping bag Carmen had shoved in the bottom of her backpack and in turn covered themselves in the night; they were two kids who had faded into the nothingness of the street. For one night, Carmen pretended she could wrap an arm around her brother and wrap him in words that shielded him from the truth of it all.

It should have been easy, for one night, to block out the thumping of her heart that left her breathless, pumping in time to *what did I do what did I do what the fuck did I fucking do?*

But it wasn't something that was so easy.

Mattie, his thick, black hair against her neck, molded against her like he had so many nights before. Trusting. She didn't need to look at him to know his dark, quick eyes were staring around them. He smelled like the cheap shampoo from the group center, like a little kid who had spent his entire day at school.

He smelled like home.

He smelled like home and everything Carmen had missed last time. Now she had him here with her, and all she had for it was guilt tripping at her stomach and panic clambering its way up her spine.

He was so young.

"It's pretty here."

The urge to laugh at the ridiculous statement was almost overwhelming, but if she blocked out the dripping behind her and the smell, it almost could be called pretty. Under the bridge, the water in front of them was a deep pool of black, and if she tilted her head slightly, the lights of the city reflected all along it. White and orange and blue rippled slightly and made it seem like reality were playing tricks as they skimmed along the surface.

So all Carmen did was hum, letting Mattie think she agreed.

"Is this where you were when you ran away last time?"

Carmen sighed, burrowing farther into the sleeping bag, the dripping of a leaking pipe behind her keeping pace with the beat of her heart, a drum to keep time to the still-repeated thought: *what did I do what did I do?*

"Some of the time." Not all of it. Most had been spent elsewhere, somewhere Carmen was beginning to think they'd have to go back to.

The feeling made her heart speed up even faster. Going back there would be like accepting that this was their reality now, that this was Mattie's life.

"I'm glad I'm with you this time."

Carmen tucked him farther under her arm and said nothing. What the hell had she dragged her little brother into? But he would have run on his own. Carmen had seen it—it had been clear in the stubborn glint in his eye, the set of his jaw, the jut of his chin. A look she knew he had learned from her. A look that told her he meant it.

And what then?

Her brother wandering alone on the street, and hoping to run into Carmen by chance? This city was huge, a maze full of kids and adults. He was five years younger than Carmen was when she had done it, and she had been far too young for it then.

Everyone on the street was too young for it. Even the old generation: the vets, the discarded who lay out in cardboard boxes and tinkled like glass knocking against glass when they moved, their hair white and skin crinkled like fruit left in the sun.

No one was old enough to qualify for this life.

But her brother had already seen his mother pass out on a bathroom floor, experienced hunger rumbling in his belly, sat in darkness and shivered because bills had gone unpaid, and felt abandonment sink into his bones, deep enough to lay a map throughout his insides. Carmen could not have stomached seeing what the streets would do to him if he had run away alone.

It changed people.

But what if the foster home had been a good one? One filled with food and meals that arrived at the same time each day, with an adult who liked to hug, where safety floated over your shoulders like a net that should have been there since forever?

Maybe Mattie would have given that a chance.

Now she would never know, and neither would he, and they lay under a bridge Carmen knew wasn't frequented this time of year: too loud with the trucks reverberating overhead and the lap of the water. Too cold—the breeze carrying a bite, the water carrying a fog that could sink into your skin and leave you trembling.

But not with the sleeping bag made for negative temperatures that she had stolen the last time she'd slept outside, independence burning in her chest and idiocy coursing through her blood. Not with a brother who could sleep through a bomb, not with the need to keep him from the things she'd seen in the squats during her first few weeks on the street, years ago.

She still had nightmares about things that had happened there.

Against her chest, Mattie's breathing evened out, his fingers loosening where they clutched her hoodie. Carmen swallowed and watched the lights play over the surface of the water, trying to keep her mind blank, to not think about what she was going to do.

But really, that was what had gotten her into this mess in the first place.

She'd done what she had wanted to do, followed the urge that had been building for years: to run, to hop a bus, a plane, to disappear. But she'd stalled in her takeoff, her eight-year-old brother's hand in hers, and realized she would never have done any of that without him anyway.

His breath washing over her skin reminded her of him as a baby—even and steady and hers. The moon was full, gaping wide, and Carmen felt as if she could fall through it, like they could both tumble through and move among the stars, stepping from constellation to solar flare, something forbidden to mere mortals, but not to them.

The last time she'd stared up at it all had been with whiskey on her tongue and the warm weight of Ollie next to her. Carmen had actually felt sixteen then, and that hadn't seemed like a bad thing.

But she wouldn't be going back to that, or falling in among the sky.

Instead, she was here, and Carmen had no idea what she was supposed to do now.

Ollie knew she was lucky—that many kids didn't like their parents or their parents didn't like them or everyone rubbed each other the wrong way. She knew there were families that had torn each other apart or parents who didn't care and left their kids alone to float along, adrift in their own mistakes.

Her family wasn't like that.

"When's Sean coming for dinner again?" her father asked, passing potatoes to Ollie before she could ask for them. He liked to regale her friends with stories about how, when she'd been a baby, she'd only eat potatoes. Nothing else. Even for breakfast.

The question grated. "I don't know. He's busy."

She needed to tell them that short thing was over, but panic lit up in her stomach that she couldn't explain.

"He could come this weekend?" Ollie's mother topped off her wineglass, ink still staining her fingers. She must not have had a day doing procedures in the hospitals but in consultation, listening to hearts and writing notes. She was insanely busy all the time.

Her parents weren't like all the ones she knew could exist, and Ollie was lucky; she knew that. But sometimes she was all too aware of the pressure of them both, one on each side of her and always pushing. "Maybe."

"Or do you have exams coming up? Maybe you should study."

"Have you thought any more about those campus tours?"

Who even knew which parent asked what?

Sometimes Ollie was awash in expectation and long-drawn conclusions. All around her, people pushed her into adulthood yet snagged her backward, holding her in place and not wanting her to move forward, while asking things of her that seemed beyond her capabilities.

"Ollie?"

Blinking, she turned to her father. "Yeah?"

"Campus tours?"

"I don't know…"

"I hope you're still thinking of law. You always talked about being a lawyer."

Had she? Or had her parents said she had? "I was thinking of art."

Her father flinched, a quick look, one that was barely discernible. "I still think it's more of a hobby."

Her mother threw him a look, and Ollie didn't know if it meant *not right now* or *stop* or *I know, right?* Whichever it was, she wanted to disappear to her room. Hopefully, Sara would come over later and they could sneak vodka from the hip flask she sometimes brought along. Or she could go out, pretend it was to study, but end up at Deon's and sprawl on his sofa while his parents were away, watching the free Netflix he hacked.

But instead, later, her mother put on a movie, and Ollie sat next to her. In minutes, her mother had pulled Ollie into her side, soothing fingers running against her scalp. Their legs sat next to each other, Ollie's dark ones alongside the white of her mother's, who joked she couldn't tan, even with stuff from a bottle. Her father joined later, next to her, and Ollie liked the way their legs went from white to dark brown to even darker. She wanted to paint it out on a canvas, the way her parents' skin tones had created hers, but instead she stayed pressed between them. They sprawled out, lost in the movie, and Ollie wished they would be this calm all the time.

Carmen woke with a jolt, adrenaline surging through her so fast that she barely noticed the ache in her neck. Everything was blurry, and she rubbed at her eyes, blinking away the last of her dream still at the edges. Something about the taste of whiskey, the splash of a ping-pong ball, the lick of a tongue at her bottom lip.

The sky was streaked with pink, the water no longer a beautiful black pit hiding secrets but a reflection of sunrise, of a new day, of something that should encourage anticipation but left Carmen tasting ash. She had wanted to get herself a life, find a job, and set herself up so that at eighteen she could get her brother back. But the chance of that had been low to begin with.

The air was cool, hinting at a bigger turn of the weather, and she yanked her hood to cover her ears, pulled the sleeping bag higher up over Mattie, and bit her lip.

"What are you thinking?"

The voice was gravelly, full of sleep, and Carmen looked down to see Mattie watching her, his breath warm against her forearm, cheeks a little ashen.

"What we're going to do."

There must have been something in her voice, something that gave her away, because his eyes widened and his voice pushed against the gravel in it. "Don't give me back."

Carmen swallowed past that damn swollen feeling in her throat and settled her hand over his forehead to smooth through his hair, a habit as old as Mattie himself. "What about food?" she challenged.

"We can find food."

Carmen laughed—just a puff of air through her nose—at his cadence, at the naivety.

"We can," he insisted. His voice was still squashed with sleep, and Carmen wished he could stay that way forever, that trusting and sure of her. She wished he could stay this safe in the security of a night with her, with food in his stomach, with warmth. "You did last time."

Carmen pressed her lips together and looked away. From there, they could watch the city come alive from a point where the city couldn't see them. How could she explain that it had been easier last time without an eight-year-old in her care, without worrying about him, worrying about preserving his innocence? At thirteen, she'd looked so young: shelters would call the authorities. Soup kitchens would edge toward their phones, trying to keep her talking, to keep her near, to make a call they thought would be helping her. How fast they'd do that if she went now with someone as small as Mattie at her side.

"I did." There was one thing she could try, but Carmen had no idea if it was an option anymore. "What about school?"

Even curled up in his sleeping bag, sleep still hanging off him like dew, he managed to shrug. "What about it?"

Carmen did laugh this time, softly, the sound grating at her ears but the feeling in her chest easing just slightly. "Said the eight-year-old."

He eyed her. "What's that supposed to mean?"

"You need school."

"Do not."

Carmen sighed and lay back down, Mattie wriggling into her side, warm and breathing and with her.

"Do too," she said.

"Nuh-uh." His voice was muffled against her shoulder. Carmen stared up at the gray cement overhead, covered in layers upon layers of graffiti. The patterns swirled, nonsensical, and she closed her eyes, the colors and curls imprinted on her eyelids. The feeling crept up her throat that that was meant to be an image of her life flowing out in front of her, leading nowhere and wrapping in on itself again and again, colliding with the past so that she never really went forward, or anywhere at all.

They spent the day walking streets Carmen hadn't been to in years, safe in the knowledge that the city was huge, that there were hundreds of kids like themselves and not enough people to find them all. Anonymity held something humbling. To know how easy it was to slip through the cracks. Especially when that was where she wanted to go. With a credit card taken from the same place as the money the morning before, Carmen bought two bus tickets to New York, gave all their details, and let their names get tapped into the computer. Without a backward glance, she dropped the tickets into the trash can outside the station, snapped the credit card in two, and dropped it in after them.

Mattie stared at her, puzzled. She gave him a wink. "The card's probably been reported stolen."

"So?"

Sometimes it was easy to forget how young he was, how much about life even he didn't know yet. "They'll know it was me that took it, and the transaction here will be flagged."

"Flagged?"

They walked down the street, and Mattie's backpack bounced with his steps.

"Like, *noticed*."

"Wouldn't that be bad?"

"Well, if we were actually going to New York, it would be a clue to them, and yes, it would be bad. But that bus leaves in twenty minutes, and they won't notice we're not on it. That shouldn't get logged electronically. They normally tick that off on a piece of paper."

Mattie chewed his lip for a second, his eyebrows scrunched together. "So they won't know where we are?" A grin was starting on his lips, and the pull of it made Carmen want to cry.

Instead, she said, "Exactly. They'll see we bought two tickets there and tell child services. They'll think we've gone there, but really we'll be here."

And that crack they were already slipping into would grow wider, a chasm to swallow a street kid whole.

Mattie stared up at her. "That's pretty smart, Carmen."

Her throat ached at his happiness that she was dragging him down with her.

They spent the day in a library, still clean and put together enough that they could slip a smile to the librarian and mention a homeschooling project. They set up in a corner, and Carmen gave Mattie a topic, one she knew he could go at for ages—the planets and the sun—and watched him walk among the aisles. His fingers plucked at books, trailed along spines. He carried back armloads.

They repeated this for days, the weather cooling around them each morning but Mattie never once muttering against it. Every night, Carmen lay awake, staring upward and begging the sky for a plan. The same one always came to her, but she rejected it every time, stubbornness hardening her jaw as she tried to figure out a way she could make things work with only the two of them.

Or maybe she was waiting for Mattie to give up on this dream so she wouldn't really be giving in to this life.

In the library, Mattie read with small movements of his lips, as though he needed to roll the words around his tongue to really get a feel for them. Carmen showed him the glossary, taught him how to find the words he didn't know. He dragged out a notebook and pen from his backpack, the childish loops to his letters rolling out from his hands and across the pages. His toes just barely scraped the floor when he kicked his legs, and the table shook gently with each movement, but not once did she tell him to stop.

Rather, she sat and mulled. Rolled thought after thought in her mind. Ideas clashed and rebounded, and she picked each one apart until it lay in a tangled mess, proven worthless to help her predicament. Her knee bounced, and she flicked a pen around and around her fingers until she stood and moved to a computer she could still see Mattie from. A colorful book with Saturn spread over its cover sat propped up in front of him.

Carmen wasn't great with computers. They'd never had one at home, and what she'd learned, she'd been taught at school. But she could do a search. She searched for shelters that didn't require your age, that didn't report to child services. None existed for children as young as Mattie, and any that could prove useful were all full.

She searched for soup kitchens. The money in her pocket wasn't going to get them far. Some she went into with Mattie, and they ate fast, keeping an eye on any volunteers who edged for their phones.

Being alone had been so much easier.

Until it hadn't been.

She kept circling back around the idea, again and again. Trying uselessly to avoid it.

During that last day of marinating in bad ideas in the library, a sound at the window drew her attention, and Carmen's stomach sank as water splattered over the glass. Fat, heavy drops started to fall, and soon it was pouring outside, the windows fogging and the rain washing the city clean. With the computer humming in front of her, she watched Mattie look outside, his body tensing, before he looked back to his book. He kept looking back, then away, until eventually he was staring, pupils reflecting the coming storm.

Sliding into a chair opposite him, Carmen tried to smile and cover her panic when his nervous gaze launched to catch her own.

"It's raining."

"It is."

With a quick glance around the library, secrecy already easy for him, Mattie lowered his voice even more. "We'll get wet if we sleep where we've been."

"We will."

He stared at her, and Carmen gave in to the only idea not left strewn and exhausted. "But it's okay. I know somewhere."

And so easily, he relaxed into his chair, pulling the book onto his lap, shoulders no longer squared but at ease. "Oh, okay."

Just like that.

When the library started to close around them, they slipped the books back where Mattie had taken them from. Outside, the cold was almost stinging, and Mattie's cheeks were damp within moments from it. He slid a hand into hers, his fingertips still warm from the haven inside.

"Can we come back here again?" He had asked that each day.

"Of course."

"Where are we going?"

"You'll see."

At least, she hoped he would. Over two years had passed. It may not even be there anymore. They walked for over an hour, the rain giving up to barely a trickle. Not once did Mattie complain or say he was tired. With the streetlights lit up around them, they stopped halfway to pull the bread out of her bag that she had bought the day before. They smeared pieces of it with peanut butter, thick in their mouths and more filling than things they'd eaten at home at times. Carmen relished in the sense of satisfaction that at least she'd managed to fill his stomach. When the rain stopped, it was like Carmen herself had willed it.

Action felt good.

They walked again, slipping into mazelike alleys, feet treading a path Carmen had never thought she'd be on again, especially side by side with Mattie. Finally, they reached a fence, the wire pulling out easily like it had years before when she'd tried it. The hole was just big enough to slide through, snagging at the bags on their backs. Mattie didn't ask a single question, and his trust was heavy on her shoulders.

They ducked under another fence, then through a gate, and eventually they came to a warehouse on the outskirts of the city. In front of them was a door covered in peeling green paint.

Mattie looked up at her, and Carmen gave him a smile. The stars peeking between parted clouds overhead were bright in his eyes, and the fog from the river started to creep up the streets around them. Taking a deep breath, she tore her eyes from the galaxy of his and knocked on the wood: twice rapidly, once after a pause, then three more quickly, a pattern she played before sleep some nights after she had returned to her mother's place, a longing for days gone by in the balled fists of her hands.

A panel slid open, and dark eyes stared out at her.

Carmen swallowed, and Mattie's hand clamped tighter in her own.

"I need your help."

CHAPTER 8

"So she has no Facebook?" Deon stared at Ollie, his collection of monitors behind him blinking and glowing like they held the answers to everything.

"Nope."

"No Twitter? No Tumblr? No...no social media?"

She shook her head again, buried in a beanbag chair with a bowl of popcorn on her stomach. Between her legs, sitting on the floor, Sara stretched out like youth personified. They'd agreed after a few days with no sight of Carmen that it was time to find something out. Now, with the rain coming down in fits and starts outside, with the three of them tucked away in Deon's basement, she was hoping for some answers. "None that I could find her on."

Deon tapped a pen against his lip, a pattern like Morse code, a codex to his thoughts. He'd skipped two grades. Scholarships were paved out in front of him. Leaning back in his computer chair, he tossed his pen behind him on the desk. He sucked at a straw inside his oversized soda and eyed her. "That's kind of weird."

"Not kind of. It is."

"What sixteen-year-old doesn't have Facebook?"

Ollie shrugged and tried not to answer that it was apparently the kind who kissed like she was on fire, who kissed like Ollie was the one who could keep her from extinguishing herself, the kind whose nails gripped at her skin; that type didn't have Facebook.

She tried to tell herself that those kisses had nothing to do with why Ollie wanted to find Carmen. It was concern—that was all. They'd stumbled over each other a few times on some path neither of them knew the end of, and Ollie just knew she needed Carmen around if she wanted to see the finale.

Carmen was…something she didn't have a word for.

"C'mon, Deon." Sara threw her hands in the air. "Can you help us?"

A look not unlike offense screwed up Deon's face. "Of course I can. You're talking child's play."

When he smiled, he looked all kinds of charming, and when he was cocky, like now, he gave a shake of his head that made his thin, short locs fall around his face. Once, when Ollie was younger, she'd had a crush on him that lasted a painful year. His cheekbones had left her speechless. And then he'd appeared in one of the school's Queer Club meetings and told her he was representing the *A* in LGBTQIA+, and that it did *not* stand for ally, but for asexual and aromantic. Some people, he explained, were one or the other. Others were both, and he was one of them; they were terms he wore proudly. Her crush had ebbed, eventually, and she'd found a great friend.

From the bed in the corner, Deon's older brother, home for a while from college, spoke up. "What he wants to say is what's in it for us?"

"Don't you mean for him, Ruin?" Ollie asked, eyebrows raised.

Ruin flashed a smile, flopping back on the bed, an older version of his brother. "No, I mean for us. I'm the brains of this operation." With a lazy wink, he dropped an arm over his face.

Ollie looked back to Deon, who was rolling his eyes. But she needed to know. "I'll buy the next piece of equipment you're after."

The hole that would make in her savings account would be huge, one too big to cover up from her parents' prying eyes, but she would find a lie to excuse it away as a school project. Something about a media assignment. Carmen had lit a want in Ollie, a need, a curiosity, and then had left her behind with nothing to sate it. Where the hell was she? And why did she kiss like the world was falling around her?

And why did Ollie care?

Deon's eyes lit up, and he swiveled his chair. Two of the monitors flashed to a wide screen, lines of code typing too fast for Ollie to follow on another. She could see now, in the determined set of his shoulders, in the rapidly changing, flickering screens, why Deon had received a visit from some cloaked government agency a year ago for his talent at finding out things he shouldn't.

"Deon, what did those suits say to you after they took you from school in that van?" Interest lilted Sara's words. When he'd come back the next day, a little wan, he hadn't said a word, and they'd realized enough to leave him alone.

Deon just shrugged and spoke at his screen. "They said a lot of things."

Sara sighed. "Enough to make you stop?"

He turned then, a smirk plastered on his lips. "Enough to make me learn how not to be caught."

Then he said something about IPs and bouncing and lines, and Ollie was lost.

"So, her full name?" He turned away again, tossing the question over his shoulder.

"Carmen García."

Maybe she said it too fast, too easily, the syllables falling from Ollie's tongue as if they weren't something new, because Sara tilted her head where it lay against Ollie's thigh, a look on her face Ollie didn't want to try to understand.

Deon's shoulders were hunched, keys clacking rapidly. "Date of birth?"

"No idea."

"She's in the year below us, you said?"

"Yeah, but our age."

"That makes it easier, to at least know her age."

For a little while, the monitors were just a blur from Ollie's position near the floor, and she ran her fingers through Sara's hair. Eventually, Sara hunted through her bag and pulled out a blunt. "You mind?" she asked.

Deon shook his head, and she lit it smoothly before offering it to Ruin, who took a hit.

Ollie shook her head when it was offered to her. Despite how it mellowed her out sometimes, she didn't like how weed sporadically left her skin itching and made her feel like the world was closing in around her. She had days in which she felt like that anyway, especially around exams—like all the air was trapped in her chest and there was no oxygen in her system. Why take weed and make it worse?

The school counsellor had used the word *anxiety*, and only certain breathing exercises could bring Ollie back to earth at times. She'd tried medication, and after six months and feeling back on top of her anxiety, had weaned off of it. The anxiety was never entirely gone, but the counsellor had given her some tools to keep it in check.

For the next few hours, Ollie lolled in a lazy afternoon, her bag on the floor behind them, the hours of study she had to do stretching out into the night ahead.

With glazed eyes and a hum in her chest, Sara fell back against the beanbag, her hand poking at Ollie's thigh, with a giggle spilling from her. "You're vibrating." A smile split her lips. "That your phone in your pocket, or are you just happy to see me?"

High Sara was always an unstoppable flirt. Ollie rolled her eyes at her, and when she saw her phone lighting up with Sean's name, she swiped it off and slipped it back into her pocket. Eyes now closed, her head a brick against Ollie's knee, Sara made a "tsk" noise, and Ollie ignored her.

"Got something." Deon said an hour later with a low whistle. "And it definitely isn't a Facebook account."

Ollie had thought they'd find a fake name, a changed surname, some link to find a mobile number, a social media account, some way to send an awkward message like:

Hey, wanna make out some more?

No, not that. More like:

Hey, are you okay?

The cloak-and-dagger had been excessive, something like a game, something she had slipped on for the afternoon to find her damsel. Instead of something so fun, Deon laid out a path of foster homes, of a runaway three years ago, of brushes with police. The confirmed death of her mother, mug shots of a white woman who looked like a shell of a person, the collection back into foster care, a group home. Swallowing past the prickling in her throat, Ollie wondered at the life Carmen led.

No firm address was filed, just a note in an online file that said a home was to be determined, one of three that were all far away.

She wondered if she'd ever see Carmen again, disappointment acrid on her tongue at the thought that it really didn't seem she would.

"Shut it off," she said. She'd seen something too private, not for their eyes. Even if she found Carmen, how would the other girl feel about the digging Ollie had done? "Shut it off, and pretend you never saw it."

Eyes just stared at Carmen through the hole in the door. Everything around her and Mattie was shrouded in shadow, only the weak light of the moon breaking through a small gap in the clouds and orange security light washing over them. Carmen felt naked, like a sacrifice: vulnerable and trussed up to stand before her maker, her brother clutching her clammy hand. Waiting to be told if she lived or died.

"One minute."

Carmen knew that voice. Her stomach dropped, something rising in her and at the same time leaving a sick, swooping feeling behind.

The window slid shut with a slam that made Mattie jump beside her, the squeeze of his hand bordering on painful, but nothing Carmen wouldn't take for him. She'd take things a thousand times worse than that, might have to soon. With a sidestep, a small shuffle of his feet, he was pressed against her side, the warmth of him soaking through her clothes. She glanced down to the top of his head, the moonlight washing over the droplets of water in his hair. It made it seem silver, a color for gods, for heroes, not for the mortal she wanted her brother to be. Not for the everyday, for easy living.

He deserved so much, and yet he only had her.

When he looked up, his eyes no longer reflected stars overhead but the clouds that were creeping back over the sky, dark and rolling and roiling with rain. A splat of it landed on his cheek, and it shone as it rolled down the slope of it. With a swipe of the back of his hand, it was gone. "Where are we?"

Carmen ran her tongue over her lip, hovering on her answer. "Somewhere with friends, if they'll have us."

"Friends you had before?"

"Yes."

He blinked, cocking his head to one side. "I'm glad you had friends before. I thought you were all alone."

Carmen's chest ached with a swelling behind her ribs, an influx of emotion at the thought that before, at five, her brother had worried for her. "I wasn't. They helped me learn how to survive."

Skills Carmen had thought she could use alone this time, not wanting to ask for help. Not even sure if they would have her, with how it had ended, with how she had left—and now she was with a boy too young at her side.

It was as if the weight of the world were pushing down to crush her bones, as if she were sixteen going on eighty. She wanted to sink into the feeling, to let it bow her, to give in to age, to sigh as she turned to ash and floated away. Instead, she straightened her shoulders and squeezed the hand in hers a little harder.

She'd learned these lessons from the cradle, and she could learn it all better this time: find food, feed your own, make sure you were warm enough, make sure people didn't find out you were alone, hungry, cold, a bit too dirty.

"Why didn't we come here before?"

Carmen swallowed and looked down again. His big eyes were still staring up at her. He smelled damp from the rain, like clothes that were bordering on needing a wash. He *had* slept under a bridge the last few days.

"Because—"

The door swung open, the hinges creaking and echoing out behind them, the sound bouncing off old walls and corrugated-iron fences.

Light flooded onto them suddenly, seemingly switched off beforehand to cloak in mystery the person who had been at the door, something that didn't surprise Carmen in the slightest. Mattie threw his hand up, covering his screwed-up eyes, but Carmen made herself squint through the shock of the light.

"Well, well. Look who's returned."

It was exactly who Carmen thought it was, voice slightly deeper after two years. Her eyes were layered in dark eyeliner. There were rips in her jeans, and she wore a jacket layered over a dark shirt.

"Hello, Rae."

The punch hurt, even though it wasn't entirely unexpected. It hit her on the cheekbone and was nowhere near as hard as Rae could hit. At least, that was what Carmen told herself to feel a little better. What hurt like a truly-meant punch, though, was Mattie's panicked shout and the way his hand tore from hers when she took a shuddering step back to take away some of the impact.

Her hand covered the spot flooding with heat on her cheek, where she knew a bruise would blossom.

She eyed Rae. "I guess I deserved that."

CHAPTER 9

"Damn right you deserved it." Rae's words held a bite, but her face was impassive.

Mattie was back at Carmen's side, his hand holding the back of her shirt. He stepped in front of her and stood sideways, looking at Rae, who stood with her back straight and her eyes glinting as Mattie stared her down. *Up*, rather, considering how small he was.

Carmen was left with anxiety in her belly, wanting to claw him back to her, to yank him safely behind her, but also in awe of what he was doing.

"Stay away from her." His other hand was a tight-knuckled fist.

The throb in her cheek wasn't abating, and the smile she was forcing down didn't help. And certainly, laughing at her brother wasn't appropriate right now.

Rae didn't bother to hold it down, though: she gave a harsh bark of laughter. Her eyes were almost black, deep and dark. "Or what, kid?"

"You'll have to go through me."

Carmen didn't know where he learned such a statement, but the audacity of it, the sheer determination, slayed her.

Rae didn't laugh this time either; instead, her face was solemn, the smile gone, though Carmen was sure it was still playing at the edges of her mouth a little. Rae cocked her head, her arms crossed, and stared Mattie down. He didn't turn from the glare in front of him, and Carmen didn't know if she should be horrified or proud.

Finally, Rae gave a nod. "Fair enough." Her gaze flicked up to meet Carmen's, obscure and hiding a wealth of secrets, most of which Carmen had never even come close to, even though she had come closer than most. "I can totally see you two are related."

Carmen finally gave in to the urge pushing at her fingers and pulled Mattie close, her hand planted over his sternum. His protective stance didn't dim, though; his chest puffed out against her palm.

A butterfly batting against a storm.

"Little brother?" Rae asked.

"Yes."

Rae looked down at him again. "It's nice to finally see you in the flesh, kid."

Beneath Carmen's hand, Mattie deflated slightly, confusion pushing his eyebrows together as he looked up at Carmen, the top of his head against her stomach.

"She's a friend, Mattie."

"She punched you."

"She did, but I kind of had it coming."

Rae crossed her arms, tatty leather jacket creaking. "She did."

"Mattie, this is Rae Muoy."

"Muoy?" Mattie was back to looking up at Rae.

She winked at him. "It's Cambodian."

"Cool."

"I'm always cool, kid."

The back alley was silent then, excluding the sound of the rain that had picked up again around them. Drops were hitting the pavement; they splattered against Carmen's skin, one after the other, a pattern to testify that she couldn't keep her little brother safe alone. She couldn't even keep him dry alone. Under her hand, Mattie shivered, the tremor rising up his spine.

Carmen and Mattie just stood together, watching Rae watch them. Finally, she gave a small roll of her eyes and stepped back through the door. "Come on, then."

Smothering her sigh of relief took everything she had, the tension draining from her shoulders as she stepped forward, Mattie's hand sliding into her own.

Rae led and they followed, their feet leaving squelching footprints on the cement floor. The door slammed shut behind them, and Mattie jumped slightly at the jarring sound. Carmen squeezed his hand once, and as he looked back ahead, his gaze darted from one thing to another along the hallway, one Carmen had stepped down so many times before. They emerged into what used to be the factory floor, two stories with battery-operated lanterns scattered about, the huge space lit as if by candlelight, shadows lurking in corners the light couldn't reach.

Everything was familiar, but little things had changed. Since the few years Carmen had last stood there, the space had been set up even more. More sofas spread out on one side, and bookshelves improvised from pallets or fixed up from the street had grown in number, books lining all of them. Taking up most of a corner and a wall was a makeshift eating space, also made with pallets and mismatched chairs and crates. Boxes filled with food lined the walls. A few gas stoves sat round.

Carmen was still amazed at how much stuff people threw out onto the street.

Curious eyes stared at them from where a few teenagers, who appeared to be around Carmen's age, were sprawled on the sofas. She recognized none of them.

Mattie stared around, taking in the huge open space, the rooms on one side that led off to what had probably been offices before, and the stairs that went up to a catwalk that ran around the walls, leading into other rooms. The whole complicated structure was all made of clanging metal that Carmen remembered reverberated with steps at all times of the night. Ropes hung from the ceiling, and Carmen had a strong memory of their burn on her hands whenever she slid down from the catwalk above, muscles in her legs aching. She'd always had to remind herself to let her feet take the burn, to save her hands.

They didn't cross the space in front of them but took a left and walked into one of the rooms. A cot was set up in the corner, and books were stacked along a wall, magazines next to them. A map of the city was pinned up, scrawled all over, some parts colored in red. Sitting at the desk, looking exactly the same as she always had, was Jia.

Carmen swallowed and stopped in the doorway, Mattie half a step behind her and pressed up against her back, his head peering around Carmen's arm.

The room hadn't changed, Jia hadn't changed either, and Carmen's heart fluttered in her throat, her palms clammy. A memory of the first time she'd stood in this spot welled up in her mind, a time when she'd had more than a lightly bruising cheek. When she'd been smaller, and fractured inside. The keening sensation had sat deep within her then—of missing the exact boy who now stood behind her.

Carmen's gaze was glued on Jia. From her periphery, she could just make out Rae watching them from where she'd plopped down on the cot, her feet crossed at the ankle and her dark eyes flitting from one to the other. Slowly, a smile crept up on Jia's face, the scar on her left cheek folding in on itself. A smile like that was one Carmen hadn't been offered very often, and warm relief pooled in the back of her throat, sliding down in a torrent to flood her insides.

"I almost didn't believe Rae when she said who was at the door."

"I'm not surprised." Carmen shrugged, the movement more relaxed than anything else about her. "It's been awhile."

"We would have worried about you, but at least you got word to us that you were fine."

Carmen bit her lip, the space of time too large between them. How to fill it up? "I didn't want you to think I'd run on purpose."

Rae snorted from the bed, and Carmen's cheeks warmed as she looked at her before looking back to Jia, who still sat at her desk and watched Carmen openly.

"I always knew you'd go back home if the chance came. I'm glad you had that opportunity."

Weak-kneed at the knowledge that, after years, the woman in front of her didn't harbor hatred, didn't feel betrayed, Carmen wrapped her arm tighter around her brother. "I was so grateful for what you did."

Jia cocked her head. "And now you're back."

Carmen cleared her throat and her cheeks grew even warmer as moisture prickled at her eyes, and she cast her gaze toward the ceiling to try to push the feeling down, to stop it from drowning her. "My—our mother, she died."

Mattie twitched under her arm, and she wished she could shield him from all of it, from everything. "We were back in the system. They were going to send Mattie to a foster home again, but me..."

"To one of those group homes." Knowledge of what that meant wrapped itself in her vowels.

"Yes."

"And you ran with an extra this time, I see." Jia's attention finally fell to Mattie.

Carmen nudged him to stand in front of her like before, and pulled him against her front so Jia could see him properly. She folded her hands over his chest.

"Hello, Mattie."

Mattie looked up at Carmen, then back to Jia. "How do you know my name?"

"Carmen told me about you when she was here last time."

"What's your name, then?"

Jia's lips quirked in what could have been amusement but she quickly squashed it down if it was. "My name is Jia Lu."

"What is this place?"

"This is…" Jia looked around the room and then back to Mattie. "This is somewhere safe for kids like you. Kids with nowhere else to go."

"You take all of them?"

Jia glanced away before looking back to Mattie.

He was watching her openly, and Carmen knew just how hard it was to have to spill hard truth to those trusting eyes.

"Unfortunately, no. I wish I could, but there's not enough space, enough resources. I take in the ones most desperate, the ones who cause the least trouble. Ones who are quick and smart and motivated."

"You looked after Carmen."

"She was especially pathetic, yes."

Carmen rolled her eyes, and Rae snorted from the bed again.

"Rae."

Rae looked to Jia, trepidation playing on her face.

"That bruise coming up on Carmen's cheek—will that be the last?"

"Yeah, I figure we're even now."

"Good."

Eyes back on the two of them in the doorway, Jia said, "Rae will take you to one of the empty rooms. You'll have to share. We're a bit packed, what with the weather."

Against her, Mattie relaxed.

"That's no problem." Carmen squeezed him closer. "We prefer that anyway."

Jia's expression didn't change. "I thought as much. We'll talk tomorrow, Carmen. We need to discuss how this is all going to work… He's young."

"Okay."

At that, Rae pushed herself up off the bed and walked past them, her shoulder brushing Carmen's. Not roughly, at least. With a final look at Jia, one hundred questions threatening to explode from her tongue, Carmen poked Mattie in the back gently, a cue to walk in front of her. They walked up the creaking metal steps and ended up in a corner room, two mattresses on the floor and a small window along one wall, rain smattering against the glass.

Rae stood against the doorframe and watched them in the small space, standing in the middle of the room. Mattie really was little for his age, Carmen thought, as he looked around the room: it was bare, the walls a little dirty, a water stain stretching across one. His gaze tracked over the mattresses, the single window, and Rae, then fell on to Carmen.

"This is way better than the bridge," he finally said.

Almost smiling, Carmen dropped her backpack at her feet. She glanced around as though everything didn't hinge on this battered building and its battered people, giving a one-shouldered shrug. "Yeah, I think so."

From the door, Rae asked, "You guys have a sleeping bag?"

"We have one."

"I'll grab you another."

She disappeared without another word, her boots clattering a little on the stairs. Carmen suddenly felt the lack of her presence, the swirling of air she left in her wake. After not having her around for so long, the last few minutes had weaseled Rae back under Carmen's skin.

"Can I have that bed?"

Tearing her gaze from the empty doorway, Carmen looked back to her brother. He was pointing to the mattress under the window, eyes lit up like they hadn't been the past few days.

"Sure." Carmen tried to ignore the way her voice rasped a little at his happiness over a ratty mattress on the floor. "Sure you can."

He dropped his bag on it, sitting down in the middle and bouncing a little. "It's comfy."

Anything was comfy after sleeping on cement, where the cold crept through no matter how many layers you wore.

"Good."

Mattie stared up at her, and Carmen sat down on her own mattress, the foam sinking under her, her eyes almost level to her brother's.

"Carmen?"

"Mm?"

"What will we do here?"

"It depends."

"On what?"

"How long we stay."

Mattie looked around again, his eyes ending up focused on the doorway where the catwalk was just visible. "I'd like to stay."

Carmen knew that look in his eyes, had seen it on her own face, reflected in dirty glass when she'd first arrived somewhere where people didn't yell at her or chase her or hit her. Somewhere that had warmth and food. Stability.

"Plus," Mattie continued, "I saw they had cereal and pasta. I'm kind of sick of sandwiches."

Carmen choked on a laugh. He said it like he was confessing something, a guilty thought that had played in the back of his mind. "Yeah, I kind of am too."

He gave her a shy smile, and something flittered between them, something familiar and soft.

"Here you go." The sleeping bag, rolled tight, hit Carmen sideways, and she looked back to the door where Rae stood, looking a little pleased with herself. "You guys eaten tonight?"

"We did."

Rae raised an eye brow. "Enough, though?"

Carmen looked to Mattie, checking his face, but he gave a nod. Eyes back on Rae, Carmen said, "Enough."

"Okay, do I need to go over the rules again?"

Carmen knew the rules. But Mattie didn't, and it seemed easier if he got the same introduction everyone else did.

Before she could say anything, though, Mattie piped up. "I don't know the rules."

Another smile was poorly smothered as Rae crossed her arms, her shoulder against the doorframe once more.

"Okay—we all contribute, in whatever way. Jia will talk to you tomorrow to find out how that will be. Clean up after yourself, and speak with Dex to find out what you need to do to help in the building as much as you can. Especially as it gets colder, we have to do a lot of work to make sure it's warm enough here. No drugs. None. You're found with drugs, you're out. No guns. Any guns, you're out. Same goes for knives." She shrugged. "That's it, they're the rules."

Mattie's face was scrunched up, a picture not unlike when he was small and trying to understand what was going on. "What's...countreebute?"

Rae, despite herself, smiled this time—a lopsided thing. "*Contribute*. It means help out."

"I can help out. I do at home, don't I, Carmen?"

Carmen hummed her agreement distractedly, not sure where Jia would want Mattie to help. There were a lot of ways of helping out there, each person's contribution a little different. Before, Carmen had scrounged food. They knew all the places people wasted a lot, threw out unopened packets because they were a day past their use-by date, malls in which you could get enough food to feed them all for a night.

There were the kids that had learned to pick pockets a little, targeting a certain type of person. Only those who were small and fast did that. Carmen had done that too. She didn't want Mattie doing it.

But then there were the books, and some of the older people that pushed kids to learn, to read, to keep up with school. Dex was involved with that. The ultimate goal was to get the kids moved on, to something legitimate and real and legal. Jia and Dex had connections, had routes to get as many of them off the streets as they could. People who would take a risk and offer leases or jobs.

"Jia will speak to you guys in the morning, then. You know how it is, Carmen. You're free to come and go, upstairs and downstairs." She cleared her throat. "I, uh, grabbed this, in case he'd want it."

Something heavy landed next to her on the bed, and then Rae was gone before Carmen could say thank you.

"Is that a book?" Mattie's eyes had lit up, the nervous look that had been constant lately fading slightly.

"It's Roald Dahl."

In moments, Mattie had scooted over to her bed, and soon they were laid out, both sleeping bags open over them. Words stuttered out of Mattie's mouth, his voice a little high and hushed as he whispered and read the story of an adventurous child. His head stayed against her shoulder, and when he fell asleep with heavy breaths, the book fell to the floor with a dull thud.

Carmen stared up at the ceiling, so like the one she'd stared up at her first night here, and she wondered if this was really the best thing she could have done for him.

Someone laughed downstairs, the sound foreign and loud. Footsteps clanged along the catwalk. Nervousness about the people who were there should have played at her stomach, but Carmen had never heard of an incident here. It was the world outside that was a threat, looming and unknown. Here, Jia and Dex kept them all in line.

It wasn't very late, and Carmen was buzzed, energy burning up her legs. She wanted to bounce them, to pace, to run.

Mattie snuffled in his sleep, rolled a little, his head falling from her shoulder to the mattress.

Carmen took the opportunity to slip out of the bed and stand in the middle of the dark room, orange light from outside spilling over the bed Mattie had chosen. Empty, as it would probably be most nights.

He was tiny on the mattress, a tiny lump made of tiny, basic needs. He was too young, younger than Jia normally had here, younger than those who normally wandered the streets. Younger kids were homed more easily, picked up faster. Carmen's stomach twisted. He could be in a house right now, going to school in the morning, not laced in uncertainty and lost in a city so big you could disappear in it.

He was sound asleep, his breathing rhythmic. When someone dropped something downstairs, the noise clattering and loud, he didn't move, didn't flinch.

Once Mattie slept, he was out.

Carmen slipped out the door and closed it behind her. No one went into rooms with closed doors here.

On the catwalk, the metal beneath her feet creaked ever so slightly, the runway old and a little rusty. When she looked over the railing, people milled near the eating area, some still sprawled over the sofas. The smell of damp people who hadn't showered quite enough hung in the air, not strong, but there. There were public showers they could access, gyms some slipped into; most didn't go enough, though.

Jia's door was closed, and after a second of wringing the rail under her hands, Carmen turned and walked as quietly as she could around to the other side of the catwalk, to a door that was always open. Her footsteps echoed a little as she climbed the stairs. At the top, she pushed open the door, the cool air from the roof spilling over her cheeks.

She gulped it down, not sure why she felt like she couldn't breathe when she and Mattie were finally somewhere safer than most other places.

The rain was still falling lightly, almost a mist. She tilted her head up, letting it coat her face as she sat on the edge of the roof, legs dangling and her heels kicking against the brick, legs flying out, only to feel that tug of gravity as they fell back down to bounce again.

Buildings lay out in front of and around her, soft lights filtering from a few. Most in this area were empty and unused. Everything smelled like rain, like cleansing, and as gravity kept pulling her feet back to the brick, Carmen thought of eyes too blue, that sucked her in and left her breathless. When they had kissed that time, Ollie's lips had been like the tide pulling at the shore, like fingers that dragged her under. Her skin had been dark and mappable and soft.

Ollie, a girl she had only really collided with twice, was someone she needed to forget and put down to coincidence. Not easy to do when her mind plucked at physics, at an undeniable pull, at something indisputable.

"Has the view changed?"

Carmen didn't even jump at the voice.

Rae plopped onto the edge next to her, her feet swinging in time with Carmen's, a rhythm they built together.

"Not at all," Carmen said. The mist was fading, the air still sitting damp and heavy over their skin.

"Does your face hurt?"

Carmen smirked a little. Yes, it did. "Not at all."

Rae huffed a laugh.

Something assembled in her stomach, slid up her chest, and sat heavy at the back of her throat. Words formed, and before she could swallow them down, Carmen let them spill out, long overdue. "I'm sorry."

The thudding against the brick paused for a moment before they gave back into it, somehow even more in time than before. "Thanks."

Something deeply etched into her ribs eased a little. Carmen turned her head, watching Rae's profile as she stared out ahead of her. Her hair was short now, pixie short, with a shaved undercut; the color of ink. The cut was fierce and soft all at the same time. "Do you need an explanation?"

Rae sighed, her breath a visible huff in the cool air. "Don't *need* one." She turned to look Carmen in the eyes. "But I *want* one."

With a nod, Carmen dug her fingers into the brick beneath her hands, letting it bite into her fingerprints. She remembered the feeling of the wind on her face, pulling at her hair, as she'd run. Rae's footsteps had purposely pushed her in the opposite direction—always the plan: to confuse whoever was chasing them. The money clutched in her fingers had been burning-hot, and Carmen had been so sure she'd get away. Then a hand had snatched out, grabbed at her sweater, and yanked her back. Her head had cracked against the pavement, light exploding behind her eyelids. When she'd been bundled into the back of a police car, not for the first time, she'd seen Rae getting pushed into the back of another, and her stomach had sunk as if it had been filled with stones.

The story they'd perfected, the names they knew, were prepared and ready. The lies wrapped in more lies, given by people who knew names they could use that didn't have rap sheets, ran around and around in her head, ready to spill to help save both their skins. Normally, they'd be given a slap on the wrist in the street, occasionally at the station.

Sitting in different cars, just before the doors had closed on both of them, they had locked eyes for a desperate second, and Carmen hadn't been able to read the look on Rae's face.

"I was angry you'd been caught. You were too young and my responsibility."

Carmen rolled her eyes. "We were each other's responsibility. I was just as angry you were caught."

Rae gave a shrug, her heart clearly not in it. The two years she had on Carmen might as well have been a lifetime.

Expectantly, Rae watched her, so Carmen kept talking. "You were driven off. But then this lady was banging on the window of the car I was in and speaking to the police. I didn't leave you behind, Rae. I didn't."

Carmen swallowed down the tone in her voice, tried to calm the desperation that pulled at her vocal cords. Carmen didn't care what many people thought, but Rae was one of the few people who were under her skin, sewn into her muscles, stretched over her bones. Family. "This lady had been one of my old caseworkers. She recognized me. She talked them into letting her take me from the station, without them charging me."

Carmen had panicked. Her entire body had gone numb. She'd argued and said she didn't want to go, but no one had listened. She'd thought they would take her back to foster care, another home.

"So...you didn't drop me in it?"

Carmen sighed, the brick still biting at her palms, her fingers. "Well, I did. Just not on purpose. It was a weird fluke: my mom's case had just passed through court, she'd somehow been given back custody, and she was on some kind of war path, saying I was missing."

The caseworker had told her that, and Carmen had gone even colder. Being back with her mother was nowhere she wanted to be. Where she had been—with Jia, with Rae—had worked, had felt like safety, a net she'd never before known. It wasn't one she had wanted to throw her brother into, but she had missed it herself the last few years.

"The caseworker told me Mattie was going back to my mom the next day... I couldn't run again, because... I couldn't leave Mattie there alone; it was bad enough at the foster home."

Carmen couldn't be with him in the foster home he'd been in, but she could be with him at home. She *needed* to be with him at home. He had been barely six at that point. Barely six and with a mother who forgot to come home, who lost herself in a bottle, who used drugs like they made her a better person when all they did was flood her and leave her floundering.

"Maybe, uh," Rae's voice was rough, "maybe you didn't deserve that punch, then."

The clouds were parting again, stars muted between them. The temperature had fallen even more in the last hour, though, and goose bumps prickled along Carmen's arms. It would most likely start to rain again soon. Carmen shrugged finally. "You didn't know. I know it looked like I'd run, or taken the easy road. But once they knew my name, I couldn't give them any kind of story that supported yours."

Sighing, Rae dropped her head back, staring at the black sky. "Yeah, once they knew I was lying, I said good-bye to any chance of talking my way out. I did thirty days in juvie, then was put back in the system."

And clearly ran from it immediately.

"I really am sorry." Carmen didn't take her eyes from the sky.

"I was so angry at you."

"I was angry at me too."

And Rae gave her a gift then, fragile; words that wrapped themselves around something deeply carved into her ribs, and somehow Carmen was able to breathe again.

"It wasn't your fault."

The book in front of Ollie's eyes was blurring, the words swirling together and swarming into nothingness. Her pen tapped rhythmically on the page, a beat she didn't recognize but that wouldn't leave her mind. This paper was due in a few days, a report on a war from years ago that her country still celebrated with vigor. As if battles and death and destruction were worth glorifying rather than avoiding at all costs.

It was a night for ruminating, for settling among her thoughts like sinking into quicksand—every time she struggled to leave them, she became further entangled.

Sara was breathing deeply behind her, wrapped in the sheets of Ollie's queen bed like she had been doing since their first sleepover. She was an utter blanket hog. Dinner had been quiet. Ollie and Sara had sat down with her mother and father. The food had been hot on her plate, and Sara had talked too much in order to distract them from the mood that had taken over Ollie since Deon's house.

Ollie's family wasn't rolling in money, not by a long shot. Her mother volunteered too much of her time with organizations that sent surgeons to faraway places or to clinics down the road to help those who had nothing. Her father was an architect who worked extra hard to make sure her mother could give time to these causes. But they were more than comfortable. Ollie had no idea what hunger really meant, had at least one parent with her every night in the house. In fact, their concern pressed in so much that sometimes Ollie wanted to crawl out of her skin to find some space to breathe. But what was that compared to what she'd seen of Carmen's life? That quick glimpse Ollie had had of foster homes and feeling lost, of losing a parent and having no one else?

But Carmen had the government looking out for her now. From the looks of it, she was going to a girls' home, would be in school.

She'd be fine.

But she wouldn't be with Ollie.

So why wouldn't the memory of her leave Ollie alone? Why did it feel like Carmen had imprinted herself over Ollie's skin, invisible to everyone else but pulling at everything that was Ollie?

Outside the rain was falling so hard it echoed throughout the house, the splattering over the glass matching the rhythm of Ollie's tapping pen. Though it wasn't that cold, the weather was starting to turn. It'd be a hard winter.

She stood and stared out the window, unable to see much of the backyard beyond the rain falling in sheets. The shrub near the window spilled drops of it, water running down its bark, dark and brown. The color made Ollie bite down the memory of Carmen's eyes, staring at her in an alcohol haze, as they were tucked into a bathroom. She had stared at Ollie with something so desperate under dirty bleachers that Ollie had wanted to tear herself open, to spill everything she was, to offer it all to Carmen, just on the small chance it was what she wanted.

With a flick of her wrist, she yanked the curtain across the window and went to bed.

CHAPTER 10

FOR A MOMENT WHEN CARMEN woke, something in her chest expanded and she thought she was home. Not home, at her mother's, but *home*, the feeling that was meant to go with the word, that feeling that slid along your insides to nestle in and beat alongside your heart.

She *knew* the sounds that echoed outside the room, the voices that murmured, the thuds that meant someone was walking up or down the stairs. Soft breaths echoed in the room, and Mattie mumbled in his sleep, rubbing his face into their shared pillow, his hair buffed into a cloud that they needed to do something with.

When he finally grumbled awake, blinking and stretching, he sat up suddenly, looking wildly around the room.

"Hey." Carmen's voice was thick with sleep, low and gravelly.

Mattie's eyes found hers as he twisted to look at her. "I wasn't cold."

The fact he was surprised to wake up and be warm made Carmen swallow and force a smile. "Good. You hungry?"

"Yup." His look darkened just slightly, eyebrows bunching together. "We don't have to have peanut butter, do we?"

Carmen poked him in the ribs, wriggling her fingers to make him squirm away, his face lighting up for a moment with a grin that warmed her. "Nope, doubtful. You said you saw cereal."

At the end of the bed, as far from her tickling as he could be, Mattie asked, "But what about milk? I didn't see a fridge."

Carmen lifted her foot and poked him in the ribs again with her socked toe, smirking when he thudded slightly off the mattress with a squawk, his lips curving upward. "They have magic milk."

Cross-legged on the floor, he eyed her. "Magic milk?"

"Yup." Carmen sat up, reorganizing her hair. It would be so much easier to manage short. Her waves of hair were nothing like her mother's straight locks. Once, when Carmen was small, she'd asked her mother if her hair had been from her father. Her mother had said something about her father's family, from El Salvador, and had left Carmen with more questions than answers.

"You're tricking me."

Carmen blinked, pulled back to a world with magic milk, and put on her hoodie. "Yup."

She smirked, and he returned it, rolling his eyes for good measure.

They walked out, Mattie close to her side. She dropped an arm over his shoulders as they walked down the stairs, their feet in time with each other.

"No, but seriously," he asked, "what about milk?"

Some teens she didn't know lolled on the sofas, and when they wandered to the makeshift kitchen, mismatched and organized and loved, Carmen's breath stilled in her chest. "Dex?"

Somehow, he looked bigger and softer all at the same time.

"Carmen."

He had no rise in his tone, just a sense of expectation. Clearly, someone had already told him she was here, and he grinned, his eyes vibrantly green. He walked up to her, and for a moment he hesitated, as he no doubt remembered the girl who shied away from hugs, remembered her backstepping, her darting eyes. But then he stepped forward, his giant arms enveloping her.

Carmen stiffened, her spine rigid. But in spite of herself, she relaxed into it. His hand, coarse and gruff yet somehow so gentle, cupped the back of her head for just a moment. Her throat tightened, prickling.

He stepped away to let her have her space. "It's damn good to see you."

She bit her lip, felt herself fight the urge, but then smiled anyway. "You too."

"You look all grown-up."

Her shoulders pulled up in a shrug, and Mattie moved closer until he was against her back.

"Not really."

A look flashed in his eyes that Carmen couldn't place. Extra lines creased around his eyes. His hair and beard were streaked with gray.

"Good." His looked down and dropped to a knee, looking Mattie straight in his cautious eyes. "Hey—I hear you're Mattie."

Mattie stared at him for a moment, then looked up at Carmen. "Why does everyone know me?"

Dex chuckled, warm and rich like butterscotch, and Carmen remembered how he would sink into one of the sofas with her and Rae, his voice a rumble as he shared stories and Rae accused him of exaggeration. "I'm magic."

Mattie gave him the same look he'd given Carmen minutes before, a look of very preteen *as if.* "Jia told you."

The laugh that burst from Dex was a surprised boom. "She did. I'm Dex. It's great to meet you. You hungry?" Dex was still kneeling. When Mattie nodded enthusiastically, Dex asked, "What for?"

Mattie glanced at Carmen, unsure, before looking back to Dex. "I think I saw cereal?"

"You did. Want some?"

"Yeah." Mattie's eyebrows knitted together. "But what about milk?"

"Important question." Dex stood. "Come on—let me show you some *real* magic."

When Carmen didn't say not to, Mattie followed Dex over to a pallet bench, his eyes curious as Dex pulled out a can of powdered milk from one of the crates and held it out.

Mattie looked from Dex to the can and back again. "That's not magic *or* milk."

Dex chuckled, and Carmen crossed her arms, letting Mattie have his moment of cheek.

"Well, Mattie who seems to know everything," Dex said, "watch and learn." Without even looking up, he added, "Carmen, Jia wanted to speak to you when you had a moment."

"Okay." Mattie was glued to Dex's side, watching him spoon powder into a small bottle of water. "You okay here, Mattie?"

He glanced up. "Where are you going?"

At the jarring edge in his voice, Carmen's feet took her a step toward him before she could stop them. "Just to Jia's office."

With a lip caught between his teeth, Mattie looked from Carmen to Dex.

"You can come," Carmen offered.

"Or," Dex said, "you can make the magic happen."

He held out the bottle and the cap, and Mattie's lips quirked up a little. He reached for it, but paused to look back at Carmen once before taking the bottle. "I'm okay here."

With one last glance back at her brother, Carmen crossed the warehouse floor, nodding at the two guys she passed who were sprawled on a sofa. They gave lazy waves back, one with an iPod in his ears and the other with a book.

The door was open, and Carmen stood in the doorway, her hand hovering to knock, but Jia turned to face her from her desk before it was necessary. "Carmen."

"Hi."

Her arms felt too long, so she buried her hands into the center pocket of her hoodie, knotting them together. With no reason to do so, her heart pounded, a drum in her ears.

"Come in."

She did, and took a seat in a spare chair, then pulled a leg up under her.

"Sleep well?" Jia asked.

"I did. You?"

"Yes. We've done a lot of work on the building. It's much warmer than it once was."

Carmen glanced around the room and partly out the door before turning back to Jia. "It's looking really good."

For a beat, they eyed each other. Jia had originally hesitated when Carmen had first turned up here with her bruised face and bleeding lip; her scrawniness, her age, the anger in her, and the way she never spoke on her own accord had all been points piling up against her.

"Your brother is young."

"He is. So was I."

"Not that young." Jia sat back in her chair. "He could be in a school, in a home. At his age, the placement is faster, easier."

A muscle in Carmen's jaw ticked, and she measured her words before she spoke. "It doesn't mean it would be a good one. Or a permanent one. He could be moved constantly—probably would have been." Carmen hesitated over the next words. "Plus, I really think he would have run away this time." She sighed. "I know he would have."

Jia didn't bother arguing. She knew that better than most. She saw it constantly. "There's really no family? Nothing?"

Carmen swallowed, too heavily, the pull at her throat unsettling her. "No one."

Carmen's mother said she didn't know who Mattie's father was: he was an unanswered question in Mattie's life that would stay that way.

"I'm sorry about your mother."

That prickling in her eyes was back, and Carmen had to look up at the ceiling again and blink rapidly before she could answer. "Thank you."

"So." Jia just watched her as she spoke, gauging her in a familiar way. Carmen had never known anyone to read people the way she did. The way she would size people up and make a decision. And that initial decision was one that never changed. "What's your plan?"

Carmen blinked again. Cleared her throat. The silence and the expectation of an answer were suffocating.

"No plan?"

The lack of surprise in Jia's voice bothered Carmen but shouldn't have, really.

"I want to be his legal guardian when I can."

Jia's eyes, black and knowing and filled with too much wisdom, stayed on her intently. "How do you think, when you apply, that will play out, when they find out you've had him on the streets with you, out of school, for almost two years?"

"I..." Carmen dropped her foot to the floor and looked at Jia, her elbows on her knees. The plan that had been itching at the back of her mind for days now pressed at her for a place to expand. "I had one idea..."

"Tell me."

"Mattie," she explained, "could lie. He could say he ran, and I'll agree, and, maybe, possibly, someone else could testify to that fact. We could pretend I'd never found him on the street. I'll petition for guardianship."

"You think they'd believe that?" Jia's expression made it clear she didn't.

"I—I don't know."

"I don't think they'd buy it. That he was alone for two years and you magically find each other?"

Someone pushing back at the only vague idea she had was not making Carmen feel any more confident. "Maybe—maybe he could just get found alone, or go to a police station? With no attachment to me?"

Jia's eyes just watched her, dark.

"I could go to social services a little while later and ask about him? Say I didn't bother earlier because I knew I couldn't have him until I was legally an adult?"

Sighing, Jia swiped her hand over her jeans. "Maybe. I think that trying to get legal custody isn't going to be easy, Carmen. Especially now you're both out here."

Did people think she didn't get that? "I *know.*"

"I'll say this once." Jia looked her straight in the eye. "It's not too late to get him back into foster care. It would make it easier for you later."

"No."

And Jia must have seen the way she straightened, the fire Carmen could feel burning in her eyes, because she raised her eyebrows. Finally, she sat back in her chair. "Okay. That's what I expected, anyway."

As she should. Carmen just couldn't do that. Not now. Mattie would never forgive her. She'd never forgive herself.

"Look," Jia said. "It *could* work. It's not the best plan, but it *could* work. But why would they give him to you? An eighteen-year-old who dropped out of school to live on the streets at sixteen? One with a record?"

"A record that will disappear when I turn eighteen."

"And the other idea?"

"I'll find a job. I'll work legitimately. I'll get us an apartment eventually."

One day, Carmen would take courses and get her high school diploma. She'd liked school. She was good at it. The year she'd spent out of it last time had been long, and missing it had surprised her.

Jia sucked in a breath. "We need to figure out a better plan, Carmen. It could work, maybe. But it also may very well not. We can help you with some of it… But what about the next year and, what—several months? With the system, at least two years before anything was finalized? What about Mattie?"

And there, that was where Carmen stuttered and stalled. He was safe with her. This place, it was safe. But he was eight and living in a crack in the system. "I don't know."

And she really, really didn't. She had no idea what to do with Mattie.

"We can think about it. There are options." Jia's voice right now was so much like Dex's. Carmen had heard it before, tight with anger, had heard her bark orders at people and watched them jump into line. But at times like this, it was flush with reassurance and hope.

"I thought," Carmen faltered, "if we could fake his record somehow, or a birth certificate, we could enroll him in school."

Jia didn't dismiss the vague idea straight away. "Papers like that, digital issues, take months. More, even. And money." She paused, then shrugged. "I can ask around. Before that, we can look at schooling him with Dex."

Dex, who had a voice as soft as feathers and pulled each kid under his wing. Dex, who had made Carmen study algebra and literature, made Rae read when all she wanted to do was fight someone with anger burning in her eyes. Dex, who chased them all for answers to questions he'd sent them out with. Who had been a teacher once before all this, who had worked in a shelter part-time and had seen the broken system, then had disappeared with Jia to help fix it where he could. They built pathways between them, used old connections, got kids jobs, helped them find apartments, helped them build a life back up when they'd all been torn down.

And they did it like this, unofficially, where the red tape was a murky gray and the law was too. At a pretty huge risk.

"Did Dex get his bar?" Carmen asked.

Jia smirked. "You didn't ask him yourself?"

"He was distracted with Mattie."

"He did. It's opened."

"He finally opened it?" He had always talked about wanting one. "Did they call it what they always said they would?"

"Floaters?" At Carmen's nod, Jia rolled her eyes. "Yes."

Carmen huffed a laugh through her nose. Dex had always called them all that.

"Mattie," Carmen ventured, "he wants to help. He wants to contribute."

Jia shook her head. "He's not working the streets."

Carmen let out a breath she hadn't known she'd been holding. In reality, he was perfect for the work: small, quick, and innocent-looking. On the other hand, his skin was several shades too dark. Carmen's had been too: many of theirs was. Black held something especially dangerous these days.

With Jia, they had never pickpocketed a lot, but it was a necessary thing, something Dex had taught them all and something he'd never explained how he knew. They had a particular client: never anyone who looked like a student, who clambered for money probably more than they did; never someone in beat-up shoes, never one of their own. Always people with a certain clean look, a cut to their clothes, wrapped up in phone conversations and appointments; a parent with brand-name sunglasses juggling a child in a stroller worth more than anything any of them had.

Not that that made it better, but it was something. You had to have standards.

"If he ever got picked up, he'd be lost in the juvie and the foster system." Jia glanced out the open door, focused on something Carmen couldn't see. "We've been trying to get to a point where we don't need the kids doing it anymore. The bar..."

When she didn't finish, Carmen asked, "How can we help, then?"

They had to help. Nothing here worked on its own. Everything was built up from a team, from sharing work and doing what they all could.

Jia's focus fell back on her, eyes a well of understanding. "You can teach him to scrounge: the areas, the places. He can team with you and with Rae; she doesn't go much anymore, though. He can also be here, cleaning. Dex and a group of the girls are doing some construction work on the building. He can help."

"Okay."

"Dex will teach you too. We have a kid the age you were when you first arrived, another a year younger. He's been doing a lot with them."

Carmen had to ask. She had to know. "And a job?"

No job meant no guardianship. No apartment. No security. No Mattie. Even with a job, those things weren't guaranteed.

Jia surveyed her then and gave one slow blink. "We could try you in the bar."

That made Carmen pause. "But I'm only sixteen. Seventeen soon, I suppose."

"As long as you aren't handling alcohol, it's fine in our state. You can waitress, clean up, do dishes, do some of the prep." Jia grinned then, her scar deepening, a shadow across her face that Carmen knew intimidated some but to Carmen was just familiar. "All that fun stuff."

"Will it be legitimate?" Something was rising up, was threatening to spill in her throat and down to her fingertips—something a little like hope.

"We can put you on legitimately. It's easy to pretend we didn't know you were a runaway if they ask. I'd say we'd pay you under the table, but if we're caught doing that, it's bye-bye bar. Besides..." Jia paused, something clouding up like grief in her face, "once you're over sixteen, they kind of stop caring. We haven't had anyone over that age ping their system yet."

Carmen wondered why she lived in a world where that was a good thing.

Life wrapped itself around Ollie, and she threw herself into studying, into friends, into anything. Especially into the parties they all had, one by one, taking turns to trash one of their houses when their parents were away. They always lay about in the aftermath, the others gone home and their core group all together. She would fall asleep among them all, friends breathing in her ear, and wake up tangled or with someone different or with an extra person there.

Some of their friends fell upon each other—lips and tongues meeting, alcohol streaming through their blood—and then muttered the next day that nothing had happened. Chelsea and Alex were repeat offenders until Deon finally rolled his eyes and asked them who they were kidding. They still just slid each other sideways glances and shy smiles, and Ollie watched them, astounded that two people so interested in each other wasted so much time dancing around each other.

Usually, Ollie ended up spooning Sara and Deon. The three of them would fall, chuckling, on a sofa or a blow-up mattress. The mornings were always filled with painful groans, with the smell of coffee and bacon and eggs, with bottles clinking together as they all pitched in to pick up the carnage. Summer was well behind them, fall long closed in and shedding golden-brown across the ground. The air had started to bite at their cheeks, and most of them were kissed ruddy by it, beanies pulled over their ears, kicking leaves up to watch them play in the wind.

Some days, she was awash in those moments and nothing could touch her. And then some nights things felt like they'd pull Ollie under.

Dinner with her parents would stir up questions, discussions. Her dad would leave a heavy hand on her head, and her mom would smile at them both. Then her parents would speak about college and bring up her aptitude—or lack thereof—for chemistry, followed by other questions falling thick and fast about a future Ollie was being pushed into feetfirst, heels digging into the ground. And she still hadn't told them about Sean.

Ollie felt everything inside her halt at the fear that she *just didn't know what she wanted.*

Some nights, she would sit at her desk, a textbook open in front of her but her pencil in her art book, and sketch out lips and eyes and hands and shadows. She'd remember the last time she'd soothed someone, really seen the pain tearing at their insides and pooling in their eyes, the way she'd literally just offered herself up with zero explanation from the other person.

Ollie couldn't help it: when she saw someone who needed something, she liked to step forward and help.

And so Carmen was someone she couldn't stay away from. Ollie was stuck in her orbit, even if it all now seemed like a distant memory, a daydream, a scene from a movie that had seeped into a deep part of her, lulled into her brain.

After weeks, she stopped glancing around for Carmen. Deon's digging had said enough: Carmen was at a different school on the other side of the city. Letting her go would be easier. Ollie couldn't stalk out her address; it would look too weird. Carmen knew where to find her, and the fact that she hadn't left Ollie a little cold.

But also feeling a little ridiculous: what had they shared, really?

Instead, she pushed Carmen to the back of her mind. Pushed the burn of her lips, the stroke of her tongue, the graze of her fingertips to a place where Ollie could ignore them—let them fade into that strange dream state and let them be.

Sometimes, when she was with her friends, Ollie didn't think about Carmen at all.

One night, thick with sweaters, Ollie stumbled through her front door. Her glasses were fogged up, and she wiped a clumsy hand over them, achieving nothing. Deon had dropped her off, and she'd weaved her way up her garden path, his car idling out front, clearly waiting until she was in the house. That's when it hit her full force:

She was really drunk.

Her key scraped out of the lock, and it was just after midnight, right on time for her curfew. Ollie had told her parents she was staying at a friend's, but Sara hadn't been able to come to the party and Deon had left early. In the end, she'd craved her house and her bed and her space.

Her glasses were really fogged up. Or maybe she was just blurry?

She closed the door behind her as quietly as she could. It snicked shut, and she breathed a sigh of relief.

Her parents slept through everything.

Light was spilling from the kitchen, but she ignored it and tiptoed to a side table to lay her keys down gently. They barely made a sound.

Her stomach roiled. Who had brought out the Jaeger?

Though every time she complained about that, someone always seemed to point out it had been her.

Boots came off clumsily, almost tripping her in the process. Her hand flashed out, and she caught herself against the wall before she could fall.

She really was kicking this sneaking-in thing's ass.

As she straightened up, Ollie took a step forward and froze. Her mom was standing in the kitchen doorway, watching her with an eyebrow raised and what could have been either a smile or an angry frown. Everything was blurry.

"Olivia. While that was highly entertaining to watch, you were louder than a herd of goats."

"I was quiet!"

"Not even a little, sweetie." Her mom stepped forward. "How drunk are you?"

She may throw up. "Not at all."

"Well, that's a lie." Her eyes narrowed. "Bathroom. Now."

Ollie barely made it. But when she threw up, her mom lay a cold washcloth over the back of her neck and rubbed circles on her back. Instead of lecturing her, she got Ollie into bed with water and aspirin.

"How did you get home?" her mom asked.

"Deon."

"Was he sober?"

"Yup." Ollie groaned in her pillow. "'Cause he's not an idiot."

"Good."

Silence, then, and just her mother's hand rubbing her back.

"Why aren't you yelling?" Ollie's eyes were closed, her bedcovers tucked in around her.

"Your head will do that enough for me tomorrow."

"Ugh."

"Yeah. Ugh." Her mom's voice was quiet, a note in it Ollie hadn't heard before. "Are you okay, Ollie?"

"Drunk."

"No, I mean…are you okay?"

For a minute, Ollie let the room spin and shift around her. Even with her eyes closed, everything was drifting. "Yes," she murmured. "But also no… I feel like I don't know what I'm doing."

She wondered if she would remember this conversation tomorrow. Her mom's hand still rubbed soothing patterns.

"None of us do, Ollie. But it'll get better."

Nights grew colder, but the warehouse didn't hold the bite it once had. Dex took Mattie and Carmen around and showed them the patched-up holes and the insulation they'd found or taken from other empty buildings. Mattie listened to it all, and one day, with a hammer in hand, he sat in the wind on the roof, Dex squatting next to him. Carmen watched with her heart in her throat as he fixed tiles in a spot in which the water had come through. Days later, when it rained in sheets and sheets, he dragged Carmen to the spot and stood under it. The rain was hammering on the windows, and none of that rain made its way inside. Mattie grinned so hard she thought they both might shatter.

For weeks, she didn't let him out of her sight, and he made no attempt to leave it anyway. Carmen and Rae led him to places they knew they could pull out bags of thrown-out food. At the end of each term, the kids at college who moved dumped enough to stock boxes for days. Supermarkets wasted too much, and a lot of workers who emptied the stock into the bins outside turned a blind eye to the kids who scuttled out, fingers desperate and bags ready. They knew which supermarkets didn't order perfectly good food destroyed when they tossed it.

Mattie learned to clean windows, to fix things, to use his hands. Jia had connections, people who helped her get hold of first aid gear, donations sent to shelters she could haul in: warmer clothes, sleeping bags, pillows, a newer mattress, extra gas for the camping stoves. Carmen did everything she could to get them somewhere to shower more than a couple of times a week.

But Mattie saw things Carmen wished he didn't. If they were out too late, with darkness in every corner, all the horrors the day stifled leaked out. Fights that erupted, people lying in corners with needles in their arms, a brutal police officer, the flash of a gun tucked into a waistband.

Most nights, Mattie slept well. But many nights, Carmen lay awake, second-guessing everything she did while Mattie sprawled out beside her, sharing her heat. She was lucky, she knew, to have the people in her life that she did—this strange collection of humans.

Dex was a constant. He was like a bear, but the first time she'd been there, Carmen had watched him bring a puppy back to life with a dropper of milk and sugar, his huge hands enveloping it and his voice a soft hum. The dog, huge now, a patchwork of breeds, bounded at her and bowled her over. Mattie was in love with it instantly.

The readings Dex gave them, the old textbooks that lined one of the shelves, the math he patiently had them repeat, all meant nothing; Carmen knew that. Nothing official, nothing that could go on their record. But knowing that Mattie had some kind of structure, anything, made her feel better. Once he got back into school, *if* he got back into school, he wouldn't be so far behind.

Some of the nights that Carmen lay awake, sleep burning at her eyes but evading her with each breath, she scooted away from Mattie and went back downstairs.

All the kids Carmen had known before had moved on, most of them to things Jia and Dex had set up for them. Yet the newer ones were nice: they were rough around the edges but good kids who deserved more than to be grasping at this version of normalcy. The youngest, Arti, was as close to a friend that Mattie could now say he had. Dex gave them the same material to look at, and Carmen often made Artie sit down to actually do it with Mattie, or dragged them during a free moment to the library. Most nights, Artie slept on a sofa, and no one made him move. He had an aversion to closed-in spaces, and even his room was too small for him. In summer, Rae told her, he'd slept on the roof with only the blanket of stars to close in on him.

On those nights when Carmen stumbled downstairs, a soft glow still lit the building, one that never really went away, due to the muggy streetlights outside. Someone was always up. Sometimes, someone would offer hot tea or coffee, or Rae and Dex and Jia would be there, and those were Carmen's favorite nights.

Dex had taught Carmen to fight when she was thirteen and angry, with fear rumbling in her stomach. Never, *never*, for fun, he'd told her—and repeatedly had to say to Rae, rolling his eyes as he did so—but to protect themselves, to fight *back* if ever need be.

They'd had to sometimes.

The day he'd first stood in front of Carmen and shown her how to throw a punch, his fingers gentle as they untucked her thumb, the bruises from being undefended had still lingered on her skin, marks that had sunk themselves deep and permanently spoiled something within her.

Now, three years later and rusty, she sparred in a back room. The space was big, one set up with filthy old mats they'd wiped down a thousand times, that were stained and splitting their insides. Dex reminded her of focus, of breathing, of momentum, and using force to deflect an opponent—to incapacitate and run.

Rae, once coal-eyed and all fire and boiling blood, now laughed at Carmen or poked her arm. Carmen thought vacantly that Rae simmered now more than boiled. Hours later, sweat cooling on their skin, they would sit in the frigid air on the roof, their feet swinging and sharing a drink of beer or a cigarette, dividing their heat under sleeping bags they pulled up with them. Most of the time, Jia joined them, grabbing the beer bottles out of their hands with a huff, putting their cigarettes out against the concrete. They'd offer her sheepish smiles, and they'd settle in, not the same as before, but different—deeper, comfortable. And Carmen knew that just below, Mattie slept in a bed with a blanket, his stomach full and a book just fallen from his hand.

In those moments, Carmen forgot to second-guess herself. She forgot that anxiety should be crawling up her throat and choking her and instead breathed easily, the heat of arms against hers and the chatter of her crew around her.

CHAPTER 11

THERE WAS A RINGING IN Ollie's ears.

It echoed, like time was bouncing against itself. Her backpack sat at her feet, heavy and filled with books she really had to get through that night. She still had her scarf wrapped around her neck, the cold from outside clinging to the fabric. The living room seemed huge, encompassing, overwhelming—even as the walls were compressing in on her. A painting hung on the wall that her mother had brought back from a trip last year. Her mom had raved about it for hours.

Her mom?

What had her father just said?

She'd walked in, and he'd been on the sofa, strangely ashen and gaunt-looking. And then he'd said something that just wouldn't register.

"Ollie. She's gone."

Her father repeated the words, standing now in front of her. When had he stood up?

"What?" she asked.

"She—she's gone. It happened this morning, right after you left. They tried…"

She'd never really know what they'd tried, because his voice broke then, painfully, and that ringing sound grew louder.

"What—" Her lips felt numb. "What do you mean, gone?"

His face was agony to look at, so Ollie looked back at the painting on the wall. She wasn't really a fan. The colors clashed. "She…she died, this morning." Her dad's voice had never sounded like this. "It was a heart attack."

The air disappeared.

That word.

Died.

Dead.

Ollie absorbed the news with a simple blink, a slight parting of her lips, and a rush of air from between them. She looked at her father again. His eyes were glittering, brimming with tears that fell too fast to be her father's. His fingers grasped her arm in a way that left five perfect circles on her bicep.

"I tried." He cleared his throat, though it did nothing. "I tried to help."

How? Her mother was a heart specialist and the only one who could have possibly done something.

"They said it was instant. That nothing could have been done."

Her phone was still clutched in her hand. The message from her father was still open, telling her to come home early.

The receptionist at school had taken her from class and whispered to her to meet her father at home. A woman known for having a raised voice and for harsh words. But still, Ollie hadn't expected this.

Her lips were numb, and Ollie wanted to ask him again what he meant. Her mother couldn't be gone. That morning when Ollie had left for school, her parents had still been getting ready for work. The entire house had smelled like her mom's shampoo, and Ollie had heard their laughter, her mother's flirtatious giggle, floating from her parents' bedroom.

Ollie had rolled her eyes and left without even shouting good-bye.

Why hadn't she said good-bye?

Were her father's lips trembling?

Ollie took a step back, shaking her head, her heart thrumming away in her chest, while apparently her mother's heart did nothing. Her father's hand was in the air, hovering now that he didn't have her arm to cling to. Did he feel like she did—untethered?

She turned on her heel and went to her room, the air gone from there too.

After that, things passed in a blur, and Ollie wanted to clutch at all those moments, to grasp them to her chest and not let them go, each of them precious because they kept her closer to the time when her mom had been alive. But it was like when she was small and tried to cup the seawater in her hands to carry home with her.

Days passed, and Ollie barely registered them. Her father ghosted through the house. Sometimes, he tried to speak to her, but Ollie couldn't even hear him. That ringing in her ears didn't leave, as if it were trying to muffle out the truth of everything around her.

The house still smelled like her mother's shampoo.

Or maybe she was imagining it.

The morning of the funeral dawned strangely bright and warm, as if it hadn't received the memo that they were supposed to be mourning. A fluke of fall weather. Not much of the day imprinted on Ollie's mind beyond that. She vaguely recalled the weary shaking of her father's shoulders, the way he looked like he hadn't slept, like he was rumpled without her mother there to put him together. There was a vague recollection of black clothes and of ground that swallowed her mom whole, leaving Ollie aching with nothing.

Sara and Deon pressed against her on either side, as if to hold her up.

Partway through the wake, she'd stumbled to her room, the door clicking shut behind her. She was gasping, gulping air, and her fingers clawed at her chest, trying to wrench out whatever the thing inside her was that left her feeling so empty, so heavy, so unable to breathe.

Sara's body against her back, her arms wrapped around Ollie's waist, saved her. It was the pressure of her best friend against her hyperactive, overstimulated nerves that slowly slowed Ollie's breathing. As her oxygen levels returned to normal, a sob cleaved from her throat, and Ollie slowly sank to her knees, Sara a puddle around her.

"It's okay. It's okay." Sara repeated again and again. Ollie didn't have the words to tell her that it really wasn't.

Deon found them later. Without a word of question, he sat down next to them, his baritone joining Sara's voice to murmur words Ollie didn't believe.

Strangely, in that moment, she wondered if had been like this for Carmen. If it had felt like something important had cleaved itself from her body.

The next month ached, if time could do that. Ollie wandered away from school when she could, her mind a cloud of grief. The weather was freezing now, and she welcomed the sting in her fingertips, the bite to her lungs as she gulped down air by the river. The cold was like some kind of retribution as it sank deeper and deeper into her bones. Even when she left school alone, either Deon or Sara always found her. One would fall into step with her, or just sit with her, their warmth soaking into her side. The other would collect all their homework and make a list of all the things they missed, and pass it to Ollie with nothing but a hug.

Everything felt like she was behind glass, muted and watching the world but unable to touch it.

The school counsellor called her down and tried to get her to speak. But Ollie had no words, just a racing heart and the feeling of anxiety, once under control, now raging. She tried to be present, to acknowledge that her father was hurting, to find out how to put them both together when their puzzle had been torn apart and the pieces set on fire.

Most nights, Ollie pulled on every jumper she could, followed by her parka, and slipped out her window to lie across the grass of her backyard, a bottle of vodka turning her eyes glassy and numbing the icy air in her chest.

She wished, in some moments, she hadn't pushed Sean away. She would have someone to cling to, lips to bite at, would at least be able to chase at something he didn't have to give. But he was gone, and it was her doing, so she curled into herself on the grass, desperation groping at her throat and frustration scorching behind it.

She never tolerated the cold for long and would crawl into her bed later, shivering and numb.

On her seventeenth birthday, she choked on a smile when her father gave Ollie her mother's old watch, the metal cool and not holding any of her warmth anymore. The watch had been a gift from Ollie's grandparents when her mother had gone to medical school. Ollie wanted to thank him, to say something, but all she managed was a tight pressing of her lips, and her father's face mirrored her own.

Looking at him was hard. When her mom had collapsed, had his face been the last thing she'd seen? Had he really tried to save her? If it had been the other way around, would she now have both her parents with her, whole and together and breathing?

That night, Ollie got a hold of another bottle of vodka and went to Sara's with the mission of trying to ignore the guilt at leaving her father. He'd been sitting on the sofa in an empty house and she left with nothing but her inability to smile. As if her mother's death had flipped the entire world and left her with no idea how to walk among it.

Sara took her out back to lie on the trampoline in a nest of blankets and watch the sky unfold.

"Happy birthday to me."

Ollie held the bottle up, and Sara pulled her harder into her side. The stars were a blur overhead, from tears or vodka or both; Ollie didn't know. Her glasses poked painfully into the bridge of her nose, but she didn't want to move. Later, she barely blinked as Sara took the bottle away.

She fell asleep with her wrist held to her ear, trying to match her heartbeat with each tick.

There was something methodical in cleaning the bar. Maybe it was because it was always somehow filthy, even after Carmen had spent hours the day before cleaning it. But whatever the reason, the action was soothing, and Carmen found a way to not think. If she was one for that type of thing, it could have been like meditation. This time was her favorite, when the bar was just closing on a weeknight, not too late, and the last of the regulars were dragging themselves from their stools, a sway in their steps.

She'd thought this place would disgust her, that watching people drink away their evenings, watching their nights fade around them as they bathed themselves in alcohol, would remind her of her mother. Would remind her of blown pupils, of the stench of a week-long bender, of cheap, spirit-laced promises that dissolved to nothing in the harsh light of day, of flashing blue-and-red lights washing the living room and casting shadows on Mattie's cheeks.

Curiously, it didn't. Instead, the entire thing was something new, something fragile, something she finally belonged to. Her hours were all over the place, adjusted depending on Dex, on Mattie, on Jia. But Carmen had signed a contract, had some kind of proof she was earning legitimate money. It wasn't a lot, but it was something. Plus, she was allowed to play around in the kitchen. They didn't do much food, just fries, mostly. But Dex had insisted they serve something: drunks needed it, and he truly believed it led to fewer fights, fewer problems.

The bar was quiet during the week, but he'd built it up for the weekend, offering half-priced beers at happy hour and drawing in a college crowd. They were lax with IDs, and some of the faces Carmen saw couldn't have been much older than her own. Some nights, inexplicably, her gaze searched the room for a face she might recognize, before she'd drag it away and tell herself not to lose her mind to fantasy.

"You're getting good at that."

A plate was balanced in Carmen's hand, piles of glasses tucked under her forearm, looking precarious but perfectly balanced. She shrugged at Dex, the glasses barely shifting. "I'm a pro."

He put down the two trays of clean glasses and started putting them away. He was a conundrum, Dex. All brawn and muscle. Yet watching him with Mattie, watching him put glasses away, watching him with his dog, he was so gentle, his fingers moving over things as if always aware of the vulnerability under them.

When they sparred, she could forget he had the ability to lay her flat, to break something. His movements were fast, his footwork resembling a dance. But then, Carmen had also seen him dark-eyed and dangerous. There was something of that buried deep that had been stitched into him, not born. She'd seen him take out people who threatened one of the kids— or Rae or Jia.

"Can you finish stacking these? I need to go out back and unpack the new order."

Carmen hummed a yes as she backed into the tiny kitchen and put the dishes down to get to later. At the end of her nights here, her fingers were often pruned from soap and water. Her back ached a little, and her eyes burned with a new kind of tiredness.

But it was *her* pain, *her* exhaustion.

It was *her* life.

Some nights, Carmen snuck behind the bar and served a few drinks. Not at all legal, but it was where Dex normally needed her on a weekend. They'd made her a fake ID, one that looked genuine, just in case. But whenever other bars had been checked, no one had ever gone as far as comparing IDs with working records. Most cops, if they appeared, just checked IDs and left.

The bar made no real money, barely managing to do anything but cover costs. They never wanted anything big. Their focus was on the warehouse, the kids, the runaways. But Dex had wanted something to his name. Jia had come around to the idea when she saw the way it could be used as a stepping stone, when she realized the plus side to having a business around, linked with taxes and doing legitimate operations. All the profits went into the warehouse, into anything for the kids who Dex and Jia tirelessly worked for.

With the glasses unpacked and Dex back behind the bar, Carmen headed into the tiny office, pushing the swinging door open and sliding into a chair opposite Mattie.

He had his DS on and was playing the one game he owned, swiped by Rae, his face screwed up in concentration. Carmen still remembered how he had lit up when they had first walked through the back door, Mattie's hand in her own, and he'd realized he had somewhere to charge the game's battery.

The table was strewn with open books, a notepad, and a pencil. He didn't even look up.

"Aren't you supposed to be doing some kind of report?"

"Did it."

Blinking at Mattie, Carmen waited for him to make eye contact. Nothing. Swiftly, she grabbed the notebook. Notes filled the pages, headings were highlighted, an occasional doodle in a corner.

Sometimes, Mattie went quiet, withdrew a little, and Carmen tended to wait for him to come back. Most likely, he'd learned it from her, and she understood the need to crawl inside your own head and live there for a while. So she would just sit near him, listen to the little beeps from his DS, and let him know she was nearby.

She always tried to be nearby, never really leaving him until he was asleep, wearing every pullover he had to try to drive off the cold. Then she'd go down to spar.

It had taken weeks, but Carmen had finally remembered the ways to move her body when Rae threw a punch. Had remembered how to duck under it, to seamlessly pop up behind her and use her body weight to drag her to the ground. Never in her life would Carmen have enough strength to take out Dex, and instead she learned how to dodge and use his momentum.

She used her speed and her reflexes, and she turned his few flaws against him.

It was addictive having something to throw her body into—to finish, gleaming with sweat, her chest working for air, her muscles somehow tight and loose all at the same. Like she had with soccer. She felt cleansed after, limber, like she could actually lie down and sleep.

Plus, it kept her warm.

With the bar finally closed that night, Mattie slipped his DS into his backpack, and Dex, Carmen, and Mattie all walked home together, Mattie tight against her side. Carmen was itching to spar that night, energy prickling up her limbs even as the cold prickled her face.

Looking completely the opposite, Mattie blinked sleepily, his stomach full after eating fries in the bar, delighted with the hot food, the salt. She had just been glad about the surprising amount of fruit they managed to get hold of, as well as some veggies. So much was thrown away. Dex made pasta in the warehouse sometimes, when they had enough of the ingredients to make some for all of them. Mattie had told her it tasted like home was supposed to.

In the warehouse, Mattie was dead on his feet. As he followed Carmen upstairs, he waved hello to Jia and Rae and to Artie, who was sprawled on a sofa. After they lay together on the mattress in their bedroom, he read to her. His voice fell to gravel, to the waves of exhaustion, until his eyes were almost closed, the book an inch from his nose as he tried to keep going. When Carmen's hand touched his hair, the book fell on his face, his eyes closed, and he was breathing heavily.

Finally, sure he was asleep, she went down to spar. Sleep rarely came without pushing herself physically for hours. For some reason, her body was always wound tight, and her thoughts raced until she stood across from Dex or Rae or one of the others Dex was teaching and bounced on her toes with somewhere to direct her energy.

The best nights were ones she spent with just Rae and Dex and Jia, and they fell into step with each other easily, something comfortable in the air between them all.

That night, like most, Carmen ended up leaning heavily against the wall of the sparring room, the brick harsh against her back. Dex's arm rested just against hers, a whisper of connection, something to melt into. A light sheen of sweat covered them as they watched Rae train with one of the older teens, a kid new to fighting. Unlike before, Rae held back, treating the session as a moment to teach him rather than letting her rage fly out. That wasn't how it had been when Carmen had first met her. These days, Rae still buzzed with something electric, but in the last few years she had mellowed.

"Mattie asked me when he could learn to fight."

Carmen's head turned so fast to look at Dex that her neck twinged. His face was impassive.

How could Mattie have asked without Carmen knowing? She was never far from his side. But sometimes Mattie and Dex were poring over a book, and Carmen had her feet kicked up on a sofa not far away, but not paying attention. "How did he know we were fighting?"

"I've seen him sitting up on the catwalk, watching from up there through the door."

"The door's always closed."

"Not always." His lips pressed into a line, just visible through the gruff salt-and-pepper of his beard. "Besides, most of them here are learning. He was always going to know."

Carmen looked away, swallowing heavily.

"Carmen. Maybe he should."

"He's eight."

Dex's voice was low, steady, a thread to cling to. "He is. But he's also an eight-year-old who lives, well…" his hands gestured vaguely, "…here."

"He has me." Carmen's voice was harsher than she had meant to make it, the words flying out of her mouth with flame.

Dex didn't even flinch. "He does. But he can't always have you."

Truth was something Dex always dropped like it was nothing. He had always littered the floor with it and left it behind for people to stumble over, gather up, or avoid as they saw fit. Something in Carmen's chest rose up, fierce and undiluted, the words forming on her tongue to fight that, to argue, to tell him Mattie would *always, always* have her. They were lava in her mouth, threatening to burst through. But then her gaze caught his, deep and honest and open, and everything stuttered.

Dex had had a brother once.

They'd all had parents of some description.

Jia had had a son.

Yet here they all were, without those people.

Blinking at Dex, the words cooled to stone on Carmen's tongue; she swallowed them down, the truth of them rasping at her throat and coming to rest in her stomach.

She gave a nod, one that hurt like she was shaking apart her insides. He laid a heavy hand on her shoulder. After a beat, she rested her head against it, the warmth stealing into her skin and the brick still scraping at her back.

Ollie felt as if she was drifting. Her house was always quiet; her father worked more and more, throwing himself into his job as if this could distract him from the reality of his dead wife.

He tried and tried to connect with Ollie, but she had shut down, not even knowing why, until he suggested she see her school counsellor and disappeared into work again. They communicated with notes on the kitchen counter, scrawled loops of handwriting that Ollie was furious with but never threw away. One night, opposite each other at the counter eating spaghetti, Ollie had said something about school. Her father had smiled and lifted a hand to touch her wrist, and Ollie had flinched. The moment was too quick to stop or take back, and guilt bubbled in her stomach at the depth of hurt that carved its way across her father's face. He tried to bury it. Ollie watched it happen. But after that, he kept his hands to himself, as if scared to feel his daughter's rejection.

Ollie didn't know why, but she couldn't bridge that gap.

She'd stumbled her way through the last few years, had pulled back from her parents' attention, yet their family had always been one for relaxed affection, touches, hugs, easy laughter. Her father was barrel-chested, and Ollie's favorite place when she had been small was in his arms, her ear against that chest, his heartbeat playing in her ears. She'd drum the beat against his arms with her fingers. At night now, with the ticking of her mother's watch, Ollie fought with the urge to crawl out of bed and to fall against her father, to listen to his heartbeat and ignore the fact that she'd never hear her mom's again.

That morning haunted her, the lack of good-bye, the roll of her eyes. The dismissiveness Ollie had felt.

Worse yet was the memory of her mother's hands on her back not long before she died. Ollie's drunkenness that night had reduced the memory to a dreamy blur. Some nights, she woke up, choked with the feeling that her mom's hands had *just* been on her back, rubbing soothing patterns.

Her mother hadn't even lectured her the next day. Just bit it down and put a plate of scrambled eggs in front of her. There'd been a smirk at the edges of her lips, playful and teasing, when Ollie had blanched at the sight.

But her mother was gone, and her father was as lost as Ollie was.

Ollie was painfully logical, able to sift through facts and to draw conclusions. She knew, she *knew*, it wasn't her father's fault. But for some reason, she still couldn't meet his eyes, couldn't offer more than tight smiles and short sentences.

He'd been there. While her mom lay on the floor and left them both behind.

The house was quiet, snow swirling in the window.

Everything was closing in on her, and Ollie turned on the television and upped the volume so loud the neighbors were sure to complain. Even so, the silence seeped in from the other side of the house. Ollie switched on the radio in her room, and then the stereo in the kitchen, and the cacophony of voices twined together to drown out that emptiness that had taken over.

But not completely. Not enough.

So she messaged Sara, who turned up instantly, fist pounding at the door.

Ollie swung the door open, and Deon and Sara, bottle of something in hand, flinched at the ball of media noise that hit them even on the doorstep. Grimacing an apology, Ollie went room to room and flicked switches and tapped buttons. Instead of silence, she was flooded with the sounds of her friends breathing, their upbeat questions. Sara and Deon flopped onto the sofa, snow still melting in their hair, and left a gap between them for Ollie to fill.

Bottles of mixers and shot glasses were dumped onto the coffee table, and Ollie burrowed between her two friends.

"Shots first?" Sara asked. A few weeks ago, she'd voiced concern to Ollie that maybe she should sleep more, try to look after herself. Then the look of drowning Ollie could feel in her eyes had made Sara close her own and pull her in for a hug. Still, at times Ollie could feel the concern in Sara's eyes.

"Always."

Sara accepted hers, and they clinked them together, spirits spilling over and Ollie's eyes burning for no reason. They all did their shots in procession, coughing at the liquor's burn.

They did another one, and then Ollie poured drinks, mixing Coke and ice. Finally, she fell back against the sofa, the touch of her friends' skin calming the heartbeat that fluttered against her chest.

"You okay?" Deon asked.

Ollie shrugged, their arms rubbing together as she did so. "No."

Sara took a pull on her straw, angling slightly so she faced them. She pulled her legs up and laid them over both Deon and Ollie's laps. "Your dad working late again?"

"Yeah." There was something bitter in how Ollie said it, a taste she didn't want in her mouth, but she had no way to stop it from spilling up and out. She sipped her drink, swilling it around her mouth, it doing nothing to erase it. "Like always."

Sara and Deon made eye contact, and Ollie noticed but ignored it.

"Maybe you should ask him to be around more." Sara turned her eyes back to Ollie, rushing to continue when Ollie opened her mouth quickly. "Even just in one of your notes."

Ollie snapped her mouth shut and shook her head. "I don't even know if I want him around anyway."

She had no idea how to word the mess of thoughts and tied-up feelings in her chest. How to explain that the hole there was huge, with her mom dead and her dad out all the time, but that when it was just her and her dad, that hole was bigger somehow. So big Ollie thought it was going to swallow them both.

"Well, Sara has a plan."

The tone in Deon's voice made something in Ollie perk up. "Yeah?" She looked to Sara, her drink clutched against her chest.

"Well…" Sara smiled a little. "Ruin is back from college this weekend, and Deon said he'd mentioned a bar he was going to go to where they don't card you." Sara's grin grew a little wicked. "So Deon convinced him to take us."

Something like interest stirred in the back of her mind. That sounded fun and like a totally stupid idea. It sounded like something she wanted to do. "And he agreed?"

"Of course he did." Deon nudged her. "I just reminded him he'd already mentioned which bar it was and that we'd go without him anyway..."

With another grin, Sara shrugged. "It worked. So we'll tell our parents we're at Deon's and we'll go out with Ruin."

Reckless with alcohol, and reckless without it these days, Ollie perked up. "Deal."

"Excellent!" Sara straightened and poured more shots. "You better?"

Ollie opened her mouth to say yes but instead, no fell out again. And she accepted the shot and threw it back without waiting for the others.

"Okay." Sara's voice was small, laced with the apprehension that never went anywhere these days when it came to Ollie. But she took her shot, and Deon took his, and they all let their night become blurry around the edges.

It was a not a great thing to do, but Ollie agreed to it anyway.

That Friday night, they piled off the bus in a neighborhood their parents would probably warn them about. Sara had dressed up Ollie, complete with makeup on to help her feel a little older. Deon had procured them each a fake ID, which sat in their bags and would hopefully not need to be used.

Ruin pushed the door to the bar open, and the music blasted out, warmth radiating into the street. A grin lit up his face. "I'm going to get my ass kicked if anyone finds out about this."

"No one will, Ru." Sara looked delighted as she walked past him.

Ruin rolled his eyes as he held the door open for Deon to follow Sara, but when Ollie started to walk past him, he asked, "You okay?"

Ollie gave him a nod, too sharp, her blood already singing a little from the pregaming.

He eyed her, then returned the motion. "Okay."

Unable to take sympathy, to look empathy in the eye, not when it was a night Ollie wanted to be someone else, something else, *anything* else, she turned and walked into the full bar, which was brimming with boisterous noise and drunken energy.

It took so long.

It took even more weeks on top of the few months that had passed, but Carmen had finally left Mattie with someone else. Her fear had nothing to do with the people—as difficult as it was to admit, Carmen trusted Dex, trusted Rae and Jia, all of them, with her life. But trusting them with Mattie's was more difficult. Anytime he was too far from her, a thick and heady unease crawled up Carmen's spine. It left her feeling like all the air had left the room. Sometimes, if she walked to the other side of the warehouse, Mattie's gaze flicked up, eyes almost black from his blown pupils as he watched to see where she'd gone.

But she always had the feeling that if she let him out of her sight, he wouldn't be there when she got back. When they'd been in the group home the last time for a night, Carmen thirteen and Mattie five, she had been sent to school one morning. Mattie hadn't been there when she'd returned.

He had been so small and young, sent to the first open home without being able to say good-bye to the only person he had in the world. Carmen had begged to see him, begged the family she was with next to see him, begged the one after. She'd always been met with silence.

So she didn't like to leave him alone.

But now, after months, Mattie trusted the others, especially Rae. For the first time, when Carmen had been about to leave, Mattie hadn't jumped up immediately to join her. He'd been sitting next to Rae on the sofa, who was busy trying to beat his top score on his DS and failing badly. Mattie had hesitated, almost hovered, as though torn between his desire to stay with Carmen and wanting to be somewhere that was starting to feel like home.

"Want to stay with me, kid?" Rae had asked, her eyes on Carmen, filled with a question.

Mattie had swallowed, had stood, had taken a step toward Carmen, and then paused and looked back at Rae. "Can we spar a bit?"

Sparring with Mattie was all footwork, teaching him to duck and weave. He loved to dance around Carmen as she taught him the signs of someone about to throw a punch, taught him to roll, to be quick. They were progressing slowly, and she still lived with her heart in her throat, but he loved it.

Sometimes he laughed mid-dodge, delight in his eyes. The sound filled the room, filled Carmen, and left her breathless.

"Yeah, we can." Rae nudged his shoulder with her own.

He'd looked back to Carmen, teeth at his lip. "Can I?"

"Of course." But she was looking at Rae. "You sure?"

The nod was certain, but Carmen's gut wasn't, and she left after ruffling Mattie's hair, trying not to make it a big deal. The feel of his hair, shorn much closer to his scalp than in the past to make it easier to maintain, left an ache in her stomach. She had liked the soft cloud it was when it grew out.

Her own hair was at her chin now. Rae had taken her scissors to it during a night filled with a few beers, the taste of them like bread over Carmen's tongue. Her hair now was jagged, shaggy, her long, dark waves a distant memory. A patch had even been shaved just above her ear like an undercut.

The bar was busy that night. Fridays always were, and Dex had beckoned her up to serve with a wink and a grin that bordered on cheeky. It was better that way. The pace was faster as she switched between pulling beers and cleaning glasses; doing it kept her mind off Mattie, off the space he left within her when he wasn't there, off the way something tugged at her to go back and get him. This was the best option: he wasn't cooped up in the back office with the sounds of drunken idiots around him. He was somewhere safe, with someone safe. But still.

He wasn't with *her*.

The crowd was getting thicker, louder.

Dex ran a tight ship. Troublemakers weren't even remotely tolerated, and on nights like this, he called in a friend, equally as large and bearded and weighty, to help him keep the idiots at bay. By now, everyone knew the rules, which meant the crowd was usually a fun one, easygoing. Carmen only had to ward off the occasional overly friendly dude.

A guy stood in front of her with cheekbones to die for, who, despite the rough stubble, reminded her of someone. His skin was like the inky black of the river she and Mattie had slept by at night, soothing and deep and endless.

"Hey."

"Hey. What'll it be?"

"Two beers and—" His face fell. "Wait. Yo!" He turned around to the crowd behind him. "What was it?"

And then a guy with matching cheekbones was standing in front of her, grinning up at the older one. He also looked familiar.

He was familiar.

Carmen knew him. She knew she did.

"One rum and Coke, and a gin and tonic." He grinned at her. Then his mouth fell open.

Panic seized Carmen so strongly she had to grip the bar top. His name was Deon. She remembered him now, laughing with Ollie at that party, an arm carelessly over her shoulder hours before the bottom fell out of the world.

Sara, who Ollie had draped her arm around at that party, pushed up next to him. She barely looked at Carmen as she went to say something to Deon. Then she noticed the look on his face and turned to see what had caused it. Sara's mouth dropped open too.

"Holy fucking shit! What are the chances?" Then Sara was grinning and grabbing someone behind her, and Ollie was in front of Carmen, thinner than before, hollow under her eyes, but still Ollie.

Something tripped over in Carmen's stomach. She paused, and the urge to ask Ollie what had taken the stars from her eyes rose up.

"Ollie! Check it out. It's Carmen. Dude." Sara's attention was back on Carmen. "You have no idea how much Ollie was trying to find you."

Carmen could only stare at Ollie, who blinked back at her, the sky in her eyes a storm. Then one thought made it through the others: they couldn't know she was here. If they told people, the school would find out, and that crack she'd merrily tripped down would widen until she was found.

Until Mattie was found.

"Carmen." Ollie's voice was all husk, surprise, and something else Carmen didn't recognize.

"Ollie." For a distracted moment, Carmen loved the way Ollie's name flowed out of her mouth, like it was meant to be there for those few seconds.

"I—" Ollie was staring at her as if Carmen had all the answers, when Carmen felt that she had nothing to offer up but confusion. "How are you?"

Before Carmen could answer, someone down the bar yelled for service, and people jostled, waiting for drinks as Dex managed his end. He threw her a look, his eyebrows thick over his brow.

"I'm really sorry," Carmen said. "I have to get your order out and serve the next people."

Sara was looking between the two of them, Deon muttering something to the guy that was clearly his brother.

"Two beers, one rum and Coke, and one gin and tonic?" she checked.

Ollie's never stopped staring at her, and she just nodded and watched Carmen the entire time she made the drinks. Carmen's fingers trembled, which she blamed on the horror overtaking her that this was the first step in being found out.

That had to be it. Because it had nothing to do with Ollie and the memory of burning skin under Carmen's hands or the urgency to her lips—nothing with the way Ollie had offered herself up like the answer to a prayer.

So many eyes were on her, brows pushed together in contemplation. Carmen was nauseated at the idea that maybe she and Mattie were going to have to run, just as he'd settled in.

The others all scooped up their drinks, but Ollie was still watching, lips parted slightly, the bow of her mouth a question.

"You guys want a tab?"

Ollie still stared at her, so Sara smiled. "Yeah, thanks."

Carmen set it up, and when she looked back over, they'd gone, swallowed by the crowd. Something had opened up, some space, and gulped down something Carmen needed. Filling up a row of glasses with beer, the guy who asked for them trying to smile at her, Carmen pushed past the hollow feeling. What could she say to Ollie to ensure none of them mentioned Carmen to anyone they knew?

"What was that?" Dex was next to her, digging into the ice bin and filling some glasses.

"What?" Carmen took the guy's cash with a glare until he got the hint and his friend helped him carry the drinks away.

"That showdown." Dex splashed gin into the drinks in front of him, and Carmen took someone's order down the bar by simply watching them gesture to the drinks in front of them and mouth, *Four more?*

"There was no showdown."

"You know them."

Carmen licked her lips. How much did you really know someone? How much could she really say she knew Ollie? She didn't really know the others, that was for sure. Just their names. Just the way they all moved in each other's orbits like they'd done it for a millennia since the first star exploded and engulfed them all. She kind of knew the drinks they liked, had watched them tell jokes and play games one night at one party.

And she knew Ollie only slightly more. Carmen knew she tasted like the fringe of summer, like passion fruit, tart on Carmen's tongue. She tasted like distraction, like everything Carmen craved but couldn't touch. She had eyes that watched Carmen through hallways, across rooms, spilling galaxies and solar flares. Ollie had felt the urgency in Carmen's fingers, the scrape of her nails along the skin of her back, and had offered herself up for more. Carmen had fallen into Ollie to forget, to feel something that wasn't her everyday. But to Carmen, it was like Ollie had driven herself into Carmen's orbit to remember how to live.

Only this time, she hadn't looked like that girl with the easy smile and eyes like the sky. She'd looked dimmed, clouded.

"You know them," Dex said again when Carmen still hadn't responded.

"Not really."

She could feel Dex's eyes on her for a moment before he simply said, "Okay," and took the money held over the bar with a thanks.

Carmen was thinking of Ollie's lips when really she should be thinking of how to hide herself from her.

They were all drunk, or past tipsy and heading there. Hazy. Slumping over each other, swaying against one another and propping each other up. Laughing at nothing, and telling stories about each other that all of them knew but that they loved to embellish every time. Two other friends had joined and shimmied in among them, their group verging on too loud and boisterous.

That grief that slicked over Ollie's insides had dulled, softened at the edges. Sara was nuzzling her hair, and a giggle bubbled up within Ollie, but she bit it down, let it dissolve into nothing. All her emotions felt just out of reach, and she wished she could forget the watch at her wrist, the look in her father's eyes, the hole in their house torn through the fabric of their lives.

Carmen had done that for her, for those moments while Ollie had blinked at her, shock curling in her stomach. A burst of elation at seeing the face Ollie had tried to forget had drowned it out briefly.

"How is Carmen working here?"

The words were slurred into Ollie's ear, and she nudged Sara with her shoulder, not roughly, just hard enough to make her sit up a little.

Sara straightened. "Hi, Ollie."

Ollie loved no one like she loved her friends. "Hi, Sara."

"So?" Sara asked.

"So...?"

"Why is Carmen here?"

"I don't know."

"Go ask her."

"I don't think she wants to talk to me..."

Carmen's eyes had held something panicked, the brown of them a wild spark. Not the consuming look like when she'd pushed Ollie up against a wall or the soft, needy look when they'd been drunk in a bathroom.

Ollie wanted to press her against the bar and run her nose over her neck right now, to be the one that plucked Carmen open this time. To be the one who spilled her secrets, who cracked open that serious mask that was always over her face. She wanted to watch Carmen soften under her mouth like she had the last time, to see the way her eyes changed, lulled into something else.

"You two seemed pretty chummy at the party. And then there was that whole, you know..." Sara waved her hand around. "...thing where you freaked 'cause she wasn't at school."

Ollie shrugged. "I thought she was a friend."

"Maybe she still is."

Ollie hummed an answer, trapped in something she had no words for. She didn't know what Carmen was, why Ollie wanted to push herself against her skin and feel the imprint of her.

"Shots!" Ruin's loud announcement inspired him to stand up and almost fall over, much to the laughter of the group.

Ollie's lips twitched up, almost a smile—a betrayal—and she pursed them together.

Sara's gaze was back on Ollie, deep and dark and soul-searching. "You're allowed to laugh, Ollie."

A lump in Ollie's throat made swallowing hard, like she could choke. She gave a one-shouldered shrug and reached for her drink.

Sara didn't push it for once, instead throwing her arm around Ollie's shoulder, pulling her in tight against her and challenging Deon to a drinking competition.

Ollie liked the bar, liked the break in the routine of house parties. She liked the fact that she was with her people, no one looking at her like she was about to break, even if she felt she was about to.

They were there for hours, crowding a table and drinking more than they should, blowing birthday cash and Ruin chipping in a lot. The room didn't seem to empty around them, and Ollie kept watching the bar, watching Carmen move from person to person. Her cheeks seemed washed out. More so than before, and she had always looked a little that way. Ollie had traced her lips along that skin on a night she wished now hadn't been so blurred by alcohol.

Whenever Carmen ducked under the bar to bus the tables, she seemed to carefully avoid Ollie's corner, and Ollie stalked her with her eyes, begging her to look over.

Finally, Ollie had had enough. "Have to pee!"

And no one really paid attention by that point. Instead, she headed for Carmen, on the other side of the room with a tray filled with glasses. "Can I talk to you?"

Carmen's eyes flew up, and traced Ollie's face, something soft at the edges before the look slammed away. She glanced around the room, made eye contact with the other bartender, then looked back to Ollie. "Okay."

Carmen dumped the tray on the bar and led the way to a door. Suddenly, they were in an office.

In the last two hours, Ollie had slowed down, had nursed her warming beer as the others worked through more. Even still, she was foggy. She wanted to remember Carmen in front of her, to remember what they were about to say. And for all of that, Ollie had no idea why.

For a moment, they stared at each other, Carmen's arms crossed, the picture of defense. Ollie wanted to tear that apart, to pull on Carmen's arms and watch her become pliant underneath her.

"I like your hair," she said instead. Which was true; she did.

Carmen softened, barking a laugh. "Thanks."

"I was worried about you," Ollie finally said, the words slipping out before she could catch them.

That look again, that soft giving, and Carmen broke their eye contact. "You shouldn't have been."

"You just…disappeared."

Carmen looked back to her. "How much do you know?"

Warmth crept over Ollie's cheeks. "I… My friend is good with computers. I asked him to find you. I expected to find a different name on Facebook or something, some way to see if you were okay. But he found… other stuff."

A muscle in Carmen's cheek twitched.

Ollie stepped forward, several feet of space still between them that might as well have been thousands. She had no idea what made her close that gap. "Are you…are you okay where you are?"

Carmen stared at her for a second as if she was considering everything she could say. "I'm fine. The group place I'm in is fine. The new school sucks, but it'll be okay."

Relief blossomed in Ollie's chest, something that filtered into that chasm inside her, months old and shaped like her mother. "Good. I'm glad."

She'd imagined worse.

"Ollie." Carmen was looking at her now, her eyebrows pushed together and a look on her face like she needed Ollie to listen. "I need you to do something for me."

Ollie stepped closer, only a foot of space between them. The air moved as Carmen seemed to sway toward her, gaze dropping to Ollie's mouth, even as she didn't take a step forward.

Ollie wanted to rub the ends of Carmen's hair between her fingertips. Her stomach flipped at the shaved part over her ear. Like this, Carmen looked edgier. Yet Ollie didn't understand how someone's eyes could be that deep, that bright, a brown that looked sun-filtered, that looked filled with every thought.

"What?" Ollie's voice was a whisper.

"Don't mention you saw me. Make sure Sara and Deon don't. I... The group home I'm in thinks I'm somewhere approved on the nights I'm here. They don't know I have a job; it wouldn't be allowed."

There was a shadow in Carmen's eyes, but Ollie didn't know what it meant, and suddenly she felt drunk again, completely drunk from the way Carmen's hand had moved to rest on Ollie's hip, her thumb running over the skin there. She was drunk on the warmth of the breath that rested between them.

"Okay." Ollie's voice was still a whisper, and then Carmen grasped at her, that dark look in her eyes darkening further, deepening, and Ollie stumbled until they were flush against each other.

Carmen stepped back to sit against the table, Ollie standing between her legs.

Their lips crashed together, the warmth pulling a moan from Ollie that Carmen swallowed greedily. Fingers were against the back of her neck, nails scratching at Ollie's scalp. That grief still thick over her insides felt quelled at the beat of blood through her veins, her heart speeding up to wash everything out.

Ollie wouldn't tell a soul if it meant Carmen would touch her like this, would kiss her like this, would drag Ollie into a place where it didn't feel like her life had imploded, where her father's eyes didn't look dead and hurt and full of pain and where Ollie didn't feel something missing so large that she couldn't cover up the hole—like she was clawing at her chest to stop the feeling in there.

Lips were on her neck, teeth grazing the place Ollie's pulse pounded. Everywhere. Carmen was everywhere. For months, nothing had felt like this, had felt real. Ollie dropped her head back as a hand fell to the base of her neck, holding her closer as Carmen bit at her skin, then soothed it with her tongue. "Please." Ollie had never whimpered like that, never begged, never asked for something in a way that left her so vulnerable.

The lips on her neck paused. "You're drunk."

Ollie shook her head, her hair whipping and she cupped Carmen's cheeks, staring her straight in the eye. "I'm not."

Carmen's lips curled up, and Ollie couldn't remember ever seeing something so fragile. "You kind of are."

Sighing, Ollie rested their foreheads together, sharing the air between them. "A little." She then caved. "Okay, a lot."

Carmen tilted her head up, her legs wrapping tighter, and kissed her again, more gently, as if they had all the time in the world and not as if they might never see each other again.

"It's okay."

Regret was tied into those words, but they were also laced with sincerity. Ollie wanted to tease Carmen's voice out of her, to carry that husk with her.

"Can I have your number?" Ollie blurted.

Carmen's entire body tensed under her, and she shook her head. "I don't have a phone."

Ollie had forgotten, heavy with the feeling of Carmen's body surrounding her and the taste of her against her lips, that she'd never been able to find a phone number. A small laugh fell from her chest. "How do you not have a phone?"

A tiny laugh puffed against her cheek, where Carmen was running her nose against the soft skin. "Just don't."

"Can I see you again?"

Carmen pulled back, and cool air swirled everywhere, the urge rising in Ollie's fingertips to keep her tight against her. Carmen's gaze darted over her face, her look unreadable, and she shook her head. "It's impossible."

Ollie didn't think she could go months without this again. Not when the rage humming in her ears and the flicker of anger that fed her grief had only really dulled for the first time when Carmen's fingers had left scratches on her back just now. "I can come back here."

Ollie hated just how needy she sounded.

Carmen stood up, the motion making Ollie take a step back. "I have to get back out there."

Without looking back, Carmen walked away. The door closed with a thud behind her, and Ollie stood alone in the office.

Carmen hadn't said yes. But she hadn't said no either.

CHAPTER 12

THE STARS WERE A BLANKET overhead, and Carmen had the urge to dig her fingers into the sky and pull them down around her shoulders. Ollie's kiss was stamped over her lips. The taste of her own lies was all that had made Carmen pull away from Ollie and push her away with words she didn't want to say. Nothing else could have made Carmen leave that room, to leave the taste and smell and feel of Ollie behind her.

Ollie deserved more than dishonesty.

When Carmen had come back in the early hours of the morning, Mattie was asleep on a sofa, wrapped in his sleeping bag and a beanie on his head. The orange glow that always filled the warehouse washed over him, and he looked bronzed. He smelled like child, like sweat. Like he used to after a day of running around school in open air. The memory made her stomach clench, and she touched his baby-soft cheek.

What the hell was she doing with her little brother? What the hell was she *supposed* to do with him?

Rae had been passed out on the sofa opposite him, eyeliner smudged under her eyes, lips slack with sleep. *Vulnerable* was never a word Carmen would have chosen for Rae, before. She was all hard lines and sharp angles with a silver tongue. But in that moment, she looked the picture of vulnerability.

On hasty feet, Carmen had headed for the roof to sit on the edge of the wall. Her entire body was thrumming, the sensation spreading from her chest and down her limbs, easing into her fingertips. Ollie had set her on fire, and Carmen was aching for something she had no words for. Her feet kicked aimlessly, heels beating a rhythm with no tune on the wall of the ledge. It was an unseasonably warm night, the kind in which you could hear the dripping of melting ice, a winter music that pattered onto garbage under the snow.

Even though it wasn't doing a lot, she pulled the blanket tight around her shoulders, glad for the extra coat they'd dug out of a donation bin. Her breath was puffing off into the night.

Months had passed since she'd taken her brother's hand in hers and led him onto the streets.

Yet still, somehow, she was lost with Mattie.

And, still, Ollie shadowed her.

Ollie looked like a shadow of herself. She was thinner, a look cloaking her that Carmen would never have pictured there before. The easy, quick grin Ollie had always given was gone.

She was still Ollie, though, with eyes too deep and too accepting, with fingers that clawed with the same *need* that Carmen's did this time. Ollie, who opened herself up for Carmen to pluck at, to take what she wanted and leave them both breathless in the wake of it. Did Ollie know she left Carmen that way too? That when Ollie surrounded her, with her hair, her skin, with the steady, fast pulse under Carmen's lips, that Carmen was left reeling?

It should have been terrifying, mind-numbingly scary. Instead, Carmen was left with a smile on her face as she sipped a bottle of water on the roof, reveling in a feeling of wanting more, of wanting everything.

Everything she shouldn't want. Not with Mattie. Not after lying to Ollie about her situation. Not when she and Mattie were balanced on a knife's edge, scared to fall either way and scared that the situation that held them up was going to slice through them and leave them in neat little pieces.

Not when Ollie looked like something had snapped inside of her.

"I can *hear* you thinking."

Rae plopped down next to her, leaving mere inches between their shoulders and legs. She plucked the bottle from Carmen's hands and took a long sip before handing it back. Her breath came out in little puffs, the two of them a duo of mist. She pulled her sleeping bag around her shoulders, gloved fingers clinging to the material.

"I'm not thinking." The words sounded lame even to Carmen's ears.

"You're always thinking. Same as your brother."

Just the mention of Mattie left Carmen with a sensation in her throat she couldn't name. He was sprawled out downstairs, trusting that Carmen knew what she was doing when, really, she had no idea. He had no school; they existed on the fringes of society, never belonging.

She wanted Mattie to belong.

After her birthday the other month, the idea that the next would be her eighteenth had left her nervous. The reality of their situation was becoming increasingly apparent. The fact that she was supposed to prove to a court that she was the best person for her brother, after being everything for his entire life, was feeling less and less achievable.

Yet Carmen was sitting on a roof, watching the stars and finding patterns in them that made her feel mushy inside as she thought of Ollie.

She couldn't afford to feel mushy, to feel undone.

Impossible, Carmen had said. And it was. "Was he good?"

Rae snorted. "He always is. We sparred for an hour and a half." Rae leaned back on her hands. "He's improving."

"He is." Too fast. He loved the dance, the movement. He ducked and wove and had reflexes that topped all of theirs.

"What's got you thinking so loud?"

Carmen ran her tongue over her lip. "Nothing."

"Yeah. Sure." She stole Carmen's water again and took a long swig, fingers picking at the label when she was done. "You've always been a loud thinker."

Carmen hummed in response, her feet still kicking that rhythm. Once, years ago, lifetimes ago, before her mother had been such a mess, Carmen had been small and squished on her lap at the table, against her chest. Cool hands had run through her hair, and a finger had tapped her nose. *"My Carmen, always thinking."*

That was it. One memory to cling to that didn't smell like spirits or wasn't jabbed through with the sting of heroin, nights alone, and learning to pull the cupboards apart to find something edible.

"You want to talk about it?"

Did she? She thought about letting the words out, of telling Rae about the fear that had laced her spine and iced her stomach at the sight of kids from her school. Or about the fact that those kids could tell someone, and then she and Mattie would have to run. Or about how she didn't think a way to ever crawl out of the crack in the system she'd burrowed into existed. No way to get Mattie into a world he could join.

Or even about the girl Carmen was making a habit of kissing, even as she knew she shouldn't.

What did they say? Once was an accident. Twice a coincidence.

Was three times a habit?

But that was something, one thing that felt like *hers*. Something to pull out and go over when she was lost, to hold close to her thumping heart, something that was all for her.

"Do I want to talk about it, Rae? No."

Rae hummed her understanding, her feet in beat with Carmen's own. She didn't need to say it. If Carmen ever wanted to talk about it, Rae made it clear just by being herself that she was available.

Twenty minutes later, half-asleep and rumpled, Mattie emerged with his sleeping bag around his shoulders. Carmen scooted back a little, and minutes later he was asleep again between them, nestled into her side, his toes under Rae's thighs, and Carmen's fingers against his scalp. Rae's arm lay securely over him, anchoring him in place.

Sometimes, Carmen thought she should have waited to see where Mattie would have ended up in the foster care system. At times, she played with the idea of handing him in. Ensuring his safety, his education.

Most of the time, though, she felt like both of them were where they belonged.

CHAPTER 13

ALCOHOL WAS AN EVIL THING.

Ollie spent Saturday hungover and tracing her fingers over her lips, as if this would help imprint the feeling of Carmen there forever. Her dad disappeared into his office, and Ollie made a nest on the modular sofa, which Sara later invaded before the grief could crawl its way through the hangover and ruin Ollie entirely. They watched Netflix and ate too much junk food. All afternoon, they napped on and off, legs entwined and equally grumpy with each other.

Each time Ollie fell asleep, she took with her the memory of how soft the skin of Carmen's stomach had been under her fingertips and the look in her eyes as she'd searched Ollie's. The entire encounter had left Ollie feeling as though someone was really seeing her for the first time in too long.

It wasn't until Sunday in Deon's basement, when Sara and Deon and some others were sprawled over a blanket and the sofa, that they really talked about Friday night.

"Ollie?" It was Deon's voice.

"Mm?" The sun was weakly making its way through the tiny window near the ceiling, just managing to hit Ollie's face, and she was trying to enjoy it. She really should be reading her book for English. It was spread open over her chest as she lay on her back, and maybe she could absorb some of it that way. That was how that worked, right?

"Did you get Carmen's number?"

And then everyone was looking at her.

Grateful for the hood pulled just over her eyes, Ollie shook her head. "No. And, uh, she asked that we don't tell anyone we saw her."

Now they were all looking at her more intently. She could feel it.

"Why?" Deon asked.

Ollie gave a one-shouldered shrug, curling her fingers over the cover of her book. "Something about the home she's in wouldn't like her working there."

"Yeah, those places can be shit."

Something brittle was in Sara's voice, and Ollie pushed up on her elbows to be able to see her. "They monitor everything you do. I'm surprised she can even get away with working there. The one I was in had a really strict curfew. We couldn't even go out for a walk in the afternoon." Sara's face clouded a little, and Ollie threw her foot over hers. "I won't breathe a word."

The rest, like Ollie had known they would, all mumbled their agreement.

Here, in the basement, for the first time in ages, Ollie didn't feel completely heavy. Since Friday night, she'd been thinking that the only time she'd managed to forget was with Carmen sighing into her mouth.

That night, Ollie and her father sat on opposite ends of the sofa staring at the television. The gap between them expanded and undulated.

"How...how are you?" The words floated out, misted in the air. Fell to nothing.

Ollie blinked at the TV and tried to ignore the way the words didn't even touch her. "Fine."

She could feel him then, his eyes on her, looking at her, and Ollie didn't know if she wanted to fall into that look or curl away from it and run.

"If you're not okay, you can... It's fine. You can talk to me."

The words sounded rehearsed. Had he muttered them to himself? How often had he stared at her, trying to work up to saying that?

"I'm fine."

That gap somehow grew broader even as neither of them moved.

Her mother had loved to sprawl over the sofa with both of them, to sit in between them, a foot buried under Ollie's father's leg and an arm around Ollie's shoulder. Or, when Ollie was being prickly, near enough so Ollie always knew she could get over herself and inch closer.

Her mother always insisted on watching B-grade scary movies, ones they all groaned about and pretended to hate. But they never went to bed until they finished them.

Some nights, Ollie had left her room for water and would find them laid out, a pair of spoons pressed close. More often than not, one or both of them would be asleep, and Ollie wouldn't even have the heart to roll her eyes. When she had been tiny, they'd pull apart and pull her between them, a created space Ollie had always slotted into perfectly.

At the memory, Ollie suddenly couldn't breathe.

Her fingertips were tingling. Her heart fluttered in her chest, and it was as if she wasn't on the sofa, wasn't really anywhere. Her fingers hooked into the material in a desperate attempt to ground herself, but she couldn't really *feel* it. The counsellor at school had suggested antianxiety medications again, but Ollie had shied away from the idea. Before, her anxiety had seemed obscure, like everything and nothing was the cause. Now it was solid, obvious to her what caused her pulse to race: a part of her worried she'd lose the one connection to her mother if she dulled the pain around her death.

So she worked with breathing exercises, but there were times she forgot how to breathe at all.

Without saying good night, and before her father could notice Ollie was having issues remembering how to function, she got up and left him to that gap, that woman-shaped hole. With gasping breaths, she crawled into bed, and choked hyperventilating breaths into her pillow, unable to even cry.

School was a blur, and still her teachers left her alone. They had for months, even with her unexplained missed classes. Now she wasn't absent as often, and they left her to stare out the window and disappear into her head. How long would they let her get away with that?

Art was the one class she let herself get lost in. She slashed color and poured herself into images even she couldn't make sense of. She filled canvases and made a portfolio dedicated to loss: reds and blacks and blues so deep they were almost obsidian. Her teacher's eyes would run over them with a look too deep and with praise on her lips even as her brows knitted together.

On one Tuesday, without thinking, Ollie painted in a color like whiskey. Eyes stared back at her from the paper, eyebrows together, a furrow between them. That look from Carmen had been following Ollie since she'd first caught sight of her near the lockers. Since she'd been pulled back behind some bleachers and seen desperation. Since she'd walked into that bar, where Carmen had looked at her as if she wanted to be her undoing.

On Wednesday, Ollie gave in.

It was six o'clock. Her father was working late, and twilight was trickling in through the windows. Ollie was trying to study, was trying to get herself back on track. She wanted to leave behind the mess she'd been in the last few months, but her leg wouldn't stop bouncing, and her mother's watch was ticking on her wrist.

She wanted to hear the door open downstairs and hear her mother call her name. She wanted her mother's hands against her neck, cool and reassuring. She wanted to hear her mother laugh or murmur or even ask her what she wanted to do when she graduated, what she was going to study—any of those questions that used to make Ollie feel like she was drowning but which she'd started to realize were actually there to buoy her up.

But Ollie heard nothing.

Then she was grabbing her bag, checking that she had her keys and phone, and was out the door. With one quick message, Sara and Deon met her thirty minutes later at the bus stop.

"On a Wednesday?" Deon asked.

"Why not?"

"I, for one, think this is a great idea."

"Of course you do, Sara." Deon rolled his eyes before looking back at Ollie. The playful look fell away to something deeper. "You okay?"

"Mhm."

The bus trip took forever, and Sara slipped out a hip flask the three passed between each other on the backseat. Ollie only took two sips. She just wanted to burn the nerves away but remembered the way Carmen's lips had stilled on her neck as she'd asked, "Are you drunk?"

And then she'd pulled away.

They got off the bus, feeling slightly less secure in that neighborhood than when they'd been flush with alcohol and with Ruin. Melting snow was layered over everything. They slipped quickly into the bar.

The difference in atmosphere was staggering. The odd patron was scattered around, the music quieter, the entire vibe less charged and more chill. They piled onto stools at one end of the bar, and the big bartender from the other night walked over to them. He looked so rough around the edges, but when he smiled, he made her think of coffee, warm over your tongue.

"Hey, Deon."

"Hey, Dex."

Apparently they'd bonded.

"Dex." Deon put an elbow on the bar and gestured to Sara and Ollie. "Do you remember my friends? Sara and Ollie?"

Dex's gaze swept over them, hovering over Ollie a moment later, and her cheeks went hot.

Did he know something?

He focused on Sara. "You're the one who did three tequila shots in one go."

Sara grimaced. "Don't remind me."

He smirked. "Fair enough. What can I get you all?"

Ollie didn't hear their answers, because she heard a door open and close quickly, and she turned a little to see Carmen walking in from the office before she stopped dead, staring at Ollie, her face completely unreadable.

Voices murmured next to her.

Carmen's hair looked damp and was curling at the ends around her face. Maybe she'd showered right before work. Would she smell like shampoo? Body wash? What type? She stared at Ollie, her eyebrows furrowed in the manner Ollie had so desperately tried to capture on paper.

No one looked at Ollie like that.

Consuming. Knowing.

And then Carmen was moving again, ducking under the bar to stand next to Dex, her hand against the edge of the bar top as she pressed against the edge.

Ollie blinked and tried to remember not to look enraptured. A beer was somehow in front of her. Sara's was already in her hand, and Deon was taking a sip of his.

Carmen looked between all of them. "Hey, Sara. Deon." Her eyes caught Ollie's and something permanent inside Ollie shifted. "Hi, Ollie."

Her name sounded like water over rocks, an ebbing tide. "Hi, Carmen."

"Carmen!" Sara grinned. "Hi. Sorry about the drunkenness the other night. You know how it is."

Carmen smiled slightly, her lips quirking. "No problem. If you ask me, you were far drunker at that party."

Sara put her beer down, her elbows on the bar, her eyes twinkling. "I think *everyone* was drunker at that party."

Carmen's gaze flicked to Ollie's before they landed back on Sara. "I enjoyed myself."

Ollie's cheeks warmed even more.

Somehow, later, Ollie was at one end of the bar on a stool while Carmen was unloading trays of glasses. At the other end, Sara and Deon chatted with Dex, or just each other when he was pulled away. Ollie still nursed the same beer, the liquid warm and a little stale.

Ollie leaned an elbow on the bar top and propped her chin in her hand languidly. She watched Carmen, the way she moved, steadily and sure. She was a little ashen, something still etched in her eyes that haunted Ollie. She didn't know what to do with the feeling—if she wanted to throw herself at a canvas or pull Carmen against her.

Out of nowhere, the desire rose up to ask Carmen if she missed her mother like Ollie missed hers.

But that would be like stripping her feelings down.

"Do you like working here?" The question was inane, but Ollie wanted to know. She wanted to know everything, if she were honest. She wanted to sit and pluck Carmen apart until she knew her inside out. Besides, if she didn't ask that question, she'd ask the mother one, and that left Ollie's chest feeling tight.

Carmen wiped water marks off one of the glasses. "I do." Ollie just blinked, so Carmen kept going. "It's relaxing and easy. It's work."

"How do you get to work? From what I heard, it's hard to have a job when you're in one of those homes."

Something faltered in Carmen's movements, something barely noticeable, and if Ollie hadn't been watching her so intently, she wouldn't have noticed. Carmen didn't stop working.

"It is," she said finally. "I guess I'm lucky."

"How's school?" Even though Ollie wanted to know everything, she didn't want to be asking questions that sounded so ridiculous. A barrier sprung between them, one always kind of there, which felt like unshared history. Ollie didn't know how to scramble at it, how to tear it down to their feet so it could be easily crossed.

"It's fine."

That answer felt hollow. "Look, if you don't want to talk..."

Carmen's gaze flew up, and her hand landed on Ollie's, who sat back down before she'd even managed to stand properly. "No, it's not that. I'm sorry." Carmen met her eyes, then studied her for a moment. "What's happened to you, Ollie?"

That barrier was suddenly shattered, and Ollie was left winded at the lack of warning. She blinked at Carmen and swallowed, unable to look away. "What do you mean?" Her voice cracked, and Ollie resented it.

Carmen pushed a tray aside and leaned against the bar, their faces a foot apart. She cocked her head, her gaze all over Ollie's face before coming back to her eyes. That look was back, the one that left Ollie with need at the back of her throat.

"What's happened to you, Ollie?" Carmen repeated, her voice low and like gravel. "Something's changed."

Fingers of panic clawed at her back, and Ollie had the urge to run away. A lump was in her throat so big that Ollie didn't know how she could breathe or even swallow as heavily as she did. She looked down at the end of the bar—her friends were completely distracted—and back to Carmen. She shook her head once, her lips a tight line. "Come with me?" She stood and started to walk to the office they had gone to last time, but fingers grabbed at her hand.

"Not there," Carmen said. "Someone's in there."

So Ollie followed her toward another room, filled with crates and pallets and cartons.

Once inside, Ollie closed the door and leaned against it, heart hammering in her chest. Carmen stood in front of her, an inch of space between them now and her gaze glued to Ollie as tears brimmed in Ollie's eyes. Angrily she swiped at them with both hands, fingers digging into the softness of her skin.

Everything in her stilled when Carmen curled her fingers around Ollie's wrists. She brushed her thumbs over the wetness of her cheeks.

"What happened?" Carmen's words were a whisper over Ollie's skin. Her breath was warm and sweet, and Ollie closed her eyes, dropping her head back onto the door behind her.

The words always hurt to say, and she didn't know *how* to tell Carmen, how to shape the sounds that formed the story of the gaping, black space her mother had left, how to explain the revulsion, misdirected and toxic, that was bubbling in her stomach at her father: why was *he* here and *she* wasn't? And then there was the blinding guilt, because it wasn't that she didn't want her father. It was that she wanted *both* of them, and only having one felt like a constant reminder of the other's absence.

How did she word the loneliness that swelled in her chest at night, when she used to hear the sound of her father tiptoeing out for water but now heard the clink of a liquor bottle against a glass? How did she communicate the utter *lost* feeling when she thought of the next year, the next two, of making decisions about her life when she had no idea what she wanted? How did she explain the way something in her had twisted and bent?

She had no words, but neither did Carmen, with her evasive answers and the way she disappeared in and out of Ollie's life yet watched Ollie like she was the only thing holding her to her own. Ollie had no words, but she did know something that helped, something she wanted.

So she threaded her fingers in Carmen's hair and pulled Carmen against her with a gasp. Their bodies melded as their lips touched, pliant and soft and somehow altogether desperate. Thighs slid between each other, and Ollie sighed into Carmen at the touch, at the flex of Carmen's leg between her own. It was a kiss that Ollie was always craving, that something in the back of her mind was always waiting to occur. Teeth grazed Ollie's bottom lip, her hips jerking at the sensation.

Carmen pulled back, just barely, her forehead against Ollie's, even as Ollie's hand fell to grab at her shirt. Terrified Carmen was about to disappear, she fisted the material in her hand.

"I meant it, Ollie. The other night." Carmen's lips were mere millimeters away, and Ollie opened her eyes, only to have her vision invaded by brown softness, a well of something Ollie would happily fall into if it always soothed the ache in her chest like this. "This is impossible."

Impossible was such a big word, one Ollie hated. And at that moment, all she could think, all she could say was, "What *isn't* impossible?"

She tugged the fistful of Carmen's shirt. Carmen melted into her, her tongue hot on Ollie's, the brush of it almost too much. As fingers slid under Ollie's shirt, as Carmen's palm slid over her waist, Ollie's skin jumped at the touch, and she couldn't feel that gaping hole in her chest anymore; when Carmen touched her, she didn't feel like she was so utterly lost.

She was where she was supposed to be.

Carmen lifted her glasses off, and Ollie didn't even care where they ended up.

Teeth grazed against her neck and her collarbone, and Carmen's fingers, one by one, flicked at the buttons of Ollie's shirt, then slid over the sensitive skin of her belly as she pushed it open. Her lips left a bruise against the swell of Ollie's breast, the feel of it tattooing itself along her nerves.

When Carmen's hand, clumsy and fast and perfect, slid into her pants, Ollie came undone with a smile on her lips, her teeth grazing Carmen's neck.

CHAPTER 14

HALF OF CARMEN WAS WALKING home as if she were skating through the sky, her footsteps light, as if gravity had been stripped away, leaving her floating. She felt dizzy with Ollie's touches, dizzy with the smell of her, with the memory of her throat beneath Carmen's lips and the pounding of her pulse against her tongue.

The other half was firmly rooted to the ground, feet dragged down by lies of omission. Ollie had no idea about the life Carmen was living, that she was drowning in struggles while trying to make everything seem normal so that Mattie didn't fall apart. Ollie had no idea, not really, no matter what she'd read when her friend had done something on the Internet. She had no idea of the ins and outs, the street beneath Carmen's feet, the brother who was along her side, his DS clutched in his hand.

Carmen had dropped lies, cloaked herself in them, and Ollie didn't even know Mattie existed. She thought Carmen was inside the system, at school and in a house with locks and safety each night. With food she didn't scrounge for, or send her kid brother to scrounge for.

Words that weren't lies had built up on Carmen's tongue, but then Ollie had looked so shattered. Something about Ollie's eyes, previously brightly lit with something untouchable, was now dimmed and cracked and broken. When Carmen had clung to her at school, sheltered by bleachers, Ollie had been pliant and warm and receiving. Her gaze had searched Carmen, looked for whatever she needed and offered it up.

Ollie still did that.

But now she was searching for something of her own too. Need sat in Ollie's fingers, absent before, and coaxed Carmen to ease it. When Ollie had shaken against her, had come apart, Carmen's name had painted her lips as they curved up for the first time Carmen had seen that night. Carmen hadn't been able to take her eyes off her.

That broken thing in Ollie's eyes had, for just a second, looked like what it had before.

"Carmen." Mattie's voice was low.

Carmen needed Ollie to go away, but instead she kept jerking her closer. "Yeah, Mattie?"

"Do you miss Mom?"

That word *Mom* punched low in her stomach, bruised something buried deep. Carmen swallowed heavily as if the motion could drown out the sensation caused by three simple letters. All the while, he adamantly stared ahead as they walked the darkened streets, as if he'd been building up to it forever, as if knowing Carmen wouldn't like it.

"I…" Carmen's breath was caught in her chest, left hanging there, leaving her feeling overinflated and unsure. "Sometimes."

It was the most truthful thing she could offer. If Carmen could help it, she didn't think of her mother. When she did, her fingers would twitch with an anger so deep, one that had been settled so low in her stomach for so long, she thought it was tacked into her. But layered just under it, tinier and smothered, was hurt and shame and need all directed at the woman who had abandoned Carmen constantly.

She licked her lips and tried to remember Mattie was a kid. His view of their mother was skewed. "Do you?" she asked. They barely talked of her, of their life *before*, as if doing so would bring forth something neither of them knew how to deal with.

He was silent for a moment, the sound of their footsteps bouncing off stone walls and overly loud in the hush of late night. "Sometimes," he said.

When his silence stretched on for what felt like forever, she thought that would be it.

"Sometimes more than sometimes."

She wished he had left it at that first *sometimes*. His voice cracked over the final syllable, over emotions too big for him. A rushing sound was in Carmen's ears, and that anger that bubbled so deeply flared and rose in her chest; her mother had failed Mattie so badly, both in life and in death.

They came to a dead stop on the street, bathed in shadows that Carmen knew they needed to get past. People and things she always tried to keep out of Mattie's sight lurked in dark places here. But the sight of him, his lips pursed together, eyes glittering and as hard as diamonds, broke her heart. She squatted with one knee on the ground, the cement biting painfully into her skin through her jeans.

"That's okay, Mattie."

He shook his head, just once.

"It is. You're allowed to miss her."

He pushed forward then. His hands fell onto her shoulders, and his forehead touched her own. When his eyes screwed shut, his breath shuddered. "Okay," he whispered. "Sometimes I miss school. And the house. I miss…"

He didn't have words for what he missed, and Carmen just let the ones he had hang between them.

They stayed there for minutes, Carmen wishing she could take everything he was feeling and mash it inside herself. They breathed in sync, and she let his fingers bruise her back.

An age later, he straightened his small shoulders, swiped at his cheeks, and gave her a nod.

When they got back to the warehouse, Dex had beaten them there on his bike. He sat on a sofa, cards in his hands, playing a game with Rae. Her face was slashed with a frown. Mattie and Carmen paused and looked at each other, then back at the pair. Mattie's hand fell to the dog that came to slump against his legs, almost knocking him over with its bulk.

"What's going on?" Carmen asked.

Rae's jaw clenched tight, and the muscle in her neck popped. "He's cheating."

Carmen snorted. Dex didn't cheat.

"She's losing and taking it badly." Dex picked a card from the pile, a grin splitting his face. "But, Rae, it looks like I win again." He dropped his cards down, faceup. "Gin."

For a second, Carmen thought Rae was going to throw her cards at him. That muscle ticked again. But then her shoulders relaxed and she dropped her cards, scattering them on top of his. "I need a drink."

Dex chuckled, a rumble in his chest. He pulled out a bottle of whiskey and poured them out a glass each. The cheap, sharp odor of spirits reached Carmen and Mattie where they stood, and they both wrinkled their noses.

"Want to spar?" Carmen had an itch in her feet, one that had been soothed by Ollie until Ollie had tried to slip her hand into Carmen's pants. It felt wrong, somehow, when Carmen hid her reality from Ollie, when Ollie had such a broken look Carmen couldn't place, when they had barely had a conversation.

She had touched Ollie because Ollie had needed it. There was something there; Carmen could see it. She just couldn't put a word to it.

Rae straightened in her chair, knocking back the drink in one hit. With a glint in her eye, she said, "Let's go."

"Can I too?" Mattie looked up at her, now cross-legged on the floor, his fingers buried in the dog's fur.

The memory of the fingers that had bruised her shoulders just moments before made Carmen hesitate, but then Dex stood up. "I think," he told Mattie, looking from Rae with her gleaming eyes to Carmen, who was rocking from foot to foot, "you and I should just watch this one."

Dex stared down the rebuttal Carmen saw rising up, and, finally, Mattie huffed and agreed. Carmen led the way to the sparring room, and slipped her shoes off before standing on the old mat in the center of the room. Rae did the same, and they faced off.

Rae could be wild in a fight, all intuition and hard fists. She was fast, and she fought like she was possessed, with no tactics. The style worked for her. No one ever saw her coming.

But Carmen knew her style.

Against the wall, Dex stood next to Mattie with the dog at their feet, his hand dwarfing Mattie's shoulder.

"Let's go." And that was all Rae said before dropping and swiping her leg out in a clean sweep, trying to trip Carmen onto her ass.

Pure reflexes saved her as she jumped over it and bounced back. Rae stood, and Carmen swung forward, a kick aimed for her knee.

They bounced between each other until they were gleaming with sweat, panting hard. Ducking and weaving, only the odd glancing blow landing. They fought with open hands and kicks, certain areas out of bounds unless you knew the other would dodge it. The rules were embedded in their brain.

Breathing hard, they wore each other down until, finally, Carmen managed to swipe a foot out from under Rae, sending her back to hit the mat with a sweaty slap. With a grunt, Rae's hand shot out, wrapped around Carmen's ankle, and took Carmen down with her. They both lay next to each other, chests heaving.

And still that itch was under Carmen's skin, roiling at her nerve endings.

Afterward, the two of them sparred with Mattie. Dex offered words of advice in a low, even tone. With Mattie between them, they threw kicks and swung out at him, slower than they had with each other, but not by much. He was fast—he'd always been fast—and after months of this, his reflexes were honed. He danced away from Rae's kick, then his arm barred Carmen's swing and he stepped into her space. In the blink of an eye, he brought the heel of his hand to her solar plexus, stopping just before it landed.

He stared up at her, his chest heaving for air. Carmen stared back. Finally, she grinned. "You're getting good."

The smile he gave her was huge. For the next hour, all she could feel was the sting of his hand where it had bounced away against her forearm and the whistle of air as he had almost winded her. She just saw that smile, all teeth and gleaming eyes and dimples that broke her heart with their innocence.

An hour later on the sofa, Carmen slid Mattie's head off her thigh and made sure the blanket covered him completely. He was heavy in sleep, floppy, his limbs askew and breaths deep. Rae had gone to bed, but Dex sat on another sofa, a book in his hand. She sat next to him, watching Mattie, his chest moving up and down, and wished she could give him more than a life of missing what had left them both with scars crisscrossing their hearts.

She wanted to give him everything but was starting to wonder if she might end up giving him nothing.

And Ollie. Carmen didn't have time for whatever she was doing with Ollie. But it turned out she was terrible at following through with that thought.

Dex's arm, heavy and warm, came around her shoulders and tugged her into his side. His never looked up from his book. "I can hear you thinking."

Carmen slowly relaxed into his side, her head falling onto his shoulder. The dog pulled himself up onto Mattie's feet, and Dex lay his hand atop her head as she fell asleep, remembering the sound of Ollie's sigh and the taste of her lips.

Impossible.

The word throbbed across Ollie's mind, over her chest, and down her fingers.

She wanted to ask why, had wanted to know why *impossible.* Such a big word. But how could Carmen use it, then let Ollie pull her forward and lose herself in their heat?

Everything was so different than how it had been with Sean—not better, not worse. Not anything like that.

It wasn't even about him at all. It was about Carmen, the way her fingers grabbed at Ollie as if she were the last thing keeping Carmen on earth, the last thing tethering her to a world that was pushing her away. About how the world had clamored in Ollie's ears since her father's words had blown them apart. About how the only time that clamoring had truly dimmed to nothing was when Carmen had smiled, had brushed a kiss to Ollie's lips.

Ollie hadn't meant to let it go so far, hadn't meant to let Carmen slip her hand inside her jeans. But her mind craved the silence Carmen brought, and instead of ending it, she'd pleaded for more.

Carmen was everything Ollie wanted to know and nothing she actually did.

The depth of her eyes hid a secret, something more to this *impossible* than simply going to a different school now. But she couldn't fault Carmen and her secrets, not when Ollie had words she kept clamped down and didn't say even as Carmen asked her, "*What's happened to you?*"

She ached knowing that something had changed so drastically within herself that it was visible. Visible to someone who kissed Ollie so hard she wanted to break, but who barely said a word herself. Yet, at the same time, the knowledge that she had been truly altered, that this feeling in her chest, this hollowness, was not something she'd invented, felt vindicating. It existed, splayed across her features in a truth too physical to pretend it wasn't real.

Ollie spent days bouncing between grief and wanting to see Carmen again. Some moments, when she was thinking of Carmen and her complicated eyes, a glow settled somewhere in the pit of her stomach, warm and almost like comfort. Her brain would jolt, and guilt would tear up her spine and split her in two. How could she feel something like that when her mother was gone and her father was wallowing in loneliness in their too-big house, grief clawing at his eyes as Ollie pushed him further and further away?

One night, with the house too quiet and her father on the sofa, Ollie got a message from Sara telling her to come over. Before she could reply to it, her father spoke.

"Maybe, uh…maybe we could go to the cemetery on the weekend."

Everything in Ollie froze, cold seeping to her fingertips.

When she didn't answer, he continued, "Someone, at work… They thought maybe it would be a good idea. To do that. Together."

That coldness was in her chest, and suddenly wet warmth was in her eyes. The contrast between the two made her want to gasp; or maybe it was the word *cemetery*. Where her mother was.

"M—maybe."

He could hear the quiver in her words, she knew, his head turning too fast to stare at her. The look in his eye was too much like what she could feel in her chest. Ollie needed to get out of there. She only took a second to decide: "I'm going to Sara's."

She left him behind on the sofa, sick with guilt for doing so.

It never ended. She felt guilty for enjoying Carmen, guilty that she wasn't thinking of her mom all the time. Most of all, in that moment, she felt guilty because her father simply dipped his head like he'd expected her response, his empty gaze slowly going back to the TV.

The bus got her to Sara's quickly, which was lucky, because Ollie thought she might break apart on the seat. The two of them immediately sprawled over the sofa, and Sara just blinked at her.

"What happened?"

"Nothing." The biggest lie Ollie had possibly ever told. She fell back, hand over her eyes and a lump too large to swallow past in her throat.

Within moments, Sara was on one side of her, squashed between her and the sofa. "Are you okay?"

Hand still over her eyes, Ollie nodded. But halfway through, she shook her head, tears spilling past her lids. Arms wrapped around her, and Sara's chin rested on the top of her head.

"Wanna marathon *Friends*?"

Ollie nodded once more against her neck, and they spent the night like that, sprawled over each other, with the lingering sweetness of ice cream light on her tongue.

She tried to remember to breathe. She tried to remember and not crack open and talk about how much she missed her mother. Going to the cemetery would feel like some kind of cosmic joke, salt in a wound.

On Saturday, when Ollie, Sara, and Deon stepped into the bar, the room was crowded, but nothing like the week before.

Deon looked around, and his eyes lit up like they always did when he realized something. "College people have finals coming up. Or midterms. Something."

At the bar, Dex gave a hello to them as they approached. She didn't want to, but Ollie found herself scanning the bar for Carmen. Her hands went clammy when she caught sight of her near the back, clearing glasses and wiping a table for a waiting group.

Carmen looked up and caught her eye, and Ollie's racing heart seemed to stop. She gave Carmen a wave, a smile on her lips. Not for the first time, she wished Carmen hadn't had to rush back to work the other night.

Belying the simplicity of her small wave back, Carmen's eyes looked deeply into Ollie's, searching her face before turning back to the table.

Sara elbowed her, and Ollie jumped.

"What?" Ollie asked.

The smile on Sara's face was definitely shit-eating. "Deon asked what you wanted to drink."

"Oh, a beer. Thanks, Dex." Ollie looked away from him, then noticed Sara was still grinning. "What?"

"Could you be any more obvious?"

"I don't know what you mean."

"Sure, Jan."

Ollie's brow furrowed. "What?"

"*The Brady Bunch*? You know, that meme?"

"Did you just speak words?"

Sighing, Sara shook her head. "We need to get you and your art on Tumblr."

"Sure, Jan."

"No. Not how you use it."

Ollie accepted the beer Deon handed back to her and tried again. "Sure, Jan?"

Groaning, Sara took her own drink. "No!"

Ollie shot her a small smirk, and something around Sara's eyes softened. "What?" Ollie asked.

Sara shook her head. "Nothing."

She could see the words, though, building in Sara's eyes. The *I missed you*. It would make things serious and maybe pull the smile from Ollie's face, so she just bumped her shoulder against Sara's for a second.

"Hello, Ollie."

Ollie's eyes closed for a moment, and when she opened them, she turned slightly. Carmen was behind the bar.

"Hi." Ollie's voice went a little breathy. The last day they'd seen each other, Carmen's hands had been in her pants and Ollie had felt as if some of her pieces were being put back together. So of course she was breathy. Kind of like in a bad romance movie. If life were a movie, everything would have slowed down, and Carmen's hair would be wafting in some strange indoor breeze.

"Hi, Sara, Deon."

The two raised their glasses at her and pulled up stools.

Carmen and Dex floated in and out, serving others and Carmen picking up glasses.

Ollie tried to focus on her friends. She watched Sara and Dex speak in low tones across the bar, watched how easily they spoke, Dex rolling his eyes as he poured her out a tequila.

"Did you hear about Sara's test?" Deon asked.

Ollie shook her head, her curiosity piqued as Sara turned to them and rolled her eyes.

"What test?"

"It was nothing." Sara's cheeks were dusky with a blush.

Across the bar, Dex chuckled, the sound a deep, rich rumble in his chest. "Your face says otherwise."

Ollie looked between Deon and Sara. "What happened?"

Sara narrowed her eyes at Deon even as her lips quirked up. "I aced some test they give to the nerds and can fast track to college if I want."

"Should I be surprised?" Ollie wasn't. Sara was one of the most scientifically minded people she'd ever met, her math scores miles ahead of anyone else's in their school.

"Well, anyway—" Sara took a sip, "—I want to stay at school."

"Why?"

Sara cocked her head. "I don't know. Everything feels...settled. Good. I like it."

"I'm not complaining if you stay."

Under their stares, Sara shifted in her chair and changed the topic. Deon brought up a party from weeks ago and their friends who had collided into a hookup and then fizzled out over a matter of hours. Ollie tried to listen but barely paid attention. There was something so different to Carmen than when Ollie had first seen her, something harder that Ollie had noticed that first night at the bar. Carmen had always been all angles and maturity, but now there was something more profound, and she supposed she shouldn't be surprised. After her mother's death, Ollie had been trampled with the effects of it. And Carmen had not only lost her mother but had been in and out of foster care, had a history Ollie couldn't begin to understand.

But still, there was *something* else besides all that. Something more.

She wanted to fall into Carmen and pry out her secrets, one by one, and uncover what lay beneath her skin.

When their eyes caught across the bar, something in Ollie jumped, ticked over, and she wished they could meet somewhere Carmen wasn't working. She wished she could drag her out of this bar, out of that group home, and somewhere none of their dead parents or cloudy pasts could touch them.

A few hours later, Deon had gotten louder, and Sara was slumped heavily on the bar. Yet the same beer, lukewarm, remained in Ollie's hand. Behind the bar, Carmen glanced at Ollie and whispered something to Dex. After a scan of the room, he gave a nod. Carmen ducked under the bar and was there next to her, close enough to touch, her eyes lidded.

"Hi."

"Hi." Ollie smiled a little.

"Would you like to have a drink out back?"

Mouth dry, Ollie said yes. She slid off her chair, and suddenly Carmen was reaching across the front of her for the two drinks Dex was holding out. She handed one to Ollie. "Gin and tonic, right?"

"Yeah."

Carmen took a sip of her own drink and froze as she looked past Ollie. Her eyebrows crashed together. When Ollie turned, someone was sidling up to their group, all dark leather jacket, dark eyeliner and, maybe, ridiculously hot.

"Rae?"

The girl focused on Carmen. Though *girl* didn't seem appropriate. She looked a bit older. "Hey."

"Where's—" Carmen looked at Ollie, then back at Rae, the set of her jaw nervous.

"With Jia."

The tension that had seized Carmen's shoulders seeped out. "Okay."

"Rae!" Dex held his hand out over the bar and she clasped it. "I didn't know you'd be in tonight."

"Had some stuff to do." Her gaze swept over the group and settled on Ollie, her proximity to Carmen clearly gaining her attention. "Who're these people?"

"This is Ollie," Carmen said.

Ollie gave a wave, and Rae just stared her down.

"And Sara, and Deon."

Rae had stopped looking from person to person as they were introduced and focused on Sara, her head cocked. Still leaning against the bar, Sara stared straight back, her jaw clenched.

"Oh…" There was something about the narrowing in Rae's eye Ollie didn't understand. "I *know* Sara." A smile was growing on her lips, but nothing about it seemed friendly.

Ollie blinked. Sara was normally open, a little rough around the edges, but she smiled easily. Not right now, though.

"You do?" Ollie asked.

"We were in a foster home together," Sara finally said.

Neither elaborated anymore, and everyone just stared from one to the other, the music and other bar noise behind them all, Carmen's shoulder warm against Ollie's side.

This Rae person knew Sara before where she was now? When she was misgendered and miserable? Ollie narrowed her eyes, not sure she should leave Sara alone right now.

"Well, that's cool—a link between you all." But the glares the others shot Deon's way had him looking like he was about to sink into the floor. His cheeks hollowed as he sucked them in.

Dex cleared his throat. "Drink, Rae?"

At her call for a beer, Sara started up a conversation with Deon. With a flick of her eyes, Sara caught Ollie's gaze and made a shooing motion with her hand. Ollie raised her eyebrows, but Sara narrowed her eyes and repeated the *get lost* motion with a sleazy wink for emphasis.

Ollie looked to Carmen. "Drink?"

Carmen led the way, and Ollie followed. The noise outside was sealed off as the door closed, and the silence fell like a brick.

Instead of sitting on the chairs, Carmen flopped onto the cot in the corner, sitting against the wall. Not sure what else to do, Ollie sat next to her, their sides barely touching and their feet beside each other on the floor.

They had barely had a conversation, and that had never been more obvious than right at this moment. But she still wanted to turn her head, though, and brush her lips across Carmen's neck, to wrap her fingers in her hair and breathe her in, to kiss her lips and feel the wetness of her tongue against her own.

Everything was easier when buried in the physicality of Carmen.

Clearing her throat, Ollie tried to think of something else. "Your friend Rae seems…nice."

"No, she doesn't."

Ollie wasn't expecting that answer, nor the amused looked that accompanied it.

"She doesn't seem *nice*," Carmen said. "I know that."

Ollie chuckled a little, the sound still not sitting right in her ears as it pushed in among the constant heavy feeling her mother had left behind. "No, okay, she doesn't. But I'm sure she is."

"She's my best friend."

"Did you know she knew Sara?"

Carmen shook her head, something in her eyes Ollie didn't know how to read. "No."

"It's a small world."

Carmen turned and looked at her properly, something quizzical on her face. "It is." Carmen rested her head against the wall, never taking her eyes off Ollie. "Tell me something."

Ollie waited, and when Carmen said nothing else, she asked, "What?"

"No, tell me *something*. Anything."

Carmen blinked at her, so sincere that something caught in Ollie's chest and held. She put her drink on the floor, if only to get a break from that sensation and from the need she had to brush her lips against Carmen's.

"Um." Ollie sat back against the wall, her head tilted to look at Carmen's. Nothing about that helped: their faces were inches apart. "I like pizza."

Carmen rolled her eyes. "Fine. To be fair, I didn't know that."

Ollie liked her like this, so relaxed. "Tell me something."

"I don't like pizza."

"No." Ollie shook her head. "You're lying."

"Nope. I don't really like cheese."

"That's tragic."

That made her huff a laugh. "Oh, it's the biggest tragedy of my life."

Ollie wanted to kiss that smile in the hopes it would be carved into her lips and she would never have to go without it again. After a moment, the look on Carmen's face became expectant. "Oh. My turn?"

At her nod, Ollie said the first thing that popped into her head: "I want to kiss you."

Her pupils blew wide, and her gaze dropped to Ollie's lips before shooting back upward. "We're getting to know each other." Carmen's voice had lowered, the timbre deep. "So behave."

Ollie sighed and tried not to think about the way she could feel Carmen's heat, so close, yet not close enough. "Fine. I never had a brother or sister, but I always wanted one."

Carmen looked away, then back at Ollie. "Which would you prefer?"

"I thought a sister, once. But now Sara is like my sister."

"Friends can be family."

"Exactly. Your turn."

"I once stole a skateboard."

"No?"

Carmen laughed, the sound low. "Yes. I was seven. I tried to go down a hill, and karma caught up with me, and I broke my arm."

The image of tiny Carmen on a skateboard was a little adorable. "That's rough karma for a seven-year-old."

Turning so she was facing Ollie a little more, her shoulder digging into the wall, Carmen took a moment to answer. "Maybe."

"Um…" Ollie's gaze fell to Carmen's lips again. "I liked kissing you."

Those lips definitely quirked up a little. "Focus."

"I climbed our Christmas tree when I was three, and it, and I, went through a window."

Carmen blinked at her. "Seriously?"

"Seriously. Four stitches." Ollie pulled her hair away from her eye, and Carmen's eyes searched until they fell on the scar that was almost unnoticeable. She ran her fingers over it so gently that Ollie closed her eyes.

"I'm scared of needles."

Ollie opened them. "You?"

Carmen's grazed her hand down Ollie's cheek and then let it fell away. "Completely. They're disgusting."

Ollie laughed, delighted. "I didn't think you were scared of anything."

"Everyone's scared of something. It's your turn."

"I once cheated on a test."

"Really?"

"Really."

Carmen frowned. "I didn't peg you for the type."

Ollie winked playfully. "There's a lot you don't know about me."

That sincerity laced itself on Carmen's face again. "I know. I'd like to, though."

"Me too."

In the gaze between them, something heavy landed, and Carmen's brow bunched, her eyebrows together and her eyes searching Ollie for something. "What's happened to you, Ollie?"

Those words, again. That question, like an arrow in Ollie's chest, piercing the exact thing Ollie was trying to ignore. There was no desperate kiss to throw herself into this time; the words harder to dodge—she might just drown in her own answer.

"My..." Ollie licked her lips. She looked away, her eyes stinging, and then back to Carmen. Their knees were touching, and they had curled toward each other a little, but it wasn't enough to feel like she wasn't going to splinter apart. "My mom died." She drew a shuddering breath and clenched her jaw.

Carmen's eyes, butterscotch in color, stared straight into her. "I'm so sorry."

A hand was on her knee, sure and steady and grounding. The fingers squeezed. "Thank you."

"Tell me about her."

So Ollie did. She told Carmen about how her mother liked to throw herself into work but was never the absent type. About that one time she'd raced through the halls of Ollie's school in scrubs she tried to hide with a trench coat, all to watch Ollie win some kind of art prize. Two seconds of an announcement and a certificate held in her clammy hands, and her mother clapped with so much force Ollie had thought her smile would break her apart. Once, her mother slapped a woman who hurled a slur at Ollie, something about her skin that Ollie had been too young to really understand. There'd been fire in her mother's eyes.

"What happened?" Carmen asked.

"She had a massive heart attack."

"I wish I could say something more than I'm sorry."

Ollie shrugged. "My dad was with her."

"That's something."

Their foreheads were almost touching, and Carmen closed the gap.

Ollie closed her eyes. "I think he hates himself," she whispered.

"Why?" The husk to Carmen's voice pulled at something in the middle of Ollie.

"She was a cardiothoracic surgeon, and Dad isn't. I think he thinks if their roles were reversed, she could have done something, but he was useless." Ollie hesitated then, her eyes squeezed shut. "And I think I kind of hate him for it too." She didn't need to say she knew it wasn't fair. The way the words choked out, the wetness on her cheeks, made that clear. They left something acrid on her tongue, a bitter taste for bitter, evil words.

"Oh, Ollie." And Carmen pushed forward, her lips on Ollie, who pulled her in harder, desperate for something that burned away the guilt at the words she'd felt every day but had never spoken.

CHAPTER 15

School seemed unimportant.

Once, it had meant a lot to Ollie. Not because she'd been overly good at it. She'd always been an average student. But she just liked it, for the most part.

Not anymore.

Ollie walked the halls scattered, lost in thoughts of the heat of Carmen's kiss and the way her lips quirked at the things Ollie said. Seeing each other was difficult; a week could go by with only one catch-up. The days spent waiting left Ollie with an ache in her belly and her mind whirring and distracted.

Before, she'd been distracted by a grief so dark and deep Ollie had thought she would drown. Now that darkness was bursting with something pushing through. It was filling with a glow that built and built and seemed as if it would overtake everything.

Sometimes, that glow was overwhelming. Ollie lay in bed with her heart racing and feeling like she was about to float away in the warmth that just the thought of Carmen caused, but then her limbs would go cold at the guilt that flooded her. Her mother was dead. Yet Ollie was starting to feel better than she had ever thought she could.

Even so, she could still barely look at her father.

Some nights, she wanted to pad down the hall and knock at his study door. To watch him look up from his computer, surrounded by models and paper he still insisted on using, even with the computer programs that could make his life so much easier. He would pretend to admonish her for being awake, even as something in his eyes, darker than hers yet the same shape, would light up. They'd whisper in the almost-darkness, awash in the light of the computer. One by one, she'd spill her thoughts for him to accept, to look through, to put together so that everything made some kind of sense.

But instead, she lay in her bed and hugged her knees to her chest, because on the nights she used to do that, her mother would eventually come in. She'd be sleep-addled and dozy, glowing white in the darkness of the room. Eventually, she'd usher Ollie back to bed, and Ollie would hear the comforting murmur of their voices as she fell back to sleep.

These days, she felt torn in two. As she lay in bed each night, her insides would writhe in her gut. She'd turn into herself and try to breathe through the grasping, choking feeling of *missing* her mother, with an ache so deep her bones rattled with it.

But she missed her father too.

She'd fall asleep, though, with a want to see Carmen, her fingers curling against her palm as she'd imagine Carmen running her own through her hair.

When she could, she went to the bar, but Carmen could never be sure of the days she'd be there. Ollie didn't really understand how she could get away with being so flaky at a job, even if her boss seemed to be her friend. Some weeks, though, Ollie would get a wink and the promise of a weekend.

The best promises came with the suggestion of a weekday, a night the place was quiet. The two of them could slip away or sometimes, even better, sit opposite each other and trade stories. That was when Ollie felt she was really learning something about Carmen. She'd bask in the questions Carmen asked, her interest in everything Ollie had to say. Carmen had said *impossible*, but whenever Ollie walked into the bar, she never uttered that word now. Rather, her face lit up, the smile curling into her eyes.

The feeling Carmen was holding something back faded but never desisted. It was a splinter deeply embedded in Ollie's mind that she wouldn't notice until something grazed over it with the slightest touch—something like the way Carmen would glance away as if pretending to scan the bar for something when Ollie asked a seemingly harmless question. But Ollie never pushed. She never wanted to see the way Carmen had reacted the first few times she'd asked more questions, the way her eyes had avoided Ollie's own, the way something in her shuttered.

Because normally, Carmen was anything but closed off to Ollie. There'd been something in her eyes that Ollie had seen that first time near the lockers and had reached for, something she couldn't keep away from. To see that something flicker away, even for a second, made her breath catch in her throat.

One night, on a Tuesday, the bar was quiet, and Carmen dragged Ollie into the little office. They surged together urgently, like stars pulled through gravity, like feet to the ground—it was all physics and inevitability. That word always left a sweet taste in the back of Ollie's mouth.

Inevitable.

It was such a better word than *impossible.*

A pattern had formed to their movements now. Ollie knew that Carmen moaned, deep in her throat, when her teeth grazed the muscle where shoulder met neck. Carmen seemed to know that if her fingers crawled along the skin at the base of Ollie's spine, Ollie's hips would jerk and they'd be flush together, always clawing to be closer.

But now, just as Ollie had melted into her, just as the memory of the way her mother's laugh used to meld with the throaty one her father gave all faded to nothing, Carmen had pulled back. Panting, Carmen cupped Ollie's cheeks, their foreheads together.

"I want to take you out."

Those were not the words Ollie had expected to hear. She looked around the room. "Uh, we're out of the bar?" That had brought out the smile in Carmen that made Ollie's insides melt.

"No—out. Like a movie. Or dinner." Carmen bit her lip, her gaze so genuine that liquid feeling became more like heat. "Or both?"

All Ollie could do was breathe, "When?"

"How's Sean?"

Ollie jerked her head up at her father's words. The remains of Chinese food littered the coffee table. Neither had eaten as much as they used to, and Ollie missed the way her mother picked at all the containers, wanting pieces of everything. Her father had always stubbornly persevered with his chopsticks, even with zero coordination. More often than not, he'd use one to stab the chicken, and a laugh would trickle out of her mother as he ate it in one gulp.

That night, he'd sighed like he was exhausted and brought out a fork from the start. She'd tried not to eye it the entire time they were eating.

Those days were before Ollie punished them both for things she didn't know she was punishing them for. Back before she knew how fast it could all disappear.

Months had passed since she'd ended it with Sean, and her father's words sliced through her. She'd never mentioned it to her parents, and she never knew why. Now she just wished she'd opened up to her mother when she could have. There was a time once when Ollie told her mother everything. Almost everything. Without her to tell, the chain of information between her and her father had broken, the rails upended and leading nowhere.

Ollie watched the TV flicker images, and her mouth dried up. When was the last time her father had laughed?

The rice she'd eaten was lead in her stomach. "Sean's fine."

Mere feet separated them on the sofa, and it could have been a valley, an ocean, an entire galaxy. Her throat ached with the urge to cross it, to slide over and lean into him, into his solid weight. To tell him something, anything: to let him in.

But they weren't at the table, because her mother's place there was like a crater, and the sofa didn't have her scent anymore, and all the air had left the room.

Ollie ignored that her father had turned to stare at her, an imploring look in his eyes in her peripheral vision.

It took no time to gather their dinner remains and then disappear out the door, claiming a group project, the lie so heavy Ollie could swear it bent her double.

She got a late bus. The window shuddered under her forehead, and she let it, hoping it would rattle free some of the anger that flickered at the inside of her chest for no reason. If she could, she'd find Carmen, but she still had no phone. Ollie could show up to the bar and end up there alone, and that thought left her cold.

Instead, she went to Sara's, who answered the door, took one look at her face, and dragged her outside. On the trampoline and under a cocoon of blankets, unnecessary now that the weather was warming up a little, they stared up at the crystal-clear sky. Did anyone else ever feel like they could bathe in the stars? Like they could pull the sky down onto themselves and roll in it, leaving stardust in their hair? She'd first sat next to Carmen in this yard, a little drunk, with those same stars mapped overhead, the only witnesses to something that had felt so delicate.

Sara was warm along her side as their breathing synced, slow and steady, letting Ollie's fingers lay over her wrist. "Want to talk about it?" she asked.

Ollie shook her head, so they stared up in silence, the sounds of crickets in the yard clicking in time with Sara's pulse beneath her fingers.

"I think you should," Sara said.

Ollie swallowed, a shooting star trailing across the sky, an urge in her fingers to grab the meteor's tail and finish its journey with it. And if not that, then at least to sprawl the image of it over paper, light it up with colors that could never quite match. "I don't even know what to say."

"Why are you here?"

Because Sara was her person. Because home was too hard. "Because some days, I feel like I can breathe again…" Sara's wrist twisted, and her fingers entwined with Ollie's. "Others, I can't breathe at all."

"Your mom?"

Just those words squeezed Ollie's throat, and tears pushed down her cheeks. She swiped them away, her fingers damp with the evidence. "Can we talk about something else?"

"Okay." Something sly played in Sara's voice. "What about Carmen?"

Another name that made something in Ollie squeeze, but not like with her mom. Carmen was not something Ollie often let them all talk about. She liked to keep thoughts of her close, something just for herself. They were moments she could pull out later and go over, like a mantra, a prayer, her own personal worry beads.

"What *about* Carmen?" Even Ollie could hear the smile in her own voice, the tears cooling on her cheeks.

"Where did that all *come* from? I mean, I knew something was up, with how badly you wanted to find her."

"I don't know. There was something about her. We kissed a couple of times. I felt bad because I'd cheated on Sean…"

"And then?"

Ollie blinked up at the sky. "And then she was all I thought about, even with Mom." Her voice cracked over that word. "Is that terrible?" The sky was a blur now, the stars a wet blob. "Shouldn't *she* be all I think about?"

"Hey…" Sara dug her arm under Ollie and pulled her closer. Warmth surrounded Ollie, and she buried herself in farther. "I don't think that at all. I don't think your mom would think that either. I think she'd just be happy something makes *you* happy."

If Ollie could pay any money in the world, it would be to have her mom saying that to Ollie herself, for her to be doling out that specific sense of comfort from Ollie's childhood—the smell of her mother, her voice soft and reassuring and safe.

She yanked her glasses off and dropped them behind her, then nestled her face into Sara's shoulder, rubbing her eyes into the material of her shirt. Sara wouldn't care. Ollie had done her first alcohol-induced vomit with Sara in range. She was like Ollie's sister—a tear-soaked shirt wouldn't bother her. "What about you?"

"What about me?" Sara asked.

"What's up with that Rae chick? The two of you looked like you wanted to kill each other."

"Nothing."

Lies were not one of Sara's talents. She was the smartest person Ollie knew, along with Deon, but lying laced her voice, bit at her words, marked her syllables. Lying came as unnaturally to her as math to Ollie.

"You guys were in a foster place together?" Ollie prodded.

Unlike Sara, Ollie had grown up in the safety of a family who cared. In fact, before her mother had died, Ollie had been busy feeling like they cared too much, like they were smothering. Now she ached to go back to months and months ago.

Foster care was a foreign idea to her. There were tragic stories, like the hints of Carmen's in those files Deon had hacked. Then there were stories like Sara's.

"It wasn't a great one," Sara finally said. "Though not the worst. Rae was there before me."

Rolling onto her back to stare back up at the sky again, Ollie made sure they were still wrapped together, her leg thrown gently over Sara's.

"You guys didn't like each other?"

"We barely knew each other."

No matter what Ollie asked, she got nothing more. Then Sara turned the conversation to a story from school. Ollie let her, questions burning at the back of her throat.

CHAPTER 16

"Do you like to read?" Ollie asked.

The glass in Carmen's hand was clean, and she dropped the rag she was using on the bar top as she looked up at Ollie, who in turn was openly watching Carmen, elbow on the surface and head propped in her hand. Days had passed since they'd last seen each other, and Carmen had found herself longing for the days of school. She'd lain on the roof of the warehouse and imagined the ways Ollie and she would be able to sneak off together—to be seventeen, smitten, and with days and days ahead of them to press close together under bleachers, to entwine themselves together against lockers, sparks dancing along their skin at the mere presence of each other.

To be seventeen. And only to be seventeen.

The bar was nearly empty. The music was low, a bass thrumming in the air that Carmen could feel in her chest. She crossed her arms on the bar top too, her arms inches from Ollie's. Everything smelled like beer. This scene felt like something from a life that shouldn't be theirs: not yet, not at their age.

"I do. I love to read," Carmen answered.

The blue of Ollie's eyes seemed to brighten. Carmen could watch the color play through them all day—the stormy sight when she was sad or lost, like when Carmen had seen her at the bar the first night. When Carmen kissed her, they turned a dark azure twilight with constellations spread throughout. A lighter blue sometimes emerged when she listened to Carmen like she couldn't imagine doing anything else, a blue just for her.

Did Ollie know she carried the universe in her eyes? Or was Carmen just a sap, a romantic newly discovered?

"Me too." Ollie's voice was low, clearly meant just for Carmen. "Though I hate when they make movies into books."

Carmen couldn't remember the last time she'd seen a movie that hadn't been in class at school, or something on the TV in the home. But she didn't want this conversation to end. "You can't capture a book the same way. You're doomed to be disappointed."

"Exactly." Ollie's nose wrinkled up, and Carmen had never seen anything so adorable. "If you were stuck on a desert island, what book would you take? Only one."

Carmen kept so much from Ollie, secrets shadowed in the back of her mind she danced around constantly, trying to get as close to them as she could to avoid lying completely. She wanted to tell Ollie about Mattie, to tell her how he devoured books. How he could read for hours. How the weight of him was all that centered Carmen some nights as he sat against her reading or—rarely now that he was a bit older—when he asked her to read to him.

But she couldn't do that, so she laid out what truth she could. "When I went into foster care this time, I grabbed a textbook... I think it means I'm a nerd."

The delight on Ollie's face planted a seed of warmth in Carmen's belly. "A textbook?"

Carmen shrugged and picked up another glass. "Yeah."

"That's so adorable."

"Shut up." The smile on her lips felt almost foreign. "What about you?"

"I'd bring another textbook so you'd have two."

Carmen slowed down the rag in her hand, staring at Ollie, her cheeks feeling as if they might shatter. "Because we'd be stuck together?"

"Of course."

Moving forward to kiss Ollie was the most natural movement in the world. Her lips were soft, and she tasted like soda and promises.

Ollie stayed until closing, and they hovered in the street, Dex yards away and pretending to ignore them. It was obvious Ollie wanted to walk her home, that she didn't want the time to end. If she found out about Mattie, about the warehouse, about the existence Carmen spent balanced on a knife's edge, maybe Carmen could ask her back, could give her a taste of normal. But none of it was normal, and it was all too perilous, too fragile.

The lies were necessary, and she hated it, especially when Ollie offered her nothing but herself.

"Does your dad know you're here?" Carmen asked, her breath mingling with Ollie's, their foreheads together.

Ollie shook her head. That darkness in her eye, the time she looked like a storm, rose up easily. It was always there, rumbling in the background of her irises. Under Carmen's arms, Ollie still felt thinner than she had the first time they'd been in a bathroom together. Sadness continued to cover Ollie like a shadow, but now Carmen knew its name, and when they were together, she loved to watch it slide away and reveal Ollie underneath.

"He thinks I'm studying."

"Are you talking to him?"

Ollie tensed under her hands, and Carmen wanted to soothe it away. She shrugged and pulled back slightly from Carmen, looking up and away, avoiding her eyes. "Not really."

"Why not?"

That look was back on her now, and Carmen met it. "I'm still... I feel..."

Watching Ollie struggle to find the words was hard, but Carmen wanted her to acknowledge whatever had formed inside her, that had taken her over since her mother died.

"I'm still angry."

Carmen nodded. "That's okay."

"Is it?" Ollie's voice was tight, a string pulled too taut.

Carmen kissed her softly. "It is."

"I want to tell him things...but I don't know how to start." The words were whispered, and Carmen kissed her again.

"Start when you're ready."

They peeled apart slowly, said good-bye, and just as she was starting to get on the bus, Carmen called out, "Ollie?"

She paused with one foot on the step. "Yeah?"

"I'm still angry too. All the time. I think it's normal."

Ollie's shoulders relaxed as she looked like Carmen had given her a gift. Whether because Carmen had reassured her, or shared something, Carmen didn't know.

"Thanks."

Their smiles didn't fit their conversation, and she watched Ollie get safely on the bus before she fell into step next to Dex as he started walking now Carmen was with him.

"Where's Mattie tonight?" Dex asked.

"With Rae."

Dex was bundled in a coat. It made him seem somehow soft, rather than bulky and big like normal. "Those two really get along."

Carmen hummed and nodded. They did. Mattie could spend hours with Rae, and Carmen suspected it was because Rae trained him harder than she did. But there was something else too, a way they just *got* each other. Something special. It was a relief to know Mattie had someone else besides her.

It had been months now. Six? Seven? Mattie's ninth birthday had been and gone. Anxiety lived in the back of Carmen's throat, prickling and uncomfortable. The closer she crawled to eighteen, the more she worried her plan was beyond fallible: Jia wasn't sold on it. To be honest, neither was Carmen.

"How am I going to prove to a court that I deserve Mattie?" She didn't mean to ask. Pushing those burdens onto someone else wasn't her style. But they burned on her tongue, and she needed to ask them aloud.

Beside her, their shoulders not even touching, Dex tensed. She didn't need to look over to know how his weathered cheeks tightened or the look in his eyes darkened. But she asked another question anyway, because they were beating against the roof of her mouth, a flood now that the tide had opened. "What if they don't approve it?"

Sometimes Mattie stared at her with so much faith Carmen thought she'd shatter open from it. What if she failed him?

Still Dex didn't say anything.

Carmen's voice was tight. "I've already... I've fucked it up for him so badly already."

Mattie moved through the streets like he had been born in them. He gathered supplies and had an intuition she'd never seen in others. School was a distant memory, but not so distant that he didn't miss it. They lived somewhere with no real plumbing. No real security. Well past the fringes of society. He was so small and so unshaped. She didn't want this life to be what molded him.

"We'll figure it out if it comes to that, Carmen."

The low rumble of Dex's voice usually soothed her. Not tonight. Tonight it left her shaken.

"Stand still."

Dex didn't say those words. Someone with a low voice, rough and angry, did.

A clicking sound sent her hair standing on end; an unmistakable sound. The cocking of a gun.

She and Dex froze, the presence behind them looming. It was as if she could feel the gun's presence hovering behind her as a tangible thing. As one, they inched their hands above their heads, their heads turning just slightly to catch each other's eye. Dex's throat bobbed as he swallowed, and somehow, her heartbeat slowed to a calm rhythm against her ribs.

Adrenaline, Dex had always told them, never actually helped in a fight. You made mistakes with it pumping through your veins, especially in the first minute. People spoke of how it amped them, but really, it led to sloppiness. He taught them breathing in a fight, calming techniques, a way to ensure they didn't lose their heads.

"Look ahead, no looking at each other." The voice was still low.

Desperation tinged its edges, and if a hadn't been pointed at them, Carmen would have empathized with the hunger she heard it in it. They did what they were told, and their hands brushed over their heads.

Footsteps brought the man closer, and the barrel of the gun pressed between her shoulder blades.

One shot. That's all it would take.

"All right, big guy. The gun's right on the girl. Empty your pockets. Cell phone. Cash. Cards."

This man had picked the wrong people. The only thing they had was maybe a crumpled bill. Maybe. Dex had a cell phone, but he always left it at the bar.

"Reach into your pockets, nice and slow."

Dex's hand, the warmth of it, left hers and she could feel him inching it to his pockets. The push of the metal still against her back wavered, and Carmen took the moment. She spun, using her forearm to push the man's, keeping the gun away from both of them, and thrusting her hand up to take out his nose.

Blood spurted, and the hair on her arms stood on end when she saw not one man, but two. A second had been quietly flanking the first. A fist connected with her cheek, the thump of it proof Rae had hit her months ago with only minor intention. Heat flared at the sensation. The force of it pushed her back a step, and she used the momentum to spin, kicking out twice—once between the legs and the second a sharp, vicious boot to the head when he fell. She gave a final kick to the gun, sending it clattering far away over the cement.

Carmen hated guns.

Dex had the other guy on the ground, and a firm punch knocked him out. Breathing hard, they looked down at them, both out cold.

What if Ollie had been with them? Or Mattie?

That thought echoed through her mind, and Carmen's aching fists tightened as she sucked in air. She looked to Dex. "Recognize them?"

"You don't?"

She searched their faces. They looked gaunt; the hungry look was one she knew too well. But who were they, actually? Their faces were young but with the hard look only the streets could give.

"No."

"That one—" Dex nudged the one he'd taken out "—was one of the ones Jia turned away when you were first with us. He'd done some nasty stuff in a shelter, and she'd been warned about him. I've seen him around."

Squinting in the darkness, Carmen cocked her head. There was something familiar there under the matted, strangely youthful beard. His eyelids fluttered.

"Let's get out of here," Dex said, his voice a low growl.

They turned as one and bolted. They didn't stop until they were at the warehouse, until the door slammed behind them. Mattie must have been asleep upstairs in their room, and Rae had thrown herself over the sofa.

A sick feeling flared in Carmen's stomach. She ignored Rae's puzzled expression, leaving Dex to explain. She pounded up the stairs, panic flickering and her cheek throbbing. As quietly as she could, she pushed the door to their room open. Her body sagged at the sight: Mattie lay in their bed, bathed in orange light, and Carmen hovered in the doorway, watching the way his chest rose and fell.

Of course he was fine. But what if he'd been there?

Voices murmured below. Jia's floated up, her syllables a whispered hiss. Carmen didn't go back down, the tremble in her fingers having nothing to do with what had occurred but rather with what *could* have happened.

With a final glance backward, Carmen went upstairs and sat on the roof, her feet kicking against the wall where she sat on the edge. The sky was clouded over, the light of the moon weak behind them. She longed for them to part, to see the stars and trace the constellations with her gaze, to stare up until the rest faded away and it was like she was there among them.

The door opened, and Carmen didn't need to check to know it was Rae who sat next to her, her feet still while Carmen's moved restlessly.

"You okay?"

Carmen shrugged.

"You're going to have a great black eye."

And a great bruise over her cheekbone. She hoped the bastard hurt his hand. "Better than the one you gave me."

Rae snorted. "Damn. You're right."

Carmen wanted to tell her to go away, to leave her to this feeling compressing her chest. The words wouldn't come, however, so she didn't force them.

"Mattie wasn't there," Rae said.

"He could've been." Carmen didn't take her eyes off the light filtering out from behind the clouds, fascinated at how it split into something like beams. She wondered where the light hit, what it led to, if the universe was highlighting the parts of the world it approved of. Her rooftop was cased in shadows, shrouded in darkness.

"But he wasn't."

"They had a gun. What's a kid to that?"

Rae sighed. "I know. But that's why we've taught him to be fast. He's on the street, as much as you've tried to shelter him from that; he's seen shit. But kids at school and in nice fancy homes see shit. Get shot."

That did nothing to make Carmen feel better. "That's different than actually having him out here, wandering around at night."

Rae nudged Carmen's shoulder with her own and didn't speak until Carmen turned to look at her. "You have no idea what situation he'd be in if he wasn't with you. He's happiest with *you*."

Was that enough?

"You should put some ice on your eye."

That finally made Carmen huff a laugh. "Sure, I'll just go to the freezer and get some."

"We could call the butler."

"Yes, please do ring for Charles, and while he's bringing forth ice, request some tea, please. Tepid."

"Tepid?" Rae raised her eyebrows.

Carmen shrugged. "I've always wanted to use that word." The tense feeling in her shoulders eased a little, and her feet slowed to a gentle sway.

God, what a mess.

It seemed like forever ago that Carmen had been lost in Ollie. Though, thinking of Ollie, she had asked Carmen about something she had no answers for.

"Rae..."

"Mm?"

"How do you know Sara?"

The shoulder brushing hers tensed. "I told you, same foster place."

"Yeah, but why the few times I've seen you together are you...you know."

Tense. Angry. Glaring. Carmen had only seen Sara and Rae together once or twice more, but it was like they circled each other, snapping, eyes narrowed. Something sparked between them. They barely spoke a word, yet Carmen watched them and couldn't understand it.

"Nothing."

Carmen waited her out, the distant sounds of cars and the darkness creeping in.

Finally, Rae offered, "We were always like that. But it was fun. We'd rib and piss each other off, but it wasn't... It was fun."

Carmen just continued to wait, the sound of a truck rumbling far away behind them and the clouds shifting overhead.

"Then one night, we stole some vodka. We were, I don't know, young. I was twelve. So Sara must have been eleven. And I kissed her. She kissed me back. We were kids. The super-religious dad found us and screamed and yelled, and she got moved, and I ran. For, like, the second time. But this time was permanent."

"So why the hatred?"

Rae shrugged. "I don't know. She didn't defend me when he blamed me. I didn't defend her when he locked her in her room, calling her an abomination for being trans. He didn't, you know, say that word. He said other things. It was a fucking mess."

Their school was not a quiet place. When Carmen had ended up back there, a year behind—more, really, after their mom had moved them around for a while—and clinging to the walls as if they could swallow her whole, she'd heard about another girl from the system. Sometimes, Carmen had watched Sara, something akin to jealousy flaming in her as she wondered how she had managed to find a foster family who actually took care of her.

So that jealousy turned out to be misplaced, and guilt rolled in her stomach. Life hadn't always been like that for Sara.

"Have you thought about, you know?" Carmen shrugged. "Talking to her?"

Rae turned to look at her, an eyebrow raised. "Does Ollie know about this? About Mattie?"

Carmen blinked and turned away.

"There's a whole world of things we all *should* talk about, Carmen."

"I'm off."

Her father's voice was timid, a ghost of the commanding, booming man Ollie had grown up with. He had no idea what to do with his seventeen-year-old daughter anymore, and it was clear in the way he hovered.

When Ollie looked up from the cereal she was crunching through for dinner, her father was trying to look at her. But his gaze kept flitting away, stuttering on Ollie like a glitch. Like he didn't trust himself. Or Ollie. Her ribs ached, as if something were swelling within them and she was about to choke on emotions she couldn't name.

Did her father see her mother in her eyes? Ollie did. Mirrors hurt. When had her family become *this*?

"Okay."

When had Ollie been unable to offer more than short syllables that seemed to grate past her teeth?

Sometimes, when Ollie was at her worst, when all the air leeched from the room, she pictured the paramedics having to pull her father off her mother, having to force his acceptance that she'd been gone before his hands had even landed against her sternum.

A moment stretched on forever before them. It expanded and contracted like the world had no thought but for the father and daughter in a room that was too small and too big all at once. And all they could do was stare at each other. Her father swallowed, snapped the moment in two, and Ollie could feel it shatter as he nodded and turned to go. In a moment of panic, Ollie wanted to pull the pieces into her lap and drive them back together, to use the look in her father's eyes as glue to make sure they didn't fall apart again.

"Sean and I broke up."

Her father paused in the doorway, and there was something stooped about his shoulder as he turned. He stared unblinking at Ollie, as if anything more could fracture what Ollie was holding out with trembling fingers.

"Ages ago." Her voice cracked over the words, not having anything to do with what she was telling her father but that she was telling him anything at all.

Her father stepped forward so he was only feet away. It felt closer than he had been in months and months.

"I'm sorry to hear that." The voice wasn't timid now but soft, with a sincerity in it that did nothing to assuage the aching in Ollie's chest. "Do… do you want to talk about why?"

His lips were quivering, and Ollie wondered at the emotion her father was repressing, had been repressing, since he'd told Ollie her mother was dead. Parts of Ollie were pulling away, screaming with white knuckles to stand up and leave, and another part was slamming her forward, urging her to fall against her father and breathe him in.

"I met someone."

No surprise lit up her father's face. He was watching Ollie with an intensity that seemed borne of a fear of chasing her away.

Ollie's heart pounded, sped up to beat a rhythm in her ears, and left her dizzy. With no warning, the lump dissolved and left her throat tight, prickling. Ollie wanted to tell her mother this. To see her reaction. To know if she would stand up and walk away in disgust or smooth her hair back with cool palms. "A girl. From school."

The parts that wanted to run almost won out, Ollie's foot twitching where it sat against the rung on her stool.

Her father took another step forward, the kitchen island separating them. With his hands on the edge, he cocked his head. "What's her name?"

"Carmen." The name whispered from her lips, and her eyes were intent on her father. Her vision went blurry, wet, and she had no idea why. Even more horrifying, her father's eyes looked the same.

"Does she make you happy?"

Ollie nodded, her lips pursed.

Haltingly, his arm jerking, her father raised his hand, hovering just against Ollie's cheek, waiting until Ollie ducked her head and pressed her skin against his palm. Like it had always been, it was rough in places. Calluses caused from always clutching something to draw with. Something sighed over his body, and he smiled, shaky with obvious, painful relief all over his face. "That's all that matters to me."

A snap in Ollie's chest, and a sob broke from her mouth. "Mom would have liked her."

Her father's eyes were still glittering and red. "I'm sure she would have."

CHAPTER 17

"What happened to your eye?"

Hands quickly cupped Carmen's cheeks, and she leaned into the touch, eyes fluttering closed. She had never wanted someone to be concerned about her. That was her job, to worry. To pull Mattie close and cover his eyes when she could, or distract him if she couldn't, or run with him when things were dire.

Ollie's concern, though?

It was nice. Sweet.

Like something that shouldn't be hers. This belonged to a girl who spent her time walking to and from school. To a girl buried in studies who stumbled over a girl who looked touched by the stars. A girl who somehow turned that star-filled brightness onto her.

Remembering where she was, Carmen pulled back, the bar separating her from Ollie. Her eyes were intent on Carmen's face. Carmen knew she looked a bit of a mess. The bruise had darkened to black, to something speckled with a purple that seemed unnatural on her skin. "Don't freak out."

Ollie blinked at her, her brow furrowed and her hands still against Carmen's cheeks.

The touch was keeping Carmen in that moment, keeping her rooted to the ground when she thought she could float away. The divide between their lives should have been more prominent than ever, but instead, Carmen felt as if they'd melded together even more.

"What happened to your eye?"

Carmen sighed. She couldn't lie. She was fed up with lies, the ash of them. "Dex and I almost got mugged the other night."

Ollie looked horrified.

Carmen hurried to finish. "But we're fine, seriously. Nothing happened."

Walking behind Carmen with a box, Dex huffed, "Yeah, because you knocked the gun out of his hands."

Carmen closed her eyes.

"There was a gun?" Ollie's voice was definitely high-pitched, and her hand fell away.

The rush of cold air against Carmen's cheek was bracing, and her stomach fell. If she didn't think it would just bounce off his overly bulging muscles, Carmen would throw something at Dex. She opened her eyes and was greeted by Ollie's wide-eyed stare. "But, uh, I knocked it out of his hands?"

Ollie was looking at her like she didn't know her, and that made Carmen's stomach ache. As much as Carmen hated it, Ollie really didn't know her. And that was Carmen's fault.

"How?"

"Fast reflexes?" Carmen tried.

She wanted to kill Dex. Though at the same time, she wanted him to spill everything for her so she didn't feel like she was holding it all back.

"But you're really okay?"

"I am."

"You shouldn't walk alone. Can't someone from the group home pick you up or something?"

If only that was the biggest of Carmen's problems. That divide filled with everything Carmen kept from Ollie grew a little at the issues and problems Carmen had submerged herself in, at the lies she'd muttered when she'd thought she'd been saving herself, protecting Mattie. But how could Ollie ever understand it if Carmen never gave her the chance?

"I'll be more careful." Because what else did Carmen have to offer but false promises? Ollie's accepting silence left something hollow in Carmen. As she sat farther back on her stool, the distance expanded between them.

The evening was a slow one, time passing in fits and starts. Even in the moments when Carmen was serving and cleaning and clearing, it dragged along. She could feel Ollie's eyes on her the entire shift. When things quieted down and Carmen sat on the stool next to Ollie, their knees knocking between them, or when Ollie stood across from her on the bar, their elbows on the bar top and mere inches of air drifting between their skin, time raced by. She was left unsteady when she had to move away from their easy conversation to serve a beer or wipe down some tables. Dex floated between them, only rolling his eyes once. That Carmen noticed, anyway.

Mattie knew she would be late today, and Carmen was just happy he had agreed to stay behind more the last few days. He'd panicked the morning he'd seen her eye, and she had told him the truth: she tried to protect him from some things, but also needed him to understand that the world they were in was filled with things that sought to bring them down. Carmen felt like she had when she'd been tiny, no more than five, and had slipped on her mother's shoes and tried to walk in them: she was carrying things too big, too adult, walking a path too large for her, yet stumbling was not an option.

Thirty minutes before they closed, Carmen slipped into the office, then slipped out again, nodding to Dex. He turned over the Closed sign and disappeared out the back with a wave.

Ollie watched him go. "Shouldn't we walk out with him?"

Carmen shook her head, her heart fluttering and her stomach a hive. "Not tonight. I'll do the final close."

Slowly, like she couldn't believe it, Ollie smiled. Still on the stool, she hooked a finger into Carmen's belt loop and tugged her between her legs. She wound her arms around Carmen's waist.

Carmen could have sighed into the contact and never left. Everything with Ollie made her feel settled and like she was reeling at the same time, uncertain with her footsteps, yet marching on determined all at once. "Come with me?"

Ignoring Ollie's questioning look, Carmen led her toward the office, her hand clammy where Ollie clutched it. She opened the door and stepped in, watching Ollie's face.

The room was lit with mismatched candles, as many as Carmen had been able to find. Dex had donated some from the ones they kept both in the bar and in the warehouse for emergencies; others Carmen had used sticky fingers to get.

The light flickered, shadows playing across Ollie's face as she stared around the room. The fingers wrapped in hers twitched. For a second, everything stood still as she waited for Ollie to say something.

She'd held her breath yesterday as she'd slipped a packet of tea lights under her jacket in a supermarket. Right now, though, it had been worth it.

Or maybe not. Ollie still hadn't said anything.

It was too much. Too corny. Too much like a bad romance movie, a cliché. But she had no spare money for movies or dinners, and Ollie deserved a date.

Ollie deserved everything.

Finally, Ollie beamed, and Carmen let out a breath, the pressure expanding in her ribs the last tense few seconds.

Candlelight was in Ollie's hair, in her eyes. As they ate the pizza laid out, the softness of the flame seemed to settle inside her, glowing in her chest. She didn't like pizza, but Ollie loved it, and Carmen would eat it with her every day if Ollie wanted to. Trading the free pints with the shop across the road was the best idea she'd had in a while.

Cheese caught on Ollie's chin, and Carmen swiped at it with her thumb, following it with a kiss.

"You don't eat your crusts?" Carmen asked.

"Nope." Ollie dropped one with a clatter on her plastic plate. "I don't."

"But they make your hair curly." Carmen couldn't remember who told her that, and with a stab in her stomach, she wondered if it had been her mother.

Ollie's eyebrows rose, and she looked up as if she could look at her own hair before she looked back at Carmen pointedly.

Carmen chuckled. "Okay. Fine. You don't need curlier hair."

Though Carmen wouldn't be opposed. She loved Ollie's hair. The tightness to its curl. Just less than Mattie's. Slightly softer. Her hair was like tiny springs. Absently, she moved closer, elbows digging into the table, and wrapped the end of a strand around her fingers.

"How's school?" Ollie asked.

Innocence in such a question. The tendril of hair unraveled from Carmen's finger, and she twirled it again gently. "Fine. Same, same. How about you?"

Ollie's gaze dropped to the table. "It's okay. I'm catching up after falling behind."

Letting her fingertip fall slightly, Carmen traced a line down Ollie's cheek. "That's good." She smiled. "Are you concentrating on more than just art?"

Ollie huffed a little, softly. She smelled like citrus. A new body wash?

"Yes. I'm being good."

"Can you bring your portfolio next time?"

Carmen had watched Ollie bring things to life on napkins on the bar, simple doodles that captured whatever she was drawing perfectly. Some were pinned up on the office wall. They marched along behind Ollie, covered with sketches of regulars. One of her favorites was Dex, pulling a pint and staring at nothing.

"You really want to see it?"

Turning back sharply, tearing her gaze from those sketches, Carmen gave Ollie's hair another gentle pull. "Of course."

"Okay." Her voice was quiet. "I'll bring it."

They ended up on the cot, their shoulders together. They sat against the wall, as they often did, feet and legs hanging off the side, forgotten pizza crusts scattered over the table.

"How is your dad?" Carmen asked as usual. She knew how it felt when your heart lit up with rage, then froze toward a person in self-protection. But she also knew that Ollie's heart held the ability to melt, and that as her grief settled, so would that rage.

Ollie kissed Carmen's shoulder and hummed, the skin heating up with the motion. Puffs of warm air added to the sensation. Carmen smiled. Did she ever need to leave this bubble?

"He's okay." Now Ollie's lips moved against her shirt, and she turned her head, her cheek on Carmen's shoulder, their sides melded together and their hands interlaced. Ollie's traced her spare hand gently over Carmen's bruised eye, her gaze following the motion.

Did Ollie know how much Carmen held back?

She didn't want to hold back.

"We talked...a little. I told him—" Ollie's fingers tightened "—about you."

Carmen turned her head completely, Ollie pulling back a little at the quickness of the movement. "You did?"

"I did. I'd like you to meet him one day."

That anger that usually coated Ollie's gaze was simmering, not raging. Carmen smiled, tighter than she meant to. Would it ever be possible to meet Ollie's dad? "I'd like that. One day."

The answering grin left Carmen warm, a tug low in her belly that she had started to think Ollie owned. They met in a kiss bathed in stuttering candlelight, and Carmen would give anything, she realized, to keep Ollie this close. She shared so much, so easily, and Carmen wanted to give her something to meet that trust and match it. Fingers plucked at her shirt, and soon it puddled on the floor with Ollie's, followed by bras and pants and underwear. With a gasp, their skin was flush together. and Carmen thought she was going to shatter apart at the touch of Ollie's fingers, the feel of her beneath her. The first time they were naked together, Carmen didn't know if it was Ollie's tears or her own on her cheeks.

Bruises, Carmen was learning, faded quickly sometimes, and sometimes painfully slowly. The bruises that smattered her insides were still tender, as they had been for years and years. Some matched the imprint of her mother's voice, and others Carmen's own bitter disappointment. The one on her eye disappeared so quickly, it was like it had never existed.

The ones that danced over her collarbone, red from Ollie's lips, Carmen never wanted to disappear. Carmen liked to carry a part of Ollie that was all hers.

The warehouse was getting hot, as it did this time of year. Too hot. It left Mattie cranky, surly, a glimpse of the person he could become in a few years. They were crawling toward her eighteenth birthday, and she had no idea how she was going to get out of there, to get Mattie out of there and back in school. Having been so long out of it, he'd be so far behind.

So would Carmen.

And he asked questions now. "Why are you smiling?"

Rae scoffed. "Yeah," she said, a smirk on her lips, "Why are you smiling, Carmen?"

Other days, it was more obvious. He liked to throw questions at her while they sparred, and cheekily use her distraction against her.

"I heard you laughing at the bar the other night, from the office." That night, Mattie had come, and Carmen had insisted both Dex and Rae walk home with them. Shadows had loomed from all sides, and not for a second had Carmen been worried about herself but for the boy who felt like a part of her. Who *was* a part of her. "You never laugh like that."

Carmen cleared her throat and bounced to the side as he threw a hit. "Sloppy," she said, and his eyes narrowed. For a second, Carmen saw her mother. The jolt of it made her pause and stare and ensured the next punch landed as Mattie took advantage of her hesitation. He crowed with his success but bounced straight back in defense, not one to rub in the shot. He was a good kid.

Dex watched them from the wall, noting the play of Mattie's feet, the way they danced and how he ducked under her arm. Dex had mentioned boxing one night. The suggestion had left Carmen glaring at him with as much venom as she could gather. Even if it made sense. Even if Mattie loved this.

Carmen didn't want that for him.

But damn, did it make sense.

"So who makes you laugh like that?" He made the face of a disgusted nine-year-old. "Do you have a *boy*friend?"

Carmen paused, her arms lowering slowly, and Mattie stayed ready but cocked his head as he looked up at her. "What if I had a girlfriend?"

Why was her heart racing?

His brow furrowed and he looked like Mattie again, small and young and confused. She really hoped that anger didn't build in him, didn't take him over.

He just stared at her, clearly thinking. "Do you?"

Carmen could feel Dex's gaze on her, intent and heavy. "I think so."

Mattie grinned, ducked close, landed a hit to the padding on her rib, then danced behind her so she had to whip around. "Okay." He shrugged. "Can I meet her?"

Carmen stepped in on his left side, taking advantage of the fact that he was a lefty and threw him off balance. She tripped him up and before he could scowl at her, heaved him over her shoulder, her knees struggling with the bulk of him. She spun them too quickly, his shriek of laughter making Dex boom out a laugh himself.

Later, Dex forced Mattie to sit down to study something mathematical that made Carmen itch to join in. She'd loved math, the formulaic manner it had, the way there was always an answer. After only ten minutes, Mattie threw down his pencil.

"I don't even need this." He looked up, the brown in his eyes scathing, painful.

Carmen met the gaze, even as something in her yearned to flinch away.

"I don't go to school anyway."

His chair scraped loudly, Jia looking through her office door, and Carmen and Dex watched as Mattie pounded up the metal steps.

The sound seemed to echo in her chest. She looked to Dex, and he looked back steadily. "He's right," she said.

"Which part?"

That question held a test. "Not that he doesn't need it."

Dex blinked.

"In his frustration. The fact that he doesn't go to school."

Dex nodded. "He's a bright kid, but that anger could end up eating him alive."

Carmen waited ten minutes and followed him up, pulling Mattie onto the roof to sit next to her until the knot of his shoulders eased and he swung his legs in time to hers, a breeze playing through his hair, now grown into a cloud over his ears again.

She owed him more than this, but her hands had nothing else to give him.

It was the type of night that wrapped its way around Ollie and left her woozy with contentment.

The table was littered with long-abandoned empty glasses, some still holding warm, flat beer at the bottom. The music verged on too loud, people straining their voices just slightly, but not so loud that anyone had bothered to ask that it be turned down. It was a Friday night, the kind that left Ollie layered in satisfaction with an urge for the future sparking in her limbs, even while craving everything to stay the same.

She breathed more easily now. Her house wasn't trying to smother her. She and her father took two steps forward and one step back, rather than vice versa, and sometimes Ollie wanted to collapse under the relief of it. Some moments, she found happiness spilling through her chest, and she took a second to enjoy it, to gasp at the shock that she wasn't drowning in grief so much anymore but treading water.

She'd even told him she was bisexual, and he'd just repeated he just wanted her happy.

Sara was trying to balance a glass on her forehead, her head thrown back, and Deon shoved her, trying to knock it off. Every now and again, one of them would throw cards down at the game they played on and off. They all kept picking it up intensely for five minutes before losing interest, only to start again.

On her break, Carmen plopped into the empty chair at Ollie's side, her cheeks flushed with the heat of busing tables in an overcrowded room. She dropped a kiss on Ollie's lips, soft and short and perfect. Ollie grinned at her in a way that should probably have been embarrassing. A comfortable kiss was almost better than the ones they shared alone, heated and gasping.

Almost.

As Carmen pulled her away, Rae, leaning against the bar with a tumbler of golden-brown liquid in her hand, caught Ollie's eye. There was something about Rae that could catch anyone's attention, a dangerous silence, an attractiveness that threatened to burn people who came too close.

The last thing Ollie saw before she left the room was Sara next to Rae at the bar, her face screwed up, no doubt dripping something frustrated in Rae's direction. Those two were like sharks sometimes, opposite each other, and Ollie was expecting one to drag the other down with a scream.

But that was easily forgotten, and she found herself against a door, a thigh between hers and hands up her shirt. She giggled, an actual giggle, one that sounded like it belonged to Ollie from forever ago, but also one she was starting to realize could still be hers.

"I have ten minutes..."

Ollie smiled at the words whispered against her neck. "Ten minutes is plenty."

There were fingernails under her bra, and it should have hurt, but instead Ollie bucked, a groan guttural in her throat. It was so easy to lose herself in Carmen.

When they tumbled out ten minutes later, maybe fifteen, actually— Ollie winced—the bar was filled with even more people. "I have to go soon."

Carmen turned back to her, her eyes sparking and deep and reminding Ollie of chocolate, the taste sweet on her tongue. "What?" she asked.

Ollie put her lips to Carmen's ear, feeling the shudder it enticed. "I have to go soon."

"Oh?" Carmen pulled back, those eyes imploring her to stay even as Ollie knew she would kiss her good night and watch her leave if that's what Ollie said she needed to do.

"I told Dad I'd be home at twelve. I'm trying a new thing..."

Carmen's lips twitched up, and Ollie shrugged, gaze on the ground. "I'm glad."

"Where's Sara?"

Ollie glanced to their table. It was devoid of her friend. Carmen looked behind her and then suddenly laughed.

"What?" Ollie followed Carmen's line of sight, and her mouth dropped open. In a dark corner near the entrance, Sara and Rae were entwined, hands grasping hair and pulling each other close. "Oh my God." Ollie couldn't look away, and it made Carmen laugh again, the sound grating against Ollie's shock. "Carmen! They're kissing."

"You're really surprised?"

Ollie turned an openmouthed look on her, hoping her expression conveyed it. "Uh, yes?"

Carmen chucked her fingers under Ollie's chin, and Ollie shut her mouth obediently.

"I don't think anyone else is," Carmen said.

Was it really that surprising? Ollie looked back to the two in the corner, and her mouth dropped open again, ever so slightly. It really was. Blindly, she followed Carmen, and laughter finally made her look at her friends at the table.

Deon was staring at her expression, occasionally flicking his glance back and forth between her and the quiet spectacle of Sara and Rae. "Seriously?" he asked. "You're shocked?"

Later, with Sara falling asleep against the window of the last bus, Ollie would arrive home when she'd told her father she would.

But she was barely thinking of that as she stared at Sara.

Finally, Sara opened one eye. "Shut up."

Ollie smirked. Sara's lips were swollen, a red mark scratched over her neck. "Didn't say a word."

"You didn't have to." Her eyes closed, and her head fell back against the headrest, even as Ollie kept smirking. "I can feel you watching me."

"Wanna talk about it?"

"No."

Ollie's snort said it all.

CHAPTER 18

BOOKS WERE STREWN OVER OLLIE'S bedroom carpet, papers littered among them all. The bright colors of empty potato chip packages and cookie boxes broke up the blandness of it all. Sara was writing complex equations on Ollie's bed. Ollie had caught a glimpse of them at one point and gone cross-eyed at the sight. Every now and again, Sara snapped her gum before going back to mindlessly chewing it. Deon was sprawled on the floor, notes piled high next to him, blurry-eyed. Finals were approaching, and the stress of it was a constant fizz in their blood.

The history book on Ollie's lap was starting to blur, dates melding until she had no idea what she'd just read. The monotony of reading clawing at her skull, she pulled out a stack of index cards and started making her own set of flash cards.

"You're procrastinating." Sara didn't even look up from her book.

"Am not."

"You're making flash cards, and you're going to spend a good few hours decorating them."

Ollie looked at the boat she was drawing, details down to the carving in the rail. It would be a visual aid to help her remember which boat and which date. "What? It helps."

Sara snorted. "And you get to doodle."

Ollie traced the sail with her pen. "Yup." They always teased her but then asked to borrow the cards later, a fact Ollie would forever remind them of.

Later, Ollie heard the front door open and close and didn't feel her entire body tense like it used to. She and her father moved around each other more fluidly now. The hole her mother had left wasn't gone, but it had shifted, almost as if it were just out of their way so they didn't trip and fall into it or accidentally push each other down it with their bitterness.

Her father knocked at the door and waited for Ollie to call to come in. It wasn't too late. Recently, he'd been trying to be home more. As he stood against the frame, he looked tired.

"Hey, all," he murmured. "How's the studying?"

His expression made Ollie think he was almost grateful to find them all there, spread out with stress on their faces. Had he thought he'd lost this? Guilt squirmed in her stomach at the thought of how angry she'd been at him, at how angry she still was sometimes.

Sara groaned. "It's hell."

He winced sympathetically. "AP Physics?" At Sara's nod, he winced again. "That's not fun. But if anyone can do it, Sara, you can."

"Thanks, Calvin."

Her father was a good person, and that guilt flared again in her insides.

"It's almost eight—have you eaten?" He asked.

"We heated up the frozen lasagna," Ollie said. "We left you some."

"Mm. Nutritious." The playful tone that curled her father's words at the end left Ollie feeling lighter. "Thanks."

"Did you say it's almost eight?" As he sat up, Deon looked around the room, hand rubbing at his eyes.

"Just gone."

"Shit—I mean, damn." A grimace and a wry look to Ollie's dad. "I'm going to be late. My brother's getting back into town." He gathered his stuff. "Thanks for the use of the floor, Calvin."

Ollie wondered how her father could smile yet still be traced with deep lines of sadness. "You're always welcome, Deon," he said.

Deon paused on his way past. "Thanks, sir."

"Ollie." Her father waited for her to look at him before continuing. "Whenever you want to invite Carmen over, she's welcome."

The genuine tone of his voice, the way his gaze wavered, as if scared Ollie would jerk back and away, left her throat tight. "I'll ask her."

He gave a last wave at Sara before turning to leave. With a hand on the doorknob, he paused. "It's really nice having you all back in the house."

And he closed the door, leaving a heaviness in the room.

"I'm glad you two are talking again." Sara had dropped her textbook off the side of the bed. She flopped onto her back, staring up at the ceiling. "I was worried there for a while."

"For a while, so was I." Ollie stood by her desk a moment, listening to the watch at her wrist that ticked steadily, a sound she still needed next to her ear at night to sleep. The bed dipped when she fell onto her back next to Sara and stared straight up at the ceiling with her.

When had everything started to feel like she could cope again? It felt tenuous, like she was balanced on a wire. Would it just fall out from under her?

"So… Rae," she began.

A pillow hit Ollie in the face, and she pulled it off, sitting up on an elbow to narrow her eyes at Sara.

Who just smirked. "You deserved that."

"You made out in a bar last week for everyone to see, and then the other day she was waiting at school for you, all dressed in leather and looking stupidly hot, and you just disappeared with her."

Something flashed over Sara's face—a look, then blankness, and Ollie wondered if she'd imagined it.

"We went to her place."

Ollie's eyebrows rose, a stab of jealousy in her gut over the fact that she hadn't done that with Carmen. "I'm impressed. You guys go way back."

Sara was blinking up at the ceiling. "We do."

"I thought you hated each other." Ollie dropped back against the bed. Movement against Ollie's shoulder told her Sara had shrugged.

"We do."

"But…?" Ollie waited.

"I don't know… Rae was the only one in that foster house that kind of… I don't know…*got* me. But there's no *but*. We're just… I don't know… getting something out of our systems."

"Naked?"

A hand whacked Ollie on the leg, and she laughed, the sound of Sara's own laughter melding with her own.

If Carmen hadn't taken Mattie's hand that day long ago, would he have been okay? Would he be at a house right now, studying, about to be called to a home-cooked meal? Would he have spent the day in the routine of school, working toward a future that was more than this?

There were teenagers sprawled throughout the warehouse. A humid storm had brought more of them in at the same time. Some were playing cards. Others were sparring, the shouts and the sound of skin slapping against mats filtering into the room past the pounding sound of rain that echoed throughout the entire building. Some were sorting food in the kitchen area, organizing pallets and making sure they had enough for the night. Two had left earlier, garbage bags over their clothes, in hope of raiding a supermarket dump spot without being chased off.

Mattie was up a ladder, Dex up one next to him, and Dex was showing him how to deal with an electrical circuit. Apparently, Dex was trying to work out a way to tap into an electrical grid outside.

Whatever that meant.

Carmen really had no idea what they were doing, but Mattie had shown an interest. That had been all it took for Dex to pull out an ancient book on wiring and circuitry and for Mattie's eyes to light up.

With her feet up on a table, Carmen was keeping an eye on Mattie while she thumbed her way through a book Jia had recommended. And stressing about Sara.

Why had Rae had to bring her here?

Today she didn't have to be at the bar, but she was going by tomorrow. Last week, she and Dex had planned for the money she would have earned. They'd opened an account for her ages ago, the money piling up there, the debit card in a safety box at the bar. The hope that at sixteen she'd fall off the radar had so far held. Even with her Social Security number being used, no one had come knocking. Other kids had all managed it too. It was a flaw in the system but one that worked well for her.

It amazed her to think she had some money in a bank, that she would be able to go to a shop and buy something. But for now, all that money needed to accumulate, to prove she could support them later. For now, they weren't going anywhere, and they wouldn't get to stop picking through the food supermarkets deemed inedible. But the day was coming.

Carmen had seen others leave, one since she'd arrived and a couple the year she'd spent here before. Jia and Dex got them jobs, used connections to get scholarships for one girl to get into community college. They tried to always make sure the kids they helped on the streets got off the streets.

It all seemed surreal, like it couldn't happen for her.

Her stomach still twisted and turned and left her raw when she thought about what it all meant for Mattie, the options for their future.

A sharp breeze blew through, and Sara and Rae walked in.

Something cold ran down her spine. She'd talked to Rae about this. Not that her bringing Sara again made much difference after the first time, but still. She snapped the book shut and set it on the table, her hands resting on top of it. Sara said something that made Rae smirk. Some of the teens turned to look at the two of them, but most didn't pay attention: if Rae brought someone in, they were cool.

Yet to Carmen, the entire world had seemed to tilt, just as it had the other afternoon when Rae had brought Sara and disappeared upstairs with her. But not before Sara had caught sight of Carmen, head cocking at the image of her poring over a book with Mattie.

"Rae." Jia's voice was like a whip, and with a roll of her eyes, Rae went to Jia's room and shut the door behind her.

For a second, Sara pretended to avoid Carmen's gaze, her hands buried deep in her back pockets, and Carmen took a moment to take her in. Way back when her life hadn't made any sense but had made more than it did now, she'd liked Sara instantly. The girl had a smile big enough to break down defenses and was unerringly loyal to Ollie.

That was what worried Carmen.

Finally, Sara caught her eye. She straightened her shoulders and walked over. After a second's hesitation, she dropped into a chair across from Carmen. She was always one for a wink and a quick joke—but now she eyed Carmen, no hint of amusement.

"Carmen."

"Hello, Sara."

They stared a minute, and finally, Carmen glanced away. She needed to know. Rae had assured her Sara wasn't going to say anything, but she needed to ask. "Did you tell Ollie?"

Sara's eyebrows rose slightly. "No. I wanted to speak to you first."

"Thank you."

"I will, though, if you don't soon."

Carmen's heart stilled for a second before pounding too hard in her ears. "I never wanted to lie to Ollie. Even by omission."

"But you did."

Carmen nodded once. "But I did, yes." Sara's stare was unnerving. "Can I ask? Why haven't you told her?"

Sara shrugged, and for a moment, Carmen thought she wasn't going to answer. "I've been you. Maybe not the same, but I've been in the system. I don't know your situation, but I'm guessing there's a reason you haven't told her?"

Carmen jutted her chin toward Mattie, and Sara turned her head to look where she indicated. Slowly, Carmen let out a breath, as if to brace herself to say the truth. "That's Mattie. He's my little brother. We...we were separated once, in foster care. Neither of us had a good experience. This time..." Carmen watched Mattie slide down the ladder, take a screwdriver and start to climb again. He was so small, still so small. "I wasn't going to let that happen, not again."

Sara was looking back at her, and the gaze almost hurt, the intensity burning through Carmen and cutting to the meat of her. "You panicked that night we showed up in the bar. You were both runaways and thought we might let it slip."

"Yes."

Sara licked her lips. "Okay. Look." She rested her elbows on the table, leaning forward, "I get how that happened. I would have done the same. I've been in the system. It can end well sometimes. I was lucky this time round. But it can be shit."

There was something in her eyes that reflected what Carmen saw in Mattie's, and in Rae's, reflected what she saw in the mirror—something hurt and beaten and bruised. Something too big for small shoulders.

"So I get it. But Ollie... She's pretty special. And she's going to think you don't trust her."

Swallowing, Carmen held her gaze. "It was for Mattie."

"I know."

"I'll tell her."

Sara stood. "Good. Because I lied to my friend the other night, and I don't do that. Not to Ollie."

They shared a look, and Sara walked away to join Rae, who stood at the bottom of the stairs. Jia followed them with her eyes as they walked up and to the roof, only looking away to share a look with Carmen.

Carmen had to tell Ollie.

She had to—now.

They were supposed to be meeting on the weekend.

Ollie was going to stop by the bar. But it had been days since she'd last seen Carmen, and her body was humming with the need to be near her. All day, she'd played back and forth between going to surprise her and sticking to the plan. When she'd left the house, she'd paused on the doorstep. She'd turn back to go inside and then faced the path again and again. Eventually, she'd sighed at herself and had gotten on the bus.

It was hard, not being able to message or Facebook her, to have no contact. But in some ways, it was refreshing. Everything about her life in every other way was instant: school, cell, Internet, people... When she saw Carmen for the first time in days, watching her smile slowly unfurl and feeling a flip in her stomach, it felt true, earned.

She couldn't stay long. Ollie had to study, and she thought tonight she'd sit next to her father on the sofa and actually watch something together, to not feel the space pulling between them. To feel that thing she had once thought was too far broken.

It was early enough in the week that the bar was almost empty, with only a few regulars Ollie recognized. With a start and an inward chuckle, it occurred to her that if she could recognize others here, she was a regular too.

Dex was at the bar, chatting with one of the men, and simply waved at Ollie as she walked in. A month ago, she'd found out he liked to draw, and the two of them had spent hours talking about art. Ever since, he seemed lighter, more casual with her.

He glanced back toward the office door, then gestured to the end of the bar. When she sat, he put a Coke in front of her with a wink, and she thanked him, watching him move up and down the bar, wiping surfaces.

"Is Carmen here?"

It would be a pity if she didn't have to work today. Ollie had taken the risk, poring over her index cards on the bus to make herself feel like it wouldn't be a waste of time if she didn't see Carmen.

Dex nodded. "She's here. She'll be out in a minute."

"Thanks."

In Ollie's bag with her index cards was a journal, every page filled with a sketch or a painting. She kept pushing against the bag to feel the sharp edge of it, heart fluttering at the thought of giving it to Carmen. It seemed intimate, personal. Like giving over a piece of herself.

Dex went to the other end of the bar, unstacking glasses. A sound made Ollie turn around on her barstool to see Carmen stepping through the office door, the door snicking closed behind her.

"*Ollie.*" The name slipped from Carmen's lips like it always did: unbidden, easily, as if anything involving Ollie, Carmen couldn't help doing.

Which was true—when it came to Ollie, Carmen was powerless.

She was on a stool, twisted around to watch Carmen, and it made Carmen's heart speed up. Carmen wondered if that feeling would ever go away. Mattie was in the office behind her, it being one of the days he'd wanted to come with her, and Carmen hadn't wanted to say no; when she knew he was close, she could focus more, relax and move through the day, even with the worries that the attempted mugging had started.

But Ollie didn't know about him. While this would probably be the perfect opportunity to tell her—especially because she'd promised Sara—Carmen had wanted to do it when Mattie wasn't there. She wanted to give Ollie time to adjust to what Carmen had to say before holding Mattie out like an unwanted surprise. Keeping it all from her now would be easier, despite the guilt that licked at Carmen's insides. Rejection wasn't an option when Carmen didn't offer anything up to reject.

Ollie smiled at her, and Carmen returned it, walking forward and kissing her, their lips melding together for too short a period.

"This is a surprise," Carmen murmured.

"A good one?"

Carmen kissed her, an answer enough to draw out a contented hum from Ollie.

"I missed you." The murmur of Ollie's words against Carmen's lips was as good as a kiss.

Later, when she was in the warehouse, too hot and tired and nervous about life, she'd pull out the memory of those words and the way they whispered over her tongue, and everything bothering her would ease.

Yet still questions gnawed at her.

What if Ollie ran? What if this truth was too much, enough to weigh them down? What if Ollie saw it as an unacceptable secret or a betrayal?

"Are you okay?" Ollie had pulled away, making the cool air swirl around Carmen's hot cheeks.

"I need to tell you something."

Ollie cocked her head, looking at her with eyes so blue that Carmen would swear she could tip forward and fall into the never-ending depths of them. When Carmen had been small, she had loved to spin as fast as she could until she fell. She'd land heavy on the grass, and the blue of the sky would swirl above. It had been endless. That's how Carmen felt with Ollie.

"Okay." Ollie's voice sounded so trusting.

Carmen was busy gathering the words that were an undifferentiated swarm in her chest. How was she going to tell Ollie that one of the first things she'd really told her had been a lie? That Ollie knew nothing of Carmen's life?

But, she would plead, she knew *Carmen*, and Carmen knew *Ollie*.

Not for the first time, she wished she were at school, maybe in the locker room and pulling off her cleats, sweaty from training and sharing a secret look with Ollie when she walked in after PE.

Or sharing kisses behind stacks of books in the library.

Or sharing notes in lockers.

Sharing a life in general, one that melded and fit and didn't clash so badly that it left everything feeling like it wavered.

Maybe they'd be arguing because they shared exam time and were stressed, unsure and panicked. After, they'd whisper apologies as they shed clothes in Ollie's bedroom, trying to be quiet, but giggles spilling over.

Later, Carmen would realize she heard the door open—pushed open so hard it slammed against the wall, while all of this was clouding her mind.

"I want everyone out!"

The voice was loud, and the words took a second to click. Carmen turned, and right then, everything inside her went cold. Under her hand, Ollie's thigh twitched as she turned to see what was going on. There were five men, their faces pasty and white and glistening with nervous sweat. Each held something in their hands, a length of metal, a plank of wood, a bat. One of them was smacking a pry bar against his leg; another against the palm of his opposite hand.

It looked like something from a bad television show: a ridiculous cliché. Yet Carmen's hands went clammy. The weight of the cement her blood turned to jarred her, froze her in place. She recognized the one in the middle. His gaze was going from Carmen to Dex and back.

He was the guy she'd knocked out when he'd tried to mug her.

She'd done everything to keep Mattie and Ollie out of this world that lurked in the streets she lived in. But certain things couldn't be kept out of the habitat they roamed.

Dex caught her eye, the muscle in his jaw clenching. Every hair on Carmen's arm stood on end.

"You heard me! If you ain't a worker here, out." The man looked back to Carmen, his gaze sweeping over Ollie. Carmen's grip tightened on her leg. "'Cept that one, since you seem so fond of her."

The regulars hovered a minute, looking from one group of people to another.

"Go." Dex's voice was low, a sound Carmen knew.

One by one, the bar patrons slid off their stools and left, all except Ollie. Carmen took a deep breath, slowly, in through her nose. She needed to be centered. The way her heart started racing meant adrenaline was hitting her system; she would get erratic.

"Let her go." Carmen stared at them, unblinking. "She's just a customer." Her heart was in her throat.

The man sneered at her. "No."

Carmen dug her fingers into Ollie's leg.

Mattie.

"Who are they?" Ollie asked, her voice a whisper.

Carmen had heard Ollie angry, sad, and, recently, happy…but never scared, and the note struck a chord that left Carmen's ears ringing.

"The men that gave me a black eye."

Their ringleader snorted. "You gave us all concussions."

Ollie was looking from them to Carmen, and everything was coming undone, unwinding in front of Carmen. Mattie and Ollie needed to leave, to get somewhere. But they didn't know Mattie was here. Should she call attention to that fact or leave him where he was, safe for now?

She looked to Dex again, who had raised his hands and was slowly walking toward Carmen and Ollie behind the bar, distancing himself from the men. "Come on, guys. The girl's got nothing to do with any of this."

"Neither do some of my boys here." The thug cocked his head. "That don't seem to matter." That sneer was something Carmen wanted to rip off his face.

Dex ducked under the bar to stand next to Carmen as they both shifted to stand just in front of Ollie. There was a back exit through the storage room. If they could distract them enough, maybe she could get Ollie to grab Mattie and get out of there.

Would there be enough time?

"What do you want?" Carmen asked.

"Payback. See, it took me a few days, once that concussion wore off, but I realized who we'd tried to mug. I realized he—"he indicated with the bat to Dex, jabbing it into the air "—was a part of that bitch's group who turned me away. Then you all had the balls to knock us out."

"You had the 'balls' to try and take our shit." Carmen stared him down. "Leave now, and it's even."

Her fist clenched. A knuckle popped.

Ollie. Mattie.

He snorted, the guys behind him shifting uneasily. The sound of a door opening behind her made Carmen close her eyes for a second and take a deep breath.

"Carmen?"

He knew not to come out. Never come out. That was the rule.

"I heard yelling."

Carmen opened her eyes, not looking away from the men in front of her. Some of them glanced at Mattie, eyebrows rising. One shifted, as if uncomfortable. "Go back, Mattie."

"No."

Dex turned. "Mattie, little dude, go back."

Steps, small and light, and then the brush of his shoulder as he stood next to her. "No."

Carmen put her arm over his chest, her hand cupping his opposite shoulder. For only a second, before she jerked him behind her to stand next to Ollie, she felt through his small chest how his heart pounded hard and fast against her forearm.

"Get the fuck outta here, kid." The man narrowed his eyes. "One chance."

Mattie and Ollie stood behind them, the men with weapons in front.

Before Carmen could tell Ollie to grab Mattie and take him through the back, the men stepped forward as one, weapons raised. Instincts brought Carmen in step with Dex as he moved toward them.

She ducked a swing and heard a crack as Dex's fist collided with someone's nose. Her knee connected with someone's groin, the skin under it giving easily and stealing all his breath.

"Get out, Mattie!" Carmen ducked again as two swung in unison, and she could feel the air caress her head as they moved over her. "Ollie! Take him out back!"

Blinding pain lanced over her back as something hit her hard. For a terrifying minute, her breath stilled, her chest spasming, until finally she gulped air, a huge, wonderful lungful of it. Unable to really enjoy it, Carmen turned quickly, her foot rounding into a kick. She hit the person as hard as she could in the diaphragm and kicked again, landing square in his chest. He went down. Her back was screaming.

Dex had blood over his eye. A fist hit her ribs, and something collided with her eye, the same one that had been hit before. She saw stars, then cleared her head just enough to see that someone was swinging again, and she danced back as a small blur stepped in front of her.

"Mattie!"

She tried to grip his shirt, to wrench him backward, and all but throw him at Ollie, but he danced forward, the cotton material falling uselessly past the tips of her fingers. He ducked to avoid a swing and landed a fist right in the man's solar plexus. It was beautiful, and it was everything they'd taught him, but he was a nine-year-old boy, and they were grown men.

The man flung his hand out, catching Mattie in the face in a backhanded motion with a two-by-four.

Her brother flew backward and landed hard, and Carmen's world bottomed out. Already, though, he was pushing himself up to sit on his knees, wavering. She stepped forward over Mattie so he was half between her legs, jabbed out with her fist to catch the man in the throat, then used his gasp for air to hit him square in the temple, the softest part. He went down hard, and she kicked again, red behind her eyelids and desperation in her swing.

Mattie was still on his knees, which meant he was okay for now. Carmen stepped forward so he was behind her. It left Carmen between the two guys left standing.

Dex was breathing hard, one eye closed, and then she didn't watch him anymore as she stepped toward one of the two guys.

Her target was her age, maybe younger. Peach fuzz just barely graced his chin, and he licked his lips, his hands twisting on the handle of the bat in his grip. His gaze darted to the floor, where his friends lay groaning, and back to Carmen.

"You can go," she offered, the sight of him, the look in his eye too much like her own.

"Fuck you." His shoulder dipped to easily indicate his swing and trajectory. There was nothing trained about him, about any of them. They all fought with fury, with anger, adrenaline clearly running their systems. With confidence in their numbers.

She ducked once, twice, stepped into his space with her shoulder, driving it into his chest. The heel of her hand came up, breaking his nose with a *crack*. When he bent forward and his hands came up to cup it instinctively, she drove her elbow down onto his neck.

He dropped like a stone. Dex was already standing over the other, chest heaving for air.

Carmen spun and dropped to a knee, cupping Mattie's cheeks, her fingers trembling. Red was blooming over one cheek and eye, the entire side of his face swollen already, his gaze unfocused. He blinked almost lazily. But it was the slightest cut, just a smear of blood. It was the swelling that concerned her. The dazed look. "Mattie. Are you okay?"

He swayed a little, then Carmen wanted to shake him as a smile crawled onto his lips, even as they quivered. "I hit him."

"You did. And he hit you. Shit, Mattie, what were you thinking?"

His lip really was trembling now, his eyes glimmering. Carmen's throat tightened, sick to her stomach at the memory of how his head had whipped back, the yelp that had fallen from his mouth.

"They hit you." His voice broke over the words.

Carmen pulled him toward her, wrapping her arms around him as he buried his face into her neck. She looked up at Ollie, whose pupils were so blown that her eyes seemed black. Her phone was to her ear as she stared at Carmen.

There were no words to drag up and give to Ollie. Carmen had nothing, nothing to say. Adrenaline was pumping through her blood, layering her arteries and leaving her breathless and sick with it. Sick with the memory of skin giving under her fist and her brother's red eye and Dex's blood. There had been a horrified shout as something had struck Carmen's back, a shout she was just now realizing had been Ollie's. "Are you okay?" Carmen finally asked her.

Ollie nodded, the motion jerky.

"Good. Who have you called?"

Ollie swallowed, and Carmen could see her fingers shaking from there. "The police."

Carmen thought her heart stopped. "The police?"

Her brow furrowed as she looked from Carmen to Dex and back again. "Yeah, of course."

Carmen didn't let go of Mattie, turning to stare at Dex.

He looked down at her. "Go through the back."

"What about this?" Carmen indicated to the groaning men on the ground.

Dex nudged one with his foot, the man already trying to get to his knees. "Get your friends up and get out. The cops are on their way."

"You called the fucking cops?" The man slurred the words.

Something angry in Carmen hoped his jaw was broken.

Dex's voice stayed low, chilled. "Get. Out." He looked back to Carmen, his eyes softening. "The back. Go. Now. I'll handle this."

Carmen wrapped her arms around Mattie tighter and stood up, grunting as she pulled him up with her. He wrapped his legs, too long for this but too small for what had just occurred, around her waist. The moment he didn't complain at being carried out, she knew something was really wrong.

Not looking at Ollie, she walked past her. She could feel Mattie's heart against her own chest, this time a comfort in its calm, steady thumping. But what had just happened? How had this happened?

"Follow me," she grunted.

And Ollie did.

Carmen went through the door to the storage room and out the back to the alley, fear crawling up her spine. Or was that pain? Her muscles were laced with fire.

Cops and an underage runaway, with her runaway nine-year-old brother.

"Carmen!"

Ollie's voice was like a whip, and Carmen thought she cracked in the middle at the sound of it. Her back was protesting, an ache so deep she was worried she'd drop Mattie. Breathing hurt. Ollie was staring at her, and Carmen wanted to move toward her, to let out this feeling filling her chest, to finally sob, to burst against Ollie's neck and let this girl run her fingers through Carmen's hair.

But that was not her life. And the police were coming. Mattie was injured and so was Carmen, and she had to move. Now.

"Ollie, I have to go." And Carmen hated that those were her words.

"Why? The police are—are on their way. They'll help."

"No, they won't." She let Mattie slide down her body, and he swayed slightly. She gripped him as close as she could. "Ollie, I really have to go. I'm not in foster care, I never was. I didn't want to do it again. I took Mattie and ran. He's my brother."

Mattie's fingers clutched her shirt, digging into the skin of Carmen's belly, grounding her, reminding her that he was why she had to walk away from Ollie in what was the worst possible moment to do so.

Ollie deserved so much more than that.

"Carmen..."

"We've been on the street." The words had built for so long they came easily, now. "Dex's been helping me. Rae too, and some others you don't know. But if they see us, a minor with her kid brother, we'll be back in the system, and I'll never see him again. I have to go."

Something was breaking over Ollie's face, and Carmen couldn't stay to see it unfold. She couldn't catch her as she fell apart, or stand while she yelled, or even take her help. Carmen needed to go. "Ollie, go up the alley to the front of the bar. Tell the cops you heard yelling and called them but saw nothing. Dex will do the rest. I have to go."

Carmen bent her knees, hauling Mattie back up and, again, he didn't protest but wrapped himself around her. Concern bounded at her temples, but for now, she needed to get them away, to the warehouse.

Anywhere but here.

A siren wailed, the sound bouncing off the walls, blue-and-red light filling the space. In her arms, Mattie trembled, his face in her neck. She heard Mattie mumble, so softly Ollie wouldn't hear from where she stood, "No. Not again."

His fingers grasped her back and pressed their chests closer together, and her heart broke at words she'd heard what felt like forever ago.

In the red and blue, Ollie looked at her like she didn't know her. Carmen turned and walked the other way, stumbling through the hole in the fence and clutching Mattie closer.

She didn't look back.

CHAPTER 19

CARMEN'S ARMS WERE ACHING.

They were like lead, heavy and useless. Against the back of her thigh, Mattie's heel bounced, his leg floppy, deadweight in her arms.

"Hey, Mattie." She grunted the words out and paused for a second in an alley, one she was only walking through to try to avoid the looks they'd get on the streets. Mattie was too big in her arms. Her face hurt and was surely bruising already; his must be doing the same. "Mattie." She gave the word a sharper inflection. Hitching him up her body, she hoped jostling him would get an answer.

"Mm?"

The sound was sleepy, disjointed, but it sent a jolt of relief through Carmen's entire body. "Stay awake," she ordered.

"Mm."

That's all she knew—hard hit to the head, and a person needed to stay awake.

She ducked through a hole in some wire, breathing easier at the sight of the warehouse ahead. Her arms were screaming in protest now. If she let herself think about it, the pain radiating through her back and ribs was extreme enough that her arms might give out.

Why didn't she know more? He could have a concussion. Carmen barely knew what that meant. Something about dizziness and their pupils? Too wide? Like dots? Or was one of those for drugs?

Her mother's pupils had done both, depending.

With panting breaths, she kicked her foot against the door in a pattern barely discernible as the one required. There was no way she was putting Mattie down now. Not until she could sit him on the sofa.

"Come on, come on."

The window slid open, Rae's eyes peering out, just as they had the first time Mattie and Carmen had stood here. But this time, when the window slammed shut, the door opened straight away. Carmen pushed past and heard the door slam behind her.

"What the hell, Carmen?"

Carmen barely registered Rae's question.

Not many people were in. It was too early. A couple of teens, slightly dirty and skinny, lounged on a sofa, watching them with their arms crossed. The space was mostly empty.

"Move," Carmen barked.

They blinked at her, then jumped up, moving back and away, their eyes trained on Mattie. At the nearest sofa, Carmen let Mattie slide down her body. He sat on the couch, eyes barely open, swaying slightly. Squatting in front of him, Carmen held him by his shoulders. His bones sank against her palms, as they always did.

He was bleeding from where the wood had split his cheek.

"Mattie?"

He blinked twice, before focusing on her, just barely. His big brown eyes were vaguely cloudy. She could barely see the injured one, the swelling was so bad. The pupils, if she squinted, looked different sizes. That couldn't be good.

"Hi," Mattie said.

Carmen swallowed, a lump in her throat so big she thought she might choke on it. "Hey."

"What happened?"

Carmen looked up. Now both Rae and Jia stood behind the couch, both hovering.

"Shit, your eye." Rae was staring at her as if the harder she looked, the faster Carmen would give her information.

Her pulse was pounding; everything hurt. God, Ollie's face. The look in her eyes. Carmen couldn't think about that right now.

Jia rounded the sofa and sat next to Mattie, cupping his cheeks, her eyes searching his face while he blinked up at her slowly. "Carmen, who did this?"

What had happened? It was already a blur in her mind.

"Five guys, one of them the guy that tried to mug Dex and me way back. They came into the bar, kicked the customers out, then tried to have a go at Dex and I—"

Jia's head whipped around, and Carmen shook her head. "No, no, Dex is fine," she finished. "We took them out, but Ollie and Mattie were both there. Mattie tried to help; he got hit by a plank of wood. Ollie called the damn cops, so Mattie and I had to run. Dex stayed behind to clear it up."

"Ollie?"

Carmen looked up sharply. Sara was there. Where had she come from? "Is she okay?"

Carmen nodded tightly before she turned back to Jia. "Is Mattie okay?"

Jia's thumb brushed over his cheekbone. Gently, she pulled back his eyelids. "He needs a doctor."

"Fuck."

It was Rae that swore, but it may as well have been Carmen.

"Get him to a doctor, then," Sara snapped. "He needs it."

Carmen gnawed at her bottom lip, one hand still on Mattie and the other wrapped around her own ribs. She bounced a little, her behind resting on her heels. It hurt, but the movement helped her focus. A minor. With another minor. Off the street with an injury. They'd call social services. He'd get taken away again.

Jia was still staring at Mattie. "It might not be serious, but I'm not a doctor. And I think any of our medical contacts would just say to take him to the ER. We can't mess around with head injuries." She finally looked to Carmen. "Did he pass out? Vomit? Say anything that didn't make sense?"

Carmen shook her head, everything spinning around her except for her brother, small and dazed in front of her. If she lifted her hand off him, she thought he'd disappear, sucked into the nightmare this evening had become. "No. None of that, but he's gotten more and more out of it."

Mattie turned to her, blinking heavily. As if on cue, he lurched and vomited over the edge of the couch, the splash of it hitting Carmen's pants. Pitching forward, she helped him stay sitting as he heaved, her hand rubbing circles on his back. A cloth appeared in front of her, and she plucked it up, wiping Mattie's face.

"That's it." Carmen stood. "I have to get him to the ER."

Jia stood too. Carmen bent and heaved Mattie up, not caring if he threw up again all over her back. He flopped against her.

A full-grown man had hit her brother in the head with a plank of wood.

"How?" Carmen asked, turning to Jia. How did she get him there? How did she deal with this? Everything was bigger than it ever had been, rearing over her: too heavy, too large. Someone needed to tell her what to do. Her throat was tight. She needed someone, for once, to do something for her.

"Ambulance... No." Jia shook her head. "Follow me."

Although she felt as if she were going to snap open and fall apart right there, Carmen did as she was told. Her ribs still ached—burned, really. Her face hurt. Mattie was like a sack of bricks in her arms as she took unsteady steps after Jia. She stopped in the doorway to Jia's office and watched as Jia slipped a brick out of the wall and pulled out a wad of cash.

"Take a taxi. This is for emergencies."

Jia shoved some bills into the pocket of Carmen's pants.

"Jia..." Carmen licked her lips, staring at her. "What do I tell them?"

Her lips pressed together as she seemed to think, her eyes on Carmen's cheek. She met Carmen's gaze. "There's no real way out of this. They'll have to know."

"Jia..."

"We'll deal with it when it happens, Carmen."

As she clutched Mattie closer, her forearms holding him under his bony bottom, Carmen wondered if she could carry him again. But she had to. "Okay."

"Do you want me to come?"

That offer, right then, meant everything. But Carmen shook her head; a prickling in her eyes made her blink and look away. "No. It's better for everything here if you don't."

And Carmen turned, almost running into Rae and Sara. She pushed past them. She needed a taxi, a hospital.

Rae walked up from behind her and held the door open.

"Carmen!"

Carmen paused. Sara was watching her, her face unreadable. "Ollie's fine, right?"

"She was when I saw her."

Guilt leaving her sick, Carmen walked down the alley. She went as fast as she could, waving down a taxi when she reached a road busy enough.

"The closest hospital." The woman up front looked at her through the rearview mirror, then turned all the way around in her seat, her gaze sweeping over them both. What did she see when she looked at them? A Hispanic teen clutching a little black boy, both looking beat-up. She pulled Mattie closer, protectiveness searing through her.

"Is he okay?"

Her voice was kind, and Carmen thought she may cry. "I don't know."

The woman gave a nod and pulled into traffic.

"Mattie?"

He groaned and shook his head.

"Mattie!"

She didn't shout, but his head lolled, and he looked up at her.

"What?" There was a slur to his voice.

Ice froze her stomach. "Stay awake."

He made a grumbling sound, his eyelashes fluttering against his cheek.

"What happened?" The driver's eyes were on her again through the mirror.

Carmen stared back. "It was…fast. We were mugged on our way home from school."

She didn't believe her. Carmen could see it. But she said, "Okay."

They didn't speak anymore. By the time they pulled up at the hospital, Carmen had spent the entire drive trying to keep Mattie awake, with fear pricking at her every limb. The driver jumped out, pulled the door open, and helped Carmen stand and get Mattie back into her arms.

When Carmen tried to give her the cash, she pushed her hand away. "Take care of him."

Throat tight, Carmen blinked. "Thank you." And she turned and walked inside.

Ollie's fingers were trembling.

Her room wasn't big enough.

The conversation she'd had with the cops was a blur, the memory of Dex explaining an accident away vague in the back of her mind.

What wasn't vague was the look on Carmen's face when Ollie had said she'd called the cops. Because why wouldn't she do that when a group of five men came in and started a fight? When one had hit Carmen's back with a piece of pipe and Carmen had cried out in pain so loudly it had made Ollie cringe? When that tiny boy who was apparently Carmen's brother had been hit in the face?

Who wouldn't call the cops?

Maybe she wouldn't have done it if she'd known the situation. If she'd known Carmen was a runaway. That her brother was one. He looked so young—Ollie was no judge of kids and ages; she had no experience with them. But he was small and skinny, even when he'd stood puffed out in front of Carmen like he thought he could protect her.

Even when he'd ducked a hit and swung like he knew what he was doing.

Like Carmen had.

And Dex. They all knew how to fight.

If she'd known that, that Carmen was hiding her younger brother, that they could hold their own, maybe she wouldn't have called the cops. Then she wouldn't have had to see such a look of anger and betrayal flash over Carmen's eyes. Directed at *Ollie*. If Carmen had damn well trusted her, maybe Ollie would have done things differently.

She clenched her fists, and her nails bit into her palm.

Who even was Carmen? What did Ollie know? She knew what she'd seen flashes of, accidentally, of foster care and mentions of some minor charges. But what did she know of her life?

Carmen's mother was dead, like Ollie's. She knew nothing of Carmen's father. She'd not even known she had a brother. All these months Ollie had thought Carmen had been in school, in a house. But instead, she was living on the streets.

Her stomach was burning. Ollie felt betrayed, and anger flashed in her gut at the betrayal that had been on *Carmen's* face. How could she be betrayed when all Ollie had ever done was given her everything she could?

Berated and angry and confused and…damn it. Worried.

Mattie had been hit hard. So had Carmen. She had turned, holding her brother and looking too small to do so, and ran, and Ollie had absolutely no way of finding out if she was okay. If that boy was okay.

The last thing she'd seen was Carmen's brother's eyes, the same shape as Carmen's, the color darker, as they stared at her, dazed.

When someone knocked at her window, Ollie jumped, her hand landing on her chest. Her heart pumped against it, thumping, as she looked up and squinted. Sara was staring at her.

Swallowing, Ollie took a deep breath. She wanted to scream, to cry, to throw something. She wanted to ignore Sara so she could be alone with the maelstrom in her chest. At the same time, she wanted to let Sara wrap her arms around her while Ollie let out a sob.

More than anything, she wanted her mom to be alive. She wanted her to be here so Ollie could stumble to the living room and fall against her, all cool hands and the brush of lips against her forehead.

Ollie stood and opened the window.

Sara stared up at her. "Hey."

"Hi." Ollie's voice was raw, emotion stripping it clean. "Why are you at the window?"

"It's late. I thought your dad might not let me in."

"He's at some work dinner, a conference thing. Come on."

Sara clambered in, Ollie helping her through. "Are you okay?" Sara asked.

Ollie clenched her jaw and shook her head. If she did it hard enough, could she shake off the weight in her chest, shake it away so she could know what she really felt about Carmen?

"What happened?" Sara asked.

Why was she asking? Ollie narrowed her eyes. "How do you know something did?"

Sara blinked and then bit her lip, looking away, looking down, anywhere but at Ollie. "No reason."

"You can't lie for shit."

Sara looked back at her. "I saw Carmen. And Mattie. I know something happened. I know you were there."

Ollie froze. "What—how did you see her?"

Sara stared at her, her lips parted and moving like she wanted to say something. But there was nothing but silence.

"Wait." Ollie froze. "Did you know about Mattie?"

Rae. Carmen had said Rae had been helping her. And Rae and Sara were...something. "Sara, did you know?"

"I only found out the other week, by accident. I—"

"You knew? For weeks? You knew she was hiding all this?" That betrayal was back, thick in her veins and thundering through her body, to sink into her muscles, her bones. It layered every part of her.

"Ollie, listen. Please." Sara's hands came up as though she was about to grab her, but then she seemed to think better of it. "I only just found out, and I told her she had to tell you soon or I would. That it wasn't fair. I just... I've been there, you know?" Her eyes were pleading. "I didn't want to let you down, but I know how scared she must be."

Breathing hard through her nose, Ollie tried to calm down. She tried to slow that slamming pulse that spread this feeling deeper inside her. "Sara." Her voice cracked. "You tell me everything."

Unshed tears were in Sara's eyes, and she shook her head. "I do, I still do. But this wasn't mine, Ollie. Can you understand that? It wasn't mine. It was deeper than that. This is serious. She's a runaway with a kid brother."

Ollie hiccupped, and finally, Sara stepped forward and wrapped her arms around her. Ollie's forehead dug into her shoulder.

"Ollie," Sara murmured, her hand running up and down her back. "I'm so sorry."

"Is she okay?" Ollie's voice was muffled, her face still buried in Sara's neck.

"She seemed it when I saw her, a bit beat-up. But Mattie..."

Ollie pulled back and looked at her. "What?"

"They think he has a concussion. Maybe more."

"God, Sara..." Ollie swallowed. "He got hit so hard." She had never seen anything like that. The violence everyone there had doled out.

And Carmen in the middle of it, more than holding her own. The fierceness in her voice when she'd shouted for Ollie to take Mattie and leave. The shock had rooted Ollie to the ground, making it impossible to move as she watched a pipe go over Carmen's back and watched Carmen shatter a guy's nose. As she ducked two at once like she knew what she was doing. The way Ollie had finally snapped back to earth and reached for her brother, who Ollie figured Mattie was, but her hand had only managed to graze his shirt as he'd ducked into the fray.

"He'll be okay." The doubt lacing Sara's voice left Ollie cold.

The room was full of sniffing, coughing, and the crying of babies. For a second, Carmen stood, blinking in the fluorescent light, Mattie's face still against her neck. With shaking knees, she stepped forward to the desk that said *Admissions*. "Excuse me?"

The man at the desk held up a finger, typing at the keyboard in front of him with the other hand. He didn't look up.

Carmen waited a few seconds. "Please, we need help."

The man finally glanced up. "Take a seat."

She flopped into the chair that was there, Mattie wrapped around her. He shifted slightly, the movement relieving her a little.

"What's happened?" His eyes were still on the screen in front of him.

"It's not for me. I'm fine. It's my brother."

The man straightened, intently looking at Mattie. He'd clearly thought he was asleep. "What's his name?"

He watched her openly, his hands over the keyboard again. Did she lie? Would they know?

"Mattie. Please, we were mugged. They hit him in the face with a two-by-four and—"

The man stood up immediately, walking around the desk and squatting by the chair. "Mattie?" he asked.

Mattie rolled his head a little to blink at him.

"My name's Viktor. Can I touch your face?"

Mattie just stared at him, and Viktor reached forward, Carmen shifting so Mattie wasn't so tight against her chest.

He gently probed Mattie's face with his fingers, then he pulled a flashlight out of his pocket and shone it in his eyes, all the while asking her questions. "Did he lose consciousness immediately?"

"No."

"Has he since?"

"No, but he's really out of it, more and more. He may have fallen asleep not long after. In the taxi, I couldn't really keep him awake."

"Mattie, follow my finger?" Viktor moved his hand like a cross, one finger held out. "Has he vomited?"

"Once."

"Good job, Mattie." From Viktor's face, Carmen knew he was lying. "Okay, Mattie. How old are you."

A pause. "Nine."

Carmen nodded, relieved, and Viktor asked, "What day is it?"

"Friday?"

No, it wasn't. That relief was gone like it hadn't even appeared. Now Carmen wanted to throw up. He always knew what day it was. It was part of the educational stuff they did with Dex, a dash of normalcy.

"Okay, and who is with you right now?"

Mattie turned slowly and stared at her. Every hair stood on end when she noticed the eye was almost swollen shut now, a grotesque purple. Far worse than before.

"Um…" He blinked at her, and Carmen couldn't breathe. Ten long seconds passed, and his words were a little slurred like they would be when he was younger and tired. "Carmen. My sister."

Viktor looked at her, and she nodded.

"All right. Great, buddy. Do you remember how you got here?"

Mattie pushed back a little off her chest, looking around, blurry and lost. "My head really hurts."

"I bet it does, and we're going to do something about that. But do you remember how you got here?"

Mattie looked around again, his gaze going back to Carmen, then to Viktor. He shook his head then blanched. "My head really hurts."

"Okay." Viktor looked to Carmen. "You're just going to wait here a few short minutes. I want to get him through straightaway. Is there an adult I can call?"

Carmen hated that question. She hated that it was always assumed someone older existed, someone more qualified than she was, for Mattie.

Maybe there should be. If there was, he wouldn't be here.

"My parents are away."

She could lie as long as she liked, but she knew it was going to catch up with her.

"Okay, well, we're obliged to call someone. Do you have a number?"

Viktor was looking at her, and she thought for a moment she saw empathy floating in his eyes.

Then Mattie vomited again, and Carmen wanted to thank him even as his shoulders heaved a third time. Forgetting bureaucratic procedure for the moment, Viktor flew away and reappeared with a vomit bag and a towel.

Five minutes barely passed before they were taken through into the ER. Wincing in the sterile whiteness of it all, Carmen sat on a bed with Mattie in her lap. A doctor appeared, repeating much of what Viktor had done, a nurse taking observations, tutting at some of the numbers.

Carmen sat, feeling his heart beat hard and fast against her palm. Who had taken all the air out of the room? Everything was bright, and the words said to her were melding together, along with the faces that appeared and disappeared. When they took him for a scan, they wouldn't let Carmen go with him. She was left sitting on the bed, everything around her crisp and white and shining. The sheets under her almost crackled. Her arms felt empty, and she bent forward, wrapping them around her chest. It hurt. She cried out at the pressure.

"Hon?" A nurse whose name Carmen couldn't remember was in front of her. "I'm Siya. Can I have a look at you?"

"Why?"

Siya laughed, a huff, her skin a liquid brown that was the perfect match for her eyes. Her accent took a moment to place, it was so soft, and then it clicked with Carmen. Indian, like one of her teachers had been at school.

Siya stepped forward slowly, as if she thought Carmen may run. Carmen didn't know how to tell her she wouldn't be going anywhere without her brother.

"Your face looks pretty bad. Not as bad as your brother's, though, but still. And I can see you're clutching your ribs. Let me take a look?"

Carmen eyed her, but Siya just stood, hands raised slightly as if to show she meant no harm. Finally, Carmen nodded.

With a flick of her wrist, Siya pulled the curtains around the bed. Her fingers were gentle against Carmen's face, and Carmen closed her eyes, only just stopping herself from leaning into the touch. The woman was plump, kind, soft. Carmen wanted to fall into her and let out the sob of worry that seemed permanently caught in her throat. She wanted Ollie. She wanted her brother back.

Carmen wanted…

"Okay, hon. Open your eyes so I can check with my light?"

The light was bright, sending a throb through Carmen's skull.

"Good, that's good. Just what we want to see. Now, can you lift your shirt?"

Obediently, Carmen pulled it up, wincing, unable to raise her arms too high. How had she carried Mattie?

Siya sucked in a breath through her teeth. "Well now, that looks nasty." Her fingers were gentle again, probing along her ribs and against her back, then again over her stomach.

"I'm fine." The words tasted like sawdust, and Siya didn't even bother to comment on them.

"Okay. I don't think anything is broken, but I think your ribs are badly bruised. There's not much we can do about that, unfortunately. It's going to hurt for a while, but we'll set you up with some pain relief."

Carmen's looked quickly to her face. She had no money for that. Even the money in her bank account wouldn't cover this visit. Especially with Mattie. That crack they'd disappeared into was spitting them back out.

Siya silently checked her heart rate and blood pressure, or possibly her oxygen; Carmen wasn't really sure.

"All of this looks good. Lots of superficial problems." She sat on a stool on wheels next to the bed, partly between Carmen's legs. With a hand on her knee, she looked up at her. "Now. Your brother is going to have to be admitted. You want to tell me what's going on?"

And Carmen did, because she saw no other way out of it. And, really, the overwhelming relief of it caught in her chest as the words spilled out.

CHAPTER 20

IT WAS LATE. THE HALLWAYS of the hospital were dim but not entirely dark. The hospital room was so silent it was eerie. Everything was in shadow, but not so much that Carmen couldn't see. It reminded her of the rooms in the group home, where the light was never really gone.

The clock on the wall said it was just before one in the morning. She was always up late—hazards of her job and, simply, the life she led. The warehouse was always buzzing until all hours.

Her own mind was buzzing now.

What she had to do.

How she could do it.

If she could do it.

Mattie lay in the bed, engulfed by the largeness of it. The sheets seemed extra white, almost as if they were glowing against his skin and the dim room. He was a little darker than Ollie, but barely. The thought of Ollie left a hollow feeling in her gut, and she swallowed past it, pushed Ollie as far back into her mind as she could.

She stroked her finger over his hand, the palm of it curling, creased with lines. The skin around his eye and cheek was already deeply purple, speckled with black.

A night or two for observation, it had been decided, what with the severity. What with him not having somewhere safe to be discharged to. That made Carmen's stomach hurt, partly with indignation: there was nowhere safer for Mattie than with her. But it was also partly with the sickening truth of it. Looking at him, it was obvious he was anything but safe.

She'd done that to him. Maybe she hadn't been the one to hit him, but her choices had led the two of them here. When she touched his hair, brushing his forehead, her fingers were trembling. What a strange thing to see in this bizarre, clean room.

A nurse would be in again soon to do his hourly neurological observations. Before they'd moved Mattie to the children's ward, the doctor had assured her he would be fine with a lot of rest. That was what Carmen was repeating like a mantra: he would be fine, he would be fine, he would be *fine*.

Carmen needed to go. Visiting hours were long over, and Mattie was mostly settled. The last time someone had checked on him, she'd promised to leave soon.

They all thought she was eighteen. She'd told Siya that.

Even if the hospital let her stay, social services would be arriving to assess the situation in the morning, and Carmen needed to be gone.

"Mattie." Her voice was hoarse, breaking past her lips.

His one good eye fluttered.

"Mattie. Wake up."

His eye opened, glassy and unfocused. The drugs were strong, especially for a kid who had never really taken anything beyond children's aspirin. "Carmen." It was a rasp, but it was something.

"Hey."

He licked his lips, and she grabbed a glass of water, helping him pull his shoulders from the bed to suck down some water through a straw. His lips were chapped. When he settled back, his one eye blinked at her. "What happened?"

"What do you remember?"

He seemed more coherent than any of the other times he'd sporadically woken before.

He swallowed, taking in the room before settling his gaze back on her. She kept his hand in hers, half on the bed to be as close as possible. His fingers wrapped around her own and squeezed tightly.

"There were some guys… They were angry?"

"Yeah?"

He shook his head, then winced. "Nothing else."

She gave him a small smile, which was lathered in her affection and exasperation all at once. "You played the hero and tried to help. One hit you with some wood. We had to get you to the ER."

"I'm in the hospital?"

"Yeah." They'd said he may never remember the actual incident.

"My head hurts."

"Yeah, it would do. You have a fractured cheekbone and eye socket. And a pretty bad concussion. They want to keep you in here a couple of days but said you should be fine."

"But…the police? What… How?"

Carmen licked her lips and tried to whisper her words like they were normal and not shredding her apart. "Mattie…you really hurt your head. They called social services."

She saw the words wash over him, the slow blink before they registered. How he started to breathe too fast, struggling to sit up.

"We have to go." His voice was high.

She pushed her hands against his chest, lifted one to rest over his forehead, trying to hold him down. "Mattie, stay still!"

He struggled for only a second more before flopping down, chest heaving, his face foggy with pain. "We have to go."

The whimper he emitted was too much for her. "Mattie, please." Her hand still cupped his forehead, and she stood, bending over the bed and resting her own forehead over her hand, their noses almost brushing.

His breathing slowed, eased a little.

"Listen to me, okay?" She waited for his full attention before she started again. "I want you to try something for me. I want you to try, like I tried with you, when we ran. Can you do that?"

She was hoping he'd say okay. Instead, he stared up at her with his one good eye. "What? Try what?"

"I want you to try a foster home." He sucked in a breath, and she rushed to keep going. "We don't have a choice. We can't run now. You're really hurt, Mattie. You need the hospital."

"But—" He gulped in air, and a tear leaked out of his good eye, followed by another.

She could feel his breath all over her face, warm and wet and filled with panic. "But I need you."

She tried not to show the way those words broke her heart, the way everything was falling apart around her. "I need you too." Her voice couldn't break over the words like that, not when he had to believe this was the right thing. "But I also need you safe. And we have no voice here—they'll come in the morning, and you have to stay. But Mattie—I have a plan, okay? One to get us back together. But you have to be patient."

He coughed a sob. "What? What plan?"

"You're going to tell them you found me the other day and that I was taking you to a police station when we were mugged. You don't remember anything about it. Okay?"

When he nodded, she smiled, shaky and painful.

"Good. And before that, you were under bridges, in tunnels, with other kids and alone. Always be vague."

"Vague?"

"It means don't give lots of details."

"Why?"

"Because." She curled her hand into a fist over his heart, the beat of it soothing. She wanted to cup his cheek but was too scared to hurt him, so she ran her hand from his forehead into his hair. "Because once I'm eighteen, I'm out of the system, like a switch. And I can get all those stupid life things sorted out, like an apartment. It was never going to work before. I was dreaming. But this *could*. If you're patient, are in the system legitimately and give me some time, I'll make sure we can be together as soon as possible."

She hoped that was true.

He shook his head. "No." He was choking on his own tears. "No. I want to be with *you*."

"I want you with me too. But think about it. I'll find out what school you're in. I'll visit. Then as soon as I'm eighteen, I'll visit legally. They can't stop me if they don't know it was me you ran off with. And then I can get you legally. With a judge in the court, and—and papers, and something permanent, yeah?"

He shook his head again, weaker, his head moving against her palm. "I don't want to be alone. I want to be with you and Rae and Dex and Jia. Not alone."

"You won't be. Mattie, you won't be. I'll get you back."

"What if you don't?"

"I will." Her voice was stronger than she felt. "I will, because you and me? We belong together." She wouldn't cry. If she did, he would lose it completely. "Can you do that for me?"

With a shudder, he nodded.

She made him repeat the story back to her. "Good. That's good."

His hand tightened its grip over hers. "Don't go."

"I'll stay until you're asleep."

He resisted for as long as he could, but medication and injury pulled him under.

Would he sleep okay, alone, in the new foster home? Would he feel safer? Was this really the best idea?

She sat stroking his head, her other hand against his chest until sure he was asleep, the type of sleep he went into when nothing could wake him. When he was breathing evenly, deeply, Carmen stood and walked through the door. She paused once, looking back and memorizing the way he sprawled in the bed, then walked down the hallway and ducked out.

The memory of his fingers clinging to hers sunk deeper. Would *she* be okay without him? She had no idea, because, to her, it was like she was leaving a part of herself behind.

The walk home was quiet, the streets dark and empty. Carmen tried not to think, focusing on the thump of her feet on the pavement, the way it echoed in some parts, much like the sound of her heart in her ears. Her side was bare, empty without Mattie, his hand clutching hers or holding on to her shirt. She'd left behind something essential.

She slipped through the fences and to the door to the warehouse, swallowing heavily and trying not the think about the panic that had choked her when she'd last walked up to this door.

Everything hurt.

She walked in. How long could she avoid going back to their room?

"How is he?" Jia looked up from the sofa, holding out ice wrapped in a cloth for Dex to take. Even as she waited for Carmen's answer, she reached into the bag at her feet, pulling out more cubes.

"The doctor said he'll be fine. His face is fractured; he's got a decent concussion."

The warehouse was silent, eerily so. Rae sat on the floor with her legs sprawled out in front of her, her back against the couch. Jia held out another cloth filled with ice, and Carmen took it, sinking onto a sofa across from them. With a wince, she drew her shirt up again and held it to her ribs.

"That was actually for your eye." Jia's lips were a tight line of worry.

Carmen shrugged. "This hurts more."

Dex watched her with his one good eye, a hand to his other, holding the ice. "Where is he?"

Suddenly, Carmen just couldn't look at them. Everyone was staring at her, and Carmen wanted to tell them all to go away. "He's at the hospital."

Someone sucked in a breath.

"What does that mean for you two?" Rae asked.

Taking in a deep breath, Carmen tried to smother the wince it induced. "I—I thought a lot while I was there. I think… He can't leave the hospital, not with his injuries. They've called social services. And if I stand a chance of getting him back once I'm eighteen, he needs to…" Carmen sighed, the cold of the ice finally starting to sink through the cloth and into her skin. "He needs to go back into foster care."

Nobody said anything. Carmen finally looked up. All of them still stared at her, gazes glued on her as if she held answers she didn't.

"He had a fractured cheekbone and eye socket. He's badly concussed. I couldn't get him out of there." Defensiveness rose up, bidden by no one but herself. "He's going to tell them he was on the street alone and finally found me, but we were mugged. Once I'm eighteen and out of the system, I'll petition for visiting time and to get him back. Before then, I'll find out what school he's in and try see him for five minutes before or after, like before."

No one said anything.

"I… I didn't know what else to do." Carmen's voice broke again, but this time it didn't recover. "He needs to be safe, and we need to find a way to be together that doesn't leave him on the fringes."

She looked from Jia to Dex, to Rae and back. She barely registered the note of pleading in her voice. "He was so small in the bed. I needed… I didn't…"

She couldn't breathe, and then Dex was there, his arms wrapped around her. Carmen dropped her forehead into his neck, trying to slow her breathing. There wasn't enough air. His fingers gripped her tightly, and the couch dipped as Jia sat on the other side, her arms around her too. At first, the pressure was too much, too hot. And then, slowly, Carmen could breathe again.

"You did what you had to do," Jia said. "You did the best thing for him."

"What if I didn't?" The words choked out of her, spilling over Dex's skin. "What if I didn't?"

"You did," he said. "And you've done so well."

Carmen tried to let those words sink in. But instead, all she saw was Mattie as his head snapped back with the blow. His face, swollen and bruised and broken. How terrified she'd been when he'd barely woken up.

"Carmen." Jia waited until Carmen pulled back, and she looked her in the eye. "I would have done the same thing."

That made Carmen feel a little better, which only made her feel worse.

It was the kind of night that was like ink spilled overhead. It was sometime around two thirty, the dead of night, and everything was silent. Goose bumps spread over Carmen's arms even though the air was warm.

She felt empty.

Mattie wasn't downstairs. It left her hollow. Questioning.

Her chest was tight.

Slowly, dragging the night air through her nose, she took a long breath in, then blew it out through her lips. And again. Her racing pulse slowed slightly, and her palms were an anchor against the cement ground that scratched them.

Just blackness. Thick clouds were obscuring the stars, and if she stared long enough, Carmen could just make out where the moon lay. She'd left the others downstairs, claiming she needed some time alone, and for a moment, she thought she'd wanted to cry for the first time in a long while, but now she sat, feeling numb and empty and alone.

The door opened behind her, and as it swung shut quietly, Carmen sighed. "Rae. I told you. I just want some time alone."

Silence. Then: "Sorry. Sara, uh, brought me. I wanted to… I'll go."

She whipped her head around, ignoring the glance of pain it provoked. Carmen's breath left her in a rush at the sound of Ollie's voice.

She stood in front of the door, a hand shoved into her back pocket while the other disappeared into the sleeve of her hoody.

For a second, Carmen forgot to breathe back in. With everything that had happened, pushing Ollie to the back of her mind had been simple. But now, with Ollie staring at her, unsure, all Carmen could remember was the look twisted on Ollie's face when Carmen had turned and walked away from her.

Ollie started to leave, her hand reaching for the door handle, and Carmen couldn't stop herself: "Wait." That couldn't be her own voice, could it? Low and as dark as the night that surrounded them.

Ollie froze a moment before turning back. Her eyes were huge, and Carmen didn't know what to do. All she could think was that Mattie wasn't here and that Ollie may very well be there to tell Carmen she wanted nothing to do with her, that she was breaking it all off. The thought of Ollie walking away from her was horrifying. Those goose bumps rose further, and the world seemed to drop out from under her.

But she had no idea what to say.

Thankfully, Ollie spoke first. "Is Mattie okay?"

Carmen nodded, then shook her head, her lips tight together; it seemed, in that moment, that if she loosened them, everything she was feeling would burst out in a torrent, too many emotions for either of them to handle.

"He's not?" Ollie's voice was high, panic lacing the edges.

"He—he will be."

Ollie had stepped forward, and she hovered again, her hands coming together, both wrapped in the ends of her sleeves now. All Carmen was aware of was her own breathing, of Ollie's eyes.

"I'm...I'm so sorry I called the police."

Carmen shook her head, the movement explosive. "No, don't be. You didn't know."

"Exactly. I..." Her voice cracked, and something in Carmen did too at the sound. "I didn't know..."

Even from where she sat, Carmen saw the tremble to Ollie's lips. The sight left Carmen wordless again. She always thought she had nothing to offer, nothing to fix the people in front of her who looked at her like they needed her to.

"You didn't trust me, Carmen."

The ache in Ollie's voice set off an ache in her, and Carmen twisted, pushing herself up and walking to her with no idea of how to make this better.

"You didn't—" Ollie cut herself off when Carmen was in front of her, hands cupping Ollie's cheeks.

"Please, Ollie. No." The whisper, the desperation of her own voice was one Carmen didn't recognize. "It wasn't that."

That lip was trembling again, and tears spilled past Ollie's lids and down her cheeks, fat drops, one by one lathing salt into the fissures in Carmen's heart. "I told you everything."

"I know. I know you did, and I told you everything I could. I did." Carmen tried to smile, the turn of her lips falling short. "No one else knows I stole a skateboard."

Ollie huffed a laugh, damp with her tears and no smile to echo it.

"Ollie, I swear it wasn't because I didn't trust you. I do, with everything." It was as if voicing the words made Carmen realize the depth of how much she did, how much she needed Ollie.

"You could have told me."

Carmen pressed their foreheads together, and, finally, Ollie's fingers gripped her back. The pressure of it felt like relief always should, even as she held in a gasp at the push against her injuries. "I was going to, right before. And I wanted to, so many times. I was scared."

"Of what I'd think?"

Carmen shook her head, their noses brushing. "No. Of losing...of losing Mattie."

And then her chest heaved, and for a second, Carmen thought she was going to be sick, but instead she sobbed. She did it again, and her arms wrapped around Ollie's shoulders as Ollie wrenched them together, her arms encircling Carmen's waist. The weight was too much; it hurt her back. But it also wasn't tight enough. Wetness was on her cheeks, and she buried her face into Ollie's neck. "But I did. I lost him. I've lost him, Ollie."

The sobs came out hot and damp and desperate. Her chest broke with it, shuddering under the stress of it all. Ollie didn't let her break apart, even as Carmen thought she was going to.

They stayed on the roof until light started to streak the sky. First, in lighter blues and grays, seeping into the world and saturating it. Then pinks and oranges lit it up. Carmen sat back against Ollie's stomach between her legs, Ollie against the door that led downstairs. Lips were at her temple, and Carmen sighed, her eyes closing, feeling tight and swollen.

"You okay?" Ollie whispered against her scalp, her arms tightening around Carmen's middle.

"Better with you." Carmen's voice sounded overused, scraped raw to match her insides. She'd told Ollie everything, and Ollie had just listened. Her head fell back against Ollie's shoulder as she watched the sun claim the skyline. "Don't you need to be home?"

Ollie shook her head against her hair. "No. Dad thinks I'm staying at Sara's. Sara's parents think she's at mine. But we're both here."

Carmen rested a hand atop Ollie's knee, tracing patterns against the denim with her fingertip. Every part of her was exhausted. Even with Ollie there, grounding her, her butt surely as numb as Carmen's was after hours sitting on the hard floor, a part of Carmen was itching to move and go to Mattie.

And she couldn't. And that killed her. He would wake up in the hospital alone. Would his heart turn heavy as he woke up and remembered?

"What are you thinking?" Ollie's words washed over Carmen's ear.

She swallowed heavily. "I don't know how I'm supposed to just…not see him."

"Mattie?" Ollie asked.

"Yeah. To not…help him and wake up with him, to not have him here every day. To not know if he's okay and what he's doing."

Ollie pressed kisses against her neck this time. A comforting touch. "I'm sorry."

"I won't… I won't even know where he is…"

Ollie's arms tightened around her, one right over her stomach and the other over her chest, that hand cupping her shoulder as well. She'd placed them in the only spots Carmen wasn't in pain, and Carmen ignored the residual twinges. "Was this your only option?" she asked.

Carmen watched as the last of the darkness left the sky, the world awake around them. "It was."

"Focus on that. Remember that. You'll find him at school, and then you'll get him back." Ollie's voice was full of conviction, sure in what she said.

"I have to."

"You'll have me to help. However I can."

Carmen twisted as much as she could, nose to nose with Ollie. In that light, she could see the depth of the blue of her eyes, the darkness around her pupils. Her hair was a mess of curls, tight and crinkly, and in that light, in the cool beauty of it, Carmen thought her heart would swell too big for her chest. For a moment, they blinked at each other, eyes red-rimmed and tired.

"I trust you." She whispered the words, a promise, letting them mark Ollie's lips.

Ollie ducked her head and kissed her. "I know," she answered when they finally parted, a soft rending of their lips. "I know."

CHAPTER 21

THE SCHOOL DAY WAS TICKING by agonizingly slowly, and Ollie thought she might fall asleep at her desk. The lights were dimmed in her biology class for a video about cell division playing on the screen at the front. She'd heard the word *mitochondria* so many times she'd lost count.

Next to her, Sara's head was on Ollie's shoulder, and from the deep breathing in Ollie's ear, it was obvious she'd started to drift off. Her own chin was heavy in her hands, and her blinking was getting slower and slower.

Ollie hadn't slept at all on that roof last night. Instead, she'd wrapped herself around Carmen and tried to show her that someone, at least, was there. She'd wanted to leave the imprint of herself behind so that when she left, Carmen could still feel her—something permanent.

The guilt and uncertainty in Carmen's gaze had forced that last lick of anger firing up Ollie's throat to flicker out. That hurt had raged within her as she'd walked with Sara to the warehouse, but it had already begun to soften as she took in the derelict buildings, the people she saw rolled up under newspapers and cardboard in the alleys and doorsteps. Then there were the haunted eyes that followed them, some completely empty, as they watched Sara and Ollie pass by. By the time she'd stared around the ratty, slightly dirty warehouse and heard Dex's gruff "she's on the roof," that small lick of anger was all that was left, fading fast once she saw those eyes, so deep and dark and everything.

Ollie had never seen Carmen cry. And if anyone needed to cry, it was her.

When the sun had started to bathe them on the rooftop, exhaustion rubbing at Ollie's eyes, she'd kissed Carmen and wondered at the delicate touch of her lips. Carmen had never seemed delicate before. She'd seemed intense, closed off, filled with something Ollie wanted to dig her fingers into and figure out.

Never fragile. Never feeling like she'd fall apart beneath Ollie.

The video on the TV kept droning. Sara was definitely asleep. Ollie's head dropped, and she snapped it back up, jostling them both. Sara jumped, straightening and looking around wildly, her gaze settling on Ollie's face. Ollie was failing to smother her smirk.

"How is this movie not finished yet?" Sara whispered as she shuffled closer and dug her chin into her hand.

"I don't know. But I feel like we're in hell."

When the movie finally finished, their teacher set homework based around it, and Ollie let out a groan. They had so much reviewing to do for finals, and he was giving them extra now?

"He's evil," Sara muttered as they walked out. They headed for a grassy spot, pushing past jostling students on their way to classes. Having the same free period was the highlight of their day. With a thump, they flopped on the grass, their heads just touching as they stared straight up.

White clouds were drifting by, and the sun was almost warm against their skin. Yesterday seemed miles away to Ollie, lost, as if it had never happened to her but rather to someone else or in a dream: the violence of it, the small kid, Mattie, and the wildness in Carmen's eyes as she'd pulled him to her in the back alley.

Time had warped.

But now, a wall came down between them on that rooftop, crumbled to nothing. That thing Carmen always seemed to be holding back had been let go, and now Ollie could see her clearly.

"You okay?" Sara asked.

Ollie considered her answer for a moment. "Thinking."

The sun was bright behind the clouds, and Ollie closed her eyes. Would it be inappropriate to nap right there? The grounds had emptied, everyone was in class, and the next hour spread out in front of her, hopefully filled with sleep. They should be in the library, but if they lay really still, maybe no one would notice them.

"I'm still sorry I didn't tell you."

Blinking against the light when she opened her eyes, Ollie turned her head. Sara stared up at the sky, hollows under her eyes. She never did well without much sleep.

"I know. But you don't have to be."

Sara turned her head a little, catching Ollie's gaze. "I am, though. But, well, I'm also not." At Ollie's scrunched forehead, she turned on her side, her head on her hand and looking down at Ollie. "I hated keeping it from you. I've never done that before. But… Carmen is from this other world in some ways. Like Rae."

She paused, and Ollie rolled over too, mirroring Sara by putting her head in her hand and staring her straight in the eyes. Their knees knocked together. "And like you."

Slowly, Sara nodded. "And me. There's something about coming from the homes we did, and being in the system, that other people just can't get. I saw her with her brother and in that warehouse, and she was trying so *hard* to protect him. I, well, I needed to have her back."

Ollie hated that there was a part of her best friend's life, of Carmen's life, that she would never be able to really touch or understand. Tendrils of it that would slip through her fingers. Inexperience and her own history would stop her from being able to really hold tight to them. But that betrayal, which had tidal-waved through her, had ebbed to nothing in the last twelve hours. How could she hold a grudge? How could she be so angry when she'd looked into the molten, dark eyes of Mattie and seen what Carmen was desperate to protect?

"I get it."

Sara blinked. "You do?"

"I do. I know I can never understand where you guys all came from, but I get why Carmen kept it from me, and I get why you wouldn't tell me for her."

"Thanks."

"Thanks for having Carmen's back."

Sara flopped back down, twisting onto her back and dropping a hand over her eyes. "Great. Now that the love-in chat is over, can we nap?"

"If you tell me if you and Rae are actually a *thing* yet or not."

Eyes still covered, Sara's lips twitched as she obviously tried not to smirk. "Don't know what you're talking about."

"You looked pretty cozy this morning."

That smirk showed a little more. "Did not."

Ollie poked her. "Did too."

"If I admit something, can we nap?"

"Yup."

"Fine… We're, like, not *not* together."

"Sara!" Ollie squealed like a stereotypical teenager but didn't care. "Really?"

Finally, Sara dropped her arm away from her eyes. "Really." She winked. "Really, really. Now, can we sleep?"

Groaning, Ollie fell next to her, throwing a leg over so her ankle hooked over Sara's in the familiar way they had. She set an alarm on her phone, though she knew the kids flooding out for lunch and heading toward the cafeteria would make it unnecessary. Slowly, they drifted off while watching the clouds move over the sky, her chest a bit lighter at the way that smile had lit up Sara's face.

The day stretched on and on, and Carmen went from the roof to walking the street to trying to sleep. None of it worked. Her mind was on Mattie and the day before and, most of all, his absence.

She was filled with a nervous energy and couldn't even spar to get it out of her system. Her entire body hurt more than it ever had. In no position to even stand for long periods of time, she was left having to try not to bounce her leg to death to get out her energy.

She was itching to know something about Mattie, to know he was okay. In her bed in the afternoon, she lay sprawled over a sleeping bag that smelled like him. Her thoughts twisted and turned on each other, melded and separated and spliced apart. All she could do was stare up at the ceiling, a hand under her head, feeling ready to tear out of her skin. Other times she'd felt like this, Mattie had crawled in beside her, the length of him along her own. When he was tiny, he'd curl up, a hand fisted under his chin and the other fisted into her shirt. He wouldn't sleep unless he was mashed against her. This had been fine when he'd been tiny and she could put him in a crib, but then at eighteen months, he'd worked out how to climb out, and that was it—he was in her bed. They'd breathe in sync, his snuffles sending her to sleep, and she'd wake with him even closer than he'd started, even if it was the middle of summer.

She'd been eight when he'd been born. Tiny and screaming and waving his fists in the air.

Before him, she didn't remember much. Time before Mattie was convoluted and meaningless. Carmen remembered time *after* him. From when she first saw him, the protectiveness had grown in her chest, a seed in her heart that took her over, the roots implanting deep, digging into the very core of her.

"Hey."

Carmen pushed herself up onto her elbows, trying not to wince at the protest from her entire body, even as the voice lightened something inside her. "Ollie."

Hovering in the doorway, Ollie gave an awkward wave. "Hi... I came straight from school." She scuffed her Converse sneaker into the ground, toeing at it. "I hope you, uh, meant it when you said to come."

"I did."

They stared at each other a moment, and Carmen slumped back against the mattress, her ribs finally winning. Everything ached. "Come in."

Carmen tried to ignore the warmth that flooded her cheeks as Ollie walked in, dumping her backpack on the floor at the end of the mattress. Ollie's eyes took the room in, no doubt seeing the stains and shedding wallpaper and emptiness. Carmen's situation, the truth of it, was seeped into the walls of this room. No belongings except for some clothes stacked into a corner of it and some books along one wall. The sleeping bags on the bed.

That was all.

But then, Ollie was only looking at Carmen, her eyes blue and soft like the sea, a rolling tide of understanding.

Carmen shuffled over on the mattress.

That was all the invitation Ollie needed. In a mere second, she was lying alongside Carmen and had propped her head on her hand. With care that made Carmen's stomach warm, she slid her leg over Carmen's thighs, hooking it over her hip. The pressure pushed Carmen's hips into the bed, and it left her centered, like gravity had finally plucked her back out of orbit and pulled her to earth.

Slowly, her hair falling to brush Carmen's cheeks, Ollie kissed her once, her lips unhurried and soft. Carmen wrapped curls of Ollie's hair into her fingers and held her there, the kiss not deepening but unfolding in front of them like they had all the time they could want. When Ollie pulled back, Carmen lifted her head, following her, then finally fell back down.

"How are you?" Ollie's words washed over her lips.

"Better now that you're here." And that was the truth. A little terrifying, but real.

"And before?"

Carmen swallowed, unable to look away. Ollie was too close and her gaze too intense. "Sore. Thinking too much. Rae made me come up to sleep, but I couldn't."

"You haven't slept?" Concern pushed Ollie's eyebrows together and filled her words.

Carmen gave a half shrug.

"Did you take those pills that nurse gave you?"

Another half shrug.

"Carmen!" Ollie sat up.

Carmen missed her immediately, the warmth and solidness of her, the way she'd finally felt tethered to the bed and the world again after floating all day, lost.

"Where are they?"

"Front pocket of my backpack."

Ollie fished them out, followed by a bottle of water from her own bag. Once Carmen had taken them, she lay back in the same position.

"Thank you," Carmen said.

"My pleasure. Though you could've just taken them."

"I was being tough."

Against Ollie's thigh, their fingers entwined, tracing over each other's palms and against the tips of each other's fingers. The motion was soothing, easy.

"Want to tell me what you were thinking?" Ollie's eyes were like the sky, looking down at her at night and open to anything Carmen wanted to offer up.

For a second, Carmen almost answered that she'd been thinking nothing. But that chasm that had separated them, that wall Carmen had built up to protect Mattie had already crumbled. So she took the last few steps to clamber over it and stumble into Ollie.

"I wanted to go see Mattie again, a last time, before he left the hospital."

"Why don't you?"

Their fingers still moved over and around each other, entwining, then slipping back apart to stroke at the insides of each other's wrists and the backs of their hands. Something behind Carmen's eyes was heavier, carrying her toward sleep now that she was the most at ease she had been all day.

"They'll be keeping an eye out for me. If they call social services... It will look worse, later. I think. Or they could have someone there, waiting. I don't know..."

Ollie bit at her lip, like she did when she was thinking, her head still heavy in her palm, hair spilling around her. "We could try to sneak you in."

Carmen hoped her smile didn't look as sad as it felt. "He's on the kids' ward, and they have a security door. You have to buzz to enter. I think anyone visiting him will be flagged."

Ollie just blinked at her, slow and heavy. Or maybe that was Carmen. Tiredness settled over her like dust. "I think, for him and for me, I need to stay away." The words were heavy as they tumbled past Carmen's lips, and she wanted to push them back in and not acknowledge their logic.

"I'm sorry," Ollie whispered.

Not an apology. Empathy.

"Thank you." Their fingers stilled, firmly entwined, and their palms stayed flush together. "I just... What if the foster home is like the others?"

Ollie looked a little lost for a moment. "Well, at least you'll know? If it's that terrible, we'll get him out and in a new one. But what if...what if it's an okay one?"

It was hard to believe, after fighting against it for so long, to accept that as a possibility. But wasn't that what she was hoping for? "True. Ollie?" She looked Ollie straight in the eyes. "What if I can't find him until I'm eighteen and can actually approach them to see him? That's months away. I can't not see him for months and months."

The idea of not seeing Mattie for such a long time left a hole in Carmen so deep that if she fell down it, she didn't think she'd ever crawl her way out.

Ollie rested their foreheads together. "I have an idea."

Carmen was so tired. Exhaustion was crawling up her spine now. The notion of sleeping next to Ollie made her want to curl into her and let sleep pull her away. "You do?" she managed to ask.

"Deon might help us."

"How?"

"Like he did with you… He, uh, is really good at hacking. Scarily so. We can find out where Mattie is placed, where he will go to school." Ollie paused. "Maybe he could hack the hospital system."

Her eyes were bright with the idea, and Carmen wanted to laugh, the urge bubbling up in her chest. "You look far too happy about the idea of doing something illegal."

Clearly trying to look abashed, Ollie gave an awkward shrug. "It's a little fun. And Deon really loved it." For a second, she stared down at Carmen, smirking. "Are you high?"

"No!"

Maybe Carmen was floating a little, yet was pinned nicely to the bed. Her eyes were closing of their own accord. She was washed in Ollie, the feel of her. She really hadn't slept at all.

"I think you're high."

"Those painkillers are strong…"

"Go to sleep."

The hand in Carmen's slipped away, and then before she could protest, Ollie's fingers ran down the bridge of her nose, slowly and so softly she could barely feel it.

Carmen's eyes fell shut. "If I sleep, will you be here when I wake up?"

"Maybe… I have to be home for dinner. But I can wake you when I leave, if you want?"

Carmen hummed her agreement. She wanted to open her eyes, but cement had set over them. Ollie smelled like something spicy—her shampoo or body wash. "Sleep with me?"

"Of course."

"But don't stop that."

The finger on the bridge of her nose didn't slow. "Not until you're asleep."

Their breathing synchronized, and Carmen hummed again. "It feels good."

"My mom used to do it to me when I was little."

Those words didn't seem as heavy as they normally would, not as explosive. Sadness at the word *mom* didn't coat the words as thickly as normal. A distant thought in the back of Carmen's mind prickled at her. "I think mine did too once. But when I was really, really small."

That was one of her last thoughts before she slept. Also, that Mattie had liked it. And the feeling of Ollie all around her.

CHAPTER 22

SUNSHINE WAS POURING OVER THE footpath, spilling out to make patterns on the cement. Walking along, soaked in light, fingers entwined with Ollie's, Carmen felt tugged in two. Guilt was colliding with pure contentment in her stomach, twisting in on each other and leaving her uncertain and walking unknown ground.

Being with Ollie, not in the bar, not throwing glances at each other, not smothered by omission, felt right. Real. Like Carmen was settled, ease slipping under her skin and soothing away the utter, gasping harshness of the last few years. But it was tainted. Because Mattie wasn't with them or waiting for them back at the warehouse or waiting anywhere that Carmen *knew*. The only reason she was with Ollie right then was because she'd left Mattie behind at the hospital.

"Are you okay?"

Carmen pressed farther up along Ollie's side. "I am."

"Nervous?"

They paused outside a house, Ollie pulling Carmen's hand to turn her so they were facing each other. Carmen shook her head. "No."

Ollie's lips twitched, and Carmen got the feeling she was smothering a smile. The fingers of her other hand slipped into Carmen's, and their foreheads came together. Ollie's lips were so close to Carmen's she could kiss her. No one else was on the quiet suburban street. They had a pocket of the universe just for them, filled with the warmth of the sun on the crowns of their heads and the distant sound of a lawn mower. But her hands were still a little clammy, her heart fluttering a bit too fast.

"Yes, you are."

"Okay, I am." Carmen let the words whisper out. "What if he can't find anything?" What if Mattie was lost to her, adrift in the system?

"He will." Ollie turned her head just slightly, their noses brushing together. "Deon's *that* good."

"He was seriously taken away and warned?"

"Yup." Ollie's eyes sparkled, lit up like the sun hitting the sea. How could someone so warm revel in such mayhem? "He really was. He hasn't told us what went down, but I think they'll end up recruiting him."

"Wow."

Ollie pulled back a little. "Wanna go in?"

The house next to them was very neat, suburban. A green bike lay on its side on the porch. Carmen took a deep breath. For a moment, she let the air settle in her lungs before blowing it out slowly. Finally, she nodded.

Ollie's fingers tightened. "Want something that will distract you?"

"Yes."

"Dad asked if you wanted to come to dinner tonight."

Carmen whipped her head around, that flutter in her chest speeding up. "What?"

Suddenly, Ollie looked away, and Carmen wanted to cup her cheeks and bring that gaze back to meet hers. So she did, her fingers gentle. "Do you want me to?"

Biting her lip, Ollie couldn't quite meet her eye. "If you want to."

"I have a black eye."

"So?"

"Won't he ask questions?"

"We could make something up?" Ollie shrugged, her hands against Carmen's wrists.

She imagined Ollie could feel her pulse, bounding away beneath her fingertips.

"Or, ah, tell him the truth?" Ollie added.

The truth? Tell an adult that she was a runaway? That she had taken her brother, even more a minor than herself, and kept him out of school? Had gotten him hurt? "The truth?"

"Or as much of it as you want to. We could tell him you left foster care but have a place to stay and a job…which is all true."

Trust Ollie? Or trust no one but herself, like usual? "Okay."

Her answer surprised even herself a little. She didn't want to keep building what she had with Ollie on lies. And that included what she told

Ollie's father. Who, despite everything that had happened between Ollie and him, was the most important person in Ollie's life. She and Ollie had started on lies, and she'd just fixed that foundation: she didn't want to rot anything further.

"Okay?" Ollie asked.

"Yeah."

A slow smile, the one that always left Carmen breathless, curled Ollie's lips up. "Great."

She stamped a kiss on Carmen's lips and turned, dropping one of her hands so Carmen was lead along by the other. Ollie let herself into Deon's house, and Carmen followed a step behind, gaze roving over the inside. The house was huge, a polished wooden staircase leading up to the second story. But they went downstairs, Ollie tramping down the steps and Carmen following more delicately. They emerged in a space that was more like a living room than a basement. On one side was the biggest computer setup Carmen had ever seen. There were four screens and multiple things she didn't have a word for.

"Hey, Deon." Ollie sounded more cheerful than Carmen had ever heard before. The thought that it was because she was going to dinner with her dad and Carmen made Carmen want to hug her.

Deon spun around on a computer chair, his smile flashing and eyes like liquid wood. "Hey, guys. Hi, Carmen. It's great to see you out of the bar."

Carmen gave a wave, her own awkwardness creeping up on her. "Hi."

Ollie all but pushed Carmen down onto a beanbag chair right beside Deon, then sat on the floor and used Carmen's legs as a backrest. Carmen would have protested, but she knew Ollie would just glare at her and stare pointedly at her ribs until Carmen sat down anyway.

The way Ollie occupied space, moved through it and settled in among it, was both beautiful and beyond Carmen's understanding. But Deon just sat heavily back in his chair, using his toe to swing himself slowly back and forth. As if it was normal for Ollie to make herself completely at home.

It seemed that for Ollie, like for Carmen, family went beyond blood and birth.

"So." Ollie threw an arm over Carmen's knee, wriggling so she was between Carmen's legs. Finally following Ollie's lead, Carmen shifted so she was more comfortable. "Any luck?"

Deon hummed. "Getting into the DCF files will be quite easy since I did it before." He grimaced an apology at Carmen. "The hospital is taking more time. And when I do get through, it'll depend on what they have on their intranet."

"What do you mean?" Ollie asked.

"Hospitals tend to use a lot of written notes. The discharge is usually online, at least. So, basically, we won't see much until he's discharged."

"That should be today." Carmen's eyes were focused on the screen. Nothing she saw made much sense to her, though.

"Great. Well, hopefully I'll be through in an hour or so. I've been trying since I left school at two."

"Free period this afternoon?" Ollie asked.

"Yup. And better, 'cause my parents work late tonight, so it's given me a really good chunk of time. But," he said, his entire face lighting up with another grin, one that reminded Carmen of a cheeky kid, "I don't think I'll need that long. I'll be through soon."

"You're awesome."

"I know." He winked and turned back to his computer, his fingers flying over keys and stopping occasionally to adjust some of the things hooked up to it all.

Ollie's legs kicked out, and she sprawled back as much as she could against Carmen. They were there for two hours, the time passing with the clacking of keys and the murmuring of their voices. Ollie's laugh trickled out like rain, and Deon occasionally snorted at something Ollie said. They shared stories of school, and somehow Carmen found herself pulled into the conversation.

Those moments at the bar, when she'd wished she and Ollie were like other teenagers, that they could spend their time wrapped in each other among friends, walking between their lockers—all of that seemed closer just then than it ever had before. Sharing her secrets, letting Ollie in, had led to something clicking between them. Something had always *clicked*; Carmen had always been drawn to Ollie. To the way she moved and smiled, to the way her eyes seemed as if they'd absorbed the sky yet turned that gravity onto Carmen. But now, the space between them was liquid, easily moved through, like it belonged to them.

"Got it." Deon's voice broke through her thoughts.

Ollie straightened, putting the bowl of popcorn Deon had procured on the floor next to her. Kernels fell off her chest from failed attempts to catch them in her mouth.

"The hospital?" Carmen asked.

He gave a quick shake of his head. "I'm almost in, but no. I meant DCF."

Carmen sat up, Ollie's hand digging into her leg, and stared at the screen. "What does it say?"

"Mattie García?"

"No, Matthew Anders." Deon typed it in without question, but Ollie looked over her shoulder, inquiry in her eyes. "García was my dad's last name. Anders was my mom's. We don't know who his dad is. I don't think Mom ever told him."

Ollie gave her a look Carmen couldn't quite decipher and a squeeze of her knee, then turned back to watch Deon. Carmen's fingers played with the ends of Ollie's hair, the feeling of it against her fingertips distracting her from the ball of anxiety sitting in her stomach.

"Date of birth?"

She told him.

"Got him." Deon was reading, his lips moving slightly. "Okay, he has a placement, due to be there tonight, which means he must be getting discharged." He looked down at her. "Still want me to get into the records?"

Carmen hesitated, not wanting to ask for too much. "Um…"

Before she could keep going, he shrugged. "Wait, of course you do. You'll want to know he's definitely cleared, right?"

Able to breathe easier since he understood, Carmen nodded. "Yeah."

"No problem." He turned back to the computer. "I like a challenge. Anyway, I'll write down the address. I imagine the school will just be the one for that district."

"Are— Are you able to look at the history of the foster family?"

Eyes down on the paper he was writing on, Deon shrugged. "Yeah, easy." He passed the address he'd written down to Ollie, who held it over her shoulder for Carmen to take. She read it three times as Deon tapped a few keys, wanting to remember it in case she lost it. "Right…the family. They've been in the system as a foster family for ten years, have one kid of their own, no complaints in any of their subfolders."

That was something. Though this might not necessarily mean they were a good family. So much was never reported. But still, it was something. "Thanks, Deon. Am, uh...am I in there?"

A few swipes and taps. "Your last update was yesterday. Some info about how you were assumed to be with your brother in New York, but it was unknown. Updated yesterday to say...that you never left the city, and your brother states he's been alone with another group of runaways in various locations. He states he was looking for you but only found you the day you were mugged. He claimed you were taking him back to DCF when it happened. He was never on a bus with you to New York and said he knew nothing about it. It says you're presumed to be in the city and that you're due to age out in a few months." He whistled slowly. "Is that not so subtle talk for they don't really care about you anymore?"

Carmen shrugged. "I think so."

Ollie swiveled so she was between Carmen's legs and looked at her, her face screwed up. "So they just *don't care*?"

Carmen blinked, not sure where that had come from. "What?"

"You're still a minor, but they just kind of...let you fall through the cracks?"

"Um..." Carmen looked to Deon, who just shrugged at her, so she looked back to Ollie, who had a roiling storm of anger in her eyes. "It's a good thing... I'm not going back to foster care."

"But they should still *care*."

Ollie was angry *for* her. Out of nowhere, a lump grew in Carmen's throat at the thought, her voice coming out too tight. "I think the system is just overloaded." She ran a hand through Ollie's hair again. "And they prefer to focus on younger kids, I guess."

"It's still wrong." Ollie was the picture of protective.

A pinging sound made them both turn to Deon. He was already looking back at the screens, his back to them.

"I'm in the hospital's system. Right." He typed for a minute that went on for an eternity. "Here it is...discharged to the care of DCF, cleared medically, needs bed rest for a few days. Needs a follow-up to check if his fractured orbital socket is healing. Headaches to be expected up to several weeks post event. Psych referral. Released only with pain medication." He turned to Carmen. "He seems fine."

Carmen let out a long breath. She'd believe it when she saw it, but for now, it would have to be enough.

On Monday, he'd be back at school, and Carmen would be able to see him.

"Thanks, Deon." She looked him straight in the eye, and he blinked, seeming surprised at whatever he saw in her gaze. "Seriously. Thank you."

There was something about Carmen. Something in the depths of her eyes that would always make Ollie think of woodsmoke and whiskey. Not of drunkenness, but of a taste that ran so deep it took days to appreciate its worth. She held a seriousness that went through to her very core. When it cracked a little, spilling over as she laughed, when she turned silly about something Ollie had said, she looked like who she was under it all: a seventeen-year-old who stared at Ollie like she herself had hung the stars in the sky.

She'd never know what had pulled her into Carmen's orbit, if it was those eyes or that seriousness or the way she'd leaned against the lockers the first time Ollie really remembered noticing her. All those sharp angles and haunted eyes and cheekbones she'd worship if she could.

Mostly, it was just Carmen and everything that made her, *her*.

And the more Ollie had gotten to know her, the more she had fallen into something she had no urge to catch herself from. She tumbled and caught up speed, and all she could do was close her eyes and lose herself to it.

Learning about Mattie should have given her pause. But instead, Ollie found herself filled with admiration. Carmen had kept her brother and herself together through things Ollie had no understanding of. She had fought for him, and she knew she'd fight for him until she died.

Sometimes, it all seemed a little complicated.

What would it mean for them? Two seventeen-year-olds melding together like they were? That one of them would have a kid they were responsible for?

But that seemed like a problem that was intangible and far away.

With all of this clouding her mind when they left Deon's, Ollie ran her thumb over Carmen's hand in her own as they walked through the door to Ollie's house.

Ollie introduced her father and Carmen as simply as she could. "Carmen, my dad, Calvin. Dad, Carmen."

And Carmen held her hand out solemnly, and they shook, the coffee table between them just small enough for her father to reach across. The smile on his face was the only genuine one she'd seen since her mother had died.

"It's nice to finally meet you, Carmen."

"You too."

Ollie watched her father's face, for once not flinching from the truth of it. He was thinner, the gray that speckled his beard a little more pronounced than before. Lines around his eyes didn't make her think of laughter anymore. But when he smiled at Carmen, he was more *him* than she'd seen in a long while. So much so that Ollie's chest ached.

"That's a nasty bruise."

In the stillness of the living room, Ollie could have kicked herself. She should have filled her father in before. But it didn't feel like Ollie's story to tell.

Carmen's gaze flicked to Ollie then back to her father. "I, uh, work in a bar, and some pretty horrible guys came in to cause trouble."

Ollie's father's eyes widened a little. "But you're okay?" At her nod, he asked, "A bar? Aren't you too young to work in a bar? What about school?"

"I don't work with the alcohol. And I don't go to school. Not, um, anymore."

Carmen slid her hands into her back pockets, but Ollie rescued one, entwining their fingers between them. Her father didn't even blink at that, and affection for him swelled in her chest.

"Carmen's mom died last year. She left school and got a job to avoid going into foster care."

For a moment, her father watched them both, his eyes deep and dark. "I'm very sorry to hear about your mother, Carmen. And about... Are you doing okay?"

Carmen swallowed, the motion visible. "I am, thank you. I have a place to stay, and soon I hope to be somewhere a bit more permanent."

"Well, you're always welcome here for dinner, or anything else."

Carmen hadn't looked away from Ollie's father, not once. "Thank you."

They sat down for the lasagna her father had made. Never the cook, her mother had left everything burned or underdone. Not her father, though. He made the best meals and had only recently been cooking again. Their forks clattered against their plates, and Ollie sat across from Carmen, their feet together under the table.

"How did you two meet, then?"

Carmen looked from Ollie to her father. "At school, before I left. Ollie ran into me."

Ollie would never admit she'd done it completely on purpose.

Her father rolled his eyes. "Always a little klutz. When she was around two, she used to climb everything. Once, we turned our backs for a second and she'd climbed the shower curtain."

The laugh Carmen gave was delighted, and it stopped short the embarrassed protest coming out of Ollie; the sound was charming.

"The shower curtain?" Carmen looked to Ollie, who crossed her arms and shrugged with a smirk. She looked back to Ollie's father. "Seriously?"

"Seriously. Before she could even walk properly, she managed to get onto the back of the sofa and roll off." He grimaced. "It didn't stop her from trying again the next day."

"What can I say?" Ollie grinned. "I'm an adventurer."

"Yet you hate sports."

Ollie made a face. "I do."

Her father made an exaggerated pout, and Ollie was giddy with how *normal* things were. She'd missed this, the ease, the way her father liked to tease and she'd push back. Unlike before, though, it was with less annoyance and, instead, with appreciation sitting heavy in the back of her throat.

"I tried so hard to get you into *something*." He turned to Carmen. "I even tried rock climbing, but to no avail. She grew out of that and just wanted to draw all over everything."

Carmen was listening attentively to everything he said.

"Do you like any sports, Carmen?"

That got them into a conversation about soccer that Ollie quickly tuned out of. She was content to watch the way those lines around her father's eyes *were* still laugh lines, despite what she'd thought. It turned out she'd only needed to see him smile to learn that. Did it ache inside him at times, like it did with her, to smile? Like it was cheating on their grief for her mom?

Carmen's hands gestured, and she smiled easily. She'd seemed more relaxed since they'd left Deon's, but to see her at ease with her dad left Ollie warm inside.

When they finished, Ollie and Carmen collected the dishes, the rule in the house that whoever cooked got out of washing duty. They bumped elbows as they rinsed them, and Ollie loaded the dishwasher, not saying anything when it was clear Carmen had never used one. Finished, she led the way to her room, falling onto her bed and yanking her glasses off. Clearly being mindful of her ribs, Carmen followed a little more gingerly. Ollie shuffled close, their chests together and their heads on the same pillow.

"That went well." She kept her voice low. Carmen had once told her she loved it like that, that it was like gravel, like the sound an asteroid would make passing by stars. The words had left Ollie dizzy for days.

Sometimes, Ollie grossed herself out with her feelings for Carmen.

"Your dad is nice."

"He is." Ollie's tugged softly at Carmen's thigh, and Carmen followed the lead, her leg going over Ollie's hip. "I wish," she said, her voice still low, a bass line, "you could have met my mom."

The look in Carmen's eyes darkened. She wriggled a little closer. "Me too."

"Carmen..." Ollie waited until Carmen was looking her right in the eyes—easy to do with barely even air between them. "If you ever want to talk about anything, you can. About foster care, before, or your mom..."

Ollie could only stare at her and hope Carmen knew she meant it, every word, and that if she didn't want to share yet, that was fine too. She'd take it in pieces, in a torrent, broken up, or altogether. Whatever Carmen wanted to share with her, Ollie wanted to hear it.

"Thank you."

Those words breathed over Ollie's lips and tasted like something Ollie wanted to preserve. Carmen closed the gap, minuscule anyway, and kissed Ollie gently, a gift in itself, a touching of lips and tongue.

Ollie never wanted it to end.

CHAPTER 23

SOMETHING WAS MISSING.

That was obvious. To everyone. Carmen could tell it was obvious. She knew that missing Mattie was layered over her smile, that the absence of him sat in the back of her gaze. Everything Carmen had done for almost a year had been with him in mind.

That wasn't true.

It had been like that since he'd been born, really.

Everyone looked at her and knew she felt as if something had been shaved away. Ollie did her best to keep her distracted, and Carmen, at times, could let herself disappear into that. The warmth of her eyes, the way Ollie kissed her like the world was coming down. Or was it like the world was being built up? Sometimes she wasn't sure which it was and wondered if it could do both, all at the same time.

Rae brought her books. Where she found them, Carmen didn't ask. But she appreciated them. It helped, to fall into another world, one so different from her own. If she could, Jia sat with her, even if it was only while Carmen read and Jia went over things in her room, papers spread out in front of her. Sometimes, Jia sat next to her on the roof and talked over the plan with her in circles until Carmen had no choice but to admit she'd done the right thing. Dex gave her more hours. As many as he could, it seemed. So, through the evening, Carmen threw herself into the bar.

It had never been so clean.

But with the information Deon had managed to get ahold of in mind, Carmen tried to relax. To accept that Mattie was okay, physically at least. But sometimes, that just didn't quite click in her brain. Her feet would start to carry her from the bar to the office, the idea of checking on Mattie blooming in the back of her mind before she could stop it. Her hand would reach for him in the bed, a reflex. She'd read something in one of Rae's books, a sentence she knew he'd like, and would want to tell him. She would look up, a flutter of panic in her chest because she hadn't checked on him, and would stare wildly around, anxious to lay eyes on him. Then the jarring knowledge that he wasn't there would crash over her, and she'd try to drag her gaze back to her book.

It was like trying to shake her shadow.

"You okay?"

Carmen looked up from the glasses she was unstacking, the blue of Ollie's eyes watching her, clouded with concern. Carmen glanced around the bar. It was Sunday evening and everything was quiet. The crowd that had appeared for an afternoon football game had slowly filtered out. They'd be closing soon. Sundays were always an early close.

With a shrug, Carmen fell against the bar, her chin heavy in her hand, elbow against the bar top. She could just say she was fine. The reflex to do so coiled in her stomach, ready to kick in. "I was thinking."

She surprised herself.

Ollie smiled, the action crinkling around her eyes just a little. She put her crossed arms on the bar, a foot of space between their limbs, and leaned forward. "That was obvious." She cocked her head. "What were you thinking?"

Carmen dropped her gaze, taking in a deep breath and trying to calm the parts of her that itched to turn and walk away from this conversation. It was as if something were crawling along her nerve endings, leaving her too exposed. "About Mattie. About the last time we were separated."

Silence stretched on a bit too long. Maybe Carmen shouldn't open up. Putting everything on Ollie was a stupid idea. There was too much.

When Carmen finally glanced up, Ollie was still looking at her steadily. Her eyes were clear and sure, and Carmen could just tell she was waiting to hear more. Even though Carmen knew the bar was empty, that Dex was out the back, doing the books, she looked around before continuing, then fixed her gaze back on the bar top. Sometimes eye contact made her feel stripped bare. She traced the grain of the wood with her thumbnail.

"It was hard then, really hard. They put us in separate homes, and I went through three before I ended up on the streets. One was okay, the others not great, but the last one was…not nice. They were angry, loud, and violent."

Her voice was low, the sound rumbling in her throat. In spite of herself, she looked up, the feel of Ollie's eyes like a burn against her cheeks. Ollie was still watching her steadily, but her eyebrows had pushed together. Something clenched in her jaw. "Being without Mattie then was the hardest part about being on the streets. But he was five, and it was so obvious then that the foster place was better for him, even if he hated it. But this time…"

Fingers brushed over Carmen's, the touch slight and warm.

Everything Carmen could say caught in her throat, mingled together, and became difficult to pick apart. The music in the bar stopped, the silence almost deafening.

"This time," Ollie spoke, and Carmen met her eyes again, "this time, you guys went through even more together. You started this together. You've had years of being his person, and now he's gone because he got hurt. It feels like a hole left behind." Too much understanding was in those words. "Something huge. And you want him back but feel bad because you think he's probably better off in a foster home. But you're worried it will be a bad one. You're worried you won't get him back. And that hole just keeps getting bigger."

They didn't break eye contact, the moment swelling around them. Carmen twisted her hand, entwining Ollie's fingers with her own.

"Yeah."

Because that was exactly it.

"Carmen?"

"Mm?"

"How did you find them, last time? Dex and Rae and Jia?"

It was hard not to smile at that. She settled against the bar top more comfortably, one knee bent so she could press her toe against the ground. Their hands stayed clasped between them, Ollie blinking at her. Attentive.

"I was a little bit of a mess. I was thirteen and angry and felt like the whole world was against me. I missed Mattie, and I even missed my mom, which made me angrier. I ran from the home one night when the guy there got drunk and angry. He threw things. He got… I had some bruises." The hand in her own squeezed tightly, and Carmen's breath caught at the feeling, at the hardness in Ollie's eyes. At someone being angry *for* her.

"I was on the street for a little over a week. Maybe two? It was horrible. I was cold and hungry, and I tried to steal some food and had to run." She laughed then, the sound light. It didn't hurt to think about anymore. "I was *useless*, Ollie."

Ollie squeezed her hand again, eyes intent and not leaving her.

"Are you sure you want to listen to all this?"

Ollie nodded, her hair bouncing around her head. "Of course I am. I want to know anything you want to tell me."

The sincerity in her voice could mend even the fractured sensation in Carmen's chest. "I ran into the wrong people, and I picked a fight. I don't know why. I was getting pummeled, when suddenly they were all running off. Someone pulled me up off the ground and dusted off my shoulders."

"Rae?" Ollie asked.

Carmen snorted. "Yeah, Rae. She seemed so *old* to me. And she stood over me with bruised knuckles, looking me up and down. Finally, she rolled her eyes and told me to come with her. I had no idea what was going on."

"Did you go?"

"I asked her, with my chest all puffed out, like I could look tough in the state I was in, what if I didn't want to go with her?"

Ollie chuckled.

"I know, right? And she just shrugged and said it was up to me. It only took a few seconds for me to run after her. She took me to the warehouse, and I almost shook in front of Jia, who asked me some questions. I don't know what she saw in me to say yes, but she took me in."

"I'm glad she did."

"So was I. I don't know where I'd be if she hadn't."

The entrance door closed, and Carmen looked up in time for Rae to grin at them.

"You were pathetic. That's why she took you in." She plopped onto a stool next to Ollie. Sara dragged up a stool between the two of them.

"I was not pathetic," Carmen said.

But Rae just stared straight at her, eyebrows crawling up her forehead.

"I wasn't." Carmen's voice was sounding sulky, even to herself. Ollie was clearly holding back a smile.

"Oh!" Rae turned to face Ollie and Sara, her hands buried in her jacket pockets.

A sinking feeling swept through Carmen's stomach.

"And if you *really* want to picture pathetic, you should have seen her at her first training session with Dex and me."

"Pathetic?" Sara asked.

"Pathetic," Rae confirmed.

Carmen grabbed a dirty dishrag and lobbed it at Ray, who ducked it easily, smirking.

"Almost as pathetic as that throw."

Ollie gave a bark of laughter, and Carmen turned to her. "You're supposed to be on my side."

Before Ollie could defend herself, Dex's voice washed over them all as he carried a crate in from the door behind the bar that led to a storage area. "You want to speak about pathetic? You should have seen Rae in her first training. Skinny little toe rag, all red-faced and fire-eyed, who threw a punch so hard she spun herself around and fell over on the mat."

Delighted, Carmen stared at Rae, who was scowling at Dex. Sara snorted a laugh, then Ollie actually burst into giggles. "Oh really?"

Rae crossed her arms. "Didn't happen."

"It did," Dex said.

"Nope."

"Yep." He stashed the crate under the bar. "More than once."

Sara and Ollie fell on each other, laughing loudly. Carmen couldn't stop her smirk. "Well, well, well."

"Not a word, García, or I tell the story of your first try at stealing from a supermarket. You know, when you—"

"Okay!" Carmen interrupted loudly, eyes narrowed at Rae. But Ollie straightened, looking interested.

"What story?" she asked.

It took five minutes to get Ollie sufficiently distracted. They ended up in a booth, Jia sliding in among them just before they flipped the sign on the door to Closed. As she sat between the wall and Ollie, with the warm weight of her girlfriend along Carmen's side and the reassuring touch of her hand on Carmen's thigh, Carmen listened to their stories and let herself sink into the safety of that circle.

Tomorrow, she would try to see Mattie at school. It had been almost a week. She would lay her eyes on him and actually have physical proof he was okay.

Tonight, her family was making sure she was okay.

Carmen's hands were clammy. Her heart was pounding too fast.

It was Monday afternoon. Finally.

The bell at Mattie's school was loud, ringing in her ears even from across the road. Mattie had to be at the school. The records indicated so. The next closest school was miles away, well out of the district. All Carmen had to do was wait and search for her brother's head. His hair had needed a cut again before this had happened. He would be easy for her to spot. She always knew him, the shape of him imprinted on her by heart.

Students streamed down the stairs, flooding the pavement.

Cars were stopping and starting; kids were piling into backseats. The sun was warm, but Carmen pulled her hood around her ears anyway, then tugged it down when she realized that would look more conspicuous. What a way to scream *nonchalance*. She rolled her eyes at herself.

Mattie was still nowhere to be seen.

The day of waiting had dragged forever. She couldn't arrive too early. Loitering around would draw attention to herself, and that was the last thing she needed. The warehouse had been hot, and Carmen had prowled around it, itching to spar and her body still way too bruised and sore to do so. After lunch, she'd tried a run, but her ribs were screaming at her when all she did was walk upstairs, so that had lasted all of five steps. In the end, Rae had dragged her to the river and they'd walked, the breeze playing over the water, and their hair flying around their faces.

And now here she was: about to see him. Excitement was crawling up her throat—more anticipation than excitement—and it made it hard to breathe.

Kids were still filtering out. Buses had started pulling up and pulling away. Hands in her pockets, Carmen crossed the road and faced the scene in front of her. Kids ran up to their parents, trailing art projects behind them that would get put up on refrigerators. One kid was crying, while another was trying to do up his shoelaces on the steps and failing miserably. Others Carmen's age stood around, obviously having rushed from the high school down the road to collect younger siblings. She fit right in now.

Where was Mattie?

He wouldn't leave without looking for her. He'd know she was coming.

He would know that, wouldn't he?

After thirty minutes had gone by, Carmen had to yank her hood back up over her head and accept he wasn't there. This couldn't be the wrong school.

With hunched shoulders, Carmen bit her lip and walked away quickly.

Was he okay? Maybe he'd had to go back to the hospital. Was the foster place one that didn't care enough to even send him to school?

No. That never happened, no matter how bad one was. School was a legal requirement, and none got out of it. If kids skipped too much school, the school contacted child services, house calls were made—there were repercussions.

So where was he?

What if something had happened?

Carmen didn't know what to do with herself. She walked, each step sending jolts up her back and settling low in her belly to twist with the worry writhing there.

Mattie needed her, and she didn't even know how to find him.

"Can you go to the foster home?"

Ollie knew it was a stupid question. She knew there had to be a reason Carmen hadn't done that. Her desperation to see her brother was obvious. She lay across Ollie's bed, an arm thrown over her face while Ollie stood uselessly next to it, hovering. Carmen had shown up at her door, her face drawn and her lip trembling, and Ollie had led her straight to her room.

The sigh Carmen gave made Ollie want to wince. So it had been a stupid question. But when Carmen pushed up onto her elbows, her brow furrowed, her teeth gnawing at her lip, she didn't look annoyed.

"I've thought about it. If they caught me, it wouldn't be worth it. Everything I want to get done later would be ruined."

Ollie tried to hide her sigh of relief. "Oh. Okay." That bruise over Carmen's eye and cheek was still dark, and her face was washed out, but Carmen smiled at her, all soft at the edges, a little sad. At the sight, Ollie was suddenly out of her depth, with no idea what she was supposed to do to help. The two of them: seventeen and drowning in life.

"Thank you for trying to help, though."

That lifeline made the feeling go away. But then Carmen broke their eye contact, her gaze jumping around the room.

"Are you okay?" Sometimes, she was learning, Carmen needed a little nudge to talk.

"I didn't know where to go. I was walking and I just…" Carmen finally looked back at her. "I ended up here. I didn't even realize it. I just wanted somewhere to…"

She didn't need to finish it. Ollie knew what Carmen wanted to say, because she felt the same way. No one or anything had ever made Ollie feel so at peace as everything with Carmen did.

When Carmen sat up and on the edge of the bed, pulling Ollie to stand between her legs, she let Carmen melt into the front of her body. Carmen pressed her face against Ollie's stomach, and Ollie wrapped her arms around her. Gently. She wanted to grip her, but Carmen still grimaced if she even so much as breathed wrong. Bruises still smattered her ribs, and her back was a solid line of dark purple that was now tinged with green and yellow. It was an ever-changing constellation Ollie couldn't wait to see faded, that evidence of violence.

For ages, they stayed like that, Ollie raking her fingers through Carmen's hair and Carmen's arms around her legs and hips. A patch over Carmen's ear was still shaved, and Ollie loved the contrasting feel of the softness of the rest of her hair and the slight prickle.

"I just want to see he's okay."

The words murmured into her stomach, warm through the material of her shirt.

Ollie hummed. "I know." Her fingers stayed in Carmen's hair. "Stay for dinner."

"Okay."

Ollie texted her dad and let him know Carmen would be there.

When he got home, they were sprawled on the sofa. A movie was playing, and Ollie wasn't sure how much attention Carmen had been giving it, but both of them seemed to be enjoying the closeness regardless. It was nice to do something like this. Almost like normal.

"Hey, Dad."

"Hi, girls. How are you, Carmen?"

Carmen smiled. "Good, thanks. And you?"

"Fine, fine. I bought dinner." He held up plastic bags.

The smell of Chinese hit Ollie, setting her stomach rumbling. Heat crawled up her neck when Carmen laughed.

"You all hungry?"

"Ollie clearly is."

They sat at the table again. Carmen was as useless as Ollie's dad with chopsticks, no matter how much Ollie tried to teach her. They both gave up and went to forks. Though Ollie could tell she was trying, Carmen was quieter this time, her conversation more sporadic. If her father noticed, he didn't say anything. Only occasionally, Ollie's stomach twinged at the empty chair her mother once used.

It wasn't a gaping hole anymore. But it was always there, like a small bump in the floor you kept scuffing your feet over, almost tripping but never completely.

Later, back in Ollie's room, they sprawled on her bed. Ollie checked her phone, and Carmen's face lay against her chest, as close as she could be. "I asked Deon to check for us."

"Mm?" Carmen's voice was heavy with sleep.

Had Carmen slept at all the night before, waiting for it to be Monday, the day she could finally see Mattie?

"There were no changes to the files at child services, and the hospital he was in before hasn't seen him again. Surely they'd be updated if something had happened?"

Carmen wiggled closer, their legs entangled. Her arms tightened around Ollie's waist, and she dropped her phone. Her head fell on the pillow. "They would, I imagine."

And that was all Carmen said. They lay, their bodies flush together. Ollie could feel Carmen's heart beating. Her face was pushed into Ollie's neck. When her breaths puffed against Ollie's skin, she knew Carmen had fallen asleep. Gradually she, too, fell under.

She woke up hours later with her glasses digging painfully into the side of her head. She'd rolled onto her back at some point, and Carmen had followed her, still close, an arm thrown over her stomach. The room was dark. Hadn't the light been on when they'd fallen asleep? Actually, a blanket was over them, one from the closet down the hall. As Ollie rolled over onto her other side, glasses safely on the bedside table and Carmen along her back, she realized her dad must have found them.

The last thing she thought, before her eyes drifted shut, was that sleeping with Carmen was probably one of her favorite things.

On Tuesday, Mattie still didn't appear.

Not on Wednesday either.

Carmen was sick each day. She couldn't eat properly, her stomach churning. Ollie watched her with worried eyes, and Rae didn't even try to soothe her, just let her vibrate with frustration next to her on the roof. The sky was cloudless and smattered with stars.

"I miss him," Artie had said on Tuesday night. With a jolt, Carmen remembered he was only a few years older than Mattie.

On Thursday, she was standing near a group of people her age, near the steps of the school he *should* be in. A backpack was looped over one shoulder in the hopes it helped her look like she belonged. Her eyes stayed on the stream of kids, and then her heart stilled in her chest.

There he was.

The sun was pouring down, and his face scrunched up at the glare of it as he stepped down the stairs carefully. One eye was still closed. The swelling looked hideous, and Carmen's heart started up again, double time, at the sight of it. The cut looked like it was healing well. But it was still puffy. Had it been too long for it to be like that? Though the injury had been severe. Maybe the recovery time was normal.

She didn't shout out. She didn't have to.

Mattie stopped at the bottom of the stairs, looking around. Carmen, trying to remember the vague plan she'd made, took steps backward. There was an alcove she could step back into once he saw her, one that would stop them being noticed as much. But each step felt as if she was tearing herself away from Mattie, like Velcro ripped apart so slowly you felt each loop break free.

She refused to blink. Her gaze stayed on him, heavy; he had to feel it. He'd be looking for her. He'd see her.

He turned and caught her eye. Carmen faltered.

His good eye widened, and Carmen saw the wet shine in it immediately. Her throat closed over, a lump growing so fast that the shock of it left her reeling. One by one, her senses came back to her, beyond what she could see and feel. She could smell the warm heat rolling off the asphalt, could hear the chatter and shouts of kids as they hit her eardrums, could taste her own anticipation, almost bitter on her tongue.

She kept walking backward, and Mattie followed her, their gazes never leaving each other's until Carmen turned the corner and she took one more big step backward. Mattie tore around the corner, and she was on her knees. He slammed into her.

She bit back her yelp of pain as her ribs and back protested and just clutched him tighter. His fingers gripped her back, the tips biting into her skin, and he gave a hot sob into her neck.

"Mattie."

It took him minutes to pull back, clutching her shoulders. They drank each other in. Carmen tried not to flinch at his face, so bruised and swollen still; it was so much worse up close. But he seemed fine. He smelled like soap and shampoo, like a kid who had been at school all day. He looked well. He looked like Mattie, and Carmen thought she may come apart right then and there with relief.

"Carmen." He said her name like he'd been holding it in since they parted. And his jaw tightened, a duskiness crawling up his neck and over his cheeks. His eye swam, and he blinked rapidly. "You just left me there."

The words hit her harder than when his hand came up, shoving her backward. Not that it hurt; he didn't push her hard. It jolted her back and ribs a little. The force of it was just enough that she fell back and sat against the backs of her ankles. But those words were what she felt slam into her chest, what made her gasp.

"You left me behind! You just walked out and I woke up and you were *gone*."

Her mouth opened, then she closed it. He shoved her again, one hand open against her shoulder. She'd never seen him so angry while looking so close to giving in to sobs.

"Carmen." He hiccupped her name.

The lump in Carmen's throat was going to choke her, she was sure.

"You left me." He gave her another push against her shoulder, but weaker this time.

She just watched him, and he glared her down, tears splashing down his cheeks.

"You left me." The venom had disappeared. Still, the fractured sound of the words made that lump in her throat explode. His hand came up again, but this time, his fingers clenched around her shirt, digging in. His chest was rising and falling fast; Carmen wanted him to keep shoving her, to keep throwing anger at her, rather than look at her like she'd broken him. "You're crying." His voice was hoarse.

With one hand, she swiped at her cheeks, the other covering the hand that clung to her shoulder. "I'm not. I'm leaking."

He choked a laugh. "Liar."

"I'm sorry." But she couldn't tell him she wished she hadn't done this, because now he was in front of her and okay, and she was sure; it had definitely been the right thing to do. But she *was* sorry.

He didn't answer that. Just tilted his head, his grip not weakening. "Whatever. You're crying."

Carmen hazarded a smile, rolling her eyes. "Well, I missed you." She deserved everything he'd just thrown at her. Giving him a minute to see if he had anything more, she repeated when he didn't, "I missed you."

His fingers twitched on her shoulders.

"Mattie, where were you the last few days? I was going out of my mind."

Swallowing, he shrugged. "My face looked really bad. When I got to the new place, I got really dizzy and threw up again. They took me to an emergency clinic, and they told me to stay home a few extra days and not move around much."

"They took you to an emergency clinic?"

"Right away."

"Are they okay? Are they nice?"

Now that he wasn't looking at her like she'd betrayed him, she couldn't stop touching him—her hands on his arms, over his hair. He let her for a moment, but then he squirmed, shooting her a slightly frustrated look. Only then did the tight ball of worry unknot, the one that hadn't left her since those men had entered the bar.

"They're okay." His voice was monotone. He stared over her shoulder at the brick wall behind them.

"Mattie?"

"They are. They're fine. There's a couple of other kids. One's an asshole."

"Mattie!" But her snort of laughter meant he just threw her a grin and didn't look chagrined at all. He'd learned that from Rae. She'd bet on it.

"He is, though." The grin was gone.

"But it's not terrible?"

For a second, he stared at her, and she had the feeling he was waging war with something in his mind. If she knew her brother, he was deciding whether or not to lie. But about what?

Finally, he shook his head. "It's not." His voice went tight. "But, Carmen, I don't know them. It's not...it's not with *you*. I..." He was staring straight at her, and her shoulder would have bruises, his grip was so tight—proof of his desperation that she could carry with her. "I want to be back with you. I could come now."

He'd obviously decided not to lie and hoped she'd still take him.

It would be easy. To duck off now. To take his hand and take him back. Her instincts screamed at her to do it. He stared straight at her, his broken face so close. When she raised her hand, her fingers trembled against his unbruised cheek. Soft. Like when he was a baby.

"I can't."

His jaw tightened, a muscle flexing in his cheek. "I knew you'd say that." That muscle relaxed. "I remember everything you said in the hospital. Everything else is so fuzzy. But I remember that."

"I'm not leaving you there, Mattie. I'm not."

He stared at her a while longer, as if he was searching her for something. "I want to come back."

And then he broke into sobs, and she pulled him into her and let him cry. Under her hands, his chest felt as if he'd break apart from the heaving, and she did her best to hold him together.

She hated that she'd have to push him back together, then push him away again.

But she'd let him have another minute before she did that.

228

Ollie never spoke to her dad about the fact that he let Carmen stay.

But on Thursday, with him on the sofa and her standing with the coffee table between them, she tried not to fiddle with her phone too much when she asked if she could stay at Carmen's.

It wasn't entirely fair, because her father knew nothing about where Carmen stayed, that it wasn't a safe house nestled in a safe neighborhood. But Ollie was nearing eighteen, and if everything worked out, she would be at college within the year anyway, not living at home. Also, he did know that Carmen didn't live at home, that she looked after herself. And maybe it was time to give him some more information? The other night, Carmen had said she could. That she *should*.

He eyed her over the book he was reading on the sofa. "You want to stay the night at your girlfriend's?"

"Uh, yeah."

His throat bobbed, he swallowed so hard.

"We want to see her brother." Ollie bit her lip. She hadn't really meant to tell him so much.

"She has a brother?"

In the middle of the living room, Ollie kind of felt like she was in the spotlight or at an interview. Nerves twisted in her belly, which was ridiculous. She dropped to the floor and crossed her legs, instantly feeling more comfortable, less formal now.

"She does. His name is Mattie."

"And where is Mattie, if her parents are…gone?"

"Foster care."

Her father put his book down, and it thunked heavily against the wooden coffee table. The dark brown of his eyes softened as he put his elbows on his knees. "That must be hard for them. Were they close? How old is he?"

"He's nine."

Her father gave a low whistle. "He's young."

"And they're very close. Carmen misses him. More than I understand, I think." Ollie picked at a hole in the knee of her jeans. "I think it's harder for Mattie. They were in foster care before. Neither of them had a great experience."

Even though Carmen had said Ollie could tell her dad, her hands were clammy. Her stomach turned over just a little. No matter what Carmen had said, were these really her secrets to spill?

"Shouldn't Carmen be in foster care?"

She could feel his eyes on her, and Ollie didn't want to lie. How long had he wanted to ask more? "She left it."

"She ran away."

The words should have echoed around the room, the truth of them thick and rebounding off the walls. An adult wasn't supposed to know this. That was the one rule. But he was always going to guess. And Ollie couldn't lie to him, not after everything.

"She's eighteen soon. She would have been aged out anyway." Ollie met her father's eyes, and that soft look was still there. She could see thoughts flashing over his face. Was he wondering if he should call someone? Did he realize it would cause more trouble than solutions? He seemed to settle on that idea, because he didn't look outraged. Rather, he just looked... concerned.

"Does she have what she needs? How does she have money if she's not in the system?"

Ollie shrugged. "She gets by."

Some days, Ollie wanted to leave money in Carmen's bag. To take out some of her savings, or leave the cash her dad left her in her backpack without thinking twice. Something, though, a small voice inside her head, told her Carmen wouldn't like that. But sometimes she sat in the ease of her house, at her table and among her things, and couldn't *not* see how absurd it was, how much she had and how little Carmen did. She wanted to give it all to her.

"Is she safe, Ollie?"

The concern in his voice made Ollie want to hug him.

"She is."

And that was mostly true. What had happened could happen to anyone walking down the street. The situation in the warehouse was like Carmen lived with a foster family anyway. Or an aunt and uncle and her hyperactive cousins.

"Is she in school?"

"No."

The lines around his eyes deepened even further.

Ollie rushed to interrupt. "She may go back. Right now she's trying to earn money, to get a good place, and to be able to prove she can look after her brother when she's eighteen. Besides," she said, testing him and not liking herself much for it, "school isn't the be-all and end-all."

At that, her father eased himself back against the couch. "She wants to look after her brother?"

"Yeah."

"She's seventeen."

Nodding, Ollie didn't know what to say.

"Ollie." What if he told her he was calling the police? "If you stay at her place, you have your phone, okay? And you call if you need anything, at any time. I know…" He squinted at her. "I know you could have easily told me you were staying with Sara or at Deon's. I—in not that long, you won't even be living at home. I don't see the point in policing your decision. But you call me if you need anything at all, okay? Or if, if Carmen does."

And he meant that. She blinked at him for a moment.

"I can help her, if she needs it," he added.

Ollie stood up and walked around the coffee table she'd used as some kind of barrier. Before either of them knew what was happening, she threw herself at her father, her arms wrapping around him. For just a split second, one that seemed to go on forever, he froze, muscles tensing. But then his arms engulfed her, tight around her shoulders. His chest was like she remembered it, under her cheek. She closed her eyes and breathed in. He still smelled the same.

For some reason, that made her throat tighten.

When she pulled away, he let her go, somewhat slowly, as if reluctant to do so. When he spoke again, his voice was tight. "What was that for?"

She shrugged. "Nothing."

Everything about his gaze was soft, and he squeezed her shoulder before letting his hand fall away. She tried a smile, surprised it was a little wobbly. The one he gave in reply echoed hers, and Ollie stood.

"Great. I'll head there soon."

"Want a lift?"

"It's okay, thanks. I think Sara is picking me up. She's going out anyway."

"Okay."

She grabbed the bag she had ready with things jammed in it for school the next day and a change of clothes. With a last "see you tomorrow" to her dad, she met Sara in her car.

"You okay?" Sara asked.

In the twilight, Ollie nodded. "Yeah, I am."

"Good to hear."

And the next smile Sara gave was so genuine that Ollie wanted to look away, even as she gave her own back.

"So," Ollie started. "You and Rae admitted you're totally dating yet?"

Groaning, Sara turned to look out the windshield and started the car. "I take it back. Go back to being moody."

Ollie laughed and settled into the seat.

CHAPTER 24

Some days, Ollie went with Carmen to the school. Carmen liked when she could go, because it wasn't often. On the other hand, Carmen went every day. She needed Mattie to know she was still there.

And she needed Mattie. Period.

But it was nice, the times Ollie did go. When Mattie would make his way to the bus, the one that left about fifteen minutes after school finished, Carmen didn't have to stand there alone and watch his tiny body get engulfed by the people in the line. The days he turned around in his seat, hand splayed over the glass as he looked to see if she was still watching— she always was—she didn't have to take a shuddering breath in by herself. Ollie's fingers, warm and firm, would entwine with her own and squeeze.

The first day Carmen took Ollie to meet Mattie, Ollie had stayed the night in the warehouse. How quickly Carmen was getting used to seeing so much of her was almost worrying. Waking up to Ollie's hair in her face, or with just a foot thrown lazily over Carmen's calf, was soothing. Carmen could lie awake and stare at the ceiling, and eventually the steady breathing next to her would lull her back to sleep.

Ollie didn't stay over often, but it was amazing when she did. Slowly, Carmen was realizing she was letting another person stitch themselves under her skin. When it came to Ollie, though, Carmen just couldn't find it in her to care that she normally needed to keep her distance from people.

So the first time they stood across from each other, the three of them hidden away in the little alcove, Mattie had cocked his head. "You're the one that called the police."

Ollie had swallowed so hard Carmen heard it. "Yeah, that was me."

His eye, the injured one, still mostly closed, narrowed. "That was stupid."

Before Carmen could tell him that was unfair, Ollie said, "It was. I know that *now*. But I didn't then."

Without answering, Mattie just stared at her again. Finally, he said, "You're also the one that makes my sister smile like an idiot. That's nice." That had made Carmen roll her eyes.

Ollie had just laughed. "Really?"

His posture shifted slightly as he slipped his hands into his pockets. "Really. She's such a sap. It's gross."

Ollie had looked at her, but Carmen ignored it. "Anyway!" She shot her brother a glare, and he shrugged. "I just thought you two should meet properly."

"I got you something." Ollie swung her backpack to her front and unzipped it. Carmen hadn't known anything about that. She watched, head cocked.

After digging around for a second, Ollie pulled out a handful of DS games. Mattie's eyes lit up like the Christmas lights he and Carmen used to watch in the city center together. When she'd mentioned Mattie's DS to Ollie, she'd never expected this.

"What—what is that?" Mattie's voice had a cautious slowness to it. The sound brought up a familiar ache in her, one that made her want to clasp him to her, to protect him from whatever disappointment he was wary of. But this wasn't one of her mom's empty promises that would leave him crushed. This was Ollie.

Ollie shrugged, and Carmen could tell she was trying to be nonchalant. "Some games I used to play, but I don't really have time to anymore." She held the fistful out. "You want them?"

Mattie eyed her for a second, still unsure, disbelieving. "Really?"

"Sure."

He glanced to Carmen, who mimicked Ollie with a shrug of her own, then back to Ollie. "O—okay."

Having smaller hands like his meant he had to take the games in both of them, clutching them to his chest. They looked like they were about to overflow from his arms. A smile started to take over his face. "Thanks."

"No problem."

It turned out Carmen needn't have ever worried about Ollie and Mattie getting along. Mostly what they did was tease Carmen. Which should have gotten old very quickly, but the sight of them both sharing that wicked glint in their eyes made warmth spread throughout her belly.

She missed having Mattie around all the time, but as the bruise faded around his eye, much slower than the one on Carmen's face, she was simply relieved to see that those smiles didn't stop.

One day, she sat on the hard cement in the alcove, her back against the brick behind them. Mattie plopped down next to her, crossing his legs and hugging his backpack to his chest. Summer school had started, and he'd been required to take part to catch up. Luckily, the bus he caught left a little later than the one during the usual school year. It was nice. They had more time.

"Where's Ollie?"

"She has her SATs real soon. She's studying."

He snorted. "Sucker. She's stuck doing schoolwork in summer like me."

"Yeah, she says to say hi, though."

"Cool. Tell her hi back. And to make sure she takes a break so she doesn't get too stressed."

Carmen smiled down at his head. A truck rumbled past on the road, and a few cars pulled up and drove away, collecting the few other kids in the summer program. "Tell me about the people in the house, Mattie."

He shrugged against her arm, but she didn't look at him. Instead, they both stared out of the little alcove, watching people pass.

"They're okay. The adults are kind of nice. They're old, like sixty or something. I met their kid. He's old too, and an accountant." He turned his head so she met his eye. His eyebrows were all scrunched up. "Do you know what that is?"

"Someone that does taxes and stuff."

"Exactly. How *boring* does that sound?"

Carmen laughed. "Really boring."

"I asked him why he'd wanna do that, and he said he liked numbers. I told him you did too. Maybe you could be an accountant?"

No words rose up to tell Mattie that to do that, she needed to be in school. To go to college. All things she couldn't do if she wanted to work and have the money to prove she deserved her brother. Anger curled in her stomach again at that thought, tingling over her limbs and her fingertips;

her temperature spiked. Having to *prove* that was still the most unfair thing she had ever heard of. "Maybe" was all she said.

"Astronauts need to be good at math. Maybe you could be one of those."

Carmen chuckled, throwing an arm over Mattie's shoulder. "That would be cool."

He nodded, his hair rubbing against her cheek.

God, she loved him. Her cheeky, frustrated, funny little brother, who looked at her like she could do no wrong "You got distracted. The family?"

He sighed. "They're fine. They're kind of like the last one, but they pay more attention. I told you, there are four other kids. But one's an asshole—" she squeezed him in warning "—fine, a douche—" she squeezed him harder. "Oof—fine, a mean guy. Better?" He didn't wait for her to respond. "He's angry all the time and picks on one of the other guys. But Rob and Faye, the parents, know he is and try to stay on top of it. They said we have to be understanding, 'cause he's been through a lot. But Carmen." He sat up and twisted to stare at her, his eyes an earnest brown like earth, rich and full of promise. "The other kids have been through stuff too. And me, I s'pose. And the girl that's there. And none of them are as much an assho—idiot as him."

Those words. *And himself,* Mattie had supposed, like an afterthought. Like the life he'd had wasn't really all that bad. Like being cold and hungry most of the time, with a mother that had left him with a sister too young to figure it all out, wasn't that big of a deal. Like the foster homes hadn't been hard, even when they were better compared to most. Like the street was easy.

But he knew other stories now. Maybe that was it.

"Well." Carmen licked her bottom lip slowly, trying to figure out what to say. "Some people don't handle things the same. Some things are too big for some people."

"Maybe he'd always been alone."

Carmen blinked at him. "Maybe."

"That sucks for him, that he didn't have a sister like you to help him."

Carmen really, really loved her little brother.

236

In a fit of uncertainty, Ollie had signed up for the SATs at the start of summer. Her school had bugged her to, and her dad had nudged her along. They were worried about her results, she knew. After the year she'd had, she was behind, and she had never been the best student anyway. If she took the SATs over the summer, she would have time to take them again senior year if she needed to. Which she would, she knew.

Maybe she should word that more as if she *wanted* to, rather than *needed* to.

Pamphlets sat in her room for colleges, and she ignored them, trying to not think about the weight of applying for things that determined her future when she wasn't sure what she wanted her future to be. She just bumbled though the exam, Sara at the same one, almost in solidarity more than anything, and hoped for the best.

Art pumped through her veins and tingled at the tips of her fingertips. It was what she threw herself into most. And, with the constant thought of what her mother would think in the back of Ollie's mind, she thought mostly about colleges with good art programs. Her dad had just nodded, a shadow in his eye, but not saying anything.

Ollie wanted to talk to her mother. To ask her what she thought. On nights following the exam, she'd lie in bed alone, her heart racing and wish more than anything she could flop onto the couch with her mom and ask if everything really did hang on these decisions she was making, or if it just felt that way.

One night, on the roof of the warehouse, Ollie and Carmen lay on their backs and stared up at the sky. With the exam over, summer stretched ahead of them. She had a job at a reception desk in one of the art museums now. Her dad knew someone who knew the director. Sometimes, she forgot that his job was linked with art, that he'd minored in it while studying architecture.

But finally, with Carmen there next to her, their legs entangled and her head on Carmen's shoulder, none of that seemed to matter.

"I have something for you." Carmen tensed under her. She didn't like gifts, or anything that felt like charity. When would she get that it wasn't charity? "Chill out, it's nothing like that," she added.

"Sorry."

Ollie sat up and stared down at Carmen, who pulled her hand under her head. The moon was full, throwing a blue light over everything. It seemed to roll over Carmen's hair like waves. Each shift made it shimmer, and Ollie wanted to draw her like that. She took a second to take her in, to imprint it all into her mind to sketch later: the colors and the slope of her cheek, the brush of her eyelashes. Charcoals, heavy with blunt lines and smudged to create the softness caused by the light. And later, she'd paint it on a canvas. Oils, maybe. Or she could play with her watercolors. They weren't her usual medium, but something about that light made her fingers itch for the brush, for the swish of water and the cloth she'd grip in her hand to wipe it clean between colors.

Blinking, she remembered where she was.

Carmen was staring at her with a soft smile. "What?"

"Nothing." Ollie traced a finger over Carmen's cheek, brushed her hair behind her ear, and smiled when Carmen shivered as Ollie ran a finger lightly over the shell of her ear. Carmen's eyes fluttered closed. "You're beautiful."

Carmen shook her head.

"You are," Ollie reiterated.

"Didn't you say you had something for me?" Carmen opened her eyes and laughed at Ollie's eye roll. Carmen could never take a compliment.

Too lazy to get up, Ollie stretched over, shuffling a little, to drag her backpack over. She rummaged inside it, and her fingers enclosed over the soft, leather lines of what she was searching for. Out of nowhere, she felt shy. Warmth flooded her cheeks. "So, I, uh, had this for you weeks ago. But it was the day Mattie got hurt, and I kind of forgot about it. And then it didn't seem like the right time. So I waited? And maybe you'll think it's really stupid—"

Carmen's hand on her knee shut her up. And then she was sitting in front of her, with her soft eyes and moonlight in her hair, and Ollie knew she was being stupid to worry like this.

"What is it?"

Ollie held out the overloaded journal she'd wanted to give Carmen ages ago. It was full of sketches, random pages filled with colors she'd played with, things she'd glued in that pulled out and made shapes and images.

Swallowing, Carmen took it, staring down.

"You—you said you wanted to see some of my stuff. More of it, I mean. So this is for you."

Carmen opened it, and she traced her fingers over the image she'd come across. The book sat in her lap, and she flicked more pages, staring down at a pastel drawing of eyes Ollie hoped she knew were her own. She touched her finger against a thick acrylic painting of a sunset. "This is amazing."

Ollie's cheeks went warmer. "Thank you."

"This entire book is for me?"

"I have a lot of them. I fill them up really fast. This is the one I started around when I met you. Some of the, uh, pages get a bit dark. In the middle."

Carmen cocked her head, nodding. She knew very well when Ollie's mom had died, and Ollie suspected it was what she was thinking about right now. "Don't you want to keep it?"

Ollie shook her head. "It's for you. It's yours more than mine. I don't know if that makes sense."

Carmen's fingers wrapped around the back of Ollie's neck and urged her forward. Ollie pushed herself up, her thighs on either side of Carmen as she straddled her and their lips came together softly.

"Thank you."

The words murmured over her lips, and Ollie breathed them in. "You're welcome."

She settled back to sit more firmly in Carmen's lap, Carmen's hand against her thigh and the other still in her hair. The book pressed between them, and neither went to move it.

"There's some of Mattie in the back."

Carmen's lips curled up even more, and Ollie wished she could see her smile like that more often. It lit her whole face up, crinkled around her eyes.

"You drew Mattie?"

"Yeah. I added them after."

A shadow fell over Carmen's face then, the smile dimming.

"What?"

For a moment Ollie panicked, thinking Carmen was about to shut down and pull back. She did that sometimes—disappeared—and Ollie let her. She always came back. But the thought of losing that open look on Carmen's face made Ollie's stomach lurch.

But Carmen shook her head, just slightly. "I'm just… I've been thinking all day. Talking with Jia."

"About how to get him back?"

"Yeah. I'm eighteen in just over a month. I'll be able to get visitations with him pretty easily, I think. I'll have aged out. Jia agrees it won't be a problem. But actually getting him back?"

Beneath Ollie's hands, one against Carmen's neck and the other resting lightly on her stomach, no longer bruised but still tender, Carmen's body froze as she held her breath for a second. Finally, the muscles under Ollie's hands relaxed as Carmen exhaled slowly, and Ollie pushed closer, shoving the book to the side, their foreheads together.

"I'm so scared I may not be able to."

"What can I do?"

Carmen shrugged, the movement shifting both of them a little. "Nothing. I need to speak to a lawyer, to someone, once I'm eighteen. Jia knows some people who will speak to me for free and give me some advice. I need to get an apartment. I need to find a job out of the bar, one more full-time. I have to prove I can look after him."

Her entire body tensed again.

"What?" Ollie asked.

"It's just…" Carmen pulled back so abruptly the cold air was a slap against Ollie's cheeks after being wrapped in her. She leaned back on her hands, staring Ollie straight in the eye, her face unguarded and her cheeks flushed. She was angry.

It took Ollie a second to recognize that look. She hadn't really seen it on Carmen's face before.

"It's that—why should I have to prove I'm the best thing for him? I'm all he's ever had. Of course I'm the best thing for him. No one—no one asked me to prove it when it was only me, and our mother was just *gone* for days and days. Do you know she once left for an entire month?"

Ollie shook her head, wanting to absorb the anger radiating off Carmen.

"A *month*. She left fifty bucks she'd probably gotten from selling crack from the very table she left it on and just went. Do you have any idea how hard it is to make fifty bucks last for food for a month? The electricity shut off halfway through. We had to have cold showers in winter. We had to make sure the school didn't notice. She raised me to do that, to know secrecy and cover-ups. And I did it, for Mattie. And I did it well. Now they want me to *prove* I deserve him? To *prove* I'm the best option he has?"

Carmen's eyes were glittering now, and when she blinked once, heavily, tears spilled over and fell too fast to count. The light caught on them, and the ones that clung to her lashes were like diamonds.

Her tongue heavy with its lack of words, Ollie hesitated. She had no idea what to say to this. To the reality of the world that had swallowed Carmen and Mattie so unfairly. "I'm sorry." She whispered the words in the hope they wouldn't hit Carmen too hard.

Carmen drew in a shuddering breath and held it a second before blowing it out. "No, I am. Sorry."

"Hey." Ollie bent forward and cupped her cheeks. "No. Never be sorry."

She pulled Carmen forward, and she relented, wrapping her arms around Ollie's waist and burrowing her face into her neck. Her cheeks and breath were warm and wet. All Ollie could do was hold her as close as possible and run her fingers through her hair. Carmen didn't shudder from sobs, and she didn't cry. She just gripped on to Ollie.

"Thank you."

"No thank-yous either."

Carmen huffed a laugh against her neck, and Ollie couldn't help the shudder, or the goose bumps that broke out over her skin.

Pulling back just a little, Carmen blinked at her. Tears still hung from her eyelashes, but she seemed calmer, the wild look that had taken over her eyes soothed. With Carmen's injuries and the stress of Mattie, they hadn't done more than press close and kiss in weeks. Carmen's gaze dropped to Ollie's lips, and Ollie's breath hitched, catching in her chest. Even fragile, with tears smudged under her cheeks, Carmen managed to make Ollie shiver.

She pushed forward, their lips colliding with more force than Ollie thought either of them had meant. The rawness of the last ten minutes, too much for too short a time, had left Ollie split open. Carmen was facing so much for Ollie to be able to help, but the uselessness that haunted her disappeared as Carmen moaned into her mouth and her tongue licked Ollie's lip.

At least Ollie was here. She could offer that.

Hands splayed over Ollie's spine under her shirt, nails scratching over her shoulder blade. Ollie arched into her.

"Of *course* they're making out."

They froze, Carmen huffing at the sound of Rae's voice.

Ollie laughed, the sound slightly strangled as Carmen's hands slid out from her shirt and rested against her thighs again. Carmen squeezed, and Ollie tried to remember to breathe. She turned around and saw Rae and Sara, who both looked far too amused for her liking. "Please. Don't act like I didn't walk in on you two in the bathroom at the bar just last week."

Sara shrugged. "You should have knocked."

"It was a *public* toilet, you animal."

"Right." Rae drew the vowels out, her eyebrows raised. "And what does that make you two? I've seen you disappear off there more times than I can count."

Well, that comeback had been Ollie's fault. She'd just gone for the insult rather than taking that fact into account.

Carmen slapped her leg gently. "She's got you there, Ollie."

"Way to take her side."

Carmen just shrugged at her as Ollie slid off her lap.

Rae and Sara walked over to the edge of the roof and sat down. With Ollie's art book firmly in her hand, Carmen hauled Ollie up, and they went and sat shoulder to shoulder with the others, their feet swinging listlessly.

The moon really was like a streetlight, lighting everything up. The stars were even drowned out a little, and Ollie felt a pang of loneliness at not being able to see them. There, with her friends around her and the world sprawling out from their feet, she could forget SATs and life decisions. Even with the salty taste of Carmen's frustration still on her tongue, the moment felt present, those decisions and repercussions a bit too far away suddenly. It was almost dizzying how much they swung from being at the forefront of her mind to far away, a problem for later.

"Hey, Ollie?" Sara asked.

"Mm?"

"Have you gotten your SAT results yet?"

Ollie groaned and dropped her head back. Next to her, knowing how much she didn't want to think about it, Carmen just laughed.

"Shut up, Sara."

The snort could have come from any of them.

CHAPTER 25

THE SUMMER PASSED TOO FAST and too slow.

Ollie worked during the day, and on days she didn't, on weekends or even afternoons, everyone came over to use the pool. In so many ways, everything was like the summers before, and in so many ways so different that it left an ache in Ollie's chest so deep it seemed to resonate.

Her mother never appeared to throw sunscreen toward her with a roll of her eyes, or gave her the special conditioning treatment she always bought Ollie for her hair. No week her mom took off to just be around the house, all up in Ollie's space in a way that had started to get irritating but now she craved.

There were things her dad didn't think of and things Ollie just did for herself.

The best difference, though, was Carmen—laid out in the sun with drops of water drying tight on her skin, brown and browning even more in the heat. There was her lazy smile when she'd roll over on her towel and throw a hot, baked arm over Ollie's stomach.

Sara and Rae came and went at their own times. Not always with each other. Sara and Ollie would still spend hours together, laid out and reading, poking each other into laughter under the twilight sky. They wouldn't go inside until one of them had to slap at a mosquito, usually too hard and on the other person with an unapologetic shrug at the indignant squeal it evoked. Some nights, Deon joined them, or a few other friends from school.

Carmen kept seeing Mattie. He was at school five days a week still, trying to catch up in some kind of summer program Ollie should really be grateful she hadn't had to do this year. Sometimes Ollie went with her to see him before he got on the bus. He was a smart kid. All dark eyes and dark hair and dark skin. He'd sized her up before he really warmed to her, and she liked his boldness. But mostly she liked the way Carmen would look between the two of them as if she had everything she wanted at that moment.

Carmen now had a standing invitation to dinner at Ollie's house. So Carmen came regularly, on the nights she didn't have to be at the bar. Sometimes, if Ollie got off from work late, she'd come home and the two of them, Carmen and her father, would be watching a soccer match on TV, yelling things at it that Ollie didn't care about. Her dad didn't even like soccer. He preferred tennis or football. She'd seen him some mornings, staring at his tablet and reading about soccer teams and cups, and Ollie had felt such a sweeping affection she'd wanted to hug him over her cereal. He was only reading up on it for Carmen.

Right before Carmen's eighteenth, he insisted she come for a birthday dinner.

"So, Carmen," he said over the meal, "you're almost eighteen?"

Ollie knew that number would be ringing in her head. She squeezed Carmen's hand under the table.

"I am," Carmen said. "In a few days, in fact."

"It's a big birthday."

Her father didn't say it in the patronizing way so many adults did when they spoke about it. His tone was low, as if he really did understand the significance it had for Carmen.

"It is." Carmen took a sip of her water.

"So. Are you going to see about your brother?"

Carmen's hand shuddered as she put her glass down. Someone's knife scraped on their plate, and Ollie realized it was hers. She put her cutlery down. Carmen knew Ollie had told her dad about most of it, ignoring as many of the more illegal parts as she could. But talking about the situation with an adult not immediately involved had clearly thrown her.

"I am. I—" Her gaze darted to Ollie, then back to her father. "I would really like to have him back living with me as soon as possible."

Her father put his elbows on the table, his hands clasped in front of him. "That's a huge amount of responsibility."

Ollie wanted to tell her dad to shut up, expecting Carmen to bristle next to her. But she didn't.

"I know it is. With all due respect, I've been looking after him since he was born. I know what I'm getting into."

He nodded, his head tilted as he took in the sincere look on Carmen's face. "I really believe you do," he said softly. "What about school? Isn't there something you'd like to do?"

Instead of just saying no like Ollie expected, Carmen relaxed back into her chair. *Relaxed* wasn't the right word; she was still tense. But she wasn't thrumming with frustration like Ollie would have expected.

"To be honest, I haven't really even thought that far ahead." Her hand trembled slightly, fingers still wrapped around the glass on the table. "I know I should, but all I can think about is getting Mattie back with me. He's the most important thing. I can look at that stuff later, when we're more set up. I know I'm young, and people will think *too* young for this. But also: yes, I'm *young*. That means I have so much time. I can study later. I can take some kind of online course, or I can look at getting my GED. But I'm young. I have ages to figure that out. People go to college late all the time. But I only have now to be with Mattie."

Ollie stared at Carmen, amazed at the conviction in her voice, the hard line of her shoulder as she sat up straighter with every word.

Her father was watching her too, a smile playing at the edge of his mouth. "Good point." He grinned now. "I would never have thought of that as a response to 'you're too young.'"

Carmen shrugged. "It's just how I feel. Everyone seems to want us all to know what we want to do and where we want to be in the next few years and then keep telling us how young we all are and how we can't make dramatic decisions because of this."

He huffed a laugh, reaching for the salad bowl. Glancing at Ollie, he said, "I like this one."

"I do too."

Carmen flushed next to her, and Ollie wanted to kiss it off her, to feel the blush under her lips. They still smelled of the chlorine from the pool.

"Well. I wanted to talk to you both about something."

They froze, and Ollie tore her eyes from Carmen's neck.

He was watching them, his expression impassive. "This is something I've wanted to talk to you about for a long time, but the more I get to know you, and especially after what you've just said, the more I'm convinced it's the right thing to do."

He took in a deep breath, and Ollie could feel that Carmen had gone completely still beside her. What was he going to say?

"I want to get you a lawyer. A good one. One who can really get you the best shot at this, but not just that. One who will tell you, realistically, what the best plan is."

If she'd been still before, now Carmen was a rock. Ollie could hardly breathe. Had her father really just said that?

"What..." Carmen couldn't even finish her sentence.

"Dad, are you serious?"

"Of course I am."

"Calvin..."

Her father turned his attention back to Carmen. "You can say no, of course. But please don't. Consider it a birthday present."

"A ridiculously expensive one," Carmen said.

He sighed. "In relation to some things, yes. In relation to the life I've built, and the one I built w—with Ollie's mother, no. I can do this, and I want to. You mean a lot to Ollie, Carmen. And I know... I know her mother would want this too."

A lump welled in Ollie's throat, and she blinked rapidly.

"I..." Carmen looked to Ollie, then back to her father. "I don't know what to say."

No one said anything, and Ollie knew her dad didn't want to push the decision. Ollie had a feeling if either of them tried, Carmen would run.

"Okay." Carmen's voice was tight. "Okay. Thank you. On one condition. You let me pay you back one day."

"No." There was a firmness to his voice Ollie rarely heard. "That's not how birthday presents work. However, there is something else that we can talk about, and this I will negotiate on if you say yes." When neither of the girls said anything, he pressed on. "I haven't talked to Ollie about any of this first, Carmen, because I want you to understand I'm doing this for you. Independent of your relationship with Ollie. So don't be mad at her for being blindsided."

Clearing her throat, Carmen nodded.

Ollie just kept staring between the two of them. Did Carmen get what he was saying? That he was offering help and it didn't matter what went down between Carmen and Ollie? That Carmen could have some security, her life not a constant tightrope threatening to snap under her feet?

"We have a small apartment we bought as an investment. We have people renting it, and their lease will finish in a couple of months. I don't know where you've been staying." Something in his tone made Ollie think he'd doubted where she was staying from the start. "But I want to offer you this place. You'll be on a legitimate lease."

"No. No. That's far too much." Carmen sounded a little panicked.

"I want you to think about it first. We can discuss how much you can afford if you say yes. With time, I'll increase the rent. We can organize, again with time, for you to pay back the extra if it means that much to you. But not until you can afford it. It's a small place, far from the center of the city. Two bedroom. Near a bus line."

Ollie couldn't stop staring at her father. No doubt Carmen looked even more shocked than Ollie did. How long had her father been considering this? She knew he had a soft spot for Carmen, an understanding for her situation, but she would never have asked him to do this.

Her mother would have, though.

"Dad…" He looked at her, and she didn't have anything else to give.

He gave her a small smile before looking back to Carmen. "Just think about it. Okay?"

Slowly, Carmen nodded, which amazed Ollie even more than her father's offer. "Okay. I'll think about it." And probably say no. It was too much.

"Good." He smiled. "So. We need to make this appointment as soon as possible. Your birthday is Tuesday, right? How is Wednesday in the afternoon for you? I can come with you, if you like, or you can go alone."

"Uh, Wednesday is good. If, if you want to come, that would be good."

"Great. We'll talk about getting you set up with visiting him. And ask everything you want about custody. Write a list so you remember everything."

"Okay." Carmen sounded so overwhelmed. Her voice was losing its edge and seeming to trip out of her mouth.

"Good."

They were all finished with food after that, so Ollie and Carmen cleaned up. Normally, they'd fool around in the kitchen, hands soapy and leaving suds in each other's hair and smothering their giggles. That night, though, Carmen was introspective, staring down at the dishes as she rinsed them, and Ollie left her to her thoughts. That had been a lot of information, and she knew how much Carmen hated being thought of as a charity case. She'd done everything alone for so long. But Ollie couldn't help it. A part of her really hoped Carmen would move past that and let someone help her.

"You had no idea he'd offer that?" Her voice broke the silence, and Ollie almost jumped.

"Nope." She closed the dishwasher and turned it on, the noise starting instantly. "None. I think he meant it—this is something between you two, not to do with me."

Carmen was biting her lip, her eyebrows drawn together. "It's too much."

"Carmen…it's not. He wouldn't offer if he didn't mean it."

All Carmen did was shrug. "I think—I don't think I'll stay tonight."

"What?"

Maybe panic laced Ollie's voice, because Carmen finally smiled at her, grabbing her hand and squeezing. "No, not because I feel bad. I think I need to talk to Dex. No, to Jia."

Ollie looked sheepish. "Oh. That's a good idea." She pouted. "I'll miss you, though."

Carmen kissed the pout off her lip. "Me too. But I need to have this conversation now."

"You won't sleep until you do. Though I do know things to help with that…"

"Hm? Really?"

"Yup." Ollie twined her arms around Carmen's waist. "Many things. Fun things. But." She kissed her again. "I understand. You should go."

"What? Tease. Now I want to stay."

"Nope. I'll see you tomorrow at the bar." She kissed Carmen again, more softly this time. "You'll feel better if you go talk this out now."

Carmen hummed. "True. Okay. Tomorrow?"

"Tomorrow."

Ollie didn't walk her out but stayed in the kitchen and tidied up more. Mostly, she wanted to let Carmen say good night alone to her dad. Murmuring voices floated into the kitchen for five minutes before Ollie heard the click of the front door. A second later, her dad cleared his throat, and Ollie spun around, dropping the cloth in the sink.

He stared at her for a second. "Was that okay?"

"Of course it was, Dad. It was…it was amazing. Thank you."

The shrug he gave was almost awkward. "It was nothing. I… Your mom would want to help. I want to too, of course. But… I just keep thinking, what would she do?"

A chasm opened up between them, the first time in a long time. So much talk of her mother, the fact she wasn't there, hit Ollie like a slap against her cheek. But Ollie found words more quickly than normal this time and managed to say them before that hole swallowed them both.

"This. She'd do this."

"She would, yeah."

Ollie walked around the island in the middle and wrapped her arms around him, her cheek against his chest and his heart racing a touch too fast against it. His arms pulled her in tighter, and they stayed that way for a while, swaying slightly.

Now if only Carmen would accept the help.

"Of course you accept, Carmen."

"What?"

Jia stared at her from her office chair, unflinching. "You accept."

Carmen had expected more questions, a bit of the uncertainty she was feeling to be reflected in what Jia had to say. Not this. "But…it's too much."

"He offered for a reason."

The chair under her was uncomfortable, biting into her tailbone, and Carmen's legs bounced. Unable to sit still any longer, she stood and paced around the room, her hands flapping a little. "But…it's far too generous. I should be able to do this on my own, shouldn't I? If, if we rely on him, it could go wrong. What if he changes his mind? And—"

"Calm the hell down."

Spinning on the spot, Carmen hadn't stopped moving when she said, "Rae! You're an eavesdropper."

Against the doorframe, Rae shrugged. "You were ranting pretty loudly."

With a sigh, Carmen flopped onto Jia's mattress. She looked between the two of them. Jia stared at her impassively, and Rae just looked amused. "What should I do?"

"Accept it," they said at the same time, neither reacting to each other and just continuing to watch Carmen.

"But—"

"Look." Jia's voice, soothing and full of wisdom, washed over her. She smiled, the scar on her face folding in and deepening. Her eyes were soft. "I understand your worries. But he purposefully tried to make it clear that this was separate from Ollie. He's not going to change his mind. And if he does, I'd imagine you'd have Mattie in your care by then and will be able to keep yourselves afloat."

"What she said," Rae chimed in.

Carmen gnawed on the inside of her cheek. She was breathless, too scared to fall into this feeling of opportunity. What if she did and she just kept falling because it got whisked away? "I'll consider it."

An apartment was too much to accept. Surely she could find one on her own.

"This is your best shot at getting Mattie into your care, Carmen." Jia shrugged. "Let someone help you."

"What she said," Rae repeated, grinning.

Carmen looked from one to the other again.

Let someone help?

As a last resort, maybe.

CHAPTER 26

TURNING EIGHTEEN WAS DONE QUIETLY. The highlight was seeing Mattie.

"A lawyer?"

"Yeah."

He hitched his backpack up on his back. "Like, one who can really help?"

"Yup." She didn't tell him about the apartment. Carmen knew she couldn't accept so much.

"How do you have the money for that?"

"It's a birthday present." The brick wall bit into Carmen's back as she shifted her weight from one foot to the other.

"Woah. From who? Jia and Dex don't have that kind of money."

"From Ollie's dad."

"Woah."

"Yeah, whoa."

He beamed then, and Carmen's stomach panged at the sight of it. Despite everything life had thrown at him, he still managed to look like every other kid around.

"That's pretty cool. So we can see each other for real soon? Like, for longer?"

"That's the plan." Carmen tried to look optimistic, and she must have done a decent job, because his smile didn't falter. She was trying to be positive about everything, to trust that it could all come together. But what if it all got ripped out from under them?

"Well, that's way better than my present."

This time, her smile was as genuine as they come. "You got me a present? How?"

"Well, I have no money."

She smirked when he said that. He could be so blunt. Sometimes she wondered if it was a kid thing or just a Mattie thing.

"So I made you a card. I had to hide it, because no one knows I'm seeing you. But, uh, here."

He looked older then, scuffing his foot on the ground, sheepish as he handed over the card. She was struck, then, with the memory of his ninth birthday so long ago, and how happy he'd been with the cake Rae had nabbed from a supermarket. Until now, she hadn't seen that extra year he'd turned in his face, the way it had thinned that bit more. The way he was embarrassed to give her something he made.

"Thanks, Mattie."

"Look at it later."

"Okay." She put it in her bag, slipping it between the journal Ollie had given her and a book so it wouldn't get rumpled. "I see the lawyer tomorrow afternoon, so—"

"You can't come?"

"No. But I'll come the next day."

"The summer school has a few days off. I'll be at the house."

Carmen's throat tightened at the thought of not seeing him until the next week. She tried to smile, and this time she knew he could tell it wasn't real from the way his dark eyebrows pushed together.

"I'll see you next week, then."

With his lips tight together, he shook his head. "That's too far away. Carmen... I—" His jaw clenched so tight she could see it, the muscles shifting.

Lowering herself to her knees, Carmen was surprised she was looking up at him a little. "What, Mattie?"

"I miss you. I—" He bit back whatever he was going to say, taking in a shaky breath.

The loss of him was like missing a limb, but everything else around her was familiar. She had Ollie and Rae, the bed they'd been sleeping in for months. The roof. The bar. Dex. Jia. Artie. Mattie didn't, though. He had nothing familiar, just the DS he'd had in his pocket when she'd left him at the hospital. He was surrounded by strangers and had nothing to ground him.

She tugged his shirt, soft in her hand and he let himself be pulled into a hug. His fingertips gripped her hard. He was still so bony. Under her hands, she could feel the knobs of his spine.

"I am doing everything I can to be with you," she said into his hair and just hugged him tighter.

"I want to run again."

"Stay focused, Mattie. It'll be worth it in the end."

Every time she promised him that, she hoped she wasn't lying.

The bus was going much slower than normal.

It stopped at another red light, and Ollie groaned. The older woman across from her threw her a look, but she just ignored it. Her leg was bouncing, and she had to physically concentrate to get it to stop. The other one started, and she glared at it.

The city had stopped zooming past, and they were finally on the outskirts. Shells of buildings rumbled past, some obviously gutted and empty; others looked simply abandoned. When she saw the sign that had faded so much that it was now all green and black smudges, she hit the Call button and bounced off when the bus came to a stop. She didn't bother acknowledging the looks thrown her way for jumping out in a part of town that was, according to most people, completely uninhabited.

All she wanted to do was get to the warehouse.

Carmen had had her meeting with the lawyer today. Such a big lead-up after a simple night of hanging out for Carmen's birthday. Ollie had bought her soccer cleats, bright orange, and shin pads. She'd wanted to do more, but Carmen had wanted something quiet, and the day had passed quickly. Now Ollie was itching to arrive so she could see how the meeting with the lawyer had gone. Any minute, she'd be back at the warehouse. And would see if that edge in Carmen's gaze had eased for the first time since that horrible moment in the bar.

Carmen didn't know it, but Ollie had tried to sketch that fight to get it out of her head—the blurs as Carmen had ducked and swung her leg out, the shading over Dex's eye that darkened their look in a way she'd never have thought she'd see on him, the sharpness when Mattie's head had snapped back and to the side.

She'd burned the pages when she was done.

Ollie turned down the final street and wove down an alley. Finally, she ended up in front of the door with peeling paint.

A knock. Three long knocks. Wait. Two knocks.

It pulled open instantly. Rae was staring at her. "She's up on the roof."

"Did she say—"

"Up to you to go ask her."

Ollie pouted, but Rae just shrugged at her. Ollie sighed. "Fine. Not even a hint?"

"Nope."

"Damn. Sara said to say she would be by later." She paused for effect. "See how I tell *you* things?" Rae simply stared at Ollie's now-hopeful look. Brushing past her toward the stairs, Ollie just yelled over her shoulder, "You suck."

"Very well too!"

Already halfway to the stairs, Ollie shouted over her shoulder, "Good to know!"

Clanking filled her ears as she pounded up the stairs, ignoring the "shut up" that drifted out of one of the rooms. Slightly out of breath, she ran up the next set that led to the roof and pushed the door open. It was bright. Blinking, she looked around.

There was Carmen, sitting on the edge, with the sky exploding in sunset behind her. Orange streaked her hair. She turned around. A smile was on her face, and Ollie took the first breath in what could have been forever.

A smile was good. Especially that one.

"Hi."

"Hey." Ollie let the door slam behind her. "How did it go?"

She closed the distance and sat cross-legged, facing Carmen, who was swinging her legs slowly over the edge. In profile, the fiery sky haloed her. She almost glowed.

"Well, I think."

Ollie waited all of five seconds. "Seriously? That's all I get?"

Carmen laughed.

That was what did it. That made Ollie realize Carmen had always held her stress in her eyes, around her lips. Because with that laugh, she looked her age. Like a girl Ollie could run into in the corridor at school. She looked like Carmen, but softer. In her chest, Ollie's heart skipped over.

"No. Sorry. I'm just overwhelmed. The lawyer, Maria, she said I can get visits next week."

"What? So soon?" Now Ollie was grinning.

Carmen nodded. "She said there's no way they'll deny sibling visits, especially because I'm independent now and it doesn't have to be organized within the system. She's sent the paperwork to Mattie's caseworker, but once it's approved, I have visits. His caseworker will go to the house with me the first time or two. Then, depending on Mattie and what they think, I can have more access."

"Just like that?"

"Just like that."

Ollie squeezed Carmen's knee. "That's fantastic. How will you set it up?"

Until then, Ollie hadn't noticed that Carmen was holding something in her lap. She held it up between two fingers, as if a little afraid of it. "With this. Your dad gave it to me."

"That's his old phone."

"He didn't make that up?"

Carmen was looking at her in a way Ollie couldn't place. "No? What do you mean?"

"I don't know. I thought he just bought me a new one. I tried to say no, but he said it was an old one that would just sit in a drawer."

Of course. Carmen didn't want more charity. "It's true. It would have. Do you have a SIM?"

"He put one in. It's a prepaid. I just top it up as I need to. I suppose I really do need one. To look more legit. And when I have Mattie, if the school ever needs to call, or emergencies or whatever."

Ollie almost smiled but didn't want Carmen to think she was laughing at her. "That's true." She shoved Carmen's arm gently. "Now we can message. Photos. Oh! Snapchat." She winked, and Carmen laughed. "And Dad just wants to help."

"I know."

She still looked a little uncomfortable, but Ollie just let it go. If she pushed too hard, it probably wouldn't help. Even if she did just want Carmen to understand that in the grand scheme of things, this wasn't a big deal, moneywise, for Ollie's dad. "And what about custody?"

Carmen was back to staring out over the buildings, still washed in that golden glow. Dimmer now. The stars would be out soon. They could lie here all night. Summer had always been Ollie's favorite time. Selfishly, she thought this one might possibly be the best one yet. Days by the pool with Carmen, her friends, the closeness they'd all built. The feel of it was tainted with the way Carmen sometimes seemed like she was missing something, with how badly she wanted Mattie back. But for Ollie, it was everything. The lack of her mom still left an aching hole, something that would never heal over completely. But it seemed smaller now, caved in on itself a little.

Maybe it would never be filled in, but things were building up over it. And maybe that was enough.

"Maria said we should wait a month or two to file for custody, to make sure I'm set up with my contract and an apartment, and that the bank things are all sorted out. To show I'm responsible and always show up to visits." Carmen wrinkled her nose.

It was the most adorable thing Ollie had ever seen.

"She liked the idea of your dad renting the house to me, and the official rental contract, how it would look."

"Did…did she say anything about the chances of you getting custody?"

Carmen shrugged, her feet swinging again, heels hitting the cement. "She said she really didn't know, that these things could go either way, and it all depended on what the court thought was best for Mattie. But she also said that in this state, you have to be registered as a foster parent to be able to take custody, whether you're a sibling or an uncle or a cousin or whatever."

"How long does that take? Does it mean you won't be able to get him until that happens?"

"That's what I asked. She said here you have ninety days to get it, even if you have custody. The only reason you have to do it is to go through the courses and things."

"That doesn't sound too bad."

"It's not. And here guardians get support payments from the government too, like a foster parent. So if I do all of this and have an apartment, I think I have a chance."

Carmen turned and looked at Ollie. The sun had sunk quickly, and the light was liquid blue.

"I hope it all works out." Ollie kept her voice at a whisper. It sounded like it all could. And then what? She didn't want to think that far ahead. Why bother if all of this worked out?

"Me too."

The way Carmen said the words, Ollie had never heard so much conviction. Not sure how to respond, she kissed Carmen instead and hoped her own conviction made it through.

It only took a few days, and Carmen had a phone call from Mattie's caseworker, who introduced himself as Ryan. She went in for an interview that lasted thirty minutes. All it involved was showing her birth certificate and address—Carmen gave her workplace, which he said was fine while she was "between places." He side-eyed her and she couldn't help but wonder if he had been her caseworker too.

"You disappeared off the radar, Carmen. It's good to see you're okay."

"Thanks." She said it awkwardly, so much so that Ryan laughed.

Though, apparently, it didn't take long to bring up the past.

Heat crept up her neck and across her cheeks. Maria had said to be vague and stick with her story about finding Mattie months after he'd run. Of course, that was the story Carmen had told Maria, who hadn't pushed for more. When they'd left, Ollie's dad had told Carmen not to tell Maria any alternative story, because she was required to not lie on Carmen's behalf.

Ryan looked a little harsh, like someone who had seen too much or was always thinking about the next thing to do. But the sound of his laughter softened him a little, and Carmen wondered if maybe he was just a little exhausted by an endless stream of kids the world was trying to break.

"No problem." He blinked. "So we thought you were in New York. Mattie, too, since two tickets were bought with a card that, by the way, no one wanted to press charges about."

She grimaced, and he kept talking like it was about the weather. "Strange that you bought two tickets, since you didn't know Mattie had run."

That had completely slipped Carmen's mind, this decoy move that had seemed like such a great idea at the time. "I, uh, had thought about taking him with me. Of getting him and leaving. I knew he would want it. But I changed my mind and decided he would be better in foster care." Carmen could only hope her face wasn't betraying her. "I had no idea he'd run away."

"Hm. Interesting. Then, it's so...lucky, you running into Mattie that day. What were you planning to do with him before you got mugged?"

Carmen swallowed. The air felt hot, warmth prickling along her arms. "We were walking to the police station. The street wasn't a place for him. I wanted him in school."

"You didn't think about keeping him with you? I bet he was pretty loud about wanting to stay with you, especially after having been on the street for so long, hoping to find you. He's certainly been loud about wanting to be with you since he's been with us."

This was dangerous territory, but Carmen still had to repress a smile at the thought of Mattie constantly bleating that he wanted to be back with Carmen. "Of—of course I *wanted* to keep him with me. Mattie is the most important person in the world to me. But I also... I knew that if I was ever going to get custody of him, he needed to be in the system."

"Smart girl." Carmen hoped he meant for that part and not for the lie. A shrug should be enough, so that's what she did.

"So that's what you hope? To get custody eventually?"

"Definitely." That was an easy question to answer. The others were like walking on eggshells, when at any moment, they were going to crunch apart under her feet.

"Great. Well, visits are a great step toward that. When do you want to start?"

"Um, now?"

"Okay." For a second, she thought he'd been teasing her with that, but he continued. "Well, I have to contact the family he's with. But maybe we can try tomorrow. It all depends on the foster family's schedule, Mattie's schedule, and yours too, of course. The first time, I'll come to observe and make sure he's comfortable and you're comfortable. I really doubt that will be an issue, though." He smiled then, everything about his face softening. "Honestly, all Mattie asks when we have contact is when he can see you. He told me he wants to live with you."

"And—he's really okay there?" Carmen had asked that as soon as she'd walked in the door. Not just to make it seem as if she hadn't seen him when she shouldn't at school, but also because she just needed the reassurance.

A few days had passed, and sometimes, in the depth of night when her thoughts were loudest, especially when Ollie wasn't there, Carmen worried that Mattie was in a far worse situation than he let on.

"He seems to have settled in fine. The family feels he is adjusting okay. One boy, well, they've had some issues with, but they have Mattie in summer school to catch up, and he's been doing well. The teachers all say he's very bright. They've asked about putting him in karate classes."

"Really?" The idea made her smile. "Karate? He'd love that."

"Good, good. So I'll call you once I've contacted the family and cleared a time."

"That's...that's it?"

At eighteen, she was supposed to be an adult. But nothing felt different from last week, or even last year. Everything about her body was uncomfortable. Did she cross her legs and look confident? Sit comfortably? How could she scream responsibility when unsure questions like that came out of her mouth?

"That's all for now. Wait." He cocked his head, dark eyes staring at her intently. "How are you doing?"

Carmen blinked at him, her mouth falling open to answer the question before snapping shut. The question had sounded so sincere. "I'm good."

"How is getting yourself set up to take on Mattie going?"

"I, uh, I have a job. But I'm looking for something more full-time. I should have an apartment soon." Which she would do alone. She didn't want to take advantage of Ollie's dad's generosity more than she already had. The phone was a stone in her pocket. She knew Ollie wanted her to take the lease he could offer, but Carmen would search for one on her own.

"Good, that's good. And you know the process?"

"I've been speaking to a lawyer. She's helping me. I know I need to register for the foster program."

"You have a lawyer who knows her stuff." He stared at her again, his head cocked, before breaking eye contact so fast that she was left blinking as he rummaged in a drawer. "Here." He pushed a handful of pamphlets across the desk. "These have information on all our registration days, the process, how to register for the foster program. May as well get that ball rolling."

Carmen started to pick them up, and he placed his fingertips lightly on top of them. "Just be sure about this. Mattie needs stability. Right now, he's in a decent foster place. And this is a huge responsibility."

She bristled at that. Spine straightening, she stared him straight in the eye. "You have no idea how aware I am of the responsibilities of taking care of Mattie."

The smile he gave her was sad, and he moved his hand. "I have some idea, I think. I've seen your files. I imagine you're what kept you and your brother going for many years. I do wish you luck in this, if it's what you really want."

He screamed sincerity. Maybe she'd flashed to her defenses too soon. "Mattie isn't a hobby to me. Or a project for a few weeks. He's my family. My only family. It is what I want. And I think it's what Mattie wants."

"Well," he said, "he has certainly made that known."

Carmen pushed the pamphlets into her bag, and when she stood up, she tried to look like the adult she was supposed to be, straightening her shoulders. It was like slipping on a costume, paying a role that didn't quite fit. Clothing she drowned in. "Thanks, Ryan."

"I'll talk to you soon, Carmen."

When Carmen walked out, Ollie was waiting by the bus stop, just like she'd promised. All the tension that had risen up in her throat eased, and she fell into the hug Ollie offered.

"Hey," she whispered into Carmen's hair.

"Hi."

CHAPTER 27

"Carmen!"

Mattie hit Carmen before she'd even managed to walk across the front lawn, pushing her a step backward. Not that she cared. At all.

Even on their fourth visit at his foster home, every time was too long since the last. He clung to her for a minute before pulling back. He was grinning, his eyes bright. And like always, she did the same. Sometimes she thought he was her mirror. Or maybe she was his.

"We really get all afternoon?" he asked.

"We do."

"All afternoon?"

"Yup."

"It's also fine to have dinner." The voice came from nowhere.

Mattie turned, and Carmen leaned to the side to look up at the front porch. Faye, Mattie's foster mother, stood looking down at them. Her eyes were so dark they were more black than brown, her skin the same shade as Mattie's. At times, she could seem formidable, but not once had she made Carmen feel uncomfortable during their visits. All of them so far had been in the house, the last two without Ryan. The last time, Carmen and Mattie had gone for a walk together. This time, she'd been given a gift, and even more of one than she'd anticipated.

"Really? That's okay?" Carmen stood up, Mattie against her side instantly.

"Ryan said we could make it up as we go from now, as long as we were sure Mattie was okay. This is his home, and most kids get to go out with their siblings, especially when they're older. Once you have a place, we can talk about sleepovers."

"That's—thank you."

Faye shrugged. "No thanks for this kind of thing. He's your brother."

Carmen tightened her grip and pulled him closer. The last few weeks, she'd been working as much as Dex could give her. Since turning eighteen, she had been allowed to serve alcohol without worrying about being caught, but couldn't drink it legally until age twenty-one. America would never cease to confuse her. But all of this meant more hours, which meant money to buy Mattie a meal with. The downside was it all meant she had to find a different job. There were too many night hours at the bar. Once the custody process finally starting moving forward, she needed something to show she'd be able to be home with Mattie.

"So what time would you like him back?"

"Let's say seven. That's five hours. Official school is back on next week. If you want, maybe we can talk about you getting him back here from there. Maybe some afternoons, he can be with you for dinner. You just make sure he does his homework."

Mattie turned to look up at her. "That'd be awesome."

"Thanks, Faye."

The extra hours at the bar meant she could afford to get him some decent food. Even if that did mean some evenings of pizza by the slice. She wasn't a millionaire, after all.

Carmen had wanted to not like Faye and Rob on principle. The part inside her that had been broken by her last few foster homes had reared up. But Mattie's foster parents were nice enough. A bit brisk, but Carmen had started to think that was just a cover. Mattie seemed to like them.

"See you soon."

They ended up at the warehouse, and Mattie threw himself at Rae and Dex. When Jia appeared an hour later, he did the same to her. Rae kept knuckling his hair, which he pretended to hate, but he couldn't seem to suppress the laugh that bubbled out. They sparred with him, and Carmen stepped back to join Dex against the wall and watch Mattie, like they used to.

Every now and again, her ribs still ached, even after so much time, but that wasn't why she stopped. She just wanted to take Mattie in. He'd pulled his shirt off, sweating in the hot warehouse, his face lit up and his eyes shining. Everything in Carmen throbbed with the knowledge that she had to get back on the bus later and leave him at his foster home. It was right, him being here.

He laughed as he ducked under Rae's arm, popping up behind her and swiping a kick.

Rae ended up flat on her stomach, huffing against the mat. "Where'd you learn that?"

"Four karate classes."

"Cheater."

Carmen and Dex both laughed when he just shrugged at that, his smile so wide Carmen thought he might burst. In one swift move, Rae pushed herself up, and then bounced on her toes a few times to loosen up before moving toward him again.

"He looks good." Dex's voice stayed low.

"He does. I..."

"What?"

"Maybe he's better staying at the foster home. Maybe it'll be better for him. And we can just do visits." Just the thought of it made Carmen's chest tight, like she couldn't breathe. But she couldn't shake the feeling.

"Maybe you should ask him that. But I don't think so. That boy and you... You two belong together."

There was no way Carmen could look at Dex after he said that. Instead, she dropped her head against his shoulder. His cheek brushed against the top of her head. He smelled like the bar, like the warehouse, a little like diesel. Like Dex.

"Oh, I want to get in on this."

Carmen didn't bother raising her head when Ollie spoke. She heard the thump of her backpack—her school had started back this week—and then Ollie was bouncing on her toes on the mat, and Rae and Mattie were looking sideways at each other, then back at Ollie, who just blew a kiss at Carmen. She waved back at her. Dex's shoulders shook with silent laughter.

"You want to spar?" Mattie was staring at Ollie like she'd just made a terrible joke. "With us?"

Carmen almost snorted, trying not to laugh.

Ollie didn't even look toward Dex and Carmen. "Yeah," she said, pulling her hair up into a ponytail that was just an explosion of curls. "What of it?"

Because he was a cocky nine-year-old, Mattie shrugged. "Okay." He launched forward with no warning, and Ollie sidestepped easily.

Mattie pulled up short and put his hands on his hips. "Has Carmen been teaching you?"

"A little."

"Hm." He stared at her. "Are you good?"

"Not even a little. I'm surprised I got out of your way."

Finally, Carmen laughed, and they all turned to look at her.

"Is she good?"

"She's learning, Mattie. Your face was priceless, though."

He narrowed his eyes at her before turning back to Ollie. "Want me to teach you some stuff?"

"Sure."

It was one of the best afternoons Carmen had had in months. In longer, even. Dex asked Mattie about summer school and his lessons, what he'd been learning. Ollie slipped him a new DS game. And Carmen sat and watched him in a space where he seemed so natural. To think she'd dragged him into this place so long ago and then worried about it.

At five thirty, she dragged Mattie away. He went quiet when they left, walking to the bus stop. Not wanting to push him, she let him stew until they were on the bus. In the back, she finally nudged him. "What's up?"

For a second, she thought he was going to ignore her, to build himself into an anger like he sometimes did, one that simmered for hours but never really exploded.

"I had fun." He kept his gaze out the window, watching the city center crawl closer where they were going to jump off for a piece of pizza before she took him back. "I had fun. And I miss it. I miss them. I miss living with you." He turned to look at her then, his eyes red-rimmed. His bruise had finally gone, a tiny pink scar left behind from the cut on his cheek. Barely a mark was left on the outside.

Carmen wrapped an arm around his shoulder so he was tight against her. She dropped her chin against his head and watched the streets pass. "I miss you too, Mattie. We all do. But you know…you know, if I get you back—it won't be like before. You'll have to go to school. We won't be living in the warehouse but in an apartment that's just me and you. I'll have to work. We won't have much money."

The silence dragged on for a long time, just the rumble of the engines beneath them and the hissing of the brakes.

"But I'll have you," he said, like that was everything.

Carmen couldn't bring herself to push it any further.

School was a rhythm that was hard to fall back into. Ollie wanted to be with Carmen, to go back to the hazy warmth of summer, the warehouse, the pool, and her friends. Yet at the same time, everything felt accelerated, like she was racing past what was supposed to be a huge moment in her life and barely had time to catch her breath.

Her SAT results weren't what everyone else had hoped, but they were better than Ollie had expected.

"You didn't score low. You did pretty well," Sara said, darting her hand out to nab Ollie's pudding off her tray. Expecting it, Ollie pulled it out of her way and poked her tongue out at Sara's pout.

Deon chuckled.

On second thought, Sara had spent days helping Ollie prepare, and Ollie probably would have failed if not for her. With a sigh, she handed the pudding over.

Sara ripped it open. "Thanks. So are you going to retake them?"

That was the big question. The one her dad kept asking her. The one the school guidance counsellor asked her. But her scores seemed good enough to get into the University of Connecticut, and they had a great art program. She didn't care about getting in with flying colors or aiming higher.

She just wanted to study art.

"No. I don't handle exams well. You know that. The stress is too much. If I don't get into UConn, I'll do art at a tech college." Ollie pushed her tray away, frowning at her cold fries.

Sara licked the back of her spoon with zero reproach in her eyes, and Deon watched Ollie unflinchingly. She couldn't imagine her dad's expression if she had said that to him.

"I think that's a great idea," Deon said. "Less stress, still art. A backup plan."

"Yeah, except I think Dad wanted my backup plan to be arts at UConn."

"Well, lucky it's not his life, then, isn't it?" Deon winked.

Ollie smiled at that, the weight that had been settling on her chest lifting. "True."

"So, it's arts, then?" Sara was grinning at her.

"Wasn't it always going to be?" Ollie asked.

Deon snorted, and Sara shoveled more pudding into her mouth. When they dragged themselves to their next class, Ollie was already itching to get home for dinner. Carmen was coming around. Now that school was back on and Carmen had more access to Mattie, they were seeing less of each other. She missed seeing Carmen every day, or, at least, most days. So, even if it was just going to be dinner with her dad, it was better than nothing. And afterward, they could disappear to Ollie's room. She'd have to study, but Carmen would pull Ollie's head into her lap and run her fingers through her hair while Ollie held a heavy book up on her chest and read. Apparently, this semester's grades were important.

Forcing herself to tune in to the teacher, she heaved a sigh.

They were all important.

"But when you applied to UConn, I thought you could maybe look more toward engineering in the end, or maybe architecture?" Ollie's father tried to keep the note of disappointment out of his voice.

Ollie wanted to disappear upstairs with Carmen, away from the hairy eyeball she was receiving over the dinner table from her father.

"I want to do art, Dad. I always have."

He pursed his lips and then finally blew out a breath. "Well, there's no point studying something you wouldn't want to. Your mother knew you'd want this from the day she found you using bubbles in your bath to paint the wall."

"She did that?" Carmen smirked at Ollie. "Cute."

Her dad laughed. "Once, she took off her diaper—"

"That's enough!" Ollie glared at him. "That story came out once, and Sara has never let me live it down."

"But I can't get half the story." Carmen tried for begging eyes, and Ollie's dad opened his mouth again. When Ollie just raised her eyebrows, he snapped it shut.

Carmen shrugged. "Fine, I'll just get it out of Sara."

"Just come by early for dinner next time, Carmen. I have plenty of stories."

Ollie groaned and dropped her head back. "I hate you both."

"No, you don't," they said at the same time. It was creepy.

They finished dinner quietly, her dad still eyeing her despite his words. She was grateful to escape upstairs later. With the door mostly shut, Carmen did exactly what Ollie had hoped she would, taking Ollie down on the bed beside her and running fingers through her hair. It didn't matter that when Ollie sat up, her hair would be a frizzy mess. Or that the feeling was making her sleepy. It felt good. She read lazily, the words almost blurring in front of her.

After an hour, she let her textbook fall to the bed and tilted her head up. Carmen's eyes were already on her. "Done already?"

"It's boring."

"It's important."

"It's *boring*. You're not boring."

A slow grin unfurled across Carmen's lips, and Ollie rolled so she wasn't sprawled over her lap anymore so Carmen could lie beside her. Like this, with their mouths gentle and limbs wrapping around each other, everything slowed. That feeling from dinner of racing forward toward something too big to handle drifted away, and it all became about the softness of Carmen and the ease Ollie had around her. She didn't feel awkward with her. Or like she was playing pretend by making life-altering decisions.

"I see Maria again tomorrow."

And then Ollie had to remember, her life wasn't the only one filled with big things, but Carmen's was too. And with things that far overshadowed her own. They were nose to nose on the same pillow; Carmen blinked at her slowly. Ollie grazed her fingers up over her neck, smiling as Carmen's eyes drifted closed at the sensation, then lazily opened again as Ollie pushed her hair back. The shaved patch over her ear was always fuzzy-soft, and Ollie often found herself running her fingertips over it again and again.

"Is this the big one?" Ollie asked. The moment called for quiet, hushed tones. The bed was their bubble, and Ollie didn't want to burst it.

Carmen nodded. "About actually going for custody."

"What happens once she petitions for custody on your behalf?"

Petitions. Custody. On your behalf. All terms that had been beyond Ollie once. But now she googled with Carmen for hours, searching for everything they could find in their state about custody and guardianship, so she'd know what was happening. Maria answered all Carmen's questions, but it was like Carmen needed reassurance: Yes, custody was possible at her age. Yes, she needed to be registered as a foster parent. Yes, Connecticut provided payments to guardians, just like to foster families. Carmen had booked her place in the week-long course immediately; she started next week.

Even when she was not with Carmen, Ollie researched to make sure she understood.

But there was so much that hinged on the line *in the child's best interests.* Ollie couldn't understand how, if you saw Carmen and Mattie together for more than a minute, you could think anything *but* Carmen was in Mattie's best interests. But Carmen was eighteen, a former street kid—well, still one, technically. Street adult?

How were they adults?

"Well, the next thing that happens is we receive the hearing date. Maria said it's not, like, dramatic court. It's just a judge and a lawyer from the state and my lawyer. They want to figure out what's best for Mattie."

"Which is you."

That deep little furrow appeared between Carmen's eyebrows. "Mattie thinks so. I want to think so…"

Sometimes, Ollie had learned, you should sit back and let Carmen talk on her own rather than ask her questions. She easily slipped into herself and fell quiet and would end up difficult to tug back into the world.

So Ollie sat and watched the furrow deepen a little more.

"What if I'm not? What if Mattie is better with adults? I don't mean 'adults' because their birthday was two months ago, but people who can really help him have somewhere stable?"

"You can do that too."

"Can I? I have to quit the bar, and the only other jobs I can get interviews for are retail and waitressing gigs. Nowhere that pays much."

"You'll have some help. They give you money for having Mattie. That will help you to get his clothes and food. Who knows? You can probably get the Internet and other things slowly set up. And once you have the

Internet, maybe in a year you can look at doing some courses online and move out of retail..."

Carmen put her head in her hand, looking down at Ollie. "How do you do that?"

"What?"

"Make me feel better? So easily that I think I can do it?"

"Because, Carmen." Ollie pushed closer. "You did it all before with so much less."

That furrow disappeared, and Ollie pulled Carmen back down.

CHAPTER 28

IT TOOK SIX JOB INTERVIEWS.

At least by the fourth, Carmen had started to know what to expect. She had to be careful her answers didn't become rehearsed.

"What do you feel you could bring to the position?"

Another person to fill your capitalist agenda? A faceless worker who is just a number to you to bring you profit in the cheapest way possible? An employee who dropped out of high school to live on the street with her kid brother and will soon hopefully have said brother living with her?

"I can bring my ability to work well under pressure, as demonstrated by over a year working in a bar during different periods. There were nights that were extremely busy, and I learned to prioritize tasks and jobs, to keep my head, and to keep customers happy and satisfied with the service, even at peak times."

"Do you work well in a team?"

No, people kind of suck. Working alone was far better.

"Definitely. I like working with others and coming up with a strategy to ensure we can all work together to complete our tasks efficiently. I also work well alone, however, and am very good at self-directed tasks."

"What other skills and abilities do you have?"

Being jaded and pretty good with sarcasm. Probably the ability to kick your ass.

"I've worked with invoices and stock, with cash registers, and finalizing tabs. I really enjoy making sure things run efficiently. In fact, I completely changed how we took in new stock and placed orders in my current position. This ended up reducing waste and saving money."

"What's your view on customers?"

They're stupid and mostly always wrong.

"The customer is always right. If I ever have an issue, I politely ask them to wait and get the manager."

"Why do you want to leave your current position?"

Because Mattie was the most important person in the world. The bar was the best place to work but took too many nights. Because this job was offering full-time, which was difficult to find at eighteen.

"I'm really interested in expanding my skill set, and while working in the bar gave me a great foundation, I'd really love to gain some more experience in the retail side of things. I'd like to be able to work my way up to a manager position one day."

Sometimes, Carmen wanted to hug Jia for the help she gave with prepping for this. At others, she couldn't believe this stuff came out of her mouth. None of it was really true. She wanted a steady job that could hold her over as she did some courses, that she could then leave to find something that paid more.

"Also, I would really love to do some further education by taking some courses. Most of these are available in the evenings, and I won't lie, this job being a day job is exactly what I'm interested in."

Six of these.

And finally, one called back.

Having a phone was nice in a lot of ways. Mostly, it was nice because she could contact Ollie all the time. The summer had spoiled them. Now Carmen not only missed Mattie's presence constantly, but found herself missing Ollie's too. But with her phone, she received streams of updates and photos. Snapchat was probably her favorite part.

But sometimes having a phone was annoying. She was constantly in contact with people now and often found herself leaving it behind in places, or jumping when it beeped at her. Still, the call to confirm she'd gotten the job at one of the only bookstores left in Connecticut came as she was walking into the bar to open up with Dex. She hung up, a little shell-shocked, to find Dex beaming at her.

"The bookstore?"

"You knew?"

"They called for a reference yesterday. I talked you up, of course. I didn't want to tell you, in case it was another dead end."

Carmen was still half holding her phone up. Her fingers were trembling a little. "They want me to start next week."

Both their grins faded, just a little. Carmen stepped forward, and Dex wrapped his arms around her. He was always so big, his embrace the definition of a bear hug. A lump swelled in her throat, easily swallowed past but still there.

"I'll miss having you around, kid."

The words rumbled in his chest against her ear, and Carmen tightened her arms. The beginning of something was always the end of something else.

Getting a lease, however, was not so successful.

Carmen was two weeks into her new job. It was strange to be getting up so early to stock shelves and go through inventory when the warehouse had only just settled down for the night. She stayed at Ollie's more often, grateful for Ollie's dad for so many reasons. Sleeping there was easier, quieter at night, and seeing Ollie more was nice.

On those days, Carmen got up and slid out of bed, Ollie rolling into the warmth left behind and not even waking up. She had another hour before she had to get up for school. Carmen would pad down the hallway, and Ollie's dad would be there already, a coffee on the counter waiting for her.

The custody process was long underway. Their hearing date was for a month from now. Mattie was nervous every time they saw each other. Mostly, though, he asked when she'd have a place. He knew she needed one.

She applied for apartments everywhere. Ollie helped her fill out the applications online, or she dropped some off at the realtor's office in person; so many of them wouldn't even consider her because she hadn't been in her current job for more than six months. Some, she was sure, passed her over for her age. There were fifteen rejections before one day, on their way back from a meeting with Maria, Ollie's dad pulled into a street she didn't recognize.

It took Carmen a second to realize they weren't going the right way. "Uh…"

"I just want to show you something."

They pulled up to an apartment block, neatly kept, old, if you stared enough to notice. They were outside the city, but not by far. A park was across the road, a big green space.

"Where are we?" she asked.

"The apartment we—I own."

Carmen blinked at it, then looked at him. "But—"

"Carmen. Just come have a look at it."

He got out without waiting for her, leaving her no choice but to jump out and hurry after him. She buried her hands in her jacket pockets, the air outside cool. Before she knew it, she was following him through the door and up three flights of stairs. She kept trying to think of things to say, of protests, of, well, *anything*, but she found herself empty of words, no matter how much she fished around for them.

They paused outside a dark wooden door, and Carmen finally found something to say. "I can't ask this of you."

"You're not." He winked at her as he slid the key home. He pushed the door open.

They stepped straight into the living room, a kitchen on their right, in effect, all one big room. Light filled the space, furniture dotted around. A soft looking sofa lined one wall, a coffee table in front of it as well as a squishy-looking armchair with a floral pattern that had to be from the seventies. The kitchen was small, with an island bench separating it from the living room. Everything smelled lemony, as if it had been recently cleaned.

"It's got most of what you need. No television, as you can see. The kitchen has the basics."

Carmen found herself lost for words again. She followed him down a hall that started opposite the entrance door, between the kitchen and living room.

"There's one bathroom. The shower's nice and big." He opened the door.

She'd forgotten that having your own shower was a normalcy. Using Ollie's was like a treat, and she'd gotten used to the public ones around the city that were usually cold. Two more doors led to two small bedrooms, one with a double bed and the other with a single. Everything was painted in a clean white. The apartment was neat, simple.

It would be perfect.

She couldn't accept more from this man. He'd done so much for her already. He was too kind, too good.

Carmen followed him back down to the living room. They stood next to the kitchen bench, and he pulled out some papers from his pockets, neatly folded. Carmen felt the opposite of that. She was messy, spread out, as if life were jerking at her from all angles.

"This is a twelve-month lease. It'll be official. I can put it in tomorrow."

"I... I can't afford this. I can't ask you to do this. It's too much."

His expression stayed open, and he cocked his head to look at her in a way that was just so *Ollie* that Carmen's breath caught. He didn't even appear exasperated with her, though she had the feeling he wanted to be.

"The rent will be low, to start, like we talked about months ago. If you really want to, as you get more settled, we can increase it. But it's not necessary for me. At all. I don't mean to say that to, uh, 'rub it in,' as Ollie would say."

He was looking at her gently, his eyes big and soft like Ollie's, only dark brown. He was looking at her like she might run away, and Carmen wasn't all that sure she wouldn't.

"I'm telling you so you understand that for me, the money isn't necessary to worry about, and the rent isn't all that less than what we were charging before. We always kept it low. Ollie's mom liked to rent it to people who normally had a harder time getting places—single parents, younger people at college." His voice was low, a rumble. "You do so much alone. And I know you always have. But you don't have to do it all that way."

He was so sincere. The lease was on the island, and he was holding a pen out to her. For a minute, she stared at it. She bit the inside of her cheek, unsure.

"You and Mattie deserve a chance, Carmen."

What had Jia said? She should take it.

She reached out for the pen.

The trial seemed to be forever away, even as school flew by. Soon December came around—cold, bitingly so. Ollie had never been more relieved that Carmen had finally accepted her dad's offer. The place had heating, even if most of the time when Ollie went around, Carmen had it turned off while wearing three pullovers instead. Christmas decorations were starting to appear in the streets, and right before the trial date, Carmen had Mattie over for his first stay.

Leaving them to their night together, Ollie went to Sara's. Before she could even knock on the door, Sara had opened it and grabbed her hand. Ollie was tugged outside and onto the trampoline. Their breath puffed out over them as they lay there, wrapped in their winter coats and a pile of sleeping bags, and the sky was a frozen stillness above, the stars like ice chips.

"We haven't done this in months." Ollie's lips were cold, almost numb. She licked them, enjoying how it made them tingle in the air.

"I missed it." Sara's arm was under her head.

"Me too." Ollie was along her side, sharing their body heat. Their nest was warm, but the air bit at her cheeks. The contrast made her think of icy white and blue slashed through with something brighter. Orange, maybe. She'd pull out her supplies when she went home, the image bubbling in the back of her mind, itching to be put to paper with soft lines. She'd use pastels, maybe. Or oils. Perhaps she'd paint the two of them under the sky, try to capture the deathly silence around them in the winter air. "Have you heard back from your early admissions?" she asked.

"Mm." Sara kept staring at the sky.

"And?" She turned her head and watched her.

"I got accepted to all of them. It's not a big deal."

It was. But Sara hated if you made it one. Though it had always been a given; she could have skipped this year and gone straight to college if she'd wanted. Most people would have jumped at the chance to skip some of these years. Not Sara, though. And the more Ollie had seen of Carmen, of the warehouse, the more she'd talked to Sara, the more she'd started to understand why.

They'd already missed so much. She wasn't in a rush.

"Well, congratulations." An ache in Ollie's chest matched her heartbeat at the thought of Sara going away to one of the Ivy Leagues, scholarship in hand and big things ahead. Not that she didn't want that for Sara. She wanted nothing for Sara but all of that, especially after everything. But not seeing her every day? That was going to suck.

"Thanks."

"Which one are you thinking about?"

"Harvard, maybe. They have the best science streams."

"Wow. *Harvard.*"

"I know, right?" And Sara laughed like she couldn't believe it.

"What about Rae?"

The smile faded a little, the stars overhead still reflected in the wide pupils of Sara's eyes. "I don't know. It's months away."

Now that Sara and Rae were together, Ollie couldn't imagine them apart. They fit, somehow. An understanding seemed to exist between them Ollie would almost be jealous of if she didn't know her best friend would always be her best friend, girlfriends or boyfriends or partners notwithstanding.

"Okay."

"What about you and Carmen?"

Her heart skipped over, and something caught in her throat just at the mention. "What about us?"

"What if she gets Mattie?"

Ollie's ears were tingling now, they were so cold. "What if she does?"

"That's, I don't know…serious. You're eighteen. You might be at college. Or working, or whatever you're doing. How are you two going to make it work?"

Ollie rolled her head back so she was looking straight up at the sky again. The stillness was broken now. A plane flew overhead, its lights blinking green and red like the holiday lights in the houses, in her own house.

Last Christmas, she and her father had just ignored the entire thing. Ollie had cried the entire day in her bed, then had left her dad alone and gone to Sara's. This year, they'd pulled out the tree and put the ornaments up. Carmen had come over later and helped them finish up. When Ollie had gotten red-eyed, her dad had wrapped an arm around her and they'd stared at the tree. Before the silence had become too much, her dad had told her a story about the time her mom had fallen asleep without putting out the presents and had woken up just before Ollie and panicked before fixing it in such a rush that Ollie had stumbled out just as she'd stuffed the last present into the sack from Santa.

"I don't know how we'll make it work," she told Sara. "We know it's complicated. But people make long-distance work. We can make it work in the same city."

"You know…you know she won't have much time?"

Something in Ollie's chest rose up to bite at that, feeling patronized. Before the words slipped out, though, she took a breath and swallowed them down. This was Sara. She wouldn't mean it like that. "I know."

"Okay."

And Sara didn't ask for more, but words were spilling up, all the things Ollie had thought about. "I do know it. I mean, I think I do." She blinked and could feel Sara's eyes on her, heard her turn her head to watch her. "When we first started, like really started, after I met her again at the bar, we rarely saw each other. She had no phone, either, or Internet. Sometimes a few weeks would go by. But it just… It didn't matter? Because she's Carmen. And with everything going on, after Mom died, she was the only thing that really made me feel better. And I think I did the same for her." She took a deep breath, wanting to measure the next words carefully. "And this time, we both know what's happening. I know she has Mattie. I know her situation. She knows I'll have school. And I still want to be there. I think I want to be there even more. She wouldn't be Carmen if she wasn't doing this."

"That's really gross and sweet."

Ollie laughed, the feeling loosening the heaviness, and looked at Sara. "Shut up."

"Well, it was."

"Oh, like you and Rae aren't gross."

"Totally different."

"Not even. We both know she'll be eagerly awaiting you when you go away for college."

Sara's grin grew, even as she rolled her eyes. "No, she won't."

"She so will. She'll show up at the airport in her beaten leather jacket and act all unaffected and like she accidentally came, when she'd been planning it since you told her your arrival time."

"Shut up."

"You shut up."

"No."

On the seventeenth of December, Carmen woke up in her apartment, warm and in a bed she still couldn't believe was so comfortable. For hours, she'd lain awake the night before, unsure if she'd fall asleep at all. When she finally had, she'd dreamed about walking through door after door after door, the handles cold in her palm as she turned them, always confronted by another one to turn.

It had been frustrating.

Blinking at the ceiling, she rolled over, receiving a face full of curly hair. She slid her hand over Ollie's warm, soft stomach. The light was only creeping in, shadows still coating everything. Outside would be overcast and gray. When Carmen gently moved her fingers, Ollie mumbled. She did it again, and Ollie groaned, rolling over onto her stomach and burying her face into the pillow.

"Morning."

"No." It was muffled, but the word was difficult to misunderstand.

Carmen chuckled. "Well, it is."

Ollie turned, her hair wild with friction from the pillows and Carmen's hands the night before. "But it's not good."

"To be fair—" Carmen slid closer "—I never said it was."

"Oh. True." Ollie was still struggling to open her eyes. They lay close to each other, the room lightening around them. "Oh!" This time, she sounded much more awake, and Carmen pulled back, blinking. "It's trial day."

"It is."

They lay on the same pillow, eyes half-open. Ollie licked her lips slightly. "It's going to be fine."

Carmen took a deep breath. With the unsettling feeling in her throat, it was like everything that had taken residence there was creeping up on her. "It will be."

"I'll be there."

"You have school."

"Don't care. Dad's coming too, and he's told the school I'll be out."

It would be easy to protest again, to act like she didn't need Ollie there. But the idea of Ollie sitting in the back, of her silent support, and of Ollie's dad there too, overwhelmed her before it could be anything more than a vague thought. She didn't know when it had happened, but she wanted them around, their help, even if it was just them being present.

Carmen nuzzled her face into Ollie's neck, glad when Ollie's arms slid around her and pulled her in tighter. Her stomach was a hive, churning over and over again. She'd never really understood the idea of having butterflies in her stomach, but now it made sense. Her mouth was dry, her heart beating just a touch too fast.

"It's going to be okay, Carmen."

She hummed as an answer, and they didn't move for another hour. Everything stilled around them, and Carmen wished she could stay there and fall into the calm and never have to make her way back out, out into a world full of adults and decisions so big that they felt as if they could take over everything.

Mattie needed her, and Carmen needed to get it together so she could be there for him.

And by this evening, she'd know: Mattie, or no Mattie.

There were people who sketched court cases for a living. Ollie had never understood that. Why would you want to use your art for *that*? So many other things existed that you could do, so many avenues you could go down.

But seated in that room, she could kind of understand it.

The room held an *atmosphere*.

It could be interesting to sit at the back like she was now and capture the defendant's face. Her fingers twitched in her lap, hidden under the warm coat she clutched there. Next to her, her father didn't seem to notice anything. She could put down on paper whatever she found in that person's face. In the victim's face. But wouldn't that be too subjective?

It was what she wanted to do now, anyway.

If only she had her sketchbook.

She'd trace the lines she could see in the profile of Carmen's face, the furrow she knew would be between her brows as she swallowed and glanced behind her at the door Mattie was behind with his caseworker. He wasn't allowed to listen in on the entire hearing. It seemed strange to Ollie that the boy who carried an entire lifetime in his eyes couldn't witness a decision that would change his life forever.

Maria sat next to Carmen, whispering words Ollie hoped were of comfort. She wouldn't draw Maria in the picture, just Carmen, small and drowning in a room too overwhelming for her.

The room she'd draw in simple, bold lines. Bold to emphasize the intimidating feeling that had settled over Ollie's skin as they'd walked in. Simple, with no shading, to bring the viewers' eyes to Carmen, hunched and diminutive at the giant desk she sat behind.

The guard who stood next to a back door made Ollie jump as his voice boomed. "All rise for the honorable Judge Falkowitz."

Her father urged her up, and she stood next to him, sharing his heat.

Judge Falkowitz had a pale face with bushy eyebrows that made Ollie think of furry caterpillars. He strode in, his black robe swishing, billowing almost, behind him. He sat behind his bench, barely risen from the ground, but just enough to give him an air of being the most important thing in the room. He didn't look mean or kind, just neutral, which made him more intimidating than if he had appeared nasty.

Ollie would sketch him from the perspective of looking up at him, surrounded by his looming, heavy wooden table, his face seeming too far away to even catch his features.

When he sat, everyone else sat, and Ollie followed her father down to their seats.

It was strange to sit and watch them talk about Carmen in formal terms. She was "Miss García," and Mattie was often referred to as the "ward of the state" or "Matthew," which was also strange. She wanted to stand and say that he was so much more than that. He was cheekiness and flashing smiles and a thrum under his skin that told of frustration. He was fluid movements and confidence in a fight, calculating looks, and a wit that made Ollie laugh.

He was Carmen's everything, and Ollie almost couldn't breathe as the hearing went on, as all the air seemed to disappear from the room.

Someone representing the state sat there, another lawyer sitting at a different table.

"He represents Mattie," her father murmured in her ear.

And again, Ollie couldn't help but wonder how that could be, because if anyone represented Mattie, Carmen did.

Maria spoke in a blur of words. She presented both the other lawyer and the judge with documents. "I submit signed statements by Matthew's current foster family about their points of view on his situation, and on Carmen's. Carmen has been having regular contact with Matthew since her eighteenth birthday, as approved by his caseworker and his foster family. She has picked him up from school, helped him study, taken him for meals. Recently, she had him in her house overnight, after clearance from his caseworker. As you can see in the statements, both foster caregivers have found her punctual, responsible, and contactable at all times. If they've called because Mattie wanted her, Carmen has dropped everything to visit him. I also submit a copy of her twelve-month lease on an apartment, her work contract, bank statements, and income reports." She walked again between both officials, handing them copies of everything.

Ollie wanted to draw her in her pantsuit, her hair in a braid like a warrior.

"Also included is her certificate of attendance to the training required of all foster caregivers, as the state of Connecticut requires. As you can see, Carmen has taken every step available to her to take Mattie under her care."

Judge Falkowitz flipped through the documents one by one, those caterpillars bunching together until they formed one long one. "And the applicant is eighteen?"

"Yes, Your Honor."

He looked up over the papers, eyes on Carmen. "And why does she feel she will make the best guardian for Mattie?"

"Well, Your Honor—"

"Actually, I'd like to hear from her."

Ollie's palms grew clammy, and Carmen stood, her shoulders straightening as she seemed to take a deep breath.

That, there. That was how Ollie wanted to draw her. That moment as she raised her eyes and set her jaw, her gaze steady on the judge, when a moment before it had been on the floor.

"Hello, Carmen." Judge Falkowitz smiled then for the first time, and a fan of wrinkles bloomed around his eyes.

"Hello...uh, Your Honor."

Any other time, Ollie would slip behind Carmen and thread their fingers together, or at least just stand close enough so Carmen would know she was there. But they were separated by seats and a wooden barrier, there to isolate those involved from those observing.

"How are you this morning?"

"I'm good."

Ollie wanted to hug her.

"Nervous," Carmen added.

He smiled again. "Normal, I'm sure. Now, I've heard a lot from your lawyer, and I did scan over your case beforehand. Lots of foster homes in your background and two removals from your mother. I'm sorry she passed."

Carmen's shoulders relaxed just slightly. "Thank you."

"A disappearance and a reappearance at sixteen and eighteen respectively. But sworn statements that you weren't with your brother. And it would seem you looked after yourself okay."

"Uh, yes, Your Honor."

"I'm assuming, though, that those two removals from your family home before weren't really the only times they should have happened. Did your mother ever have any other support? Anyone else there with the two of you?"

"No." Carmen shrugged a little. The added, "Your Honor."

"Did she ever leave you alone for long periods of time?"

"Yes."

"For how long?"

"Anything from a few days to a few weeks. I think the longest was around a month. Though that was just once."

"And how old were you when she left you alone for this long?"

"I don't remember a time she didn't."

He just nodded, and Ollie wondered how many things he had to have heard in his career to be able to react to that with a neutral face. Her father had tensed next to her.

"And what type of care did she give you when she was home?"

"Um." Carmen looked down at Maria, who gave a nod. "Not a lot. Sometimes she tried. They were nicer weeks. But generally, she didn't do a lot. There were a lot of drugs, which I tried to hide from Mattie. Mostly, it was Mattie and me. Mattie was born when I was eight. I remember her leaving me with him when he was tiny, still a baby. I learned to rock him to sleep and give him bottles. I cooked and, later, got him to school and cleaned the house. I tried to make sure we were together."

"And when you were put in separate foster homes, how was that?"

"Horrible. They were supposed to try to get us to see each other, but it happened once, I think. Maybe twice."

"And how do you think Mattie was?"

For a moment, Carmen didn't answer. Finally, she said, "When we were sent back home, he was really withdrawn. He was always shy with people he didn't know, but this was different. I couldn't get him to leave my side, and he cried when I tried to take him to school. He was six when we got back the first time. He—he wet his bed a few times, which he hadn't done in years."

His face was impassive. "I have to ask you a question, though I think I know the answer from what you've already said. But I have to ask you anyway, okay?" He waited for Carmen's agreement before he continued. "Do you really understand what taking on your brother would mean? You're eighteen. You could go back to school, which I see you've dropped out of to work. You could have a life and still see Mattie, like you do now."

Carmen's shoulders straightened again, and Ollie knew there'd be a fire licking at her gaze. "I am fully aware of what having Mattie would mean. I know it would mean it'll be hard to finish my education. I know it would mean I won't be hanging out with friends or seeing my girlfriend often at all. I know Mattie will always have to come first. But the thing is, he always *has* come first. And he always will." Carmen dropped her gaze, biting at her lip as she thought for a second. "I wondered for a while if I should do that—leave him in foster care." She looked up again. "Not for me. I want Mattie with me. There's never been a second I've wanted differently. But for him? For what a steady foster home could do, with two adults in the house, and everything they can provide?"

She didn't say anything more until Judge Falkowitz prompted her. "And?"

"Mattie made me realize that wasn't true. All he's said to me the last few months is that he wants to be back with me. He wants to be at home, and we're each other's homes."

"Well then." The judge sat back in his chair, head cocked as he gazed at Carmen. "Let's hear from Mattie. It is, after all, his life."

One of the guards walked over to a door and when it opened, disappeared for a moment before he led Mattie out.

Carmen had sat back down, but the second he was in the room, she stood up. Before the guard could even move, Mattie had ducked in front of him and dashed into Carmen, her arms around him instantly.

The guard had moved to intercept, but Judge Falkowitz said, "Can we get a chair for young Mattie, please."

The guard produced a chair, and Mattie pushed it even closer to Carmen's before sitting down. If Carmen had looked small, he was tiny. He had always been small for his age, but the room seemed to swamp him. Even from her view of his profile, Ollie could see how huge his eyes were as he stared up at Judge Falkowitz.

"Good afternoon, Mattie."

Carmen nudged him and he finally said, "Hello."

"So, how old are you?"

This always seemed to be what adults asked kids.

Mattie straightened a little. "I'm almost ten."

"Big age. Now, do you know why we're here today?"

Mattie nodded.

Carmen nudged him again.

"Yes."

"Good. Can you tell me why?"

"To decide if I can live with Carmen or not."

"That's right." Those lines around Judge Falkowitz's eyes deepened a little again. He wasn't smiling, but he did look friendlier. "Do you know why it's complicated?"

Mattie shrugged, his voice small when he spoke. "I think because Carmen's not really an adult. Though that's not true." His voice gained some volume, his chest expanding a little. "She's eighteen, and that makes her one. And, um, because I need to be somewhere safe, like a house, and she needs to have money. But she has a house and a job. She looked after us without money before."

"That's all true." Judge Falkowitz put his hands together on top of the table. "It's all about something called *the child's best interests*. It's complicated, as that can mean a lot of things. Tell me, Mattie, do you like your current house?"

"It's okay." The unsure posture was gone, and the Mattie who Ollie had come to know was back, straight-spined and sure. "It's better than the other ones from before."

"I'm sorry the others were like that, then." Judge Falkowitz cocked his head. "Where would you like to live, Mattie?"

"With Carmen." The answer was instant.

Judge Falkowitz nodded slowly. He took his time with Mattie, Ollie could tell, to watch him. He had to see the way Mattie was as close to Carmen as he could be. He had to notice the way Carmen watched him. "Even if that means you may not have as much as in this house?"

Mattie's nose wrinkled up. "I don't need much. I'm pretty small. I don't really eat a lot."

Judge Falkowitz smothered a smile, but not before it showed itself. Both the lawyers huffed a laugh, and Carmen rolled her eyes. Next to Ollie, her father snorted softly.

"Yes, well, what about other things? Clothes and toys? Extra classes? Extracurriculars? Pocket money?"

"I've never had that stuff. But I've always had Carmen."

The room was silent for a moment, and Judge Falkowitz said, "Okay."

Ollie looked at her dad, and he widened his eyes at her and shrugged. What did that mean?

A silence went on for a minute, and, finally, Judge Falkowitz cleared his throat. "It is unusual to grant guardianship at eighteen. However, it is unusual to find an eighteen-year-old who has clearly done everything in her power just to gain that custody. She has an apartment and a job and has completed foster parent training even before knowing if she would receive guardianship, despite Connecticut allowing ninety days after receiving guardianship to attend the training. She has demonstrated her ability to take care of her brother since he was born."

He paused, and Ollie thought that moment would stretch on forever. "I'm going to grant guardianship of Matthew Anders to Carmen García."

Mattie was grinning as if he hadn't expected anything else, and Carmen's mouth had fallen open, disbelief written all over her face. Ollie's eyes welled up, her breath catching.

Judge Falkowitz just kept talking.

"This is dependent on home visits by his caseworker twice a week for a month. After that, if the caseworker is satisfied, it'll be twice a month for two months and then monthly for the rest of a twelve-month period. After this, the usual home visits for a foster family will start if the case worker is unconcerned. Carmen García will receive the weekly support sum given to all foster families as deemed by the state of Connecticut."

Maria had put her hand on Carmen's shoulder, and Mattie was staring at Carmen, and Carmen was still just staring at the judge.

"You can close your mouth, Carmen. I'm not joking."

Mattie stood up, face alight, and turned with his hand held out to Carmen. "Finally. Let's go home."

Ollie's dad snorted again, and Carmen gave an incredulous laugh.

EPILOGUE

SOMETIMES, CARMEN GOT OFF WORK a little late and met Mattie at the library near his school. That was rare, though. She normally finished just before three o'clock and made it to the school to get on the bus with him. Ollie's dad had been trying to get her to have driving lessons, but she never had time, between work and Mattie and the course she'd just started to get her GED. Besides, a car cost too much money, and the buses worked fine. She liked sitting next to him on the bus, talking or watching the city go by, feeling the press of his shoulders.

He was almost eleven now but still sat as close to her as he could. It made her think of nights winding through alleyways, the city quiet around them and the warehouse ahead of them.

Today, though, she didn't have to rush. Working Christmas Eve was never fun, but there'd been no way to get out of it. Luckily, the art store Ollie had taken a job with six months ago was closed today, for some reason, and she'd said she'd be happy to hang out with him since he had no school.

Which meant they'd probably sat on the couch all day watching the television Carmen had managed to find secondhand on Craigslist. Ollie usually brought over a cable and her laptop and hooked up movies for them to watch.

Just as she suspected, the smell of popcorn hit her as she walked into the apartment with heavy grocery bags in her arms, and her two favorite faces stared up at her from under a blanket on the couch.

"Uh...hi." Ollie grinned.

Something inside Carmen's chest melted at the sight. A year had come and gone since Carmen had moved into the apartment, but coming home to find Ollie on her couch waiting for her still had the same effect as the first time it had happened. It didn't occur as often as they'd like, but when it did, it made the wait worth it.

"Are you home early?"

Carmen shook her head. "A little late, actually."

"Oh." She nudged Mattie, who was staring at the TV. "We've been busted."

He finally looked at Carmen, his head turning before his eyes followed the movement. He flashed a smile. "We were going to turn the TV off and pull out our homework and pretend we'd been studying all day."

Unwinding her scarf from her neck, Carmen scoffed. "Yeah, because I would have believed that."

Ollie looked wounded. "I study."

"I know *you* do. But getting Mattie to do that when he still has two weeks of vacation? Not a chance."

"I did some." He was back to not looking at her.

Carmen put her coat and scarf over the back of her chair and raised her eyebrows. "I'd believe that more if you took your eyes off the TV."

"If I did that, you'd see the lie in them."

In spite of herself, Carmen laughed. He was too clever for his own good. "Just make sure you sit down with me with that math stuff before school goes back."

He grunted an answer.

"Seriously. It's awesome you're so far ahead with English and social sciences, but we need to work on your math."

He was behind. Not drastically, but enough. He'd spent all year catching up, even after the summer school, and had done really well. He got distracted sometimes. But Carmen was just glad he seemed to have adjusted.

"I will."

It would be better if it hadn't been said as a groan, but Carmen would take it.

Smirking, Ollie stood up and left him to his movie. She grabbed one of the bags Carmen had put on the floor and followed Carmen to the kitchen.

"Hi." Ollie's attention was all on Carmen.

Carmen pulled her forward. "Hey." She kissed her, resisting the urge to sigh against Ollie's lips. They were both so busy that times like this felt precious. She splayed her fingers over Ollie's back, wishing she could pull her even closer. "Thanks for hanging here today."

Ollie's arms wound around Carmen's waist, their foreheads coming together. "No problem. We actually did do some stuff besides watch TV."

"I know—I saw the books on the table. Thanks. I really appreciate it."

"You know I don't mind. Anyway, I wouldn't have done much today anyway. No work and no school? I was a bit lost."

"Well, feel free to come around anytime."

"Yeah?"

Carmen smiled, her lips curving up against Ollie's. "Yeah."

They kissed again, slowly, lips barely moving.

"Ugh."

Pulling apart, they turned their heads and leaned to see that Mattie hadn't even taken his gaze off the movie to make the disgusted noise.

"You can't even see us," Ollie called.

"Don't need to," he said.

Ollie looked back at Carmen and rolled her eyes. "So. You ready to cook up a storm?"

"I think so." Carmen had never cooked as much food as they were planning that night. "What time are your dad and Deon coming again?"

"Around six. What about Dex and Jia and Rae?"

"Same time. It's a pity Sara couldn't come."

Ollie actually pouted when she said it, and Carmen had to stop herself from kissing the expression off her face. "It really is," Ollie said. "And Rae has just been moping around the apartment since she found out. Though she thinks she looks badass and broody. Really, she looks pathetic."

Snorting, Carmen finally moved away from Ollie and started pulling out groceries. "Still glad you're living with Rae?"

"It's been six months, and we haven't killed each other."

That made it sound like they barely got along, which was a huge lie. The two of them had become friends since Ollie had asked Rae to move into the apartment she'd taken around the corner from her tech college. Ollie's dad just tried not to twitch at the fact that she'd *chosen* part-time tech college and part-time work while she figured out what she wanted to do.

Ollie grabbed the fresh turkey out of the bag and eyed it with a fortifying breath.

The original plan had been to skip the traditional turkey. Pulling off that dish had seemed beyond them. But Ollie, her jaw set, had decided she was going to do it. Somehow.

Carmen had never even cooked a chicken, let alone a turkey. But Ollie had looked it up on the Internet and swore she could do it. Carmen had her doubts, but she'd never say that.

They stumbled around the small kitchen, Carmen focusing on the vegetables and Ollie on the meat. She was painting a brush over it, and Carmen wanted to laugh at how she did it with a flourish, like she'd seen her do with a canvas under her hands.

Carmen loved to watch Ollie create. She'd taken to tall canvases lately, a pallet knife and chunky lines casting colors over a sketched design. She'd pull a scarf over her hair, curls spilling out the end, and Carmen would smile to watch her so focused. Ollie was so often sporadic, moving from one thing to another, her ideas all over the place. But once art came into it, her concentration was surprising, deep. Moving to watch.

Her work got attention at the tech college.

She still filled sketchbooks, though. Carmen had another one of Ollie's now. She kept the two of them next to her bed, and sometimes at night she traced her fingers over the lines, unable to believe how Ollie saw the world. Saw Carmen.

With potatoes boiling on the stove and gravy with lumps as big as pennies next to it, Carmen finally walked over to the TV and switched it off.

Mattie didn't even bother protesting. "What do I have to do?" Resignation was thick in his voice.

"Vacuum and set the table and the coffee table—we're going to be eating spread out—we have no room. Also, make sure the tree lights are on, and find a good Christmas playlist."

"I vacuumed last week." Whining was never his strong suit.

"Cool. And you can vacuum now too."

Muttering, he pulled himself off the couch.

"Take the blanket."

He rolled his eyes and dragged it behind him to his room.

"Enjoy that in a few years," Ollie called from the kitchen.

"Yeah, har har."

Eventually, they had food laid out that was definitely going to be cold by the time everyone ate, and the room filled up with people. The lights flashed on the Christmas tree, and Mattie kept fiddling with the settings so they went off like a rave. Everyone pretended the turkey tasted good, even though parts of it were so dry that chewing it was like eating dust.

Rae looked a little lost without Sara and sat next to Ollie on the sofa, shoveling in sweet potato. Dex, Jia, and Ollie's dad sat at the table, Dex poking Mattie into agreeing to some tutoring. Twice a week they all sparred these days—more when they could—and Carmen had promised Mattie that next year she would get him into karate classes again. Money was tight, though, with having to work a little less while doing her GED courses. But Ollie's dad had convinced her it was important and that she'd be able to find a job that paid a little more if she had some qualifications behind her.

When they all finished eating, someone knocked on the door, and Carmen opened it, mouth dropping open at who she saw.

"Sara!"

The shout came from behind her, and then Ollie was bowling past her and throwing her arms around Sara while Rae stood holding plates, frozen.

"Hey," Sara said from over Ollie's shoulder.

"Hey," Rae replied, the way her lips quirked up betraying her.

"Surprise."

They spent the entire night hovering near each other—more reserved with each other than Ollie and Carmen, whose hands were always touching some part of the other when they could—but steady. The year managing long-distance, Carmen noticed, had barely seemed to shake them.

Ollie glowed. She missed her friend all the time, Carmen knew. They skyped and messaged. But having Sara near her again lit Ollie up.

Gifts were handed out, most going to Mattie. Eventually, he unwrapped a PlayStation from Ollie's dad and fell over himself trying to say thank you. He kept eyeing the TV like he wanted to set it up then and there, but Carmen's stink eye quickly put a stop to that. By nine, everyone was rolling around half-asleep, hands on rounded bellies.

It was as perfect a time as any for what Carmen wanted to do.

Carmen had dreaded doing this formally, but she had only just been told yesterday, and she had wanted to talk it over with Mattie before telling everyone. And each person there, well, they deserved to know. They'd all played a role, and sometimes, on nights when everything felt too scary and overwhelming and she lay there thinking too much, she wondered where she'd be without any of them.

She stood in front of the fake tree, crammed next to the TV and bought in a secondhand store. Ollie and Mattie had covered it with old aluminum cans she'd turned into art and Mattie had butchered. The metal reflected the blinking lights along the walls. She used Mattie in front of her as a barrier, resting her hands against his chest. He leaned into her as she did. Slowly, everyone stopped talking and stared at her.

Heat crept into her cheeks and she swallowed hard. Ollie smiled at her from the sofa, pressed against her dad's shoulder.

"So, uh, thanks, everyone, for coming."

"Thanks for the food!" Deon said.

"Yeah, it was an…adventure." Dex snorted, and Jia slapped his arm.

Carmen let herself smile at that, and some of her nervousness melted away. "I just, I was hoping to be able to let you all know this when I asked you to come over. But, ah, now I know for sure."

Everyone blinked at her, except Ollie, who just kept smiling because she knew. "Yesterday, Mattie's caseworker came, and, well, it's been a year, and—"

"And that weird year is over," Mattie interrupted, "and I'm definitely staying with Carmen." He tilted his face up, the back of his head tucked against her neck—so different than the way he'd done it when he was tiny, when his head had rested against the backs of her knees, then her thighs, then her stomach. He'd grown so much.

Even as Carmen thought that, with a pang in her chest, the room erupted into noise and cheers. They all stood to hug Mattie and her, and Mattie stayed with his arm close to hers, their heat swapping between each other like it would when they used to share a bed.

From the sofa, Ollie stared up at her, eyes a sky. She smiled, achingly wide, and Carmen matched it.

All the pieces of her life in one room, making up their own constellation.

ABOUT G BENSON

Benson spent her childhood wrapped up in any book she could get her hands on and—as her mother likes to tell people at parties—even found a way to read in the shower. Moving on from writing bad poetry (thankfully) she started to write stories. About anything and everything. Tearing her from her laptop is a fairly difficult feat, though if you come bearing coffee you have a good chance.

When not writing or reading, she's got her butt firmly on a train or plane to see the big wide world. Originally from Australia, she currently lives in Spain, speaking terrible Spanish and going on as many trips to new places as she can, budget permitting. This means she mostly walks around the city she lives in.

CONNECT WITH G BENSON
Website: www.g-benson.com
E-Mail: gbensonauthor@gmail.com

OTHER BOOKS FROM
YLVA PUBLISHING

www.ylva-publishing.com

ALL THE LITTLE MOMENTS

G Benson

ISBN: 978-3-95533-341-6
Length: 350 pages (139,000 words)

Anna is focused on her career as an anaesthetist. When a tragic accident leaves her responsible for her young niece and nephew, her life changes abruptly. Completely overwhelmed, Anna barely has time to brush her teeth in the morning let alone date a woman. But then she collides with a long-legged stranger...

FUTURE LEADERS OF NOWHERE
(Future Leaders – Book 1)

Emily O'Beirne

ISBN: 978-3-95533-821-3
Length: 253 pages (74,000 words)

Finn and Willa have been picked as leaders in the camp game. Finn doesn't know what's throwing her more, the fact she's leading a team of unenthusiastic overachievers or coming up against Willa. And Willa doesn't know which is harder, leaving her responsibilities behind or opening up to someone. Soon they must balance their clashing ideals with their unexpected connection. And find a way to win.

THE LIGHT OF THE WORLD

Ellen Simpson

ISBN: 978-3-95533-507-6
Length: 357 pages (107,000 words)

Confronted with a mystery upon her grandmother's death, Eva delves into the rich and complicated history of a woman who hid far more than a long-lost-love from the world. Darkness is lurking behind every corner, and someone is looking for the key to her grandmother's secrets; the light of the world.

FRAGILE

Eve Francis

ISBN: 978-3-95533-482-6
Length: 300 pages (103,000 words)

College graduate Carly Rogers is forced to live back at home with her mother and sister until she finds a real job. Life isn't shaping up as expected, but meeting Ashley begins to change that. After many late night talks and the start of a book club, the two women begin a romance. When a past medical condition threatens Ashley, Carly wonders if their future together will always be this fragile.

COMING FROM YLVA PUBLISHING

www.ylva-publishing.com

ALL THE WAYS TO HERE

(Future Leaders – Book 2)

Emily O'Beirne

In this sequel to *Future Leaders of Nowhere*, Finn and Willa come home from camp to find everything is different. Even as they grow more sure of their feelings for each other, everything around them feels less certain.

When Finn gets involved in a new community project, she's forced to question where her priorities lie at school. Meanwhile, her dad has moved interstate, her mother is miserable, and her home feels like a ghost town.

Willa's discovering how to navigate the terrains of romance and new school friendships when an accident at home reminds her just how tenuous her family situation is. Suddenly, even with her dad in town, she's shouldering more responsibility than ever.

As they try to navigate these new worlds together, Finn's learning she has to figure out what she wants, and Willa how to ask for what she needs.

Pieces
© 2017 by G Benson

ISBN: 978-3-95533-805-3

Also available as e-book.

Published by Ylva Publishing, legal entity of Ylva Verlag, e.Kfr.
Ylva Verlag, e.Kfr.
Owner: Astrid Ohletz
Am Kirschgarten 2
65830 Kriftel
Germany

www.ylva-publishing.com

First edition: 2017

Credits
Edited by Astrid Ohletz and Michelle Aguilar
Proofread by Paulette Callen
Cover Design by Adam Llyod
Print Layout by Streetlight Graphics